CLEVER FOX

ALSO BY JEANINE PIRRO

To Punish and Protect:
A DA's Fight Against a System
That Coddles Criminals

Sly Fox:
A Dani Fox Novel

CLEVER

A DANI FOX NOVEL

FOX

JEANINE PIRRO

HYPERION

NEW YORK

Library of Congress Cataloging-in-Publication Data has
been applied for.

ISBN: 978-1-4013-2458-2

FIRST EDITION

10 9 8 7 6 5 4 3 2 1

THIS LABEL APPLIES TO TEXT STOCK

We try to produce the most beautiful books possible, and we
are also extremely concerned about the impact of our manu-
facturing process on the forests of the world and the environ-
ment as a whole. Accordingly, we've made sure that all of the
paper we use has been certified as coming from forests that
are managed, to ensure the protection of the people and wild-
life dependent upon them.

To Kiki and Alex
My inspiration

A NOTE TO READERS

As an assistant district attorney, the first-ever woman elected county judge, and, later, District Attorney in Westchester County, New York, I have always fought for the underdog in a legal system that often favors the accused.

This book is fiction, and the events, incidents, and characters are imaginary or are used in a fictitious way. Nevertheless, much of this book was inspired by actual events and criminal cases that I personally prosecuted.

I'm using this fictional venue to give readers an intimate glimpse into what really happens inside and outside of courtrooms and to describe a time not long ago when women, children, and the elderly were treated as lesser citizens.

Helping victims has always been my calling. I don't want justice to be blind. I want her to see the victims, to feel their loss and their pain, and to make sure that those who are responsible for causing those losses and suffering are rightfully punished.

The great judge Learned Hand once wrote, "The spirit of liberty remembers that not even a sparrow falls to earth unheeded."

I see myself as a "sparrow catcher"—no matter how small or insignificant, the fallen sparrows in our society deserve to have their day in court and a champion determined to fight for their rights.

—Jeanine Pirro

CONTENTS

God has given you one face,
and you make yourself another.

—WILLIAM SHAKESPEARE

CLEVER FOX

PROLOGUE

THE GAG KEPT HER FROM SCREAMING AND BEGGING for her life. He didn't need to hear her cries or pleas to know how terrified she was. It showed in her dark eyes. Earlier, he'd bound her hands with an electrical cord that he'd cut from a bedside alarm clock and lassoed through an eye-hook that he'd screwed into the ceiling. She was now squirming helplessly in front of him on her tiptoes like an animal waiting to be killed and gutted.

He started with her clothing, savoring each twitch and tremble that she made as he cut through the expensive fabric. He wondered: Did she know what was about to happen? Fear was the ultimate rush. Better than heroin. Better than sex. He took a step backward to admire her now-nude body.

This was the moment he'd been waiting for. The drawing of first blood is what he most enjoyed. There was no reason to hurry. He would inflict as much pain as humanly possible before she took her last breath.

As he reached forward with the knife blade extended, he felt true euphoria. He was God, only, rather than creating life, he was about to end one.

PART ONE

A NEW YEAR'S PROMISE

There will be killing till the score is paid.

—HOMER, THE ODYSSEY

Twelve minutes before midnight, December 31, 1979

"GET READY!" WILL HARRIS EXCLAIMED AS HE WRAPPED his left arm around my waist while hoisting a plastic cup of champagne to his lips with his other hand. "I can't think of anyone who I'd rather be spending New Year's Eve with."

He leaned down and gently kissed my cheek.

"I feel exactly the same way," I replied.

But his comment made me curious. It sounded as if he had done a mental inventory of all the women in his life before he'd decided that I was his best choice for the evening. Or maybe that was just the prosecutor in me coming out, reading too much into what was clearly supposed to be a compliment. Maybe it was because I had been hurt and lost at love before. My former boyfriend, Bob, had taken away my faith in men. Could I ever believe a guy again? How would I know if it was real?

. Both of us looked upward at the glittering ball on the rooftop of One Times Square. It was a clear night, the stars visible in a dark blue sky.

Will had wanted to spend New Year's Eve at my house in suburban White Plains, New York, lounging in front of a cozy fire counting down the final seconds of 1979 along with Dick Clark.

But I'd insisted on escaping into Manhattan to watch the ball drop in Times Square.

My name is Dani Fox and I'm an assistant district attorney in Westchester County, a wealthy suburban enclave. I'm our county's only female prosecutor. Just 110 male assistant district attorneys and me. My specialties are crimes against women and children. Two years ago, I created one of the nation's first Domestic Violence Units and I often spend my days prosecuting husbands who believe their marriage vows give them the right to beat their wives senseless.

These last few months have been especially difficult. My boyfriend, Will, is a reporter at the *White Plains Daily* and he chronicled several of the incidents that have turned my life topsy-turvy. My troubles began after I filed charges against Carlos Gonzales, a popular Hispanic businessman who'd beaten and raped his teenage daughter. It was a high-profile case and as soon as I got a jury to convict him, our esteemed Federal Bureau of Investigation rushed in to save him because they wanted Gonzales's help in a Manhattan drug case and that was considered more important than punishing a father for beating and raping his own daughter. The Justice Department offered Gonzales a free pass. In return for his testimony, he was told that he'd get a new identity and a fresh start in the Federal Witness Protection Program. Oh yeah, the Feds were also going to relocate his younger kids with him. I was horrified, did some digging, and discovered that this dirtbag had also murdered his wife. Her death had been considered a suicide. I got a jury to convict him again, which stopped the FBI from turning him loose. As you can imagine, that case hadn't made me any friends in the FBI.

On the same night that Gonzales was convicted, I was attacked in my own house by a deranged husband intent on carving the word *bitch* into my chest. Fortunately for me, Detective Tommy O'Brien, a big Irish cop who works with me at our unit, arrived just in time to stop the attack by firing a gut-ripping round of buckshot into my knife-wielding assailant.

Like I said, 1979 was a tough year.

There were some good things, though. My pet pig, Wilbur, had survived a nasty encounter with pneumonia and nearly died. And I'd started dating Will, although I doubt Will would appreciate being lumped together with my pig's nearly fatal cold when it came to recalling the year's highlights.

Being with him—Will, not Wilbur—in Times Square tonight was exactly what I needed to take my mind off the pain and suffering that I witnessed every day in my office. It is heartbreaking to see the violence that men commit against the very women whom they'd promised to love and cherish as long as they both shall live.

"Five minutes!" Will said, sounding like an excited schoolboy.

I glanced at him. No one would mistake him for a fashion model, but Will was nice looking, tall, and fit. He had a strong jaw, a mop of sandy brown hair that always seemed to need a trim, and wore wire-rim glasses that he was constantly pushing up on his nose. It was his personality that first attracted me to him. Will was curious and smart, a workaholic—just like me—and passionate about his job. If you asked Will who he worked for, he wouldn't answer with the name of the company that owned the *White Plains Daily*. A corporate official might have signed his paycheck, but Will said that he worked for the public.

The mob in Times Square crowded together more tightly. A tipsy, tall brunette bumped against me, spilling her champagne on my new black leather coat. I didn't complain. 'Tis the season. "Nineteen eighty is going to be our year," Will declared.

Our year? What, exactly, had he meant? There were still parts of Will that remained a mystery; parts that I felt he was keeping hidden from me. Maybe he is just more private than I am. I say what's on my mind and rarely hold anything back when I'm in a relationship. Maybe Will is just more cautious about protecting himself from being hurt.

"Ten, nine, eight, seven," everyone began chanting in unison.

Will and I joined in.

"Six, five, four."

I felt wonderful. It wasn't the cheap champagne that Will had brought with us. It was a feeling of anticipation, renewal, and saying goodbye to one hell of an awful year!

"Three, two, one!"

A roar of "Happy New Year!" enveloped us as Will pulled me close and we kissed. I stood on my toes with my hands around his neck.

We held each other tightly for a minute and were about to kiss again when I felt the pager in my coat pocket shaking. The pager in his jacket began vibrating, too. We reached for them simultaneously. The only pages I get are emergencies so I knew it was not some New Year's Eve greeting from a friend. When the police call, they use a number code on my pager to tip me off. Will's newspaper does the same. We glanced at our codes and both said, "Shit!"

Without uttering another word, Will guided me through the sea of loud partygoers who were completely oblivious to the fact that someone had just been murdered. From a pay phone in a jammed bar on Forty-Third Street, I called the Yonkers police dispatcher who'd paged me.

"The vic's a woman," he said matter-of-factly. "Murdered and more."

"And more?"

"Some asshole cut pieces of her skin off."

"Butchered?"

"Tortured."

I handed Will the phone after I finished my call. He dialed the newspaper's city desk. After he finished, he said, "Sorry, Dani, this isn't how I expected the first night of our new year together to end."

"Me, either," I replied, grabbing the lapel of his coat, pulling him close, and kissing him. But my mind was already miles away. Someone around us broke into a chorus of "Auld Lang Syne."

"How you getting there?" Will yelled above the singing.

"The usual. Squad car. Lights and sirens."

Will knew better than to ask for a ride. Arriving together would have crossed a line. "I got to go," he said. "It's going to take me much longer to get to Yonkers than you."

As he started to leave, I said, "See you at the homicide."

2

THE DUNWOODIE NEIGHBORHOOD IN YONKERS IS known as Little Italy for obvious reasons. It's a long-established Italian immigrant enclave.

Over the years, Yonkers has not kept up with the wealthy Westchester villages that edge it. The neighborhood is more middle-class New Jersey than upper-class New York.

A black-and-white drove me to a brick building in the 800 block on Midland Avenue, where a half dozen uniformed Yonkers officers were loitering near the front entrance. The cops directed me to Apartment 306, where another uniformed officer was guarding the door. He studied my credentials for several moments before stepping aside. Cops still aren't used to seeing a woman prosecutor, especially at a homicide, and especially a prosecutor who still had tiny shreds of ticker tape on her coat from an interrupted Times Square celebration.

As soon as I entered, I spotted Detective O'Brien speaking to one of our county's medical examiners in the apartment's tiny living room, which didn't contain a single piece of furniture. How odd.

O'Brien was a real-life cliché of an Irish detective in his midfifties, with graying red hair, a beer belly dangling over his belt, and an ever-present toothpick tucked into the corner of his mouth. We hadn't hit it off when we'd first met, mainly because he belongs to a generation of dinosaur cops who think women do not belong on a police force or in the D.A.'s office. I consider him a work in progress.

"A new year—a new stiff," O'Brien said. "I've kept 'em out. That way you'll see what the killer saw. Take a deep breath before you go in." He nodded toward the apartment's only bedroom.

"Dispatch said she'd been cut up," I replied.

"Cut up? Skinned and filleted, I'd say."

I stepped inside. The victim was dangling from an electrical cord as if she were a side of beef hanging in a meat locker. I put her at about twenty-seven, my age, but I couldn't be sure because of her condition. At first glance, it looked as if she were wearing a bright red jumpsuit, because of all the blood. Her attacker had slashed her face and cut pieces of skin from her breasts, abdomen, thighs, and buttocks. He'd made surgical cuts, removing swatches about the size of a standard envelope.

I tried to keep focused and ignore the gore. Because she was limp, it was hard to guess her height, but I estimated she was about five foot, four inches, and weighed about 120 pounds. She was busty and although the killer had removed skin from her breasts, they were perfectly formed. Too perfectly formed. She'd definitely had breast augmentation surgery.

I stepped closer for a better look, fighting the urge to gag. The victim had shoulder-length raven hair and, judging from the clothing that had been cut from her body and dropped on the floor, she had been wearing a pricey designer label, along with a sexy black bra and panties. There wasn't a bedspread on the double bed. It's cream-colored satin sheets were sprinkled with blood like a Jackson Pollock painting.

The large gold band and huge diamond on her finger showed she was married. Her left pinkie finger had been amputated by her attacker. He'd probably dropped it on the shag carpet just as he had done with the pieces of flesh that he had cut from her body.

"Judging from the spatters," O'Brien said, coming up behind me, "she was alive when he did this to her."

Blood on the bed, walls, and carpet showed clearly that she'd twisted and possibly even tried to kick her attacker, in the process raining blood all around her. The pain must have been unimaginable. By the time death had finally come, it would have been a relief.

"She got a name?" I asked.

"No purse. No ID. The building's manager and superintendent is waiting downstairs for us. As you probably guessed by now, no one actually lived here."

I glanced at the open bedroom closet. Empty wire coat hangers were all that was inside it. The double bed was the only piece of furniture in the entire apartment.

"A love nest?" I asked.

"Love?" O'Brien scoffed.

"What would you call this?"

"A nookie nest," O'Brien beamed, clearly proud of the alliteration.

"Nookies?"

"I'm trying not to say 'fuck' so often. You know, a New Year resolution. I've been told the word offends women."

I thought for a moment about O'Brien's uptight girlfriend. I could imagine her lecturing him about his salty language. "I'm glad you're getting more sensitive," I replied. "Now, who the fuck found her?"

"Nice," he said, smiling.

"The super found her. The victim showed up here twice a week in the afternoons, regular as clockwork. Stayed a few hours. He came in here just before midnight and found her."

"Why'd he come in?"

"Looking for leaking water. Upstairs unit flooded. He was worried water was leaking down."

"Did he know her name?"

"She went by Vicky. That's it."

"How about her boyfriend?"

O'Brien shrugged. "Super never saw the man's face until today."

"C'mon, O'Brien, how could she rent this place—or he rent it—without telling the superintendent a name?"

"This apartment," he replied, "is rented by a Yonkers law firm."

I shot him a surprised look. "Anyone we know?"

O'Brien smiled. "Gallo & Conti. Ring a bell, counselor?"

The law firm of Gallo & Conti was infamous for having only one client, Nicholas Persico, better known as "the Butcher." He was a capo in the Battaglia crime family, one of the five New York Mafia families. Persico ran

"Little Italy" with an iron fist from a family-owned butcher shop in the heart of Yonkers. Wielding a cleaver was also how he reportedly liked to end the lives of his victims, although no one in law enforcement had ever been able to tie any murders directly to him.

"Seems a bit obvious, doesn't it?" I replied.

"Sometimes a cigar is just a cigar. They aren't all mysteries."

"But they are tragedies," I replied, "especially when someone dies like this. Strung up and tortured. We're dealing with a real sicko here."

O'Brien pointed toward a radio alarm clock on the floor next to the bed. "I'm guessing he started cutting on her around three-thirty."

I glanced at the time on the radio.

The killer had used its cord to bind his victim's hands. The dial was stopped at 3:35. "Nice observation," I said.

"I have my moments. Let's go talk to the super."

"Give me a second."

I looked at the dead woman. It was so sad. A life snuffed out. Why? And why so cruelly? I wanted to make sure I remembered every cut, every piece of missing flesh, every torture that her killer had inflicted. I wanted to be able to describe this scene to jurors so vividly that they would understand how much this woman had suffered before she'd finally welcomed death.

"I just made a New Year's resolution," I announced, when I walked out of the bedroom and joined O'Brien. "I'm going to make sure this fucking bastard doesn't get away with this."

3

ROMAN MANCINI MET US AT THE DOOR OF HIS FIRST-floor apartment wearing a sweat-stained wife-beater T-shirt, baggy brown pants, and well-worn slippers.

"Me and my wife, Maggie," Mancini said, "have been managing this building for fifteen years and never had no trouble like this." His apartment reeked of cigarettes, old coffee grounds, and booze. He nodded toward two threadbare chairs in a musty living room and plopped himself down on a lime-green couch across from them. Two long-haired cats were curled up on the sofa.

"My wife's not feeling well," Mancini explained. "She's got respiratory problems. Asthma. She went to bed early tonight, around ten, so she don't even know nothing happened. If it's okay, I'd rather not get her up."

"Let's start with you," I said, sitting in the blue chair. The yellow one had a third cat sleeping on it. O'Brien made eye contact with the feline as he walked over. He scooped up the cat and placed it on the floor before the pet could react. Mancini was short, stocky, and hairy everywhere but on his bald head. The stench of alcohol in the room implied a drinking habit.

"What can you tell us about the woman upstairs?" I asked.

"Not much. I mean, whenever I saw her, she always just said 'hello' but nothing more. I knew what they was doing up there, though."

"Doing up there?" I repeated, playing dumb.

"Her and that man—meeting there for sex twice a week."

"When did these trysts start?"

"Trysts?"

"Meetings."

"Oh, sex. Three months ago. This young fellow comes around and looks at the apartment. Now, I run a respectable place. Most tenants are older. We don't attract a young crowd in this building. The kids want someplace modern."

Based on the Mancinis' unit, I guessed the place hadn't been remodeled since the 1940s.

Continuing, Mancini said, "I asked this young fellow why he wanted to move into our building. That's when he tells me, it ain't for him. He works at this law firm and he's renting it for a boss. He says the boss works late and needs a place to stay. The check he gave me didn't bounce, so I figure, what the hell?"

"I'd like a copy of the rental agreement," I said.

"I already pulled it out of the file. Now, my wife, she's the one who keeps track of the paperwork. I fix things up around here and keep the place running, you know, unclogging toilets, putting in lightbulbs, that sort of thing. In this job, I get to know all our tenants and which ones are okay and which ones are never happy."

Mancini fetched a manila file folder from a nearby desk. Inside was a standard rental agreement filled out on October 1, 1979, and signed by Alberto Bianchi. Under the renter's address, Bianchi had written: Gallo & Conti, LLP, Attorneys at Law, 50 S. Broadway, Yonkers, New York, 10701.

"Did Alberto Bianchi ever show up here again?" I asked.

"That kid? Naw. A couple days after he rents the place, a moving company brings in a double bed and mattress, but I don't see them hauling in any other furniture. Then this woman—the one upstairs who's dead now—she shows up carrying towels and sheets and pillows. When I see her, I figure she's either a secretary at the law firm or the boss's wife fixing it up for him, you know?"

"You didn't think she was the law partner?"

"C'mon," he said, breaking into a grin. "A woman attorney in charge?"

He suddenly realized that he was speaking to a woman attorney in charge and said, "I mean, no offense, but, I just figured she was a secretary. Anyway, I did notice she had a wedding ring on and she dressed way too nice for a maid service or any other service—if you get my drift."

"I don't," I said. "You assumed she wasn't an attorney because she was a woman so you immediately decided she either was a secretary, the boss's wife, or what? A hooker?"

Mancini twisted uncomfortably in his seat. "Yes, I thought she might be a hooker, but then, I got to thinking that hookers don't bring their own satin sheets." He grinned, revealing a crooked row of cigarette-stained teeth.

"Did you learn this woman's name?"

"She told me it was Vicky but I didn't buy it because one day when she was walking up the stairs, I called, 'Hey Vicky,' and she didn't turn around or nothing. Then she must've realized it because she looked down at me and said, 'Sorry, I wasn't paying attention.'"

"Tell me about her boyfriend."

"The front entrance to our building is right next to our apartment so I keep a pretty good eye on who comes and goes around here. The neighborhood has gone to hell recently so the tenants appreciate the fact that I just don't let people wander around our halls."

"I get it. You notice strangers," I said, trying to hurry him up.

"Damn right. Strangers stick out and this guy stuck out."

"In what way?"

"Vicky comes in every Tuesday and Friday afternoon at exactly two o'clock. Fifteen minutes later, a limo arrives and a man gets out and goes up to the apartment. We don't get many limos coming here."

"A limo?"

"The same one every week. Anyway, around four o'clock, this man comes out of the apartment and gets in the car and leaves. Then Vicky would come down a few minutes later. You could set your watch by them two. Twice a week for two hours."

"Did he ever tell you his name?"

"No. He never said 'boo' to me. Now here's the odd part. He always showed up here dressed in a long coat wearing a hat and sunglasses and he kept his collar up. It was like he was trying to hide his identity. One day, I made a point of being in the hallway when he comes in and I tried to talk to him. I said, 'How's it going, buddy?'"

"What did he say?"

"Nothing. He walks right by me and doesn't say a goddamn word. Not even 'hello.' I told my wife, 'Hey, they pay the rent each month and they aren't causing no trouble so why should we care if they're cheating on their spouses. It ain't none of our business.' "

O'Brien joined our conversation. "Tell her about the car."

"My wife and me thought it didn't make sense. Here's this guy who wants to keep his face covered and won't tell us his name, but he arrives every Tuesday and Friday in the same damn limo with the same damn driver and the driver always parks directly in front of our building by the entrance. I went out one day and tried to speak to him, you know, engage him in a bit of polite conversation. But all he said was he was from the law firm."

O'Brien said, "Go on, tell her what else you thought."

"I thought he was one of those guys—you know." He raised his index finger up and pressed it against the side of his nose.

O'Brien said, "You mean connected."

"Yeah," Mancini said. "A mobster. That's exactly what he looked like. But it's bad luck to say it."

"Did the driver ever tell you who his passenger was?" I asked.

"I didn't ask."

"And you never saw the passenger's face?"

"Not until today."

"You saw his face this afternoon before the murder?"

"That's right. Vicky shows up right on schedule at two o'clock and she even wishes me a happy New Year. She's got a bottle of bubbly and seems like she's in a great mood. I check my watch and she's right on time. Two o'clock."

"It's good that you know the exact time," I said encouragingly.

"Yeah, I was working on one of our building's front porch lights. I had my ladder next to the door and I notice the limo hadn't arrived when it usually did. It always showed up at two-fifteen but it didn't show up until two-thirty. Same car, same driver, only this time they're fifteen minutes late. And this time when the man gets out of the backseat, he's not wearing his trench coat or his hat and he doesn't have his coat collar turned up. I was able to get a real good look at his face."

"Can you describe him to us?" I asked.

"I sure as hell can because I was surprised by what I seen. He was older than me. Must have been in his seventies and he's got a real ugly scar down the left side of his face and he's fat. He looked like someone I should have recognized, you know. Like I'd seen him before, but I couldn't place his face and it probably was just as well." Again, Mancini raised his finger next to his nose.

I shot O'Brien a knowing glance.

Mancini said, "I looked down from my ladder and said, 'Happy New Year,' but he ignored me and went inside."

"Did you see him later, when he came out of the apartment?"

"No. Maggie and me went down the street to a little place that serves an early-bird special. It was having an all-you-can-eat New Year's Eve dinner for ten bucks. Drinks were half price. The only limit was you had to clear out by seven to make way for new customers. We both got a bit tipsy and by the time we got back here, the limo was gone."

"What time was that?"

"We got back around six-thirty."

"When did you find the victim's body?"

"Just before midnight. Actually, it was exactly eleven-fifty-five. I know because I'd fallen asleep here on the couch with my cats when I got a phone call. I'd left the television on and there was a clock in the corner of the picture tube counting down the New Year. The time on the television was eleven-fifteen—that's when I woke up."

"Why'd someone call you that late?"

"It was old lady Miller. She's a widower and she's always calling to bitch about something. She's in her eighties and has cats, too. She called because her toilet was clogged and overflowing and she needed me to come right away."

"You got her call at eleven-fifteen?" I repeated. "Seems late for a woman in her eighties to be awake."

"Not old lady Miller. She stays up all night and sleeps during the day. She's afraid of someone breaking in on her at nighttime. Besides, it's New Year's Eve, remember?"

"You went up to check her toilet?" O'Brien said.

"Yeah, I got up to her apartment and there was a good inch of water on the floor. I've shown her before how to use the shut off value under the commode, but them old ladies, they don't remember and they're too old to get on their knees and reach under the toilet. Anyway, I shut off the valve, unclogged the toilet, and then mopped up the water. I checked my watch when I left her apartment because I wanted to see if I had missed the ball drop in Times Square. That's how I know it was exactly ten minutes before midnight when I left that old lady's apartment."

"Did you go straight to your apartment?"

"No. Old lady Henry lives in 406, directly above Apartment 306. I decided to check to see if water from Miss Henry's place had leaked through the floor down into Vicky's apartment. I was planning on just peeking inside because I knew no one stayed there overnight. If the place was flooded, then I would need to mop it up."

"You used your master key to get in?" O'Brien said, leading him along.

"That's right. I opened the door and went directly to the bathroom because I was in a hurry. I didn't even look in the bedroom, which was dark anyway. The apartment was quiet and, like I said, I didn't think anyone was in there. I turned on the bathroom light and checked the ceiling and sure enough water was dripping down. I'd left my mop and bucket in the hallway so I turned around to go get them and the bathroom light shone into the bedroom and that's when I saw her. Vicky. Hanging there all bloody and cut up. I couldn't believe it. I thought maybe I was hallucinating because of the drinks from dinner but it wasn't any damn dream. I ran down to our apartment and called the police right away because Vicky's apartment don't have a phone and besides, I wanted to get the hell out of there."

"You didn't wake up your wife and tell her?" I asked.

Mancini shook his head, indicating no. "Truth is, my wife likes to take a little nip now and then. She was pretty loaded when we got home. I'm not sure I could have gotten her up." He hesitated and then added, "In fact, I could really use a drink now, too, if you don't mind. My nerves are shot."

"We're almost done," I said. "What happened next?"

"The Yonkers cops arrived. I took them up and then you came," he said, nodding at O'Brien. "I talked to you and you told me to come back here and wait and that's what I've been doing. There really isn't any more for me to tell you." He started to fidget.

"Thanks," I said. "We'll be in touch."

O'Brien and I didn't talk to each other until we were outside on the sidewalk.

"You know who that super described, don't you?" he asked me.

"Yes," I replied. "The ugly scar on his cheek is a dead giveaway."

O'Brien said, "Nicholas 'the Butcher' Persico."

"Mr. Untouchable himself," I replied. "Seen visiting Vicky—our New Year's Eve corpse."

4

O'BRIEN DROPPED ME OFF IN WHITE PLAINS, WHERE I live in an older craftsman-style house that will be mine after I make another twenty-nine years of monthly payments. Rather than going inside through the front door, I walked to Wilbur's pen in the backyard.

Wilbur was only a few weeks old when I got him. He's a Vietnamese pot-bellied pig, with upright ears, a straight tail, and a swayed back because his big belly drops within inches of the ground. Wilbur is always hungry. Always. My neighbors think it's odd for someone to own a domesticated pig, especially in wealthy Westchester. But Wilbur has proven himself to be smarter than most dogs and he is as clean as any cat—that is, until he begins rooting for snacks. Once he gets a sniff of food, nothing slows him down.

Wilbur greeted me with a chorus of excited grunts and then happily waddled behind me into my kitchen—the only room he's allowed to enter. While I fixed him a bowl of pig pellets, he wiggled at my feet and listened intently as I described my morning.

"This could be a big homicide case if we discover that Persico killed that girl," I explained. I avoided using Persico's nickname out of deference to Wilbur. I'm certain the Butcher had carved more than one pig into cutlets inside his family-owned shop.

Wilbur grunted, which I took as a sign of agreement. I placed his bowl on the tile floor. Now that he was gobbling his breakfast, I was free to take a shower and get dressed for work. As I passed the refrigerator, I grabbed a Dr Pepper and a half-eaten box of Junior Mints. I'm lucky to be able to eat just about anything and still weigh in at 105 pounds at five feet, five inches tall. Sweets are one of my vices and I would kill for dark chocolate, but then again, I still go for a run most mornings to even things out. I'm less lucky in the hair department. I have naturally curly black hair that has a mind of its own.

By the time I emerged from the shower and returned to the kitchen, Wilbur was ready to go outside for a nap. I was ready to nap, too, but it wasn't in the cards. It was nearly 8 a.m., which meant I was going to be late. That happens a lot.

I got behind the wheel of my racing-green Triumph TR-6 sports car, which I will own after twenty-six more months of payments. But when I turned the ignition, nothing happened. "Damn it! Start!"

I turned the ignition again and this time the Triumph fired up without hesitation. Who knows why? As I backed down the driveway, I thought about my father. Having had no sons, he'd done his best to teach me about cars. I'd bought the Triumph shortly after he died from cancer. It was a silent tribute to him because he'd always loved English sports cars.

The 8 a.m. news came on the radio.

"The body of a still-unidentified young woman was found in a Yonkers apartment on New Year's Eve," the newscaster breathlessly announced. "According to Yonkers Police Department sources, the woman was found naked and tortured."

I sped up. This was going to be a major news story and that meant that my boss, District Attorney Carlton Whitaker III, would be itching to preen before the cameras. He'd want to be briefed ASAP.

Our offices in the Domestic Violence Unit are located across the street from the main Westchester County Courthouse. Moving outside the courthouse had been my idea. Battered women don't want to traipse through the courthouse to file complaints: they would feel embarrassed and intimidated.

In the past, many of them had gone to the police or sought help from judges only to have their complaints minimized and dismissed. They would be sent right back to their abusive husbands. But, as Bob Dylan put it, "the times they are a-changin'." I'd made our lobby into a welcoming place that looked more like a living room than a traditional prosecutor's office, with sofas and playpens to keep children occupied while their moms recounted the hell their husbands put them through.

O'Brien was already pacing near my reserved parking spot at the back of our building when I arrived. He tapped on his watch dial. O'Brien likes to remind me that he's never late. "Your boss was expecting us ten minutes ago," he said. "Maybe being punctual should have been one of your New Year's resolutions."

I ignored the dig.

For the record, District Attorney Whitaker was also O'Brien's boss, ever since O'Brien had transferred from the White Plains Police Department's homicide division to work as an investigator in our Domestic Violence Unit. But O'Brien still thinks of himself as a street cop. He's also not a fan of Whitaker, who he thinks is more sizzle than steak.

"Car trouble," I said, shrugging.

"Should have bought American. What the hell do the Brits know about building cars?"

"You mean the Brits who make Rolls-Royce, Bentley, and Jaguar?" I asked sarcastically.

O'Brien glanced at my Triumph and said, "That ain't a Rolls, now, is it?"

Whitaker and I have an unwritten understanding. He leaves me alone to handle what he calls "women's issues" and I make myself available whenever he needs a woman's help campaigning. He didn't really want a "skirt" in his office prosecuting cases because he didn't think women had the "chops" to prosecute tough criminal cases, but Whitaker was smart enough to realize that the women's movement was sweeping in a new era across the nation and he was going to need women's votes to keep getting reelected. One of his favorite sayings was "If you know which way a parade is going, it's easier to jump out front and be the bandleader." Whitaker was always ready with his trumpets and drums—and the token female attorney. At first, he'd stuck me at a desk job in the Appeals Bureau, our office's equivalent to Siberia. It took the Carlos Gonzales rape and murder trials to change Whitaker's mind about my legal skills.

I knew Whitaker would be eager to milk our new murder case. His reelection campaign was still a couple of years away, but Whitaker got up every morning campaigning and kept at it until he went to bed. The biggest question in his mind would not be who butchered this woman, but how to fully mine the case politically. Especially if the Butcher Persico became our prime suspect. I had to convince my boss to keep me involved in the investigation and ultimately the prosecution.

I may be the only female A.D.A. in our office, but those 110 male A.D.A.s also work for Whitaker, who didn't hire them because they were shrinking violets. Nearly all of them had graduated from top-flight law schools, many had more courtroom experience than I did, and several could be as cutthroat as our former chief assistant district attorney, Paul Pisani, when it came to office politics.

Pisani had been a legend in Westchester County for his courtroom skills. He was such an effective courtroom prosecutor that he was dubbed "Mr. Invincible." But he had a massive ego, an arrogant attitude, and trouble keeping his zipper up. He crossed a line when he impregnated a young courthouse intern in the closing days of Whitaker's reelection campaign. As soon as Pisani became a potential liability, he was shown the door.

Whitaker's obsession with getting reelected also explained his management style. He called himself a "hands-off" manager and left the running of the office to his chief of staff, Mark Steinberg, and his new chief assistant district attorney, Henry Myerson. Whitaker spent most afternoons at the Westchester Country Club in nearby Harrison playing golf and kissing up to the club's elite. He could easily fit in with that well-heeled crowd but he also had enough sense to highlight his less egalitarian ties when he was mixing it up with ordinary types at a local watering hole.

With each of his four successful reelection bids, Whitaker expanded his office. The additional space at one end had been made into a large conference area with a table big enough to seat sixteen. On the opposite side of his expanded domain, he installed a lounge area. Directly in the center of the room is a hand-carved mahogany desk from the 1800s rumored to have been owned by one of New York's robber barons. He had a fondness for antiques, and one of his prized possessions was an antique regulator clock whose ticking had distracted him; he'd stopped the pendulum, which always struck me as a fitting metaphor for his sexist, old-fashioned attitude. In addition to heirlooms, he'd covered the walls with photographs of himself with local, state, and national politicians along with honors and awards that he'd received. His office was a giant monument to himself.

The chamber outside Whitaker's office was guarded—not by a fierce guard dog, but by something even more terrifying. Miss Hillary Potts was prim, proper, formal, and, quite frankly, intentionally bitchy. She regarded the other women in the courthouse with disdain, because she felt that her job as Whitaker's personal secretary made her more important than the other secretaries. "You're late," she announced with a scowl when O'Brien and I entered. She sounded like a schoolteacher lecturing two wayward students.

"We're here now," I replied, without offering an excuse.

Potts scowled at me, rose slowly from her desk, made certain her cashmere sweater was tucked into her pencil skirt, and disappeared behind the double doors that led into Whitaker's office. Out of the corner of my eye, I took note that O'Brien's eyes were taking in her every step.

When he saw me smirking, he popped his toothpick out of his mouth and said, "Don't start."

When she reappeared, Miss Potts said, "Mr. Whitaker will see you now."

"Thanks, Hill," I said as we breezed by her. She hated being called that, but she couldn't complain because I knew a secret about her and O'Brien that neither of them wanted their courthouse coworkers to discover. Last year during the Gonzales case, I'd called O'Brien at home at 3 a.m. and had been surprised to hear Miss Potts answer his phone, tipping me off to their sleepover ritual. What O'Brien saw in Miss Potts was none of my business. All I knew was that I owned both of them.

As soon as we crossed the threshold, Whitaker yelled from behind his desk, "Where the hell have you two been?"

I scanned the massive office. As usual, Chief of Staff Steinberg was sitting in one of four leather chairs across from our boss. Next to him was Chief Assistant District Attorney Myerson, who was not as talented nor as devious as Paul Pisani had been in a courtroom but was a decent trial lawyer who went home at night without seducing naïve interns and secretaries.

Whitaker snapped, "Tell us about the dead girl."

O'Brien and I sat between Steinberg and Myerson and I briefed them about what I'd seen in the bedroom and our interview with superintendent Roman Mancini. When I mentioned that our suspect was a man in his seventies with an ugly scar on his cheek, all three exchanged excited glances.

"Are you telling me," Whitaker asked, almost giddy, "that you got an eyewitness who saw Nicholas Persico going into a Yonkers apartment before this woman was butchered?"

"We haven't positively identified him as Persico," I replied, trying to calm his growing prosecutorial hard-on.

"You'd better be sure if you do," Steinberg warned. "Charging a Mafia capo with murder makes this more of a sensational case than it already is."

Steinberg was good at stating the obvious.

"How so?" I asked, just for fun.

Whitaker ignored me and asked, "Any idea who the dead girl is?"

"The super said she used the name Vicky, but we suspect it's a fake name."

"Hooker?"

"Doesn't seem so. She had an expensive wedding ring and looks more Scarsdale than Times Square."

O'Brien decided to join in. "Someone at the law firm that rented that dump knows her name."

"Gallo and Conti are tough mob lawyers," Chief Assistant Myerson volunteered. "They'll do whatever it takes to protect the Butcher."

"For the money he pays them, they should," Whitaker replied. Addressing me, he said, "Let me guess, you want a piece of this, don't you?"

Without any hint of embarrassment, shyness, or fake modesty, I replied, "You're damn right, sir!"

Whitaker was enjoying himself. He leaned back in his chair and locked the fingers of his hands behind his gray hair. "So if I let you run with this, what's your first move? Questioning Persico?"

"Not without your permission," I immediately replied, giving the politically correct answer. "Obviously, in a case of this magnitude, Detective O'Brien and I would have to work closely with Myerson and the Yonkers homicide detectives assigned to investigate the murder. But just because Persico is a Mafia capo and has an entire law firm on retainer certainly doesn't make him any different than any other murder suspect."

"Yeah, right," Myerson said sarcastically.

Addressing Whitaker, Steinberg said, "Boss, the tabloids are going to go nuts over this. A young woman butchered on New Year's Eve. Pieces of her flesh sliced clean from her body. If she's married and this was a love nest, as

Miss Fox has suggested, it's going to be leading the news and papers for days."

Whitaker unlocked his fingers and leaned forward. "We'll need to hold a press conference to show we're on top of this," he said.

Myerson jumped in. "You're not going to mention Persico's name just yet, are you?"

"Not yet," Whitaker replied. "It's premature."

"Besides," added Steinberg, "we can always save that angle for the next day's headlines. Stick with the murder today, talk about suspects tomorrow."

Looking at me, Whitaker said, "I'll need you available at today's news conference. Mark will arrange it. I'll do the talking. You just stand behind me and smile."

I wasn't surprised. It wasn't the first time I'd been used as a prop. Since I was going to be paraded out before reporters, I decided to be a bit pushy.

"So does this mean that you want O'Brien and me to oversee this investigation and possible prosecution?"

I noticed Myerson flinch. He'd want to be in charge of prosecuting this murder, especially if it involved the Butcher.

Much to my surprise, before Whitaker could reply, Steinberg weighed in. "You know, boss, having a woman seeking justice for another woman who was butchered might not be a bad idea, especially after Miss Fox's performance in the Gonzales case."

"Isn't it a bit early to be deciding who's going to prosecute?" Myerson interjected, hoping to exert his power as chief assistant district attorney. "Any decision you make now might change depending on whether the Butcher is indicted. Don't you also want Vanderhoot brought in?"

"That's right," Steinberg declared. "Vanderhoot should be told it's possible the Butcher will be a suspect in this case."

Chief Steve Vanderhoot was head of our office's Organized Crime Bureau. A former military prosecutor in his early forties who kept a short-cropped haircut, he was well respected, aggressive, and had the authority to jump into any case that had the slightest hint of being linked to the mob.

Whitaker addressed Myerson. "You're right on both counts. It's premature to decide who's going to be prosecuting this murder. You're also right about the need to bring Vanderhoot into the discussion. I'd like you to go talk to him right now. Tell him to keep this under wraps and also tell him that I'll be sending Miss Fox and Detective O'Brien up in a few to answer any questions that he might have."

Myerson nodded and rose from his chair. He looked at us, incorrectly assuming the meeting was over.

Whitaker said, "Go ahead, Henry, there's a few issues I still need to speak to everyone else about."

A tinge of concern appeared on Myerson's face, but he left as directed.

"Miss Fox," Whitaker said, "I didn't hire you to be a detective. But there are times when a good prosecutor has to think like a cop. You've got to put all of the puzzle pieces together. In a big case, the best way to do that is by being part of the actual investigation. So I'm going to give you another hat to wear: I want you and O'Brien involved in every goddamn step of this case. I don't want you sitting in your office reading reports. I want your eyes and ears in the field. I don't trust the cops in Yonkers to go after someone as powerful as the Butcher. Who knows how many are on his payroll? I'm holding you responsible for making sure this is done right. If you do a good job, then maybe I'll let you handle the actual trial. But regardless, I want you to learn everything there is to learn about this murder. I don't want any surprises popping up later and if there are, then it's going to be your ass that's on the line."

"Yes, sir," I replied. "But what about Vanderhoot? He's not going to want me butting into his turf."

"Whose name is on the door to this office? You let Mark and me handle Vanderhoot. You just do what I told you."

Who was I to argue, especially since it was starting to sound like I'd get a chance to actually try this case?

5

O N THE ELEVATOR RIDE TO VANDERHOOT'S OFFICE IN the Organized Crime Bureau, I asked O'Brien what the hell was going on. I'd never heard O'Brien gossip but I also didn't know anyone in the courthouse who knew more gossip than he did. Despite his gruff, macho exterior, people generally liked O'Brien and told him things they didn't share with others. He knows how to read people and make them feel at ease. This quality makes him an excellent homicide detective.

I'd gotten to know O'Brien during the Gonzales rape/murder case. During a long road trip to Attica prison, he told me a few nuggets about his past. His father had been a prison guard who often took his anger out on his family—at home—with his fists. When O'Brien was old enough to stand up to his old man, the two of them had squared off. The teenage O'Brien had left his father lying beaten and bloody on the ground and had been shocked when his mother, who he thought he was protecting, told him to move out. I'm not a psychiatrist, but I think O'Brien learned how to read people out of a sense of survival when he was a helpless child. In addition to O'Brien's built-in radar, he also has a gaggle of loose-lipped courthouse secretaries, bartenders, waitresses, and other street sources feeding him information.

"I've heard Vanderhoot is lobbying for a U.S. Attorney's job. Wants to move on to bigger and better things. Whitaker found out and is none too pleased. Feels Vanderhoot is being disloyal. I doubt your boss is gonna want him juicing up his résumé by bringing down a capo as powerful as Persico."

O'Brien's comment reminded me of how isolated I was across the street in my office and how little I cared about office politics. Just the same, I'd learned in the Gonzales case that what happened behind the scenes in the D.A.'s office was often more important than what played out in a court-room, and that justice frequently came second to political ambitions.

Myerson and Vanderhoot were still talking when O'Brien and I arrived. Vanderhoot, true to his Marine training, got right to the point. "This isn't a domestic violence case, so why the hell are you still involved?"

"The district attorney has specifically asked me and Detective O'Brien to be involved and monitor every aspect of this case. And no one really knows if the Butcher had anything to do with any of this."

"If he did, then it's an organized crime matter. Isn't that right, Henry?" Vanderhoot asked.

"One would think so, wouldn't they?" Myerson responded in his typical wishy-washy fashion.

"No disrespect, Vanderhoot," I said, meaning just the opposite, "but this is above my pay grade. I'm only doing what I have been instructed to do. Our boss sent us up here to brief you. Are there any questions that you might have about the murder?"

Vanderhoot gave me an irritated look and I could almost see the wheels spinning in his head. The fact that Whitaker had sent Myerson and us to speak to him was a clear message. Ordinarily, Whitaker would have had Miss Potts summon Vanderhoot as soon as the Butcher's name had been mentioned dur-ing our briefing. After all, organized crime was Vanderhoot's specialty and he had extensive connections with the FBI and other organized crime task forces. It seemed obvious that Whitaker's second-class treatment of Vanderhoot was a rapping on the knuckles, telling him that if he no longer wanted to work in the D.A.'s office, then he wasn't going to be part of a potentially career-making case. "If District Attorney Whitaker wants you two handling the in-vestigation," Vanderhoot said, "then by all means, be my guests. I don't see why you need to bother briefing me."

Apparently, if Vanderhoot wasn't going to be in charge, then he wasn't going to help us. He was shrewd enough to realize that if he wasn't going to be given the football, he sure as hell wasn't going to take any blame if things went bad.

"I'll tell District Attorney Whitaker that you didn't have any questions for us," I said quietly.

"No, you won't," he replied with a grunt that essentially said, *Who the hell do you think you are?* "Myerson and I will be talking to him later today. But thanks for stopping by."

In the elevator, O'Brien said, "Goddamn it, Dani, why do you get me dragged into this shit?"

"Get ready for more," I said.

He shook his head and let out a sigh. "There always is with you," he said. "Let me guess. Our next stop is Gallo & Conti in Yonkers."

6

THERE WAS NO SIGN OUTSIDE THE FIVE-STORY OFFICE building advertising the mob law firm of Gallo & Conti. The directory in the lobby listed the firm as being on the second floor. A twenty-something receptionist, answering phone calls while smacking gum, greeted us with a cheery "Gud mornin'."

"Alberto Bianchi, please," I said, showing her my identification badge. "Westchester County District Attorney's Office."

A concerned look appeared on her young face and for a moment, I thought she might swallow her gum. She hit a button on her phone and whispered, "There's two people from the D.A.'s asking to see Alberto." She waited for a response, then put down the receiver and said, "Take a seat."

Another five minutes passed before a well-dressed man in his sixties and a much younger man—probably in his thirties—wearing an off-the-rack suit appeared.

"I'm Anthony Conti, one of the firm's senior partners," the older man explained, "and this is Mr. Bianchi, one of our younger associates. You asked to see him."

They made an odd couple. Conti was tall and thin, with salt-and-pepper hair. Bianchi was short, heavyset, had stringy, shoulder-length hair, and still bore remnants of teenage acne.

"We'll be more comfortable in our conference room," Conti volunteered, leading the way.

The fact that we'd asked for Bianchi but had gotten him and Conti irked me.

"Are you Mr. Bianchi's attorney?" I asked flippantly.

"Does he need one?" Conti replied.

"You tell me."

"We prefer to have either Mr. Gallo or myself present whenever law enforcement personnel come to our office. It's standard procedure."

"How do you ever get any work done? There must be a ton of law enforcement coming here," I replied.

He ignored the jab and said, "How can we help you?"

"We're here about the homicide in a Yonkers apartment on Midland Avenue last night," I said.

"Yes," Conti replied, "I heard about it on the morning news. A woman was found in an apartment building with pieces of her skin missing. Tragic, just terrible. What's the world coming to?"

"Mr. Bianchi rented the apartment where the victim was found," I said.

"Your law firm is paying for it," O'Brien added, tag-teaming them.

Without the slightest sign of surprise, Conti said, "Our firm rents an apartment in that building, that's true. But I can assure you that no one in our firm was involved in a murder there."

"How can you be so certain?" I asked.

"Because no one in our firm has ever used that apartment," he replied. "We rented it in case Mr. Gallo or I needed a place to stay when we were working late. But I don't believe either of us has put a foot in the place."

"Never been inside it?" O'Brien asked suspiciously.

"I haven't."

"And Gallo?" O'Brien asked.

"Ask him," Conti said. "But I doubt he has."

"You're telling me that your firm rented an apartment and has been paying rent for three months, but no one ever used it. Nobody stopped by for a nap or at night. Must be nice to throw away money like that," O'Brien said.

"Thanks for your concern," Conti said.

"We've been told," I said, joining the conversation, "that the victim arrived at the apartment at two o'clock every Tuesday and every Friday."

Conti shrugged his shoulders indifferently.

"And," I continued, "that an older male arrived fifteen minutes later in a black limo at the apartment to visit her."

"I don't know what you are talking about," Conti said. "But I can tell you this: our firm doesn't use limos."

"Huh," O'Brien said, sneering. "You can afford to rent an apartment for three months that you never use, but you take cabs to save money."

Conti gave him a stern look. "Detective, I don't spend your money. Why are you trying to spend mine?"

"Is it possible," I asked, "that you rented this apartment for one of your clients? Someone who prefers to keep his identity a secret?"

"If we were," said Conti, "then we would be violating our client's trust if we talked to you about it, wouldn't we? Besides, I don't believe renting an apartment is against the law—not yet, at least."

"Do you know the name of the woman whose body was found there?" I asked.

With an exaggerated sigh, Conti said, "Are you planning on charging someone in our firm or is this just a fishing expedition?"

"A young woman was strung up and butchered in an apartment that your firm rented," I said. "This is hardly a fishing expedition. It would seem logical that you might know her name."

Conti gave me another smug look. "I don't think that's logical at all. Our firm rented the apartment but we never used it. So why would we know who this woman was or why she was in our apartment?"

Clearly, we were getting nowhere.

Apparently Conti agreed. "This conversation is a waste of time," he announced. "I think we're done here."

"No," I said, letting my temper show, "we aren't really done here. Does anyone in your office have a scar across his cheek?"

Conti's facial expression stayed expressionless. But I detected a nervous glint in Bianchi's eyes.

"Why would you ask that?" Conti said.

"Because an older man—someone in his early seventies—was in that apartment at the time of the murder. He had a scar on his face and we are trying to locate him."

"You have a witness who saw a man with a scar on his face going into that apartment at the same time that girl was killed?" Conti repeated.

"I'm not telling you whether we do or do not have a witness," I said. "I'm asking you if anyone on your payroll here is an older man with a scar on his face."

"No one in our firm fits that description," he replied.

"Doesn't your firm represent Nicholas Persico?" I asked.

Before Conti could answer, O'Brien said in an innocent voice, "Huh, I seem to remember that Persico does have a scar on his cheek."

"It's no secret that Mr. Persico is one of our firm's clients," Conti said drily. "We have represented him for many years."

"And the scar?"

"I've never noticed."

At that moment, the door to the conference room burst open and another older, well-dressed man came in.

"I'm Alonzo Gallo," he announced. "What's the problem here?"

"This detective and Ms. Fox," Conti said calmly, "are hinting that a witness saw Mr. Persico entering an apartment where a girl was murdered."

"You people are outrageous!" Gallo snapped. "Every time there's a sensational crime in Yonkers and you cops want to make headlines, you come running in here, trying to drag Mr. Persico into it. For you to mention his name in the same breath as this murdered girl is nothing but a cheap publicity stunt."

In an indignant voice, Conti added, "We've been cooperative and civil with both of you, but now I think I'll have to ask you to leave."

I glanced at Bianchi, who hadn't spoken a word, and asked him, "Is there anything you want to say? It's your name on the rental agreement."

He shook his head.

"You ever go in that apartment after you rented it?" O'Brien asked him.

Bianchi glanced at the two senior partners. "I have nothing to say," he said.

"Who'd you give the key to?" O'Brien said.

Bianchi was starting to sweat.

Conti saved him. "We're done answering questions," he said.

"Thanks for being a model of cooperation," I said.

"We always try, especially with law enforcement," Gallo sneered.

Once we were outside the building, I said, "Judging from the way Gallo came bursting into that conference room, I'm guessing he'd been listening to us in an outside office. The room must have been bugged."

The police radio in the console of O'Brien's unmarked cruiser crackled with a message as we both entered the car. "We got a positive on Jane Doe," the Yonkers dispatcher said. "Got a home address too. Name is Isabella Ricci."

O'Brien interrupted the dispatcher before he could announce the address. "Isabella Ricci?"

"Ten-four," the dispatcher replied.

O'Brien looked at me and said, "What the fuck?"

He was breaking his New Year's resolution to avoid saying the F-word, but in this case, it seemed fitting.

"If this Isabella Ricci is the girl I think she is," I said, "then this case just got even more sensational."

"And dangerous," O'Brien replied.

7

WHITAKER PAGED US AS SOON AS HE LEARNED THE identity of the victim. What I didn't expect when we walked into Whitaker's office was that there would be an entourage waiting. Whitaker's three chiefs, Steinberg, Myerson, and Vanderhoot, were seated around the conference table, as well as two outsider guests. O'Brien and I were outnumbered and outranked.

The lanky fellow with capped teeth and carefully groomed hair sitting closest to Whitaker near the head of the table was Jack Longhorn, Special Agent in Charge of the FBI's New York field office. I despised him. He had done everything he possibly could to stop me from prosecuting Carlos Gonzales and was the backstabbing son of a bitch who had tried to put Gonzales into the Federal Witness Protection Program.

Longhorn had that good ole boy act down pat, sprinkling folksy sayings into his banter to call attention to his Oklahoma roots. But if you pricked his southern façade, underneath you'd find a blindly ambitious opportunist who didn't play fair and never let facts get in his way. Being the agent in charge of the New York field office was the final stepping-stone before an administrator became a confidante in Washington, D.C., of the all-powerful FBI director.

The younger man with him was a stranger, but his clean-cut appearance, chiseled features, and the tiny American flag in his coat's lapel pegged him as an FBI agent, too.

Without waiting to be introduced, he rose, extended his hand, and said, "Ms. Fox, I'm Special Agent Walter Coyle. I've heard a lot about you."

"I bet you have. Knowing your boss, I'm sure none of it was good."

Longhorn faked a pained expression. "Oh Miss Fox," he said, "we've locked horns in the past, but I've buried the hatchet."

"And I'm sure it's in my back."

"Time to pull in the claws," Whitaker said. O'Brien and I both found chairs across from Longhorn and Coyle.

Whitaker began the meeting. "Special Agent Longhorn and Special Agent Coyle have come with new information about our murder."

"We're here to join the team," Longhorn declared in an enthusiastic tone.

Great, I thought. How lucky can we get? The Feds want to partner up and "help" us out, which means they'll steal our case, all our work, and then take credit. Wow. I couldn't help myself from replying in his language. Staring at Longhorn, I said, "Only problem, Jack, is this isn't Dodge City, you're no Wyatt Earp, and we don't need your guns. We locals can do this one just fine."

True to form, he ignored me, turned to his colleague, and said, "You're up to bat, Walter."

"I work for a task force that is part of a Justice Department effort to break the back of organized crime here in the New York City metropolitan area. The team I'm assigned to has targeted Nicholas Persico in Yonkers. I'm certain you recognize his name," Coyle said.

He hesitated in what seemed a very practiced way, apparently to see if any of us wanted to make a comment, but no one did. Continuing, Coyle said, "I thought I had drawn the short straw in the office the other day when I got stuck running surveillance on Persico over the New Year's Eve holidays. But when I heard about that woman who got butchered over on Midland Avenue, I realized that wasn't the case after all."

"What do you mean?" Whitaker asked, clearly hoping to hurry him up.

"On December thirty-first, I followed Persico in his limo to the apartment where your murder victim was later found. I saw the Butcher go inside the Midland Avenue building. Of course, it wasn't until I heard the news this morning that I made the connection that Persico had been at the scene of a homicide."

"You actually saw him entering the dead girl's apartment?" Whitaker asked.

"No, I didn't see him enter the apartment, but I did see his limo drive him to the building and I watched him go inside."

It's protocol in meetings such as this one not to speak or ask questions until after the D.A. has finished asking everything he wants. I knew this, but I couldn't help myself.

"Maybe he was there visiting his mother," I said.

Whitaker shot me an irritated look. But Coyle smiled and said, "I checked and his mother doesn't live there. None of his family members do."

Coyle was self-assured. And he really was cute.

Since I had spoken out of turn, Vanderhoot apparently thought he could, too.

"What time did you see him get to the building?" Vanderhoot asked.

"Two-thirty," Coyle replied.

I jumped in. "You know the exact time?"

Now it was Vanderhoot who shot me a nasty glance.

"We keep logs," Coyle explained. "I wrote it down, of course."

At this point, Whitaker decided to retake control of the questioning. "How long was Persico inside the apartment building?"

"Almost three hours. He left around five-thirty p.m."

Whitaker continued, "And you're certain it was Persico who went into that apartment building?"

"Yes, sir. Persico didn't try to hide his face. There's something else you need to know. When he left, he was in a rush. He came running out of the building's front door and jumped into the limo. I followed him from the apartment back to his butcher's shop, where I watched and waited. When he came out of the shop a short time later, I noticed he'd changed clothes. He'd put on different pants, a different shirt; it even looked like he'd changed his socks and shoes."

"Are you suggesting he destroyed evidence?" I asked.

If Whitaker was irritated at me for butting in, he didn't show it this time. He must have been as eager to hear the answer as I was.

"Why else change clothes in the middle of the day?" Coyle asked rhetorically. "After he left his shop, I followed him straight to his home. He didn't leave his residence the rest of that night, so it wasn't like he was dressing up for a New Year's Eve party."

Satisfied that his young protégé had whetted our appetites, Longhorn declared in a booming voice, "It looks like we finally have a chance to wrap Mr.

Persico up in a nice neat little package and send him off to the federal pen in Leavenworth. All you fellas need to do is invite us into this homicide investigation so we can officially saddle up with your organized crime chief."

Coyle added, "I can provide Vanderhoot our daily logbooks that show Persico's recent activities." Glancing at Vanderhoot, Coyle said, "I've heard you have an excellent reputation in organized crime cases."

Longhorn said, "What do you think, Carlton? You want to partner up here, ride the same horse, and catch us a bad guy?"

"Let me think about it," Whitaker said.

"What's to think about, Carlton?" Longhorn replied with a slight edge to his voice.

"We already have an eyewitness who saw Persico at the apartment yesterday," Whitaker said, reminding Longhorn that our office could handle this case without him.

The political game-playing had begun.

"Interesting," Coyle said. "Who is it?"

"The building's superintendent," Vanderhoot volunteered. "He spotted an older man with a scar on his face ducking into the building yesterday afternoon."

Whitaker looked irked. Vanderhoot had volunteered more information than the D.A. had wanted. In his eagerness to impress the FBI, Vanderhoot had dug another shovel's worth of dirt for his own grave.

"That's Persico, all right," Coyle chimed in. "His scar's a dead giveaway."

Longhorn said, "Carlton, I can have Coyle in Vanderhoot's office this afternoon with a stack of daily logs and other intel that will nail Persico's hide to the barn door, then we can all be heroes. Or you can do this case solo and if you fail to get a conviction, you'll be standing alone on a hill with your britches down and your butt showing."

That was not an image I wanted in my head. Apparently Whitaker didn't, either. I knew him well enough to know that he didn't like sharing the limelight and he didn't trust Longhorn. Whitaker smiled slightly and said in a polite but firm voice, "Jack, that's a most generous and tempting offer. But at this point, I think we'll do this one on our own. Of course, now that we know Agent Coyle is a witness, I'm sure Miss Fox and Detective O'Brien will want to speak with him."

A frustrated look flashed across Longhorn's face, but he shook it off and said, "Okeydokey, Carlton. You can lead a horse to water, but you can't make him drink." He slapped his knees and rose from the table, a motion his side-kick echoed. But Longhorn wasn't quite done. "Did you say Miss Fox and Detective O'Brien were handling this investigation? Not Vanderhoot, your expert organized-crime prosecutor?"

Whitaker stuck out his hand. "Thanks for stopping by, Jack. We'll be in touch."

This time, Longhorn made a point of shaking my hand as he made his way around the table.

I wanted to vomit.

As soon as they were gone, Whitaker exploded. "Who the hell does that son of a bitch think he is, trying to weasel into my case?"

"The FBI does have a task force and tremendous resources," Vanderhoot said. "Agent Coyle is an eyewitness. I think it might be smart to—"

Before Vanderhoot could finish his sentence, Whitaker snapped, "I'm sure you think it would be great to team up. But you're not in charge, are you? I'm calling the shots and right now, Miss Fox and O'Brien are going to continue pursuing this investigation."

Like a puppy who'd just been caught next to a puddle on the kitchen floor, Vanderhoot bowed his head.

Whitaker addressed Myerson, who had remained silent up to now. "What do you think, Henry?" he asked. "You're the courtroom expert."

Myerson said, "You're making the right call for now. But someone needs to meet with Agent Coyle. We'll need him down the road when we take this to a grand jury, along with the super, Roman Mancini. Two eyewitnesses are better than one."

Chief of Staff Steinberg jumped in. "You're making the right call here, keeping the FBI out for now. We need this case. It's big news."

Whitaker's mood immediately lifted. "Damn right we do! Rudy Giuliani isn't the only guy who can go after organized crime in this state." He glanced at me. "Ms. Fox, meet with Coyle and see what he has to offer, but don't share too much information."

Sitting there, I understood why Whitaker was sticking with O'Brien and me. That FBI creep had tried to cut a sweetheart deal with a known child rapist and murderer. I wondered if Whitaker was afraid Longhorn might try to do the same with Persico if the FBI got control of our case. And if Vanderhoot was positioning himself for a U.S. Attorney's job, then his loyalties might lean toward Longhorn, not us.

None of this political wrangling had anything to do with solving our murder. But I'd learned early on as an A.D.A. that this sort of backstage politicking played a key role in the success or failure of cases. From the moment a victim was identified, factors such as who was assigned to investigate the crime, prosecute the case, defend the accused, and sit on the jury influenced whether justice would be served.

O'Brien broke the silence around the conference table. "Those guys don't have a clue yet who that victim is," he said.

Steinberg nodded. "When he finds out it's Tiny Nunzio's daughter, he's going to push even harder to get control of this case."

Their remarks confirmed what O'Brien and I had suspected. Our murder victim, Isabella Ricci, was the only daughter of Giuseppe "Tiny" Nunzio, a capo in the New Jersey–based Gaccione family. In mob hierarchy, Nunzio was Persico's equal, only he operated across the Hudson.

"People could start killing each other over this," O'Brien warned.

"That might not be a bad thing," Steinberg said.

"Aren't we getting ahead of ourselves?" I asked. "I'm not so sure Persico killed her."

"What?" Vanderhoot said in a surprised voice. "Of course he did."

"Doesn't it seem a bit too obvious? The Butcher leaves Isabella's body hanging in an apartment rented by one of his own law firm's stooges? Does anyone else think this might be a setup?"

"Who'd want to frame him?" Vanderhoot replied. "Persico probably was going to send a cleanup crew over this morning. Even gangsters celebrate New Year's."

"I want to see those FBI logs," I said. "The building's super said Isabella and her lover had been using that apartment for a rendezvous twice a week for the past three months. If Persico was her lover and the FBI was tailing him, the logs should reflect that, but right now, we simply don't have enough facts."

Whitaker checked his Rolex. "All right, on to the press conference. I've changed my mind about having you there, Miss Fox. It's more important for you and O'Brien to keep working this case before Longhorn finds out our victim is Tiny Nunzio's daughter and tries to muscle in." Standing from his chair, he said, "If the Butcher is our man, bring me his head."

His three chiefs responded approvingly in "Aye-aye, sir" tones, but I kept quiet. Something just didn't smell right about this case.

8

VANDERHOOT WALKED BRISKLY TOWARD THE ELEVA-
tor when we exited Whitaker's office. I hurried up to catch him.
"Chief, I'd like any files you have on Persico before we go see
him," I said.

Vanderhoot glanced around the hallway to make sure that only O'Brien
and I were in earshot. "I bet you would, wouldn't you, sweetheart," he said
sarcastically. "Let me clue you in, Ms. Fox. You are not getting squat. You
want to play with the big boys and show us how brilliant you are by taking
one of our cases, guess what?"

The elevator arrived.

"I'm only doing what I was ordered," I said.

But he wasn't in any mood to listen. As the doors began to open, he said
"Fuck you" under his breath before stepping quickly into a group of courthouse workers already inside the elevator.

O'Brien and I waited for the next lift down and headed across the street
to our offices. The lobby of the Domestic Violence Unit's office was crowded
with witnesses whom I needed to prepare for upcoming cases. There was a
huge stack of messages waiting on my desk, too.

O'Brien followed me into my office and asked, "How we handling this?"

I let out a frustrated sigh and said, "I don't feel comfortable turning over my
trial scheduled for tomorrow morning to someone else." I checked the time
and said, "Look, I've got to prepare, but I'm going to work through lunch and
should be done later this afternoon. Then we can pay a visit to the Butcher."

"The boss said this was a priority," he gently reminded me.

"So is tomorrow's trial."

"Got ya. I'll check in on the Yonkers detectives," he said. "But first, I'm getting coffee. That's a priority, too." He disappeared while I began reading the pink return-call slips on my desk. Will had telephoned from the newspaper three times so I dialed his direct number in the newsroom and when he answered, I gave him a cheery "Good morning! I didn't see you at the murder scene last night."

"I stopped there but didn't recognize any of the cops so I moved on. They wouldn't let me inside anyway," he said. "Can you believe the victim is Isabella Ricci?"

There was something about the tone of his voice that made me suspicious.

"Are you trying to get me to confirm it was her?" I asked him bluntly.

The phone went quiet for a moment until Will said, "Sorry, Dani, but the city desk is really pushing me and no one will say on the record whether it was her. I, just, well, yes, I thought if you confirmed it, I could run with it. Right now, all I've got are rumors. So tell me, is it her?"

My face felt flush. Maybe it was inevitable for there to be conflict between our jobs, but I'd trusted Will and thought he was above this sort of cheap reporter's trick. Shortly after we'd started dating, we'd agreed that we would keep our professional lives completely separate from our personal ones. Now I was beginning to wonder if that was even possible.

"In my defense," Will said, "I wasn't asking you to tell me her name. I was just floating a rumor by you. If it is her, this is going to be one hell of a story—the sort of scoop that gets a reporter noticed."

"First, I'm not just another courthouse source," I replied. "I'm your girlfriend, remember? Second, you didn't ask me directly. You pretended you knew it was her and tried to trick me into confirming it."

"Will you?" he said in a sweet voice.

"I certainly will not either confirm nor deny it. I cannot and do not want to be a source."

"Okay, calm down, Dani. I apologize. You must be having a bad day. How about if I take you to Roberto's for dinner tonight?"

Roberto's is my favorite restaurant.

"Let's check in later today," I said, still peeved. "Right now, I'm busy."

"You're busy investigating the Isabella Ricci murder, right?" he said, apparently trying to make a joke. Or was he?

I hung up.

O'Brien returned with his coffee. "Trouble in paradise, huh?" he said, smirking. "I told you not to date a reporter. He's not one of us."

"And Miss Potts . . . is one of us?"

"How many times are you gonna break my balls about her?"

"Until you get something on me," I answered, grinning.

"Oh, believe me, I'm looking." As he left, I told the receptionist to send in the first witness for the next day's case.

9

IN THE BIG PICTURE, *THE PEOPLE V. HAROLD RYAN* WAS NOT a major criminal case. I could have easily passed it over to another A.D.A., but most of my peers were more interested in prosecuting cocaine dealers and armed robbers than husbands who beat their wives. Such abuse wasn't even considered a crime between married couples until 1977 in New York. But I felt a special obligation to handle the Ryan case personally.

I'd first met Anna Forsano a year ago when her mother, Sarah, literally dragged the twenty-one-year-old into my office. She had a busted lip and two black eyes that her boyfriend, Harold Ryan, had given her. Apparently, they'd been drinking with friends in a bar when Anna had said something that irked Harold. He backhanded her, splitting her lip, and then began punching her in the face. The only reason that Anna had agreed to accompany her mother to our office was that she was afraid that her father, Albert Forsano, would find out and go after Harold. Apparently, Albert disliked him and had an equally hot temper.

I'd interviewed Anna that morning at her mother's side—or I'd tried to interview her. She'd done exactly what most victims of domestic violence do: she blamed herself. "I provoked him," she said. "I know he's got a temper. I shouldn't have nagged at him."

I hear this over and over. A push turns into a slap that turns into a punch. By the time there's a full-scale beating, the victim really believes she deserves it, because her abuser has destroyed her self-esteem and confidence. By the time the physical bruises and scars appear, the emotional and psychological damage has already been done.

Because of that, many of the women who come through my office are reluctant or refuse to testify. They need help, but they're convinced they're to blame. Most of them also don't want me to lock up the family's sole breadwinner, further anger him, or take him from his children.

And that is exactly how Anna had been when we first met that morning. I tried to warn her that abusers don't stop, despite all the promises that they make and the bouquets of roses that they bestow after violent arguments, along with a litany of "It will never happen again" and "I love you."

No matter what I said, Anna refused to tell me anything more than that the bruises were her fault. After a few moments of gentle prodding by me, Anna broke into tears and promised me and her mother that she would seek psychological help. Our meeting that morning ended with Anna promising that she'd have Harold come see me.

Of course, he didn't, but I had a little trick of my own waiting for Mr. Ryan. Under New York law, I had no authority to force him to do anything. But shortly after our unit opened, I had stationery printed with the heading WESTCHESTER COUNTY DOMESTIC VIOLENCE UNIT emblazoned across the top of each sheet. I addressed a letter to Ryan and directly under this name, I wrote: "In the Matter of the People of the State of New York against Harold Ryan." I suspected that my wording might scare him. And it did.

Had Ryan taken my letter to a lawyer, he would have been told that there was no case pending against him nor had any criminal charges been filed and that he absolutely did not have to show up. But Ryan assumed the worst and he reported to my office a few days after my letter arrived. If he had been candid with me, I might have handled him differently. But when I asked him about Anna's busted lip and swollen eyes, he lied. He said that he'd never touched her. She'd gotten drunk and fallen at a bar when they'd been out with friends.

"She's clumsy like that," he said. "Especially when she's had a few."

"Bull," I said. "You hit her and that's a crime. Period."

At that point our conversation had gone from being merely unpleasant to downright ugly. No one was going to tell Harold what he could or couldn't do with Anna.

"She loves me," he bragged, adding that she would never press charges or testify against him. "And you can't make her," he taunted.

"Look, buster," I snapped, "I don't know who you think you are, but I represent the People of the State of New York, and I can file charges and prosecute you whether Anna testifies or not."

Having gotten his attention, I said, "You either go into counseling and anger management, or I'll prosecute you. If you can't afford the counseling, my office will make arrangements for you. I expect you to report back to me because I will be keeping an eye on you."

Harold did not immediately reply. "I want to talk to a lawyer," he said after several moments, then stormed out.

A few days later, I got a call from a local attorney who told me that Anna and Ryan had gotten married. If they were thinking that as husband and wife, she couldn't be forced to testify against him, they were wrong. But neither of them would talk to me unless his or her lawyer was present.

In my line of work, I've come to trust my gut when it comes to judging people. Harold Ryan struck me as a dirtbag whose abuse would only get worse if I didn't step in and do something. So I got O'Brien to help me get the bartender to come forward as a witness. I now could charge Harold with several felonies.

As with most criminal cases, I assumed there would be a plea negotiation with Harold's attorney. My goal was to get him into treatment before he hurt Anna again. But Harold and his attorney dug in their heels, leaving me no choice but to indict Ryan and take him to trial.

I worked through lunch and into the early afternoon, preparing witnesses who had seen the beating. By three o'clock, I was feeling confident. I was nearly finished when our receptionist announced that she was putting through a call from defense attorney Richard Coppola, who was representing Harold Ryan.

Ah, I thought, a last-minute plea offer. Harold had finally come to his senses.

"This is Dani Fox," I said into the receiver.

"Have you heard?" Coppola asked me.

I felt a sense of dread and immediately suspected the worst—that Harold had killed Anna.

"What's your client done?" I asked.

"My client?" Coppola asked. "My client is dead."

Coppola explained that Anna's father, Albert, had fatally shot Harold in front of Anna and their neighbors. The cops were questioning him in lockup. There would be no need for a Ryan trial.

As I was putting the phone back in its cradle, O'Brien sauntered into my office.

"Harold Ryan just got himself killed," I said.

"No great loss there," O'Brien replied.

"Albert Forsano killed him in broad daylight with a shotgun."

"Good for him," O'Brien said.

"C'mon, O'Brien, you don't believe that."

"Hey, the kid was beating his daughter. If your father was alive, he'd have done the same thing."

I thought about Leo, my father, and wondered if O'Brien was right. Dad was a World War II veteran who'd seen combat but who also was one of the most peaceful men I've known. But the truth was that I didn't really know how my own father would have reacted if one of my boyfriends had given me a busted lip or black eye. Fortunately, I've never had to find out.

"No one has a right to take the law into their own hands," I said. But it sounded halfhearted. "C'mon," O'Brien said. "Look on the sunny side. We can get back to catching Isabella Ricci's killer. Unless you plan on putting a dead man on trial."

10

TRAFFIC WAS HORRIBLE AND IT TOOK US MORE THAN an hour to reach Persico's family-owned butcher shop in the heart of Yonkers's Little Italy. Fortunately, the shop catered to customers on their way home from work who needed to pick up dinner: it didn't close until 8 p.m.

Persico's storefront looked much as it probably had when it first opened in the early 1900s, when immigrants from southern Italy were pouring into New York in great waves. There were four patio tables with folding metal chairs on the sidewalk out front, where customers could sip coffee and eat freshly made deli sandwiches. Above the door was a painting of a big pink pig with a curly tail that spelled out the name PERSICO.

I told a chubby clerk that we wanted to speak to Mr. Persico and he disappeared into the rear of the store. There was a camera mounted in a corner, so I assumed we were being watched. About two minutes later, the clerk reappeared with a husky, short man in his fifties who was wearing a thick gold chain and an open-necked shirt that was exposing a black and gray mat of chest hair.

"Whaddya want?" he asked.

"I'm an assistant district attorney," I said loudly. "This is Detective O'Brien. We need to speak to Mr. Persico."

"Hey, I recognize youse," he declared. "You're that broad who was all over the papers. The prosecutor who got that child-molesting bastard put away." He seemed genuinely appreciative. He eyeballed O'Brien. "You got a badge or something?"

O'Brien showed him his ID.

Satisfied, he said, "So why youse two want to see the boss?"

I said, "And you are who, exactly?"

"I'm the man who decides whether youse two get through that back door and see Mr. Persico," he replied defiantly.

"You got a name?" I asked.

"Carmine Caruso," he replied. "I sorta run things for Mr. Persico."

"We're here about Isabella Ricci. Tell him we can talk here or we can do it up at the D.A.'s office."

Caruso gave me a long, hard stare. I stared right back at him. He had a big gap between his two front teeth, and tied around his protruding belly was a white, bloodstained apron. As he wiped his sausage-sized fingers on his apron, he walked through the door behind the counter without further comment.

For a good ten minutes, customers, mostly older women from the neighborhood, came and went.

I was beginning to get irritated at the lack of respect and was just about to tell Carmine that we would be back with a subpoena when I heard a voice speak quietly behind me. "Ms. Fox and Detective O'Brien. A call to our office would have been in order." It was Alonzo Gallo from the law firm of Gallo & Conti, along with his younger sidekick and apartment renter, Alberto Bianchi.

Continuing, Gallo said, "You're trying to blindside us, counselor. You know that Mr. Persico is our client."

With a smirk, O'Brien said, "Why's he need an attorney? We're just here for a friendly chat."

Gallo glanced at the video camera so that his face could be clearly seen. Then he and Bianchi stepped behind the meat counter and the chubby clerk swung open the door that led into the back for them. I decided to fall into step behind them.

Neither Gallo nor Bianchi noticed, but good ole Carmine blocked me.

"Nobody goes back unless the boss says so," he announced.

I noticed that he was still holding a large butcher knife that he'd been using to trim a sirloin. I also noticed that O'Brien was looking at the cuts of meat in the locker. I stepped back and after a few minutes, a buzzer behind the counter sounded and Carmine, who was still holding the carving knife, said, "You can go back now."

He opened the door and I saw Bianchi on the other side. He led us through the oblong back room where four men in white coats and paper hats were chopping pieces of beef from the sides of freshly slaughtered cows hanging from hooks. A fifth employee was using a band saw to cut through the bones of a large hog. None of them looked up as we walked by. I figured they were good at not seeing who came and went here.

Bianchi led us into the office in the back of the store, which contained a large table and folding chairs and featured a large plate-glass window—mirrored so people on the outside couldn't see in. The photographs on the wall were no different from portraits that might have decorated any family-owned shop: Five men in bloody aprons standing outside the front of the butcher shop in the early 1900s and then a series of similar snapshots taken at different years as the business grew and the number of employees expanded. In the center of each photo was a man wearing a suit. The Persico family patriarch, father and son. I also noticed a large crucifix on one wall next to a color photo of the pope. I wondered if they said grace whenever they met here late at night after killing someone and chopping up the corpse.

Attorney Gallo and number-one henchman Caruso were seated on either side of a portly, older man with snow-white hair and a jagged scar on his left cheek. Bianchi took a seat next to Gallo, nodding toward an empty chair apparently meant for me. The table could have accommodated all of us and I could see folding chairs stored in a half-opened nearby closet. They had made sure O'Brien would have no place to sit. A calculated snub.

I looked at the old man and said, "Mr. Persico, my name is Dani Fox. I'm an assistant district attorney in Westchester County and this is Detective O'Brien." I made no effort to shake his hand and he didn't bother to extend his or even make eye contact. No one sitting near him uttered a word. In fact, Persico looked bored, as if he had been through this before with a dozen other prosecutors. He probably had, although I didn't know how many had dared to enter his butcher's den. I met their group silence with a demand. "Detective O'Brien needs a chair."

Caruso smirked and Gallo broke out in a grin, but Persico remained stone-faced. No one moved nor spoke. And neither did I. I remained standing behind the lone chair at the table as if on strike. After several uncomfortable moments, Persico lifted the second finger on his right hand, which was resting in front of him on the table. Caruso immediately said, "If youse want a chair, there's the closet."

O'Brien pulled out the chair at the table for me. I sat down and then he rested most of his butt on top of the conference table next to my chair, keeping one foot firmly planted on the floor. He now towered over the rest of us. He unbuttoned his jacket, casually letting it open, exposing the holster on his belt and his .38-caliber police-issued revolver. Slipping his toothpick from his mouth, he said, "I'm good. But thanks for noticing."

Macho games now over, I got right to it. "Isabella Ricci was found murdered yesterday in an apartment rented by Gallo & Conti."

Persico stayed mute.

"Mr. Persico, you were seen entering that same apartment building at the same time as the murder."

"Who says my client was there?" Gallo said loudly.

Did Gallo really think I was that stupid? I wasn't going to tell a Mafia capo the name of an eyewitness. Ignoring Gallo, I said, "Mr. Persico's limo delivered him to the Midland Apartments at two-thirty. We'd like to know why you visited Mrs. Ricci."

"My client has nothing to say about this matter," Gallo snapped.

"Your client was seen leaving the building a few hours later in a hurry. He was later observed changing his clothes before he went home."

I wanted Persico to know that he'd been watched. I wasn't worried about Persico going after FBI Agent Walter Coyle. But I was concerned that he might go after Roman Mancini, since the Midland Apartments manager had been outside the building, fixing a light fixture, when Persico's limo had arrived.

My ruse didn't work.

Persico didn't show any emotion or even open his mouth. It was pretty obvious that the only reason he had agreed to meet with us was that he was curious to learn what evidence we might have on him.

I decided I was being too subtle. "Mr. Persico," I said, in my most polite voice, "how long have you and Isabella Ricci been having an affair?"

My question clearly irritated Gallo, but before he could answer for his client, Persico looked into my face and said, "Me and her?"

"Twice a week, regular as clockwork," I said. "Every Tuesday and Friday."

"You think I was banging that broad twice a week?" Persico chuckled.

"We've heard enough," Gallo said.

But Persico lifted his right finger again and his paid counselor abruptly stopped talking. "Listen, who I sleep with and when I do it is none of your damn business. Unless I'm banging you," he sneered.

I refused to react and instead asked, "Then tell us why you went to see Isabella at the Midland Apartments."

Gallo leaned over and whispered in his client's ear.

Persico nodded.

"Miss Fox," Gallo said, "unless you are prepared to charge my client with a crime, he has nothing more to say to you."

Bianchi immediately stood to escort us out of the conference room. I got up from the table and said, "Gentlemen, this has been interesting."

O'Brien slid from the table and stepped behind me. I could feel their eyes following me as we left the room and assumed they were still watching from behind the tinted glass as we made our way to the front lobby.

O'Brien and I had just rounded the meat counter's corner and were walking out the front door when Carmine yelled after me. "Hey you," he said. "The boss wants you to have this." He held up a white package of meat. "It's pork chops."

I wasn't certain if Persico was making a joke about law enforcement or if he knew about Wilbur back at my house. Either way, it wasn't funny.

"Tell your boss, 'No thanks!'" I said loud enough for a handful of waiting customers to hear. "I take my arsenic with beef."

PART TWO

EENY, MEENY, MINY, MOE: SUSPECTS APLENTY

My husband and I split up because I finally faced the fact that we're incompatible. I'm a Gemini and he's an asshole.

—ANONYMOUS

11

B Y NOW, IT WAS 6:45 P.M. AND I WAS SUPPOSED TO MEET Will for dinner at 7, but we wouldn't meet until closer to nine.

"Let's interview Isabella's husband," I said.

O'Brien replied, "Makes sense. Always an obvious suspect."

As we drove toward White Plains, I asked, "What the hell was all that folding chair bullshit at Persico's about?"

O'Brien shrugged. "Telling me I ain't worthy of sitting with them."

"Men and their mind games. I don't get it."

"Oh yeah, like women don't play 'em."

As we neared the gated driveway of a lavish French-style house in a pricey neighborhood in Scarsdale, O'Brien exclaimed, "Hey, I know him!" He pointed toward a burly, uniformed security guard posted outside the driveway entrance at the home of Isabella Ricci and her husband, Marco. "Hey, Pete, you bastard!" O'Brien hollered through his rolled-down driver's-side window.

The guard strolled over to the unmarked police cruiser. "Tommy Boy, fancy seeing you here," he replied in a thick Irish accent.

"What the hell you doin'?" O'Brien asked.

"And you call yourself a detective, Tommy Boy? What the fuck you think I'm doing standing out here. I'm getting rich. Time-and-a-half just farting in the wind."

"The easy life of a rent-a-cop," O'Brien said. "A crying shame. A mediocre cop turned hired babysitter."

"What's that? The way I heard it, you work for the tit patrol now. You and a bunch of bra-burning broads tormenting their poor husbands. Homicide to pantycide. Tell me, Tommy Boy, who's worse off?"

"Pete," O'Brien said without missing a beat, "say hello to Dani Fox, my boss."

Pete leaned down and peered into the car. "Oh, sorry, ma'am, I figured you was just another cop."

"No, I'm the chief of the tit patrol," I said. "Is Marco Ricci in his house?"

"Yes, ma'am," he said with a reddening face. "No disrespect intended."

"How long you been standing out here protecting the pavement?" O'Brien interrupted.

"Dr. Ricci called our office first thing this morning—as soon as he heard it was his wife who got butchered yesterday in Yonkers."

"Wait," I said, interrupting. "He didn't know until this morning that his wife had been murdered on New Year's Eve?"

"That's what I heard, ma'am."

O'Brien asked, "Who else is standing guard here? Anyone I'd know?"

"Naw, bunch of kids. Got one inside the house and two walking the grounds. Dr. Ricci's up there shaking like a one-dollar-a-pop whore after she's done a platoon of Marines." He suddenly remembered that I was there and lowered his head down to the window again. "Sorry, ma'am."

"He's shaking because he knows you're protecting him," O'Brien said.

"Don't let this gray stovepipe fool you, Tommy Boy. I can still take you with one hand while enjoying a cold one at O'Toole's with the other."

O'Brien said to me, "Pete retired two years ago and me and the boys gave him one hell of a send-off. He was arm-wrestling anyone who'd put a ten-spot on the pool table. Drunken bastard."

I looked at Pete and he flexed his right arm. "I beat this youngster twice that night," Pete said.

"If you think he's a youngster," I replied, "then you needed to retire."

O'Brien guffawed. "She got you good on that one, Pete."

I decided to interrupt the frat boy reminiscing. "Any idea why Dr. Ricci and his wife didn't spend New Year's Eve together?"

"I heard a few theories," Pete said. "The doc and his missus weren't exactly on peaceable terms. Nasty divorce in the works."

"Who's divorcing whom?" I asked.

"She was dumping him, according to Adalina."

"Adalina?"

"Pete's better half," O'Brien volunteered. "She owns the Bellissimo Beauty Boutique over near Scarsdale."

"We call it the Three B's for short," Pete said proudly. "Best salon around. Ain't much Adalina don't hear from her clients and Mrs. Ricci is, well, she was a regular."

"At the precinct," O'Brien said, "if we wanted to know who was cheating on who, we'd check with Adalina. She was our Deep Throat."

"Whoa, that's my wife you're talking about," Pete said, in mock horror.

"Pete's wife is a looker," O'Brien continued. "He robbed the cradle. What, twenty, maybe thirty years between you?"

"Ten, but I'll tell her that, Tommy Boy. I'll say you called her a child bride." Once again, he leaned down so he could look inside and see me. "You should go by the Three B's and ask her to fix you up. She does a lot of the guys' wives from the precinct."

"Thanks," I said, feeling a bit insulted but also wondering what those cops' wives' hair looked like after a visit to the Three B's. If Adalina was anything like her talkative husband, I'd be afraid to let her get close to me with a pair of scissors. I said, "Did your wife say why Isabella was divorcing him?"

"Either he was poking his pepperoni into places it didn't belong or she was playing hide-the-wiener with someone else. Adalina said lots of insecure women came through his office, him being a plastic surgeon, you know. A nip and a tuck and maybe a bit more."

"Like a dip and a stick?" O'Brien said, laughing at his own joke.

"You'd think if you looked at tits and ass all day you'd get tired of seeing them," Pete said. "But then, I never would, right, Tommy Boy?"

I tried to elevate the conversation. "Has anyone been out here to interview Dr. Ricci?"

"Yeah," Pete said. "Some Yonkers detectives."

"Why the heavy security?" O'Brien asked, emphasizing the word *heavy*.

"You still a detective, Tommy Boy?" Pete asked in a mocking voice. "It's as obvious as dots on a Dalmatian. The doc's dead wife is Tiny Nunzio's daughter."

I said, "Can I assume Nunzio isn't a fan of Dr. Ricci?"

"Whenever there's a nasty divorce and one of them that's getting divorced ends up dead, who do you blame? I heard Tiny wasn't real buddy-buddy with his son-in-law anyway, 'cause of his cheating ways."

Without waiting for either of us to reply, Pete added, "It's a real shame, Tommy Boy, how young people today are getting divorced. Me and Adalina, we got thirty-five years in."

"She's a saint," O'Brien said. "And if you cheated, Adalina would turn you into a soprano."

"I'm a lucky man, Tommy Boy. I ain't going to bed alone at night with only my pillows to comfort me."

"Neither am I," O'Brien said. "Your mother and sisters can testify to that."

I'd heard enough. "Let's go interview Ricci."

As we drove up the circular drive, I said, "Why do men, who are friends, show it by insulting each other? Are you afraid of being called a homosexual if you exchange niceties?"

O'Brien jammed on the brakes. "Homosexual? What the hell? I didn't say nothing homosexual to him. You got that? We was just busting each other's balls."

"Okay, okay."

Another security guard was standing at the front door. Pete had already alerted him so he opened the front door for us without asking for IDs. The foyer led into a cavernous living room, where a man was sitting all by himself smoking a cigarette and drinking coffee. Marco Ricci was small-framed, with black curly hair, delicate features, and a panicked look in his eyes.

Before either of us could ask a question, he began talking. "I've not seen Isabella's body yet. They called but I've not dared go to the medical examiner's office or to a funeral home. I'm not leaving this house."

"Why?" I asked, playing dumb.

"Why? Why? Because her father is Tiny Nunzio, for God's sake! Isabella and I were getting a divorce. He hates me and isn't going to want me anywhere near her body. I doubt he'll even let me attend the funeral, especially after he sees what happened to her."

"You mean how she was butchered?" I said.

"Yes, that's exactly what I mean," he replied in an irritated voice. "The Yonkers police told me the man who did this cut off pieces of her flesh. It was on the radio, too. To tell you the truth, I'm glad her father is going to take charge of the funeral. I don't want to see her like that."

"How far along were you in the divorce process?"

"She'd filed papers against me last year and we both had lawyers but we were a long way from getting everything settled. It should have been a snap since we didn't have any children together."

"Then why the holdup?"

"We're dealing with a big estate."

"How big?" O'Brien interjected.

"About five million, plus this house."

"Where was she living?" I asked.

"Right here. It's a rather large house—more than seven thousand square feet. She was staying on one floor and I was staying on another. The lawyers warned each of us to stay put; otherwise we might be forfeiting our claim to the property. Naturally, we did our best to avoid each other."

Marco Ricci looked around his massive living room. "Isabella decorated this house and wanted it. But I wasn't going to hand it over, because I owned it before we got married. As you can see, we had different tastes. I like period pieces; she liked Andy Warhol."

The furniture and wall coverings were modern, which didn't match the French architecture at all. But Isabella's choice in art and furniture showed she had a good eye.

"Where were you New Year's Eve between two and six?" I asked.

"Oh please. You don't really think I killed her, do you? I was in my office."

"Witnesses saw you?" O'Brien asked.

"My secretary was there. She'll vouch for me. And patients."

I asked: "Do you know of any reason why someone would want to kill your wife?"

"No, not one," he replied, nervously smashing his cigarette in a black ceramic ashtray by his chair. "But Tiny will blame me. I know he will. That's why I need protection. I asked the Yonkers cops for help but they said I had to hire guards. You need to find out who did this so Tiny will leave me alone."

Ricci fired up another cigarette, took a quick puff, and then continued talking. "Isabella was trying to take me for everything I own in the divorce.

Everything I built. The definition of hell is being divorced by an Italian woman. There's no reasoning with them. It's all emotion and anger. I've been divorced twice and never had the sort of fight that she was giving me."

"She was wife number three?" O'Brien asked.

"Yes, and to answer your next question, Detective, both of my ex-wives are still alive and collecting alimony."

"You don't seem too upset that Isabella has been murdered," I noted.

"Would you prefer crocodile tears? I've met someone and there will be a fourth Mrs. Ricci. Hopefully, the last."

His candor surprised me. "Did Isabella file divorce papers after you met the fourth Mrs. Ricci?" I asked.

"I wasn't cheating on Isabella, if that's what you're asking."

"So you were just platonic friends with this woman," I said.

"Don't be ridiculous. We were sleeping together, but Isabella didn't object. We agreed when we got married that we'd have an open relationship."

"Are you saying that Isabella didn't mind you having sex with other women?" I asked in a surprised voice.

"That's right. Where is it written that you can't have other sexual partners in addition to your wife? It's already the eighties, not the Dark Ages."

"Actually, it's written in the Ten Commandments," I said, adding, "since you asked."

"Neither of us gave a good goddamn about religion. She was raised Catholic but didn't go to church. Anyway, it hardly matters now, does it?"

"Adultery," I said, "can be a motive for murder."

O'Brien jumped into our conversation. "Let's get this straight. She didn't care if you was balling other women and you didn't care if she was screwing other men. Is that what you're telling us?"

"Why should I care if she saw other men?" Ricci said. "In fact, I encouraged her to liberate herself."

"So you weren't jealous she was banging another guy every Tuesday and Thursday in Yonkers?" O'Brien said.

"Twice a week? Is that how often they were meeting? Huh. Do you know how long this affair had been going on?"

"At least three months," I said.

"No wonder he killed her," he said smiling. "Three months with Isabella would be enough to make anyone go berserk." He pressed out his cigarette and immediately lit another. "Isabella was spoiled rotten. I blame her father. He gave her everything she ever wanted."

"Do you know the name of the man she was seeing?" O'Brien asked.

"Don't have a clue. Do you?"

I ignored his question and asked, "Do you know the names of any enemies that she might have had?"

He shrugged. "She didn't have any enemies or any friends. When people found out who her father was, they tended to stay away. Her father and her family were the only people who she wanted to socialize with."

"She ever say anything to you about problems that her father was having with some other mobster?"

"She never said a word about family business," Ricci said. "But you're barking up the wrong tree. These guys don't mess with each other's families. It's a big taboo. They're smart enough to know that once you start killing wives and girlfriends and kids, then your own wife and girlfriend and kids are going to become targets."

"You seem to know a lot about them," I said, "for someone who wasn't accepted by the family."

"Call it self-preservation," he said. "When we were first married, I tried to impress her father. I mean, I'm a doctor, an accomplished plastic surgeon, but every time I saw him, he'd make some crack about how I was the 'breast man.' If he was cooking pork, it'd be, 'Save the teats for the breast man' or 'Grab a chicken breast for the breast man.' I got sick of it. He runs a garbage collection business! Who's he think he is? He's bitter because I took his daughter away from him and I changed her."

"Changed her? How?"

"Not her personality," he replied. "I physically changed her. I improved her appearance. I worked on her legs, her abdomen, and got rid of her big Roman nose. I made it smaller and I made her breasts bigger."

"Daddy didn't like that?" O'Brien asked.

"He was furious. He took me aside and threatened me one day. It was after I had enhanced her breasts. He told me that I'd better never take the knife to his girl again or he'd take one to me. Now you see why I have guards here. Do you think I should leave town?"

"That's not a good idea right now," I said.

"Not until we get this sorted out," O'Brien added. "But it's probably smart to keep the guards around."

"Listen, my marriage was on the rocks but even if I had killed her—and I didn't, but if I had—I wouldn't have cut her up. I made her beautiful. Cutting her would have been like Picasso pissing on one of his own paintings."

O'Brien gave him a business card and told him to call if he thought of anything else. We left him puffing on yet another cigarette.

When we were back in the car heading down the driveway, O'Brien said, "Talk about a Napoleon complex." Mimicking Marco Ricci's high-pitched voice, he said, " 'Cutting her would have been like Picasso pissin' on one of his own paintings.' "

"It also would have been a way for him to stick it to her daddy, wouldn't it?" I replied. "Marco Ricci made her beautiful and then he took back his work. All the cuts the killer made on Isabella were at locations on her body where her husband had done plastic surgery. He takes back his work, makes her ugly, all the while knowing that the cops will blame the Butcher?"

O'Brien removed his toothpick from his lips. "For a lawyer, you're getting pretty damn good at police work."

"I have my moments."

— 12 —

WHEN I GOT TO ROBERTO'S, WILL WAS NOWHERE to be seen. This could only mean that he was still at the *White Plains Daily* finishing some sensational story. When he finally showed up fifteen minutes later, he explained, "It's your boss's fault. His press conference ran overtime."

"What'd the Westchester D.A. have to say?" I asked.

"He announced that the murder victim was Isabella Ricci and described how she'd been tortured, which the New York tabloids loved, of course. He also dropped your name."

"What'd he say about me?"

"That since you are the only female assistant D.A. in his office, and this was a brutal crime against a woman, he wants you to prosecute," Will said. "He's clearly out for the women's vote again."

In addition to being the newspaper's crime reporter, Will wrote about local politics on occasion. There were times when I suspected that he knew more about Whitaker than I did.

Continuing, he said, "What he didn't announce was why Isabella was in that apartment. In fact, he didn't say a word about the affair that she was having." A big grin appeared on Will's face as he waited for me to ask the obvious.

"Okay," I said, taking the bait, "if Whitaker didn't mention that Isabella was having an affair, then how do you know that she was?"

"Because I did my own digging and interviewed the apartment building's super. A fellow named Roman Mancini," he declared.

"Mancini is talking to reporters?"

"No, he's not talking to reporters. He's talking only to me. I got an exclusive. It's on tomorrow's front page. Banner headline. That's the real reason I'm late. Your boss's press conference ran long and is good stuff, but it is going to be a sidebar to my Mancini interview. Boy, is Whitaker going to be angry at being knocked under the fold."

"He won't be the only one," I said, "especially if something happens to Roman Mancini because of your exclusive. You do realize, don't you, that he's an eyewitnesses in an ongoing homicide investigation that involves the daughter of a known Mafia capo?"

"That's why this exclusive is so cool. Lots of reporters knocked on his door, but he slammed it in their faces. He slammed it in mine, too, the first time. But after I got a whiff of his breath and saw his watery eyes, I pegged him for an alcoholic. An hour later, I went back to his apartment with a couple of fifths and got myself invited in for a drink."

"You bribed him with booze?" I asked in a stern voice.

"I didn't bribe him. I simply suggested we have a few drinks together and chat."

"And you didn't see anything wrong with that?" I asked in a disapproving tone.

"Why should I?" he replied, somewhat irritated. "Look, Mancini is an adult and I certainly didn't hold a gun to his head. He invited me inside his place to have a few friendly drinks. No harm in that."

"What, exactly, did Mancini tell you?"

"Are we changing the ground rules here, Dani?" he asked. "Earlier today, you got upset when I asked you to confirm that Isabella Ricci was the murder victim. Now you want me to tell you what Mancini said before my story is published in tomorrow's paper."

"There's a difference. I'm an officer of the court. You're a newspaper reporter. A man's life may be at risk. Besides, you're going to tell everyone on the front page tomorrow what Mancini told you during your interview—so what's the big deal about telling me now?"

"The big deal is that I know you and you might try to do something about it," he replied.

His answer concerned me. "I'd really like to know what Mancini told you. Are you identifying him by name tomorrow in your story?"

"You bet I am. We're publishing a front-page picture of him standing outside the Midland Apartments."

"You do realize that you could be putting him in danger, especially if he said anything that could help identify the killer."

"Hey," Will said in an exasperated voice. "My job is to get the story and this is a big one. I thought you'd be impressed with my ingenuity. I didn't think you would criticize me about this."

"This is important to me," I said. "I need to know exactly what Mancini told you about Isabella's murder."

"Okay, so we *are* changing the ground rules," he repeated. "Can I assume that the next time I need information, you are going to tell me?"

I was getting exasperated. "No, it doesn't work that way. I'm asking because I don't want anyone going after Mancini. Don't you get that?"

Will hesitated and then said, "Mancini said Isabella Ricci was pretending to be a woman named Vicky and that twice a week, she met her lover in the apartment where she was found murdered."

"Did Mancini describe her lover to you?"

"Yes, he said he was an older man who always came to the apartment in a black limo."

"Anything else? Anything about his appearance?"

"Only the most important part of my exclusive interview," Will said, triumphantly lifting up his beer. "Mancini said that he thought Isabella's lover was a mobster. How's that for a kicker? My editors are going nuts over this story. Can you imagine, the married daughter of a New Jersey mobster found dead in Yonkers, where she was having an affair with another mobster?! You've got to wonder why they were meeting in Yonkers and the logical answer is that her lover must be a member of a New York crime family, not a New Jersey one. Rival families. This is sensational stuff!"

"Will, you need to call your editors and get that part of the story cut out," I said.

"Are you crazy?"

"But it could get Roman Mancini murdered. If she was seeing a New

York mobster, that mobster isn't going to want Mancini identifying him in court at a trial. Your story also could stir up trouble between the New Jersey and New York mobs. Tiny Nunzio is no one to fool with."

"Dani, my job is to get the news—not hide it from the public. It's your job to protect Mancini, isn't it? And I don't give a damn if some New York mobster who was screwing Isabella Ricci ends up being killed by her outraged father."

"I can't tell you everything that I know about this investigation, but you need to cut out that part of the story because it's going to cause problems," I said.

"Dani, I'm not going to do that. C'mon, I'm a reporter. I can't decide what is and isn't news based on what my girlfriend thinks may or may not happen in the future. Mancini is an adult. I asked him questions and he answered them. End of story."

Our entrées arrived, which was good, because it gave me a second to collect my thoughts. "Did Mancini say anything more about the older man who visited the apartment?"

"He just said he was an older gangster. Why? Did I miss something?"

"No," I replied, lying and grateful that Mancini had not mentioned anything about a facial scar. "But after we finish dinner, I'm going to call Whitaker and urge him to call your editors. I'm also going to suggest that he arrange for Mancini to get immediate police protection."

"Aren't you getting a bit melodramatic here?" he replied. "Besides, my editors aren't going to cave in just because Whitaker calls them—if he does."

"That's how serious I think this is."

"Do me a favor," Will said. "If you put Mancini under protection, let me know so I can get a paragraph inserted in tomorrow's newspaper saying that Mancini needed protection because of my exclusive story."

I glared at him. "You want to give yourself credit for putting a man's life in danger?"

"Dani, if anything, having Mancini's face and name on the front page will probably protect him. I mean, who's going to go after him when he's in the public spotlight like that?"

Our conversation was clearly grating on each of us.

"You know, I really don't want to talk about this anymore," Will said. "I thought you would be happy for me because I just got a big exclusive. But instead, you're worried about how it's going to impact your case. This isn't about you, Dani. It's about me."

His words stung. I said, "Will, it isn't me and it really shouldn't be about you. It's about Roman Mancini. Your story could get him killed."

Both of us picked at our food in silence. "Whether or not Mancini has put himself in danger is not my responsibility," Will finally said. "I report the news. I don't make it happen."

"But you got him to talk to you by getting him drunk."

Will put down his fork. "Don't go all judgmental on me. I don't need you criticizing me because I did my job."

We sat in silence for a few minutes longer until the waiter cleared our plates. I didn't want dessert but Will ordered coffee. I decided to offer an olive branch. "You know a lot about the mob, don't you?" I said. "Tell me about Isabella's father. Why's he called Tiny?"

"Nunzio got his nickname from when he was a kid. He and his pals used to do a lot of break-ins and burglaries and their specialty was getting into stores by climbing up on the rooftops and dismantling large air-conditioning units. Nunzio would slip inside through the vent holes because he was such a tiny guy. Or, at least, that's the story that went around."

"Why don't you give me a Who's Who?"

"Okay, here's a primer. Everyone knows there are five New York crime families, plus a New Jersey crew—the Gacciones. All of the families are living under a truce since the last big war. But there's always been bad blood between the Gacciones in New Jersey and the Battaglia family here in Yonkers. It dates back to Sicily and some reason that no one even cares about today. But it's like the Hatfields and the McCoys."

Warming to his subject, Will continued: "The capo in Yonkers is Nicholas 'the Butcher' Persico. I'm sure you've heard of him. One of his brothers, Anthony Persico, was murdered about a decade ago by a hit man from Rhode Island hired by the New Jersey mob—the Gacciones."

I said, "So Nunzio and Persico—they're both capos in two families that absolutely despise each other—is that fair to say?"

"I'm not sure that the word *hate* really captures how much these two families detest each other. After Persico's brother was killed, Nunzio's oldest son disappeared. Completely vanished. His body has never been found. Naturally, Nunzio suspects Persico. It would be difficult to find two capos who hate each other more than they do. In fact, I've been trying for months to write a story about how much Nunzio and Persico despise each other."

"You have?" I said, surprised. "You never mentioned it to me."

"I don't tell you everything just because you're cute," he said, smiling for the first time since we'd sat down to eat. "At one point, I actually followed Isabella Ricci around for a while because I was trying to get her to speak to me about her father. I was practically stalking her! I went out to the mansion where she and her husband live and spoke to him. You should see the inside of that place. All French on the outside and modern inside. Anyway, he was polite but told me that he doubted she'd talk to me. I never got anywhere with that story, but now that she's dead, maybe I can get a new angle on it, especially if she was sleeping with a mobster in Yonkers."

I quietly wondered if Will had any idea how close his imagination was to the truth. The waiter brought our bill and we split the check. I preferred to pay my own way.

"You want to head over to your place for a while?" Will asked. "We can reconcile. Besides, we still haven't officially welcomed in the new year."

My head was in a totally different place. Our earlier exchange about Mancini was still nagging at me and I was disappointed in how Will was handling the whole matter. I also needed to call Whitaker. Will's work was done at the paper. But mine was just beginning.

"Sorry, but I'm really beat," I said. I should have left it at that, but I couldn't. "Besides, I need to call Whitaker and O'Brien to see if I can get someone over to protect Mancini or at least get him and his wife out of that apartment."

"Dani, I can read you. I know you're upset with me," Will said, "but I'm not going to change anything about my exclusive."

"And if Mancini ends up getting killed?"

"Then I'll write a page-one story about his murder and you'll have another murder to prosecute. It's what I do, Dani, and you've got to learn to live with that."

13

FIVE-FORTY-FIVE IN THE MORNING ARRIVED EARLIER THAN expected. My alarm jolted me out of bed. I threw on my running clothes and tied my sneakers, stretching my legs at the same time. I put my mane in a ponytail and headed out into the morning darkness. It was two miles from my house to a coffee shop where they sold the *White Plains Daily*. I scooped up a copy but didn't bother to open it until I dashed back into my kitchen. After bringing Wilbur in to snack on my leftover salad from Roberto's, I sat down at the table, took a deep breath, and looked at the front page.

As Will had promised, his exclusive interview with Roman Mancini was printed across it under a sensational banner headline: GANGSTER'S SECRET SEX DEN! In smaller letters was a secondary headline: MURDERED BY "GODFATHER" LOVER? A photo of Mancini standing proudly outside the Midland Avenue apartment building with his arm pointing skyward at the window of Isabella's third-floor "love nest" took up the entire top half of the newspaper.

When I got to the third paragraph of Will's exclusive, I grimaced.

Mancini said that the murdered woman, who called herself "Vicky," met twice a week in the apartment with an older man.

"He was a real-life Godfather," Mancini declared. "He always arrived in a limo and had his chauffeur wait outside. I tried to talk to the driver once but he wasn't friendly. There's no question in my mind that he and his driver were both mobsters."

When asked, Mancini said he'd only seen the face of "Vicky's" lover once because the older man generally wore a hat and turned up his collar. But on the afternoon of the murder, the woman's "boyfriend" arrived without a hat and turned-up collar, Mancini said. "He had the eyes of a stone-cold killer. Looking at his face scared me."

"Fuck!" I exclaimed out loud. The anger in my voice caused Wilbur to flinch.

Will's article had created a legal problem. It would give a defense attorney all the ammunition that he needed to create reasonable doubt in jurors' minds if we tried to use Mancini to identify Persico during a trial. How could Mancini have looked into Persico's "stone-cold killer" eyes and not notice his ugly scar? How could he have not mentioned it to Will for his story?

I still also suspected that Will's story had put Mancini's life in danger. I let loose with another expletive. My phone rang just as I finished the last sentence of Will's story.

"Why's your witness's face splattered across the front page of the *White Plains Daily*?" a male voice asked.

"Who's this?" I replied in a suspicious voice.

"FBI Special Agent Walter Coyle."

"How can I help you, Agent Coyle?"

"I want to offer you some friendly advice. Send someone to tell that idiot witness of yours that he needs to stop posing for newspaper photos and to keep his mouth shut—at least until after you arrest Nicholas Persico. He's going to get himself killed."

I didn't appreciate Coyle referring to Roman Mancini as an idiot, even though he clearly was. Just the same, Mancini was my idiot witness, not the FBI's. And I didn't need Coyle telling me how to do my job.

"I informed the Yonkers police last night that a newspaper story was coming out this morning and that Mancini might need protection," I said. "I also urged my boss to call the newspaper and try to get parts of the story cut."

"Well, that didn't work out too well, did it?" he said sarcastically. Then he chuckled and said, "Although it is funny thinking about District Attorney Carlton Whitaker III actually calling a newspaper to get a story cut. Jack Longhorn told me that Whitaker is a news whore."

Who did Coyle think he was? "And Agent Longhorn isn't?" I said.

In a more relaxed voice, Coyle said, "Point taken. Look, I just called to ask if Mancini and his wife are under police protection. A dead witness isn't going to be good for this case."

For a moment, I considered telling Coyle that it wasn't any of his damn business if the Mancinis were under wraps. Instead, I said, "The Yonkers cops said they couldn't afford to assign an officer to babysit Mancini round the clock, but their chief did promise to step up patrols near the Midland Avenue apartment complex until we make an arrest."

"That's why you locals need to join forces with us," Coyle said. "We have all the resources you'll ever need. We can move the Mancinis out of Westchester County so that Persico can't get to them."

I thought for a moment about what he was saying. Maybe the couple needed to be put into a short-term federal protection program to protect them from Isabella's killer and the mob.

"Are you prepared to take them into the Federal Witness Protection Program?" I asked.

"I don't have that authority. There's a special office in the Justice Department that decides who gets to disappear. But I could file a request if you convince me tonight at dinner that I should."

"I didn't say anything about us having dinner tonight," I said.

"I know, but I just did. Look, we need to get together to compare notes about Persico anyway, so we might as well mix work with pleasure—I'll even pay."

"I generally have dinner with my boyfriend," I replied.

"What a lucky guy," he said coolly. "But I'm sure he'll understand, since it's work related. What time is better for you, seven or eight?" Agent Coyle certainly was pushy. But he also had information I needed.

"How about seven at Bistro Bistro in White Plains?" I replied.

"It's a date, then," he said.

"No, it's not a date. It's business."

"Oh, I totally understand, counselor, but tell me one thing before I hang up," he said seriously.

"What's that?"

"What are you wearing?" He laughed and put down the receiver before I could reply.

I didn't know what to make of Walter Coyle. Clearly, he was cocky, and as a general rule, I hate FBI interlopers, mostly because of Longhorn. But I wasn't certain what I thought about this one.

My phone rang again. This time it was O'Brien. We talked for a moment about the newspaper and the problems that Will's story had caused.

"I'm heading over to Yonkers," he announced. "Maybe now we can get the chief to beef up security for the Mancinis. Assuming the chief there can read."

"Great," I said. "I'm getting my hair done."

"What?" he replied. "We got a murderer to catch, remember?"

"The Three B's."

I got to the Bellissimo Beauty Boutique on the outskirts of Scarsdale a few minutes after it opened at 9 a.m.

"You have an appointment?" asked the receptionist.

"I'm a walk-in. Is Adalina available?"

"Oh, honey, she never does walk-ins. She's booked weeks in advance. But Liza can do you in about an hour. We're swamped today."

"Tell Adalina that her husband, Pete, sent me. It's important."

"This really isn't about your hair, then, is it?"

When the receptionist left her station to find Adalina, I surveyed the shop. Every chair was filled. The customers were draped in bright pink cover-ups monogrammed with three B's and a flying bumblebee. The sole male stylist was wearing a Hawaiian shirt, had a Tom Selleck mustache, and was using a straight razor rather than clippers to sculpt his chatty client's hair.

The receptionist returned with a fortyish-looking woman wearing skin-tight Gloria Vanderbilt jeans, a sexy lace top, and inch-thick makeup. Her hair was huge, teased, and sprayed into place. She looked as if she were about to attend an Aerosmith concert.

"My Petey sent you?" she asked.

"Yes, Adalina," I replied. "My name is Dani Fox. I'm an assistant district attorney."

"Oh, let's go back to my office." She nodded toward the rear of the shop. I followed her into a cluttered cubbyhole. "Sorry, it's pretty dumpy in here," she apologized. "I spend my time at my station cutting hair. I only come here to do book work."

"I'd like to ask you about Isabella Ricci."

"I know. Although, you could use a newer look if you don't mind me saying it, honey. I could work you in for a cut next week."

Instinctively running my fingers through my ironed-out hair, I said, "What would you do? I had a total makeover several months ago, but there's not much I can do with my hair."

"I'd make it bigger. Use your natural curls. The straight look is dead now. Maybe a nice big Afro."

"I'll think about it," I said. "What can you tell me about Isabella?"

"She had gorgeous hair. Black and silky."

The image of Isabella dangling from a rope with her hair splattered with blood popped into my head. "I'm more interested in hearing about her marriage to Marco Ricci," I said.

"I bet. And I could tell you plenty about Dr. Marco Ricci. To begin with, he's a bully and a real sleaze. You know they were getting a divorce, right? She'd come in here crying because of how he abused her."

"He beat Isabella?"

"Oh, not physically. Her old man would have cut Marco's balls off if he laid a finger on her." Adalina paused. "You know who her old man is, right?"

"Tiny Nunzio in New Jersey."

"God, if he knew what Marco was doing, he'd have killed him years ago. Isabella was too ashamed to tell him. That Marco was a mean son of a bitch. He beat her down emotionally until she believed she was a worthless piece of shit. He went out of his way to degrade her just so he could feel like a big shot."

"Degrade? How?"

"He forced her to fuck other men. Again, excuse my French."

"She told you that?"

"Therapy here is cheaper than on some shrink's couch, and I'm a hell of a lot better than most of them Sigmund what's-his-name types."

"Freud."

"Yeah, him. Hey, you read that book called *Open Marriage*? One of my clients gave me a copy. Petey got angry when he saw me looking at it."

I sat quietly. Adalina was on a roll.

"My client tells me there's couples all around Scarsdale who are swapping and that same day Isabella came in and I mentioned it. Turns out she was one of them—she broke down and told me the whole story. Marco forced Isabella to fuck, ah, screw these guys because he wanted to screw their wives. And it wasn't just men, neither."

"He wanted her to have sex with another woman?"

"Kinky stuff. Listen, if my Petey wanted to start swapping, I'd cut off his balls, even though there are a few guys around here who I wouldn't mind getting down and dirty with. You know, I'm married but that don't mean I can't look, right?"

I nodded. "What sort of kinky stuff?"

But Adalina ignored my question.

"Isabella's problem was her old man. He'd ruled the roost. She always did what she was told. No backbone. No fight. Plus, she had that whole Catholic guilt thing. You Catholic?"

"Yes. I went to Catholic schools."

"But you ain't Italian, right?"

"No."

"Being Catholic and Italian makes you crazy. You got all that pent-up Catholic guilt about no sex unless you want a baby popping out. Then you're Italian, which means your husband expects you to be a virgin like his sainted mother but wants a whore in bed. I think sex confused her, you know. She really hated it when Marco took her to sex parties."

"Sex parties? Where? In Westchester County?"

"Please! They're everywhere. But Marco hung out in Scarsdale. A better class of pervert, I guess. Isabella said Marco heard about this one party at the country club. Couples would meet there on a Friday night and then go to a house. Everyone started shedding clothes and screwing. Mostly guys on girls, but also girls and girls, some three-ways—even daisy chains."

"Daisy chains?"

"Gosh, you need to work here a week. A daisy chain is a circle on the floor where men and women lie down and perform various sexual acts on each other. Marco loved it but not her. She cried the first time he forced her to give another man, well, a blow job. But once she did it, Marco went wild."

"The kinky stuff you mentioned," I said. "Was it at these sex parties?"

"Yeah, but there was a different house he took her to. Some bondage place."

"He tied her up?" I asked timidly.

"Oh, honey, much worse than that."

I could feel my face turning red.

Adriana noticed and laughed. "It's okay, honey. Isabella said Marco and her went to a house in Scarsdale where the men tied a woman onto a table spread eagle and raped her, only she'd agreed to it first. Then they spit on her. It made Isabella vomit because that's what her sicko husband wanted her to do."

I was half afraid to ask. "Did she do it?"

"She said she didn't. Threatened to tell her dad. Then Marco came up with a new idea. He told her to strip, put on just a coat and heels. Then he drove her to some sleazy hotel and blindfolded her. That way, she didn't know who was doing things to her. I warned you, the guy is a fucking pervert."

"Isabella told you that she went to a hotel room where she was blindfolded and had consensual sex with a stranger?"

"If you're asking me if someone screwed her in a hotel while she was blindfolded, the answer is yes."

"Adalina," I said, "is it possible that Isabella secretly enjoyed bondage and having sex with strangers?"

"I know why you're asking me that," she replied. " 'Cause I wondered the same thing when the cops found her tied up and tortured. I thought to myself, if she really was disgusted with it, then why didn't she tell Marco to go fuck himself."

I suddenly thought about the women who'd come through the Domestic Violence Unit and how they often were blamed because they hadn't left their physically abusive husbands. If Marco had destroyed Isabella's self-esteem, standing up to him might not have been as easy as it seemed. I said, "Well, she did finally stand up to him. She sued him for divorce. That must not have been easy for her, especially since she kept living in the same house."

"She'd met someone. That's why she was dumping him. It's easier if you got someone waiting."

"So Marco lost his power over her because of her new lover?"

"That's right. Three months ago, she comes waltzing in with a big, happy smile. She was in love but she said they couldn't be seen together. You know what that means?"

I wasn't sure.

"He was married. That's what it always means when a woman says her new guy can't be with her."

"What did she tell you about him? A name? Anything that I could use to identify him? Do you know, for instance, if he had a scar on his face?"

"She didn't say. I got the impression that he was older and much more thoughtful than that jerk she married. But she never said a name. She did say that her father would kill him if he found out. Her family knew his family and they hated each other. That's what she told me. Marco must have suspected that she was having an affair. I mean, she was suddenly happy, really happy. That would have really pissed him off."

"You think Marco was angry enough to kill?"

"Marco? I'm not sure he has the balls because he was scared to death of her father. But that don't mean that little shit wouldn't hire someone to do his dirty work. It all makes me want to puke. She was such a beautiful human being. Like a flower." Adalina paused to collect her thoughts, then grinned and said, "Oh, now I remember. You're working with Tommy Boy. Pity you, getting stuck with that lunkhead. And please tell him I said that."

"I will. Actually, the two of us get along fine."

"What's wrong with you, then?" she said, laughing softly. "Just teasing. Tommy Boy is like an old teddy bear. All he does is work, work, work, and drink. He needs a woman in his life to straighten him out."

I thought about Miss Potts back at the courthouse. I guess Adalina didn't know all the juicy gossip. "Back to Marco Ricci," I said.

"Let me tell you what he did one day here at the shop. He was flirting with my receptionist and when I told him to get lost, he hit on me. My Petey would have decked him if I'd told him. I heard he's already found some stupid bitch to marry him. Plus, Isabella was divorcing his ass, which is not something that someone with a giant ego like Marco Ricci is going to like. And then there's that whole life insurance policy thing."

"Isabella had a large life insurance policy?" I asked.

"Only two million bucks' worth! Pretty good motive, I'd say."

"Only if you live long enough to spend it."

"Yeah, Tiny Nunzio. I had to laugh when Petey told me how Marco had called, all terrified, asking for twenty-four-hour protection. If Marco did hire someone to kill Isabella, he sure as hell would have made sure that he had an airtight alibi—not because of you, but because of Nunzio. That's the only way he could save himself."

"Adalina, I need you to do me a favor."

"Honey, I don't cut anyone's hair for free."

"No," I said. "I want you to talk to your husband. Have him tip off O'Brien if it looks like Marco might be fleeing town late some night." I stood up to leave.

"Sure. But how about your hair?"

"I'm not sure big hair would look good on me."

"You should try it. I don't have to go real big. Just bigger than what you got."

Five minutes later, I was driving away from the Three B's, with an appointment for the next month. Adalina was not easy to refuse and I wanted to keep her as a source. The more I learned about Marco Ricci, the more I began to doubt that the Butcher was our man. All this talk about swingers, gang rapes, bondage, and blindfolded escapades with strangers in hotel rooms had not only turned my stomach, it had also put several new twists in what already was a bizarre murder case.

14

I DECIDED TO DRIVE TO YONKERS TO HAVE A FRIENDLY CHAT with Roman Mancini. I wanted to scold him for blabbering about Isabella's death to Will and I also needed to interview his wife, Maggie. Mostly, I wanted to make certain they were both safe.

The Midland Avenue apartment building looked less dreary in the noonday sun than it had in the rain on New Year's morning. The building's entry was pretty standard for an apartment building. I pressed the top button and waited. I pressed it again and waited a bit longer. It was nearly 1 p.m. and I figured they were at lunch or simply didn't want to deal with any more strangers.

I turned to leave when I got a queasy feeling. I'm not a big fan of the supernatural, but I've always trusted my instincts and my gut was telling me something was wrong. I decided to try the front entrance and it opened. So much for security.

When there was no answer at the Mancinis' door, I knocked louder and called out, "It's Dani Fox from the District Attorney's Office!"

The door directly across the hall opened and an older woman peeked out. "You the police?" she asked.

"District Attorney's Office. Do you know if they're home?"

"One of them should be. Whenever Roman and Maggie both leave, they tell me and put a card on their door so people know to speak to me if it's an emergency. They're real good about that."

I tried the door to their apartment, and when the knob spun around in my hand, my gut tightened even more. Its locking mechanism was busted.

Bracing myself, I drew the pistol I kept in my purse and pushed open the apartment's door. "Mr. Mancini, are you here? It's Dani Fox, from the D.A.'s office."

The only light in the apartment came from sunshine streaking through the tiny cracks in a set of aging venetian blinds.

"Mr. Mancini? Mrs. Mancini?" I took two steps into the room but froze when my shoe hit something soft on the floor. It felt like a body so I stepped back, fighting the urge to run. With my left hand, I felt the wall for a light switch. It was an old push-button type but nothing happened when I hit it. I waited, gun out, for my eyes to adjust to the low light; when I looked down, I fully expected to see one of the Mancinis sprawled on the floor.

Instead, it was one of their cats, eyes wide open and lying in a pool of its own blood.

I'd seen enough.

Backing into the hallway, I told the neighbor still peeking out of her doorway to call the police.

"Are they hurt?" she asked me.

"Please call the police now!" I repeated.

She disappeared into her apartment while I took a moment to catch my breath. I knew that I had to go back inside. If someone was injured, every second could matter. I wasn't going to have Roman or Maggie Mancini die because I'd been too afraid to search for them.

With my handgun leading the way, I quietly reentered the dark living room, careful to step over the cat. When my eyes adjusted, I scanned the room and noticed that someone had slaughtered the two other cats, as well. Was it cruelty or was this supposed to be some sort of a warning?

"The police are coming," I announced in a loud voice.

There was no reaction.

Moving quietly down the hallway, I stopped outside the first bedroom's closed door. With my left hand, I turned the knob and opened it. Something shifted in the darkness. A pair of eyes suddenly appeared and something dropped from above my head to the floor. A fourth cat leaped down from a shelf.

I felt for a wall switch. This one worked and I found myself looking into a room stuffed with cardboard boxes, clothing hanging from racks, and two shelves crowded with dolls. Chatty Cathy and Barbie stared blankly at me. I pulled the door closed and moved down the hallway to the second bedroom, perspiring and breathing fast.

When you don't know what you are about to find behind a closed door and you've just seen several dead cats and been surprised by a live one, you tend to be a bit shaky. The good thing about fear is that it seems to slow down time and you become keenly aware of every sight, smell, movement, and sound. I could hear my own heart racing as I began to open the door. I hoped the room was empty. I wanted the Mancinis to be out to lunch. I pictured them at a nearby restaurant and hoped the dead cats had been left merely as a warning by someone who'd broken in.

I used one hand to open the bedroom door and then quickly returned it to the grip of my pistol. I instinctively bent my legs slightly at the knees, assuming a firing position.

The door slowly swung open. There were no windows. The interior was completely black. I listened but heard nothing. With my left hand, I reached into the darkness and felt the wall-mounted light switch.

Light flooded the room, causing me to squint.

Through half-lids, I saw a completely naked Roman Mancini propped against the wooden headboard of the couple's double bed. His arms had been tied to the bed's corners, making him appear as if he had been crucified. Dried blood covered his hairy chest and the bedsheets. His skull had been pushed back and was resting on the headboard's wooden top bar. From where I was standing, it looked as if he was wearing a tiny red necktie. But it wasn't a piece of clothing. His throat had been slit just above his Adam's apple and his tongue had been pulled downward through the opening. I had to look away.

A plump woman wearing curlers, a flowered muumuu, and pink fuzzy slippers was tied to a chair next to the bed facing Mancini. Her throat also had been slit, but thankfully her tongue had not been dragged through the opening. There was nothing I could do to save either of them. With my gun still drawn, I slowly retreated out of the apartment and back into the building's entryway. As I was standing there, catching my breath, two uniformed Yonkers police officers came through the front door and assumed the worst when they saw me holding a pistol.

"Freeze!" one yelled, grabbing his sidearm.

"I called you! I'm with the D.A.'s office."

"Drop the weapon!" the cop nearest me demanded.

It was no time for an argument.

Bending down, I placed my .38 on the tile floor. "My ID's in my purse. There's a dead couple inside that apartment."

One of the officers darted by me into Apartment 1. "Oh shit," he yelled. I knew he'd stepped on the dead cat.

"Show me your ID," the other officer ordered.

I reached for my ID as O'Brien came in behind them. "What the hell?" he exclaimed. "She's my partner."

The cop lowered his pistol and started toward the apartment door to join his partner.

"Watch out for the dead cat on the—" But before I could complete my sentence, he too had stepped on it, and cut loose with a profanity.

"You okay?" O'Brien asked me.

I nodded.

O'Brien said, "The chief agreed to assign two officers to guard the Mancinis. I followed them over."

"Too late," I replied. "We've got to make sure they don't mess up the crime scene. C'mon. And watch out for the dead cat on the floor."

"The what?" he said rushing in behind me. "Oh, shit!"

He'd stepped on it, too.

O'Brien and I found both officers in the bedroom.

"You need to keep everyone out of the apartment," I said.

One of them shot me a "Who the hell are you?" look.

In a firm voice, I said, "I'm an assistant district attorney who will be prosecuting these murders. You need to leave this room immediately. Call your dispatcher and get a photographer and medical examiner over here. Now!" Just as I had done when I'd seen Isabella's mangled body dangling from the ceiling in this very same apartment building, I did a careful sweep of the scene, trying to create a mental photograph.

Why was Roman Mancini nude? There was a pair of men's flannel pajamas on the floor next to the bed. Why had he been tied to the headboard? I ran my eyes down his nude body and noticed something that I had missed earlier. Someone had cut off his little toe on his right foot. Had he been tortured before he was murdered? Was it premortem or postmortem? I looked at Maggie and noted that her right thumb had been amputated. Why had their killer or killers tortured her? "Why so brutal? Slitting their throats, pulling down his tongue?" I said.

"That's an Italian necktie," O'Brien said. "A mob signal."

"A what?"

"You slit someone's throat, grab their tongue, and pull it through the hole."

The message seemed obvious. I thought about Will and his all-important exclusive, front-page story. Why hadn't he listened to me? Now our witness and his wife were dead and as far as I was concerned, Will had blood on his hands.

15

FBI Special Agent Walter Coyle was waiting at a table in the back of Bistro Bistro when I arrived ten minutes late for our 7 p.m. meeting.

"Thought you were standing me up," he said, rising from his chair when the maître d' escorted me to our table. "I heard your key witness and his wife got their throats slit this afternoon."

I told Coyle that O'Brien was still at the crime scene but that I'd seen enough. "Cops prefer talking to other cops anyway, not assistant district attorneys," I added. "There's still a line there."

"Especially when it comes to women prosecutors," he said in a sympathetic voice. "Being the only female A.D.A. must be difficult. You're a woman in a man's domain."

"The whole world is a man's domain."

"Must be why it's so screwed up," he said, smiling.

I liked his comment but wasn't going to let it pass without adding my own. "One reason is because of people like your boss, Jack Longhorn."

"Ouch. Tell me how you really feel," he said. "Longhorn warned me about you. He said you two clashed over a case. But that's between the two of you, not me."

"You're still FBI, he's your boss, and based on what I've dealt with in the past, that makes me skeptical of you and cautious . . . very cautious."

"I get that," he said. "And I'm actually fine with it. I've been proving myself all of my life."

Our waiter interrupted. Coyle ordered calamari fritti as an appetizer to share. I chose linguine with clam sauce as my entrée. Coyle ordered a filet mignon.

"This is my treat," he said. "Don't worry, I'll put it on my bureau expense account since it's an official meeting and not a dinner date. Besides, it sounds as if the FBI owes you."

"Thanks, but I pay my own way."

"And if this were a date, I suspect you'd pay your own way then, too, right?"

"My boyfriend and I split it most nights."

"Would it make a difference if I told you that you'd be doing me a favor by letting me pay? I can only use my bureau expense account if I take a source to dinner."

"A source? I'm not your source and I will definitely be paying my own tab. I sure as hell don't want to be identified on some slip of paper somewhere as an FBI informant."

"You really are a stickler for the rules. And you really don't like us, do you?"

I thought perhaps I was being a bit too rough. "Saying you're different from Longhorn is easy. Proving it is another matter."

He smiled. "Well put. No problem. I like a challenge, especially when it comes from someone as attractive as you. If this works out, maybe we can be more than professional colleagues. Maybe we can become friends. Imagine, Dani Fox with a friend in the FBI."

"Then you are in for a big challenge," I said. "Now, what can you tell me about Nicholas Persico?"

"Would you like wine with our dinner?"

"I'll stick with water, thanks."

"You Italian? You look Italian. Dark hair, sparkling brown eyes. You look European. I like that."

This was the third time in recent days that someone had asked me if I was Italian. "I'm not Italian," I said. "My parents are of Lebanese descent. But we're not here to discuss my looks or ethnicity, are we? Let's talk about the Butcher."

"I didn't mean to pry. Just trying to melt the ice, you know, get comfortable with each other. I think it's important when I'm working with someone in law enforcement to get to know a bit about them. A lot of what we do depends on trust, you know, protecting each other's backsides."

He opened the wine menu. "I guess I'll have a glass by myself. You sure you don't want to have some? They say red wine is good for your heart. And it might help you to relax."

"I am relaxed and my heart is fine. Now tell me about Persico."

He closed the menu and shook his head good-naturedly. "So much for small talk. As capo of the Battaglia crime family, Persico oversees all of Westchester County. But the Butcher is much more important than his title suggests. The actual head of the Battaglia crime family is Johnny Battaglia, but he's in prison serving back-to-back life sentences. Since he's in the joint, Persico is calling the shots on the streets and in charge of holding the family together. That makes him the de facto leader of the entire family."

"For how long?"

"He'll be in charge until Johnny Battaglia wins an appeal, which is un-likely, or cedes his power, which is even more unlikely."

"No, I mean, how long has Persico been running the Battaglia family?"

"Oh, about two years, and he's done it with an iron fist. His people are all loyal or afraid of him. Any threat comes from outside—namely Giuseppe 'Tiny' Nunzio over in New Jersey." He hesitated and then said, "I'm sure you recognize the name."

"Yes, he's a capo in the Gaccione family," I said.

"Speaking of Nunzio, my boss wasn't happy when he realized your boss didn't share the murder victim's name with us. It would have been nice of you to have told us during our meeting that the victim was the daughter of a New Jersey mobster."

"I'm only an A.D.A.," I said, passing the buck.

Coyle smirked. "Well, Longhorn was furious, if that pleases you."

Actually, it did.

Coyle continued: "Nunzio and his crew have had their eyes on several lucrative garbage contracts that bleed over into Staten Island."

"Which," I interjected, "likes to call itself the largest landfill in the world."

"You know about garbage," he said appreciatively.

"I know there's big money in collecting it."

"And in finding places to dump it."

The waiter arrived with a glass of pinot noir. "Agent Coyle," I began.

He interrupted me. "Please, call me Walt. Sometimes it's good to break a few rules, Dani."

"At taxpayers' expense?" I asked.

For the first time, Coyle frowned. "I don't want to argue. If it makes you happy, I will pay for my own meal and wine, but the two of us work hard for the public. We put our lives on the line every day. So forgive me if I order a glass of wine now and then, or use my expense account to take an attractive colleague to dinner."

"So you do this often? Take women to dinner on the taxpayers' dime?"

"I can see why you're a good prosecutor," he replied. "You don't let up, do you? What's next? Handcuffs?"

"What's next is more conversation about the Battaglias and Gacciones."

He took a sip of his wine. "Our task force has been using wiretaps and some low-level snitches to monitor the two crime families, and from this intel, it appears that Nunzio has been getting bolder and bolder about encroaching into Persico's domain. A lot of New Jersey trash companies dump their waste in Staten Island so he's using that as an excuse to establish a foothold in New York."

"How so? I'm not up to date on interstate transfer of waste."

"Nunzio already forces trash companies in New Jersey to pay him a kickback for doing business. Now he wants the landfills, which charge the New Jersey trash companies a fee to unload their waste in Staten Island, to kick back a piece of the action for every truck that he sends across the river. The landfill operators already are paying kickbacks to Persico. So that means they now have two hands dipping into one pot. When that happens in the mob, one hand gets chopped off."

"Do you think Persico murdered Isabella as a warning to Nunzio or to punish him for trying to move into Staten Island?" I asked.

"It's a good question. Who knows?" Coyle said. "What I do know is that he did it. Has the medical examiner given you a time of death?"

"The killer cut an electrical cord from an alarm clock in the bedroom that he used to tie her. The clock stopped at three-thirty-five. The coroner says the death happened sometime between then and about six o'clock that night."

"That window means the murder happened at the same time Persico was with her in that apartment," Coyle said. "He got there at two-thirty p.m. and left three hours later. Seems open-and-shut to me. When are you planning on having him arrested?"

"That's a bit premature," I said. "We've got some loose ends that need to be resolved."

"Like what?"

"Isabella was meeting someone in that apartment twice a week over the past three months. We suspect she was having an affair—"

"And you're having a tough time," Coyle said, interrupting me, "imagining a crusty old codger like Persico having a fling with a younger, attractive woman."

"That's part of it."

"Maybe Isabella had a daddy complex or maybe she wanted to get back at her own father. What better way to punish your father than to sleep with someone who your old man hates—someone even older than he is? But why does any of that really matter? We know he was there at the time of her murder. Arrest him, sweat him, and make him talk."

I thought it was an odd comment coming from an FBI agent. Mobsters like Persico didn't sweat when the police arrived and they rarely talked. "It just feels off to me," I said. "My gut tells me—"

Coyle chuckled. "You can't base investigations on your gut. It's facts that matter. Persico was there. I saw him. Why else would he rush out of that building? Why else would he change his clothes before he went home that night? It's circumstantial, but it all fits."

"Leaving in a hurry and changing clothes are hardly signs that you committed a murder," I argued.

"What my gut is wondering," he replied, "is why are you so intent on defending a known mob killer?"

"I'm not defending him. I'm trying to catch a killer and I don't want to put an innocent man on trial even if he's a scumbag like Persico."

"I want to catch bad guys, too. I'm just surprised you're throwing up roadblocks."

I was quiet for a moment to collect my thoughts. "Explain this to me," I said. "Why would a capo butcher a woman who he was having an affair with? Better yet, why would Persico risk doing his own dirty work? Why not send some of his goons to do it?"

"It was probably personal, especially if they were sleeping together. Maybe he wanted to punish Nunzio. Maybe he did it because his nickname is the Butcher. You're attempting the impossible: trying to rationalize the actions of a psychopath."

The waiter brought our entrées.

"When we met in Whitaker's office," I said, "you said the FBI has been tailing Persico every day for several months and had logbooks about his daily activities."

"That's right. We do tail him but we alternate agents. Everyone takes a turn."

"But those daily logs would show where Persico has gone every day for the past several months, right? So they would tell us if Persico was meeting Isabella at the Midland Avenue apartments every Tuesday and Friday afternoon."

Coyle said, "Yes, they would. Unfortunately, I don't have them with me. I meant to bring them. But I completely forgot."

I was suspect and let him know it. "Wait a minute. That's why we were supposed to be meeting here—so you could show me your entry about Persico being at Isabella's apartment."

"Sorry. I had them on my desk and then I got a call and got distracted and dashed out without them."

"You brought your memory with you, didn't you?" I said in a voice that sounded harsher than I'd intended. "Did you ever follow Persico to the Midland Avenue apartment when it was your turn to watch him—other than the day of the murder?"

"I can't help you," he said. "I watched him mostly on weekends because I'm the only single agent in the New York office. The others like to be home with their families on Saturdays, Sundays, and holidays."

I suddenly felt as if I were questioning an evasive witness. I wondered if Jack Longhorn had ordered Coyle to keep the logbooks from me.

"Is there anything useful about Persico that you do remember?" I said sternly.

"Lighten up, okay? It was stupid of me to forget the logs. But that's an easy fix. We'll just meet again for dinner," he said. "Besides, the point of this evening wasn't just for me to show you the logbooks."

"What other reason could there be?"

"I wanted to meet so we could get to know each other as people and build rapport. We'll need that when your boss finally realizes that he needs our help and asks the bureau to join in."

I gave Coyle a puzzled look and said, "I'm not certain my boss wants the FBI to be involved in our murder case."

"He might not have a choice but to ask," Coyle replied confidently. "Your eyewitness and his wife were found dead just a few hours ago. I'm your star witness now." He had a point.

"There's another reason why the two of us should be friends," Coyle continued. "You don't have jurisdiction outside Westchester County and I think Tiny Nunzio and his goons are the ones who killed Roman Mancini and his wife—not Persico."

"What?" I said, not hiding my surprise. "Why would Nunzio want to kill an eyewitness who could help put his daughter's killer in prison? That doesn't make sense."

"It might not make sense to a regular citizen, but if you knew more about the mob, then it would be obvious," he replied with a touch of arrogance. "Tiny Nunzio's only daughter is dead, and not only is she dead, she's been butchered. And she's been butchered in an apartment building in Yonkers—his most hated rival's turf. Nunzio gets up in the morning and reads in the newspaper that Roman Mancini saw the man who killed Isabella. He looked into his eyes. According to the newspaper, the killer and his limo driver were both in the mob. So now Nunzio knows the killer is someone in the Battaglia family. What's the first thing he's going to do?"

Without waiting for me to answer, Coyle continued. "Nunzio is going to send a crew over to get information out of Mancini. He's not going to wait for the cops to solve this case and make an arrest. He knows how powerful the Battaglia family is in Yonkers and knows they probably got cops on their payroll. Nunzio is going to handle this completely on his own and he is not someone who leaves witnesses behind. He doesn't care about leaving Mancini alive to testify against Persico, because if Nunzio has his way, there won't be any trial."

While I mulled over Coyle's theory, he kept talking.

"What you've got to understand is that Nunzio might suspect that Persico killed Isabella. Nunzio might even suspect that Persico was having an affair with her. But rumors and suspicions would not be enough for him. Nunzio's got to have proof, just like you do. The other family heads are going to demand more evidence than a jury would. If Nunzio made a move against the Battaglia family without getting permission from his own godfather in the Gaccione family and the other families, then he'd be signing his own death warrant and possibly starting a war. Wars between families are bad for business."

"What happens if Nunzio gets his evidence?" I asked.

"If Nunzio can prove it was Persico, then the Gaccione family will present its case to the other families and there will be a sit-down between the Gaccione and Battaglia families to see if bloodshed can be avoided. Persico and the Battaglias might have to pay reparations."

"Do you really think Nunzio is competing with us to find Isabella's killer?"

"Yes, I do," Coyle said. "What's brilliant about all of this is that Nunzio knows that the local law enforcement is going to jump to the obvious conclusion that Persico killed the Mancinis to eliminate an eyewitness. That explains the Italian necktie. Nunzio is playing with you."

"He might be, but there's an obvious flaw in your scenario," I said.

Coyle gave me a puzzled look. "Oh, really. Let's hear it."

"Roman Mancini would have told Nunzio anything he wanted to know. There was no need to torture him and his wife."

"What makes you think they were tortured?" Coyle replied.

"Roman's little toe on his right foot was cut off and someone amputated Maggie Mancini's right thumb. That suggests torture. But why?"

Coyle shrugged. "You got to stop thinking like a prosecutor and start thinking like Nunzio. Let's assume I'm right. Nunzio and his men paid a visit on the Mancinis. The husband and wife both begin squealing as soon as he ties them up. But he wants to make sure they're telling the truth. So he tortures them. Then he kills them because he knows they can identify him and his men if he lets them live. He then stages the crime scene to make it appear that Persico killed them. The Italian necktie is a dead giveaway."

Having supported his theory to his own satisfaction, Coyle then said, "How's your linguine?"

I'd been so enthralled by our conversation that I hadn't touched it, but I said, "It's fine." I really didn't want to talk about food. "Let's go back to Isabella," I said. "Since we are tossing out theories here, what if Persico is innocent? What if Isabella's husband hired someone to kill his wife and make it look like a mob hit? Marco Ricci is terrified of Tiny Nunzio. What if Marco had the crime scene staged so that Tiny Nunzio would blame Persico and go after him? He might think his best chance at getting Tiny Nunzio off his back is by pitting the two capos against one another."

"That strikes me as a good B-movie plot," Coyle said. "But I saw Persico leaving the apartment at five-thirty. Do you really think someone else had time to slip in there afterward and kill her? I'm telling you, Persico butchered Isabella and I think Nunzio murdered the Mancinis. Two Mafia capos on rampages. It's as simple as that."

Coyle ordered another glass of wine and said, "How long have you been an assistant district attorney?"

"Nearly three years. How long have you been a *special* agent?"

"Almost seven years. My first assignment was in our Detroit field office. I spent four long years there and before you ask me, no, I don't know where Jimmy Hoffa is buried." He smiled and I noticed a row of perfect teeth. He really was handsome. Even though my guard was up, I found myself warming to him.

I said, "Being transferred to the New York field office must have been a big promotion for you."

"It was. I jumped over a long list of veteran agents, but there were plenty of good reasons why I got the bump up."

"Such as?"

"I deserved it. Detroit was being torn apart by street gangs. They were out of control and the city was the murder capital of the country. I was on a task force that helped bring down the various gangs' leaders. The brass in Washington noticed and when they needed a new face in Manhattan, who the mob wouldn't recognize, they called me up from the minors. They told me to target the Persicos and the Battaglias."

"Then it really was your lucky day when you saw Persico on New Year's Eve going into the Midland Apartments," I said.

"A great day for me, not so much for Isabella Ricci. Persico has been a difficult target because he keeps himself pretty insulated. He lets his underlings handle the everyday stuff. Until Isabella's murder, our task force was feeling frustrated. Nothing stuck on this guy. Which is why helping you is so important to the bureau and our task force. We can't risk having this case screwed up by the locals."

"Screwed up?"

He either hadn't realized how demeaning his comment was or didn't care.

"Hey, don't take it personally. Look, no matter how good a prosecutor you are, the truth is we can handle this magnitude of a case better than your office—and I think you know that. We could have protected the Mancinis. And we have the expertise to see things—like how Nunzio is probably behind their deaths. We just are better at this than your office, especially since Whitaker has you and O'Brien handling the investigation rather than the chief of your Organized Crime Bureau."

His words stung.

And he wasn't finished. "We need you to get Whitaker to invite us into this case," he said.

"We need?" I replied. "As in you and Jack Longhorn need?"

Coyle took another taste of his wine and didn't answer my question. "I'm going to be frank," Coyle finally said, "because I like you. I'm going to let you in on a little secret. Longhorn wants me to find out from you why Vanderhoot is not in charge of this homicide investigation. He's not happy that you and O'Brien are handling it."

"I bet he's not," I said, but I wasn't going to discuss office politics with him. "But you'll have to ask Whitaker."

I decided to turn the tables while Coyle finished his second glass of wine. I might as well pump him for FBI intel.

"What's Persico like?" I asked.

"A rather boring guy, actually," he replied. "He's been married to the same woman for fifty years. They grew up in the same Yonkers neighborhood. Her parents owned a stand at the Fulton Fish Market. His grandfather and father opened the butcher shop. Persico earned his bones when he was still a kid."

"Earned his bones?"

"Committed his first murder. Although nothing was ever proven."

"Does Persico have a reputation as a womanizer?" I asked.

"Not that we know of. But then our files about his early days in the mob are rather incomplete."

"Seems a bit out of character," I said. "Three months ago, this seventy-year-old man suddenly begins cheating. How'd they meet? Where'd they meet? Do you have anything in your files that could help me prove they had a relationship?"

"You're talking about a man who is quite comfortable living a double life," Coyle said. "Persico goes to Mass each Sunday and at the same time, he has hookers walking the street, breaks the arms and legs of people who owe him money, sells dope, has trucks hijacked, deals in contraband cigarettes, and kills people. I doubt he's one to worry much about breaking his marriage vows."

"People cheat all the time," I said. "Most don't butcher someone when the romance dies."

"Most men aren't nicknamed the Butcher," he said. "Only Isabella and Persico know what happened between them in that room, but let's try to imagine it from his point of view. He meets her. He's intrigued because she's younger and the only daughter of his much-hated rival. She's tempted. Maybe she transfers her daddy complex from Nunzio to him. Maybe she wants to hurt her father. Who knows? But she clings to him and when he wants to end it, she threatens to tell her father. Or she threatens to tell his wife. Pretty typical stuff when people have affairs. Only Persico's way of dealing with problems is by killing people."

"Why cut her up?" I asked. "For a guy who doesn't like to get his own hands dirty, that seems like a dumb move—especially for someone whose nickname is the Butcher."

"Maybe to make the cops believe her plastic surgeon husband killed her. Maybe to humiliate Nunzio. Maybe he just likes cutting people up. Who knows?"

"Why kill her in an apartment rented by the law firm that represents him?" I said, continuing to play the role of devil's advocate.

Coyle shrugged and looked for our waiter. He was weary of my questions. "You want dessert?" he asked.

I shook my head no. "It's been a long day. I'm going home to bed."

"Alone? I'll go with you," he said, and then before I could reply, he said, "Just kidding."

But I wasn't sure that he had been. I looked away, embarrassed. He got the message and said, "I'm sure seeing Roman and Maggie Mancini with their throats cut wasn't easy. You must be exhausted. Roman Mancini should never have talked to that reporter. You can't trust them. They're pond scum."

"They're just doing their jobs," I said, "and the reporter who wrote that piece happens to be a pretty responsible guy."

"You know him?"

"He's my boyfriend."

Coyle leaned back in his seat. "Really? Do you realize your boyfriend is responsible for getting two people murdered?"

I felt like I needed to defend Will, but I didn't. I just wanted to go. I was tired. "Thanks for telling me about Persico," I said, reaching into my purse. I put two twenties on the table. "That should cover my dinner. You're on your own with the wine."

"I'll walk you to your car," he said, ignoring the money.

"I'm parked directly out front. Besides, I carry a gun."

He rose and started to move toward me. I sensed that he was going to give me a hug, so I stuck out my hand and said, "Thanks again. It's been interesting."

"I'll tell Longhorn that I didn't get any answers out of you," he said, with a wink.

"That won't surprise him."

"And I'll call you about the logbooks," he said. "We can meet again. It will be our second date."

"This wasn't a date."

"Yes," he said, smiling. "It actually was."

16

BY THE TIME I LEFT BISTRO BISTRO, IT WAS 10:15 P.M. AND it had been a very long day. But I still wanted to talk to my best friend and confidante. Not Will Harris. My mother, Esther. She's a night owl, so I knew she would still be awake.

I drove to her house, which was only a few blocks from my own. My mother has an uncanny knack for recognizing sounds. As soon as she hears the engine of my Triumph on her street, she knows it's me. She was opening her front door as I came walking up her steps. "I have leftover grape leaves with cucumber yogurt in the fridge," she said. "I'll pull it out for you."

"No, no, Mom," I protested. My mom always tries to feed me and because she is such a tremendous cook, I often let her. But not tonight. "I just had dinner at Bistro Bistro."

"Oh, how's Will doing?"

"I didn't see him. I had dinner with an FBI agent."

"You had dinner with someone from the FBI? It wasn't that horrible Jack Longsteer fellow, was it?"

"His name is Longhorn, not Longsteer, although I've certainly called him much worse," I replied with a smile. "But no, I met with a special agent named Walter Coyle. He was supposed to be sharing information with me, but he really was trying to see if I would help the FBI get invited into our murder case. I think he's also interested in dating me."

"And that surprises you? You're a beautiful woman. What man wouldn't be interested?"

"All mothers think their daughters are beautiful. You thought I was beautiful when I had skinny legs, wore my hair in braids, had buck teeth, and fat lips."

She replied, "Not always. But you are now."

"I got good genes from you and Dad, Ma."

It was true. My mother was a natural beauty with huge brown eyes, great cheekbones, black hair, and a great figure. She could have attracted a number of suitors after my dad died from cancer a few years before. But she hadn't shown any interest in remarrying. Whenever I asked, she'd said, "I gave your dad my whole heart. There's no room for anyone else."

My mother has always been my muse. I admire her, in part, because of the obstacles that she faced as a child. My grandfather had sent my grandmother back to Lebanon after she disappointed him by giving birth to four daughters but not a single male heir. My mother grew up in her uncle's house in Beirut. He'd treated her well, but he was a product of a culture that didn't much value women. Despite this, my mom refused to think of herself as a second-class citizen. And she made sure that I never thought of myself that way, either.

Mom led me into her kitchen, where we always have our best discussions. "How about some baklava?" she said. "I know you can't say no to that. We'll sit here and talk about your new case and this mysterious FBI agent who finds you attractive. Does Will know about him?"

"Okay," I said. "It's late and I shouldn't be eating but I also know you won't give up."

She smiled and said, "Is this a wine or coffee visit, Dani?"

I'd rather have a cold beer than a glass of wine, and I get my caffeine from Dr Pepper. She was asking me if we were going to have a happy mother-daughter chat, in which case, she'd pour herself a merlot, or if this was instead going to be one of those all-night crying sessions like the one we'd had when I discovered that my first boyfriend, Bob, whom I had always thought I would marry, was cheating on me, in which case she'd make a pot of coffee.

"You can pour yourself a merlot, Mom. No tears tonight."

She uncorked a bottle and asked, "Now, give me the details about this dinner. I hope there's not a problem between you and Will?"

"Dinner was supposed to be purely business. And I don't think there's anything seriously wrong between Will and me, but he did something that bothers the hell out of me. It's our jobs."

She frowned at my language. "I thought you two worked out ground rules about your jobs."

"Me, too, but there's been a murder in Yonkers—"

"I read Will's story in the morning paper," she said. "Isabella Ricci and how she might have been killed by her Mafia lover. All the ladies are talking about it. Just tonight, the television news said a Yonkers superintendent and his wife were murdered in that same building. Their throats were slit because they were going to be witnesses."

"Mom, I was the one who found their bodies."

She immediately put her glass of wine on the kitchen counter and walked over to give me a hug. "I'm so sorry, dear. It must have been just horrible to see that."

"It was. You know how hard it is for me to get those images out of my head."

"You see so many awful things at your job. I hate it. But you knew what you were getting into when you became a prosecutor."

This was typical of my mother. Sympathetic but direct. When you made a decision, you dealt with the consequences, good or bad.

"What do these three murders have to do with your problems with Will?"

"His story today is why those two witnesses were killed. I think the murderer read it and went after them."

"Oh, poor Will."

"Poor Will?"

"I'm sure he feels terrible but you can't blame him, really. He was just doing his job."

"That hardly lets him off the hook. If his job was being a Mafia hit man, would you use that same logic?"

"Dani, we're talking apples and oranges. I don't think Will twisted that super's arm and forced him to talk."

"He did—sort of. Will told me the super shut the door in his face at first but when Will smelled the man's breath, he knew he was an alcoholic. So Will went back later with a bottle of whiskey and that's what got him into that apartment for an exclusive."

"Oh, my. You think Will shouldn't have done that?"

"Don't you? It was manipulative. But that wasn't the only thing Will did. He tried to trick me into telling him that Isabella Ricci had been murdered."

"Trick you, how?"

"He acted like he already knew it was her and then he tried to get me to confirm it. He knew what he was doing, even though he tried to laugh it off."

"That was wrong."

"There's more. After he told me about his exclusive, I warned him that it might put the Mancinis in danger, but he refused to call his editors. He said protecting them was my job, not his."

"Did you try to protect them?"

"I called O'Brien and he called the Yonkers police. But the chief refused to send anyone over to the apartment building, until it was too late. I called Whitaker, too, and urged him to call Will's editors, but he wouldn't."

"Then you did everything you could to protect them. Their deaths shouldn't be on your conscience."

"How about his conscience? I'm not sure I can trust him, and if I can't trust him, how can I love him? I was deeply in love with Bob and he cheated on me. He broke my heart and I thought I would never find anyone or stop hurting. Then Will came along."

"You need to talk to Will about this. But you can't assume that Will is untrustworthy because Bob betrayed you."

"Mom, it's complicated. It was simpler for your generation. You had clearly defined roles. You didn't have a career that put you into conflict with your husband and his career."

"You don't think we had conflicts? Come on, Dani."

"You had conflicts, but you didn't have to deal with intimidating a man because you earn more than he does. Maybe a prosecutor and a reporter are like oil and water. That's what O'Brien says."

"And you're going to listen to advice about relationships from a divorced, grumpy cop? Is this argument really about your careers or is it about Will trying to manipulate you?"

She was right. I didn't care that he was a reporter. I cared that he'd tried to trick me and that he'd taken advantage of Mancini. My mother and I talked for another hour and she raised issues, but she didn't tell me what to do. She never did.

Just when I was about to leave, she brought up Agent Coyle. "Are you sure your only interest in this FBI agent is a professional one?"

"Mom," I said indignantly, "I was cheated on by Bob. I'm in a relationship with Will. I'm not thinking about Walter Coyle any way but professionally. Besides, you know how much I hate the FBI." My answer sounded convincing, which was somewhat unsettling because deep down there was something about Coyle that I did find attractive.

I got home just before midnight and found Wilbur sleeping soundly in his pen. I was envious. I went through the back door into the kitchen and checked my answering machine.

"Hey, darling. How was your FBI date?" It was Will and he had emphasized the word *date* as a joke. He'd placed the call at about the same time I had been at the Bistro restaurant. "I'm still at the paper writing. I heard from a Yonkers cop that you found the bodies today. My God, I can't imagine what you saw. Do you want to talk about it? My editors actually suggested that I interview you about it. How about giving me some quotes for my story? I can write a sidebar about you finding the bodies. It will make Whitaker green with envy. If you can call me, we'll do a quick interview. But remember, I'm on deadline so you'd have to call me back before eight o'clock." Will paused, then lowered his voice and added, "I hope you aren't mad at me or blaming me because of my exclusive. I don't want this to become a problem between us. Call me, even if you don't want to be interviewed." His voice again became upbeat. "Okay, love ya! Gotta run! Call me soon if you want to be quoted. I'm on the front page again tomorrow. This is fun!"

The blinking light on my machine indicated that someone else had telephoned after Will.

"Dinner tonight was really special, Dani. I know you're not a fan of FBI agents but we could work well together. I'm determined to change your opinion about us. I'd like to set a time for our second 'nondate' date. If I don't hear from you tomorrow, I'll call you. This time I'll bring the logbooks. Hell, I'll even let you buy me dinner. Oh, one more thing. Tell your newspaper boyfriend that he's a horse's ass. You deserve better."

17

DISTRICT ATTORNEY CARLTON WHITAKER III WAS fuming. "I've got three dead bodies and we're only one week into the new year! What the hell is going on?"

The murders of Isabella Ricci and Roman and Maggie Mancini must have been wreaking havoc on his tee times at the country club. While the killings presented him with a wonderful opportunity to make headlines, he also understood that the reporters whose favor he was constantly courting would soon turn against him if an arrest wasn't made soon. I knew Whitaker was not about to let his poll numbers slide.

O'Brien and I had been summoned to Whitaker's office for a morning briefing. We'd arrived to find Myerson, Steinberg, and Vanderhoot looking as unhappy as our boss did. "Are we ready to indict Nicholas Persico for murder?" Whitaker asked.

"No, sir," I replied. "We don't have enough yet."

Whitaker let out an exasperated sigh and I noticed Vanderhoot roll his eyes—a nonverbal rebuke that I interpreted to mean: "Hey, if the Organized Crime Bureau were in charge of this, we would've already arrested Persico."

"What do you mean, 'not enough'?" Whitaker asked. "You have an FBI agent as an eyewitness who can put Persico at the Midland Apartments during the Ricci murder. Plus, Persico has got to be behind the murder of Roman Mancini and his wife."

"I'm sorry, but we haven't gathered up any physical evidence that ties him to either crime."

"What about the Yonkers cops? Have they found anything?"

"I'll let Detective O'Brien answer that since he's been dealing with them," I said.

"They got seven detectives working the cases," O'Brien explained. "But they got squat."

"No prints, no hairs, no fibers?" Myerson said, joining the conversation.

"Squat means squat," O'Brien answered. "Whoever whacked that couple knew what they was doing."

"Anyone else in that building come forward?" Myerson asked, thinking like the trial prosecutor that he was.

O'Brien shook his head no. "The medical examiner says the couple was murdered between midnight and five a.m. It's like a geriatric ward in that building. Most tenants weren't up that late and the ones who were ain't gonna stick their noses out now that Roman got himself an Italian necktie."

"Wait a minute!" I said. "Did you just say the M.E. put the Mancinis' time of death at between midnight and five a.m.?"

"Yep. Got the call early this morning."

"Why's that matter?" Whitaker asked.

"Because it means the Mancinis were murdered before the *White Plains Daily* hit the streets at six a.m."

In an accusatory voice, Vanderhoot said, "Trying to defend your boyfriend, Miss Fox? Trying to say it wasn't his front-page story that got them killed?"

"No, Vanderhoot, I'm not trying to protect my boyfriend. I'm pointing out that the killer must have already known that Roman Mancini was an eyewitness before his photo was splashed across the *White Plains Daily.*"

"That's right," O'Brien said. "The killer had to know Mancini had seen him. Roman was outside the building's front door fixing a busted light when Persico and his driver got there. The Butcher must have seen him and put two and two together."

"There's another piece of circumstantial evidence for you that points to Persico!" Whitaker interjected. Warming to his own words, he added, "Plus, you got Persico's nickname 'the Butcher' and all three homicides involved mutilations."

"A skilled prosecutor should be able to get that nickname in front of a jury somehow," Vanderhoot volunteered, hoping to impress Whitaker. "That would be another piece of useful circumstantial evidence."

I thought forward to the trial and realized that Vanderhoot either was a lousy lawyer or had been out of the courtroom for too long. If a prosecutor tried to make a big deal out of Persico's nickname, a judge would give a curative instruction to jurors, warning them against interpreting the "Butcher" moniker in any prejudicial way. The defense would also explain to jurors that Persico owned a butcher's shop. I blurted out, "You don't need to be a skilled prosecutor to get his nickname introduced in front of jurors during a trial. All you would have to do is indict him as Nicholas Persico aka 'Butcher.' That way the jurors would hear it when the charges against him were read in court and would draw their own conclusions without a judge issuing a curative instruction."

Vanderhoot shot me a spiteful look, but Whitaker was impressed. "That's clever," he said. "Much like a Fox," he added, smiling at his double entendre with my name.

Chief A.D.A. Myerson decided to dampen the mood. "It's going to take more than cleverness and innuendo to get Persico convicted. He's beaten every charge that anyone has ever flung at him."

"We've got to do something to calm the public down," Whitaker snapped. "Every day that passes without an arrest makes us look incompetent."

"Why not get a grand jury to indict Persico now on what we have," Steinberg offered, "and hope that by the time there's a trial, we'll have enough to make the charges stick?"

I was about to object to charging someone with a crime that we couldn't prove, but I didn't have to. Much to my surprise, Whitaker spoke out against the idea.

"If Miss Fox doesn't think we have enough evidence, we'll hold off," he said. "But we are running out of time. We need to find a way to show we're on top of these homicides before the press turns on us."

It probably wasn't the best time for me to mention my doubts about Persico being the killer, but I did anyway.

"What if Persico isn't behind any of these homicides?" I asked.

"Why are you bringing this up again?" Vanderhoot hissed. "Persico was there when Isabella Ricci was butchered and he's the only one with an obvious motive for killing the Mancinis."

I decided to address the two murders in reverse order. " 'Obvious' would be the operative word here, wouldn't it? Besides, FBI Special Agent Walter Coyle doesn't think Persico killed Roman and Maggie Mancini. He told me last night he thinks Tiny Nunzio killed them."

"Why in the world would Nunzio kill the Mancinis?" Vanderhoot scoffed.

"Agent Coyle believes Nunzio is conducting his own private investigation into Isabella's murder—trying to find enough evidence to convince the other families to let him kill Persico."

Whitaker said, "Wait a minute! Why were you meeting with Agent Coyle last night?"

"To see the FBI logbooks."

"Did Coyle show 'em to you?" Myerson asked.

"No, sir, he said he forgot them."

Vanderhoot laughed loudly. "Agent Coyle is playing you. He's stringing you along."

Whitaker looked unhappy. "Those FBI bastards are trying to use you to worm into our cases," he said.

Steinberg jumped in. "Miss Fox, if Nunzio crossed state lines—going from New Jersey into Yonkers—to commit a murder, then the FBI doesn't need an invitation from us to get involved in these homicide investigations. That's why Coyle is claiming Nunzio murdered the Mancinis. It's a ruse."

Whitaker picked up on that theme. "Jack Longhorn is putting ideas into your head because he wants to take charge of these cases and make a grab for the headlines. He's using Coyle to spy on us through you."

"There's rumors the FBI is about to file a big RICO case in Atlantic City. The five families, including the Battaglias, are involved. Adding three homicides to that RICO case would give Longhorn more to brag about and turn the spotlight on the bureau."

RICO was the Racketeer Influenced and Corrupt Organizations Act, a federal law enacted in 1970 that allowed the Feds to arrest Mafia heads even if they didn't actually pull a trigger or commit a crime. All the FBI had to do was show that the family's godfather had given an order to an underling.

That was enough to create a RICO conspiracy. I knew the FBI had been watching Atlantic City gambling ever since the city's first casino opened two years ago on its legendary boardwalk.

Addressing me, Whitaker said, "Don't get into bed with Agent Coyle."

"What?" I asked.

"Rhetorically, not literally."

"You need to brief me every time you meet with Agent Coyle," Steinberg ordered. "I want to keep on top of what he is asking of you."

"That's right," Whitaker boomed. "Let's have you spy on those FBI bastards. I want you to squeeze as much information as you can out of Coyle." Whitaker turned his attention back to the murders and Persico. "This is the second time you've said Persico might be innocent. How's that possible given that Coyle can put him inside the apartment building when Isabella was being carved up?"

"What possible reason would Persico have to murder her?" I asked. "What's his motive?"

"Because you're not part of the Organized Crime Bureau," Vanderhoot said in a condescending voice, "you may not realize these two families hate each other."

"I assume you're talking about how Joseph Persico was murdered by a hit man a decade ago who'd been hired by the Gaccione family?" I replied. "And how the Persicos got their revenge by making Nunzio's oldest son disappear."

Vanderhoot had underestimated how much I'd learned about the mob. Thank God for the tutorials that I'd gotten from Will and Coyle. Continuing, I said, "Detective O'Brien and I are looking into possible motives that would pinpoint Persico as the killer. He's still our prime suspect. But we've come across other suspects, too."

"Like who?" Whitaker asked.

"The most obvious is Isabella's husband, Marco Ricci," I replied. "They were in the midst of a bitter divorce. Plus, a close friend of Isabella's told me that Marco was forcing his wife to have sex with strangers as part of a swinger's club. Marco tried to interest her in bondage, too."

For the first time since I'd gone to work for Whitaker, I saw a look of total astonishment on his face.

"Isabella Ricci and her plastic surgeon husband were sexual swingers?" he asked. "They were into bondage?"

"Her soon-to-be ex-husband. Yes, they were, or, to be accurate, he was. Plus, Marco has a two-million-dollar life insurance policy on her and he's the lucky benefactor. Like I said, there are legitimate reasons why Marco should still be a suspect, maybe even a better one than Nicholas Persico."

"I'll be damned," Whitaker said.

"Look, the guy may be a pervert," Myerson said, joining the conversation. "But Persico was still the one who was seen entering the apartment building. We know he was there. Was Marco Ricci anywhere near the apartments on the day of the murder?"

O'Brien decided to answer him. "Marco's got a pretty solid alibi but that don't clear him. He's the type who'd hire someone to do his dirty work."

I said, "We can't answer all of your questions about Marco yet. That's why it's premature to focus only on Persico."

Whitaker was still reeling from my swinger's and bondage comments. "Tell me more about this swingers' club. Did your source tell you any other specific names of swingers? Prominent people I might know?"

"A group of couples that meets at your country club," I replied.

Whitaker's eyes nearly popped out.

"But I didn't get any names," I said. "The only other detail was that Isabella and Marco went to a swingers' party in Scarsdale."

I knew better than to say anything more, but I couldn't help myself.

"You nervous, boss?"

Anger replaced the astonishment on Whitaker's face. "Watch yourself, young lady," he said. "I'm still the boss here."

"There was something else," I said. "My source said Marco not only took Isabella to a house in Scarsdale for a sex party, but they also went to a different location to watch a consensual rape."

"Consensual rape?" Myerson repeated. "What the hell is that? I don't believe it is legally possible to consensually rape someone."

"A woman agreed to be tied up and violated. Several men had sex with her in a mock rape and then spit on her."

Steinberg said, "A mobster's daughter is murdered and her husband turns out to be a swinger who attends deviant sex parties. That's dynamite news for reporters."

"Do you think the Butcher might be a swinger?" Whitaker asked, clearly hoping for a tabloid trifecta.

I decided to pop their balloon. "I seriously doubt it. Persico is a family man and is in his midseventies. Unless science has come up with a tiny blue pill that will turn an older man into a jackrabbit, I can't see him attending sex parties in Scarsdale."

Whitaker looked disappointed.

"All of this," I said, "is why we have to look at suspects besides Persico. Agent Coyle may be correct in saying it was Tiny Nunzio who killed Roman and Maggie Mancini. Maybe Marco Ricci paid to have Isabella Ricci murdered. If those theories are true, then Persico wasn't involved in any of these homicides."

"And maybe you're making this much too complicated," Myerson said. "You could be chasing red herrings. When all the smoke clears, your best suspect is still Nicholas Persico."

"I'll give you another twenty-four hours," Whitaker said. "Then we got to make some sort of announcement about a new break in this case."

O'Brien and I were the first to leave the morning briefing. Whitaker had asked everyone else to stick around for a few moments to discuss an idea that he had and apparently felt we didn't need to hear. Although I was curious, leaving first was fine with me. I was eager to get back to the hunt.

18

WE HURRIED FROM THE COURTHOUSE TO OUR OF-fices, where a stack of pink "While You Were Out" slips was waiting on my desk. I popped a Junior Mint into my mouth from a box left over from the day before and fanned through the slips like they were playing cards. When I saw Adalina's name, I immediately reached for my phone.

"I forgot something important," Adalina explained excitedly. "Really, it's a someone. Donnie Gilmore. He was stalking Isabella. His name just popped into my noggin this morning."

"Donnie Gilmore. Who is he and how did Isabella know him?"

"Oh, he's one of them swingers in Scarsdale I was telling you about. Isabella didn't know his real name when they met. They all use fake names. But he really was bugging her about doing it with him and she didn't want to. She said he got real mad."

"Mad enough to kill?"

"He was the sick son of a bitch who took them to that house where they raped that woman and took turns spitting on her. She told me that Gilmore told Marco that his wife was a stuck-up bitch who needed to be put in her place."

"Is Gilmore from Scarsdale? Do you know where he works? How'd she find out his actual name?"

"That's why I called you first thing. Isabella knew who he was because she bumped into him at the Midland Apartments. That freak lives in the same place where she was murdered. How's that for a coincidence?"

"It doesn't sound like one," I replied.

"I know. I can't believe how stupid I was not to tell you earlier. But this morning, Petey was getting dressed and I shot up in bed and told him, 'Donnie Gilmore.' Petey thought I was dreaming but it was my brain working while I was asleep. Sometimes I go to bed thinking of a problem and wake up with the answer. There's been—"

"Adalina," I said, interrupting her, "this is really, really helpful. Now, do you know if Isabella ever had sex with Gilmore?"

"Well, let's see. She told me about having sex with two guys at swingers' parties but he wasn't one of them. That's why he got mad. She thought he was creepy, especially after he took them to that house where the rape was. She said he was always bugging her and Marco. He really had the hots to get into her panties."

A few minutes later, I thanked her for calling, put down the phone, and hurried across the hall to where O'Brien was drinking coffee. We left before he had a chance to finish.

The names Donnie and Rachel Gilmore were printed on the registry next to Apartment 104. I tried to open the building's front door but someone had repaired the broken lock. I pressed the intercom button next to the Gilmores' names and a woman's voice responded. "Can I help you?"

"Is this Rachel Gilmore?" I asked.

"Who's asking?"

"Dani Fox. I'm an assistant district attorney with the Westchester County District Attorney's Office and I have Detective Thomas O'Brien with me. We'd like to speak to your husband."

"Donnie? He's at work, but two detectives already talked to me."

"We have a few follow-up questions," I said. "Can we come up?"

She buzzed us in and was waiting with her apartment door half open.

"I expect Donnie to get home any minute," she said, greeting us. "He usually is here by now when he works the early morning shift."

I checked my watch. It was nearly 10 a.m.

Rachel Gilmore was a painfully thin woman in her twenties with long brown hair and blue eyes that looked as if they were all pupil. Their apartment was identical to the Mancinis' two-bedroom place, only freshly painted and not dreary. Nor did it reek of alcohol and cigarettes. Instead it smelled like dirty diapers. I didn't know which was worse.

"This is our son," Rachel said, hoisting up a tubby two-year-old wearing only a diaper. "His name is Charles Henry Gilmore, but we call him Chucky."

Chucky was wearing a milk mustache and holding the remains of a soggy Oreo cookie in one hand.

"I was just finishing feeding him. Donnie wants to eat lunch with me when he gets home from his shift so I try to have Chucky fed and put down for a nap. Only all he'll eat today is cookies."

Chucky smiled, burped, and held the half-eaten cookie out toward O'Brien.

"No thanks, kid," the detective said, patting his stomach. "Watching the waistline. You might want to do the same before your folks begin calling you Chunky."

Rachel didn't smile.

"This seems like an odd hour to get home from work," I said. "What exactly does your husband do?"

"He sorts mail at the post office. But they only have been calling him in to work split shifts, you know, four to six hours, at peak times. It's tough 'cause I can't work now since Chucky is such a handful."

She reached for a paper towel from an end table and wiped Chucky's face but he refused to surrender the remains of his cookie. By this time, we'd moved into the living room, which was littered with baby toys.

While Rachel deposited Chucky into a playpen next to a lounge chair, O'Brien and I sat on the sofa.

Rachel ran a finger through her hair and said, "I'm a mess. I never knew a baby could be such hard work."

"Have you lived here long?" I asked. "Your place looks like it was recently painted."

"Only four months. I still got boxes to unpack. We were at my parents' place in Queens before Donnie found us this apartment."

O'Brien said, "You talked to the police, you said. Was your husband here for that?"

"Two Yonkers detectives came on the day after that woman's body was found. Donnie was at work. But I'm afraid I didn't help them much. I never met her. And when I mentioned that the cops had been here, Donnie told me that he'd seen her in the stairwell once but that was it. I heard she stuck out when she was here."

"Stuck out?" I repeated.

"Mrs. McCurry next door said the woman didn't really live here. Donny and me are the only young tenants in this building so when someone younger than sixty is in the halls, people notice. Mrs. McCurry said her granddaughter saw her, too."

"This granddaughter, does she live with your neighbor?" I asked.

"That's right. She babysits for us sometimes. She saw the woman, too, but she never spoke to her. That woman didn't talk to anyone. This building is like a small town, so everyone knew she was coming here to meet her boyfriend."

"Did you ever see the boyfriend?"

"Naw, I don't go out much because of Chucky. He likes playing here."

I glanced at Chucky, who had fallen asleep in his playpen still holding his soggy cookie.

"The detectives never came back to talk to your husband, is that correct?" I asked.

She nodded and asked, "Why do you want to talk to Donnie?" Just then, the apartment door opened and a man wearing a postal service uniform came in. "Donnie," Rachel said, "this lady is a prosecutor from the D.A.'s office and he's a detective."

Donnie was a few years older than Rachel, with a slender build, kinky black hair, a thick mustache, and long sideburns.

"Hello," he said. "The police were already here." If he was worried, he didn't show it.

"We have a few follow-up questions," I replied. "Did you know Isabella Ricci well?"

"No, I just bumped into her a few times in the building," he said. He sounded confident, cocky almost.

It was time for me to crack that façade. "You hadn't met her earlier in Scarsdale?"

Gilmore's eyes widened and his lips parted slightly as he glanced at Rachel and then back at me and said, "I'm not sure what you mean."

"She's asking if you ever met her at any parties," O'Brien said. "Like when she was with her husband, Dr. Ricci?"

"Scarsdale? Parties?" Rachel repeated. "What are they talking about?"

A look of panic appeared on Donnie's face. "Can we step out to talk? In the hallway."

"Why do you want to talk to them without me?" Rachel asked, looking concerned.

I had no interest in helping Gilmore keep secrets about his sexual swinging from his wife, but I also knew he was more likely to talk freely with us if she wasn't listening.

"Let's go for a walk and then you can talk to your wife about all this later," I said.

"Why can't you talk about it now, Donnie?" Rachel said harshly. "What are you hiding?"

"It's nothing," he said. "I'll explain later."

Gilmore nearly ran out into the hallway with O'Brien at his heels.

As soon as I joined them, Gilmore said, "Rachel doesn't know anything about Scarsdale. Can we go get coffee down the street? I can explain everything. I didn't do anything wrong."

We walked in silence to a coffee shop, where we settled in a booth near the back.

"You might as well tell us the truth because we know about you and Isabella and her husband," I said.

"It will go better if you don't hide nothin'," O'Brien chimed in. "Lying isn't going to win you any brownie points."

"Let's start with you telling us about your relationship with Isabella," I said.

"Relationship? It wasn't a relationship," he protested.

"I just told you not to lie," O'Brien replied.

"But I didn't have a relationship with her. I met her and Marco when they came to a party in Scarsdale, that's it."

"A sex party," O'Brien added. "Right? You think we don't know that?"

"Some people call them that, but it's just a group of people who are more open-minded. A guy and his wife at work invited me but I knew Rachel would never agree so I've been going by myself."

"Without telling her," I said. "I'm guessing she has no idea you've been cheating on her with other women?"

"I'm not cheating. I mean, this is about my needs and to tell you the truth, I think Rachel probably will be happy when I tell her because since the baby, she's not really wanted to have sex that much. She'll probably be glad."

Sure, I thought. Keep telling yourself that when she kicks you out of the apartment. "Mr. Gilmore," I said, "we're not here to discuss your marriage. We're here to ask about your sexual relationship with Isabella Ricci."

"Relationship?" he replied, his voice rising in fear. "You got the wrong impression. We never did it. I wanted to, but she said no. She and Marco were first-timers—cherries, is what the group called them when they showed up at Scarsdale. Isabella wasn't really into having sex with other men. She left without doing it with anybody and I didn't think they'd ever come back. I mean, he was ready to swing, but not her."

"When was that?" O'Brien asked.

"Maybe six, seven months ago. I was shocked when they showed up later and this time, she did it with two men while Marco had a party with their wives."

I noticed he was keeping his eyes on O'Brien, avoiding contact with mine.

I said, "Mr. Gilmore, is that when you first tried to have sex with her? At the second party?"

Still looking at O'Brien, he said, "I guess so. I mean, I asked her if she wanted to party but she said no. I figured it was because she already had been with these other two guys. But everyone respects it when you say no. You don't have to say yes to anyone you don't want to do it with."

"Being rejected like that must have hurt your feelings," I said.

"No, not really. I mean, sure, it was the first time I'd been turned down. Most women are all over me even though I go stag. But it was cool. I mean, I wouldn't touch some women there with a ten-foot pole."

He was beginning to get his confidence back and I didn't like that.

"Maybe the first time, you didn't mind, but you sure as hell did the next several times, didn't you?" I asked.

Gilmore must have assumed that we only knew about Scarsdale and not the rest of his attempts to bed Isabella. He finally glanced at me and I saw both fear and anger in his eyes. "Okay, she said no a couple of times. I kept thinking she'd changed her mind so I kept asking. No crime in that."

"But she didn't change her mind, did she?" I said.

"That's right," he said, with a flash of anger now in his voice. "She kept saying no. I never got to party with her."

"Maybe not in Scarsdale, but you did have sex with her, didn't you?" I continued.

His jaw dropped and he realized that I knew much more than he'd thought. Or did I? I was quietly enjoying the fact that we were keeping him twisting in the wind.

Glancing down at his coffee, he said, "Isabella never agreed to have sex with me, if that's what you're asking."

"But it's not what I'm asking," I said. "I said you had sex with her. Are you denying that now? And by sex, I mean consensual or otherwise."

Gilmore still thought he might be able to dodge my question. "I'm not sure what you are asking."

"Don't play word games with me," I said.

O'Brien piped in, "Tell Miss Fox here if you fucked Isabella, with or without her consent."

"I did not rape her," he replied.

"But you did have sex with her without her consent, didn't you?"

"No. I mean, yes. But she knew what was happening."

"You'd better start from the beginning," I said. "And don't lie to us or leave anything out."

"Her husband asked me about this house. He'd heard another couple talk about it. It's where men and women act out fantasies."

"What sort of fantasies?" I asked.

"All kinds. But mostly being tied up, spanked, stuff like that. Some broads like being dominated. Some men do."

"Are we talking about rape?" I said.

"Not really, but yes. I didn't think you'd know about that."

"Stop trying to figure out what we may or may not know, because, right now, you're sounding like a prime murder suspect."

"Murder? I didn't kill that broad!"

"But you told her husband that Isabella needed to be taught a lesson," I said. "That she needed to be raped. That it would be good for her."

Gilmore glanced around to see if anyone had heard my accusation. "That don't mean I killed her."

"Then you'd better tell us what you did do to her and tell us fast," O'Brien said.

"Okay, okay. I thought she was a snob, that part's true, and I did take her and Marco to a private S-and-M thing that happens around here from time to time."

"Go on," I said.

"You want to know if I had sex with her," he said in a whisper. "Yes, I did, but not in Scarsdale and it certainly wasn't rape. She just didn't know it was me."

"How'd you manage that?" O'Brien asked.

"Her husband brought her to this hotel. She was blindfolded and he told her to keep it on. Then I came in and he watched us do it. Marco watched and then I left before she took off the blindfold. Like I said, she never knew it was me."

"When did this happen?" I asked.

"Maybe five months ago."

"Did you ever have sex with her again?" I asked.

"No, she and Marco disappeared."

"C'mon, stop lying," O'Brien said. "You began stalking her. That's why you moved into the Midland Apartments with your wife and baby."

"No, no, that was a coincidence. I didn't know she had a place here. I bumped into her coming down the stairs one day."

"That's one hell of a coincidence. Did you speak to her?" I asked.

"I said hello but she acted like she didn't remember me. I understood why. Later, I asked Mr. Mancini about her and he told me about how she was meeting someone at the apartment. I figured it was one of their rich friends. But that was the only time I ever saw her in our building—that day in the hallway."

"You mean stairwell?" O'Brien asked. "You just told us that's where you saw her, not a hallway."

Gilmore was avoiding eye contact with me and I was losing patience. "You're lying again. Look at me when you talk."

He glanced up and I could tell he was getting angrier.

"It would have been a snap," I said, "for you to learn her schedule, especially if you talked to Roman Mancini. He probably told you she came twice a week to the building."

O'Brien joined in. "You wait until her visitor leaves the apartment. You see him get into his limo and then you knock on her door."

"No, no," he said. "That never happened."

"She answered and you forced your way in and attacked her. You brought a knife with you, didn't you?" O'Brien said.

"I wasn't there! I never touched her!"

"Where were you," I asked, "on the afternoon when Isabella was butchered?"

"At work. I was getting lots of extra hours."

"That should be easy to check," I said. "You'd better be telling the truth."

"Wait, wait, I wasn't at work," he replied, sounding panicked.

"Changing your story, huh?" O'Brien said.

"No, I was confused. I took the day off because Rachel had to visit her mother. I stayed with our baby. But, I swear, I was in the apartment the entire day. I never went near that woman's apartment."

"Your baby isn't going to make a very good alibi witness," I said.

"Which is it: Were you at work or at home? You go out that day or not?" O'Brien asked. "Think about your answer because, so far, you ain't been too convincing."

Gilmore hesitated. "I was definitely at home and I only went out once. The baby and me went down to a park, after he got up from his nap. I wasn't even in the building when that murder happened."

"How do you know when it happened?" I asked.

"One of the police detectives. He told Rachel it happened in the afternoon, between two and six."

"You took Chucky to a park for four hours?" I asked.

"No, no. I don't think I should say anything more now without talking to a lawyer."

"Why do you need a lawyer?" O'Brien asked, somehow making it sound like an oddball request when, in fact, a detective and A.D.A. were grilling him about a homicide.

"Because I'm innocent."

"Then you got nothin' to hide," O'Brien said. "She didn't want to have sex with you and you couldn't stand it."

I joined in, tag-teaming Gilmore. "You got angry, told her husband that she needed to be taught a lesson, to be raped and humiliated."

"No, you've got it wrong."

"You find a way to bump into Marco, you befriend him, you plant a new idea in his head: going to a hotel with Isabella wearing a blindfold. Sounds erotic to him and you finally get to have sex with her."

O'Brien said, "But that wasn't enough, was it?"

"You're putting words in my mouth," he said.

"You started stalking her," O'Brien said.

"When you discovered she was meeting someone else—someone better than you—in the apartment twice a week, you got jealous," I said.

"You moved your family into the same building," O'Brien said.

"You watched her come into the building on New Year's Eve," I said, "and you got furiously angry. Who did she think she was, rejecting you?!"

O'Brien had taught me about what cops called the Reid Technique, a nine-step process that included providing a suspect with a justification or rationale from the criminal's viewpoint during an interrogation. "You got to get inside their skull," he'd told me. "Make them think you know exactly why they did it." Once O'Brien had gotten a murderer to literally talk himself into a jail cell without any physical evidence. The killer had become so wrapped up in O'Brien's account that he began correcting the cops, revealing details that only the murderer would know. As we continued to pressure Donnie Gilmore, I noticed that his hands, which he was warming with his coffee, start to shake.

"You tied her up," O'Brien said, "because you knew she wouldn't have sex with you any other way. You began cutting off her clothing."

"And then you really decided to teach her a lesson, didn't you?" I added. "You really decided to humiliate her. Maybe she laughed at you. Maybe she spit in your face."

"No, no, no!" he protested.

"Things got out of hand, didn't they?" I continued. "You only meant to scare her with your knife. Terrorize her."

"She kicked you," O'Brien said.

"No!" he declared, suddenly slapping the table with his hands. "I don't want to talk to either of you anymore."

"Then let's go back upstairs and we'll talk to Rachel," I said. "We'll tell her about your little outings in Scarsdale and how you had sex with a blind-folded woman in a hotel who later ended up cut to pieces in the building that you just happened to move into."

Gilmore raised his hands, covering his face, and said, "I need a lawyer. You can't keep talking to me without a lawyer. Rachel's my wife. You can't talk to her, either. I watch television. I know my rights."

We were entering touchy territory. As soon as Gilmore told us that he wanted a lawyer, we should have stopped interrogating him. At least that is what they always did on television. But he was not in custody and he was free to stand up and walk out of the coffee shop. Therefore, we technically were not violating his rights, nor were we required to give him a Miranda warning. That subtly was not something he would have learned from watch-ing *Hill Street Blues*.

"You don't own your wife," I said. "I think she'll want to talk to us, espe-cially when she hears about Scarsdale and your hotel sexual escapades."

"Please, please. I didn't kill her but you're going to destroy my marriage."

"You've got no one to blame but yourself," I said.

O'Brien said, "I'll check the rental records at the apartments and if you moved there after Isabella Ricci began shacking up with her lover, we're go-ing to be coming back."

I added, "You will most definitely need a lawyer then."

19

A BOUQUET OF TWENTY-FOUR RED ROSES WAS SITTING on the front porch of my house when I got home after work. It was Friday night and, although Will and I had not spoken since our last awkward conversation, I was expecting him for dinner. We took turns fixing dinner on our Friday "date nights." I always prepared something in my kitchen, because I love to cook. On Will's nights, he either made a reservation at a local restaurant or arrived armed with Chinese carry-out. I picked up the roses and smiled when I reached the kitchen and saw the message light blinking on my answering machine.

"Sorry, I'm running late tonight," Will's familiar voice announced. "I've got another big story on page one tomorrow, but I'll get to your place as quickly as I can. I'll bring Chinese because it's my turn. Can't wait to see you!"

Will hadn't said anything in his message about our argument. It must have been bothering me more than it did him. It didn't seem as important to me now as it had been, in part because I now knew Will's exclusive story hadn't been responsible for Roman and Maggie Mancini being murdered. Just the same, we still needed to discuss how we were going to keep our professional and private lives separate.

It was our work that had brought us together in the first place. Will had contacted me a few days after I was hired as a prosecutor. He'd wanted to write a story about me since I was the first and only woman prosecutor in Westchester County. Will had accepted my initial "No thank you" answer but remained interested. When my office got a federal grant to open our Domestic Violence Unit in 1978, I agreed to let him write about me.

It wasn't love at first sight, although I'd found him attractive enough. It was more of a slow, gradual affection. I admired his desire to make a positive difference in our society. He'd been a teenager when President John F. Kennedy had issued his famous call: "Ask not what your country can do for you, ask what you can do for your country." And Will tried to answer that challenge.

During our interview, Will asked me why I felt so strongly about domestic violence and I'd told him about an incident in my own family. As a young girl, I'd been extremely close with a cousin who was a few years older, and I was thrilled when she and her boyfriend got married. In my innocent fourteen-year-old eyes, it was a fairy tale come true. But years later, they'd fallen on hard times and he'd started drinking. When my mother and I saw the bruises and tried to intervene, my cousin got angry and stopped talking to us. That experience had shown me how smart women were often unwilling or unable to extricate themselves from violent relationships.

As soon as I told Will about my cousin, I'd wanted to take back my words. I knew my mother would be horrified if she read about our family's problems in the newspaper. I'd asked Will to keep it out of his story, even though I'd cited it as an example of why I cared about battered women. The night before his article was scheduled to appear, I assumed the worst and prepared a speech in my head to deliver the next morning to Mom.

But Will didn't write a word about my cousin. The only line that Will put in his story that embarrassed me was a flattering description. He called me a snappy dresser with a great pair of legs and "bee-stung lips." The secretaries in the office teased me endlessly about it. Within a few months, Will and I began dating.

Will arrived late, carrying a paper bag stuffed with take-out containers, as promised. "I got beef and broccoli and General Tso's chicken," he declared, giving me a peck on my cheek after I answered the door.

He was clearly in a good mood. "I've got another exclusive tomorrow," Will announced. "We're running ten thousand extra copies of the morning edition and my boss says it should sell out. This is gnarly."

"That's great! What's this one about?" I asked.

Will smiled broadly and said, "Sorry, counselor, but I'm sworn to secrecy. I got a tip from a source and I promised that I wouldn't tell a soul until after it's published. It was part of our deal."

"Is it about the murders?" I asked suspiciously.

Will held a finger up to his lips and said, "Secrecy means secrecy. My lips are sealed, but you'll definitely want to read it, I guarantee you that."

Although curious, I decided to let him keep his secret and instead said, "I've got some great news, too. Your exclusive story about Roman Mancini didn't get him and his wife murdered."

Will stopped arranging the carry-out on my kitchen table. "What?" he said.

"The coroner has determined the Mancinis were murdered between the hours of midnight and five a.m., which was before your front-page story hit the streets at six o'clock. That means the killer didn't learn from reading your story that Roman Mancini was our key witness."

Will looked more disappointed than relieved.

"I thought," I explained, "that you'd be happy to know you didn't have their blood on your hands."

"I never thought I did," he replied, sounding irked. "Dani, I think you just don't get it. Sure, I'm sorry that the Mancinis were murdered. But I don't care if the murderer read my story or if he didn't. My job is to get a great story and that's what I did. It was your job to protect Roman if he said something stupid. I don't understand why you keep trying to make me feel guilty about what I do for a living."

"Will," I replied sternly, "like it or not, you are responsible for what you write in the newspaper and what gets published. Even the U.S. Supreme Court agrees that speech can and should be limited. The fact that you put our key witness on the front page—even after I asked you not to do it—and quoted him talking about what he'd seen on the day of the murder should give you pause."

"I reported the facts and I take no responsibility for what someone else decides to do because of those facts. Don't lecture me about ethics. The *New York Times* didn't worry about how President Nixon would react when the Pentagon Papers showed that the president had lied to the American public about the Vietnam War. Woodward and Bernstein didn't call up the White House to ask for permission to write about Watergate. I don't decide what the public should and shouldn't be told."

"That sounds noble, but it's bullshit!" I yelled. "You decide if something is a news story. You decide how important it is by putting it on the front page. You decide if the public needs to know. That makes you responsible for what you print and tell people."

Will crumbled the Chinese carry-out bag in his hands. His face was flushed and then, suddenly, he seemed to relax. "Let's not fight," he said. "Let's have a nice evening."

But I wasn't ready to surrender.

Lowering my voice, I said, "I want a nice evening, too, but we can't just ignore this tension. Let's put aside your defense of the First Amendment and talk about how you tried to trick me into confirming that Isabella Ricci was our unidentified murder victim. You're not supposed to be manipulating me. You're supposed to be someone I can trust."

"C'mon, Dani. You're making too big of a deal about this." He walked over to where I was standing and put his arms around my waist. "You can trust me, okay? I'll admit, what I did the other morning was stupid. I shouldn't have done it. I apologize. No one is perfect. And I won't do it again. My editors were on my ass and I gave in. But I didn't commit a felony."

"Will, you have to realize that every time you write something about the courthouse, Whitaker and Steinberg automatically assume it came from me. Until the other day when you tried to trick me, I didn't give a damn about their suspicions because I knew you kept our conversations private. I could assure them that I wasn't your source."

"You still can," he said. "I always protect my confidential sources."

"That's not the point."

He smiled mischievously and said, "Dani, relax. I've got plenty of sources in the courthouse besides you. Just wait until tomorrow and you'll see that."

"I'm not one of your sources!" I exclaimed. "Don't you get that? We're sleeping together."

"So? What makes you think I don't sleep with my sources?" he asked, but when he saw my face, his smirk vanished.

"Stop joking around," I said. "Clearly, we need to reestablish some ground rules between us."

"You sound like a lawyer now. You want to type something up and have me sign it in blood." He released his grip around my waist. "And what if I refuse to go along with your demands?"

I winced. "Will, I want to work this out. It's what professional couples do when they have jobs that conflict."

"It's not our jobs that are conflicting, it's us," he said, folding his arms across his chest in what was clearly a defensive stance. "Go ahead. Tell me your demands."

"First of all, we've got to be completely honest with each other. No more tricks. No manipulations. You don't try to worm information out of me. We keep our professional lives out of our relationship."

"I agree on one condition," he said haughtily. "If I don't tell you about a story, like the one that is coming out tomorrow, then you can't get angry at me for keeping it secret."

That was the second time he'd reference tomorrow's story but I wasn't going to bite and ask him about it. Instead, I said, "Okay, what you write is your business and you don't have to tell me about it in advance."

"Great," he said. "You just told me what rules I need to follow in our arrangement. What rules apply to you?"

"You tell me," I said. "What do you want from me?"

"I don't want you to blame me if I quote someone like Roman Mancini and my story ends up putting him in danger or impacts one of your cases. I don't want you trying to censor me like you did the other night. I don't want you punishing me if I write something that you happen to dislike."

"Punishing you?"

"Yes, getting angry at me for doing my job."

"Doing your job is okay with me," I said.

Both of us had agreed, but the wounds were still fresh. There was only one way to de-escalate the situation. Reaching out, I returned his arms to my waist, leaned up on my toes, and kissed him. "I just don't want our jobs to cause us problems in the future," I said.

"They won't," he said, holding me tightly, "because if I decide to make an honest woman out of you someday, you'll stop chasing bad guys and start chasing after kids."

This was news to me—and it was both presumptuous and disparaging. "First, I don't need you to make me an honest woman."

"It's just a joke."

"An offensive one. Second, I definitely want children but I'm not about to give up my career. I worked too hard in law school to become a prosecutor. Besides, I love my job."

He kissed me.

"And you're great at it. But my parents divorced when I was young and I never really knew my father. I don't want my kids to grow up in a home where everyone fights and the parents aren't around."

"I'm not sure why the fact that your father abandoned your family translates into me having to give up my career," I said. The visual in my head was awful. Me with my Janis Joplin frizzed-out hair with a kid on one arm screaming, a pot boiling over, and Wilbur grunting with longing for the old days when it was just the two of us.

Eager to switch subjects, Will asked, "How hungry are you?"

I was tired of fighting. "Not that hungry."

"Good," he said. "This has been a very long week for both of us. We need to reconnect."

I agreed. Taking his hand, I led him into my bedroom and started to undress.

Later, lying in bed, Will and I both collapsed. I put my head on his chest. The tension was gone. We were Will and Dani again, two people completely exposing themselves to each other. No longer the prosecutor and reporter.

"You hungry now?" I asked. "Or do you want a repeat?"

"Let's eat," he said. "I don't want to insult General Tso."

I said, "More later" as I slipped from his arms into a white robe. He put on his blue denim jeans without bothering to grab his boxers or a shirt. We returned to the kitchen, where Wilbur was curled up on a mat, taking a nap. He glanced at us through half-closed eyes and then went back to sleep.

"Who sent you roses?" Will asked. "Your mother?"

"I thought you did," I answered, not having to feign surprise.

He tugged a tiny florist card from deep down between the stems where it had fallen and read it aloud: " 'Can't wait for our second date. Affectionately, Walt.' Who the hell is Walt?"

"FBI Special Agent Walter Coyle," I replied. "The FBI guy I had dinner with the other night to talk about the Ricci murder."

"Who sends someone roses after a business meeting? Did you mention that you were already taken?"

"Actually, I did. I told him I had a boyfriend."

I hoped my comment might ease any insecurity Will was feeling. But it didn't. "And this son of a bitch still sends you roses!"

I stepped toward him and put my face against his naked chest, holding him. I could hear his heart. "Honey," I said, "we just made love. It was incredible. As long as we're honest and open with each other, you'll never have to worry about me. No matter how many men send me flowers."

But Will was still fuming. "Men don't send flowers unless they pick up some sort of vibe."

I instantly pushed him away. "What? That's not fair. Obviously, he's making a play for me. So what? That doesn't mean I sent him any vibes," I said. "In fact, I defended you."

"Defended me?"

"Yes, when he discovered you were the reporter who wrote about the Mancinis, he called you an asshole. I defended you. You're the one who is jealous. Don't blame me for your insecurities."

As I was lecturing Will, I was thinking about my dinner with Coyle. Had I sent out any vibes? I found Coyle attractive, but I was certain that I hadn't done anything to lead him on. Will was being paranoid.

General Tso's chicken went uneaten.

Will and I argued for twenty minutes, and then he left angry.

All I could think was that this new year had to start getting better because so far, it had been just awful.

20

"WE'VE BEEN SHAFTED," O'BRIEN DECLARED WHEN I
answered my phone. I peered at my bedroom alarm, which
showed that I still had another fifteen minutes of precious
sleep before it went off at 5:45 a.m.

"What are you talking about?" I asked.

Usually, I was the one waking O'Brien up with early morning phone
calls.

"Whitaker, the chiefs, and your boyfriend," he said. "They fucked us."

Now he had my full attention. "O'Brien, I don't have a clue what you're
talking about," I said.

"A buddy at the Yonkers precinct just called," he said. "There's gonna be
a big story coming in today's paper. Whitaker sent us out of that meeting
early the other day for a reason. He and his chiefs had their own little pow-
wow and they didn't want us to know about it."

"Damn it, O'Brien, tell me what's happening."

During the next ten minutes, O'Brien explained that Vanderhoot and
the Organized Crime Bureau had arranged a police lineup at the Yonkers
precinct. The Butcher was part of it. Lineups are done discreetly because
there's no need to publicize suspicion of a potentially innocent person,
but someone, who O'Brien and I both suspected was Steinberg, had
tipped off a reporter. Not just any reporter. Will Harris. He had been
waiting behind the station with a photographer, who'd snapped pictures
of a very angry Persico and his equally angry lawyers scurrying into a
waiting limo.

"Where did they find an eyewitness?" I asked. The only one that we knew about was Agent Coyle and he already was familiar with what Persico looked like. Unless someone else had seen Persico entering that apartment building, a lineup was a pointless exercise.

"Nobody was behind that glass," O'Brien said. "The whole thing was a stunt."

"What!?" I exclaimed.

"You heard me. They wanted to get Persico's mug on the front page. All that crap about making sure the citizens feel better."

As soon as I hung up the phone, I slipped into my running gear and headed to the neighborhood store to buy a newspaper. Only this time, I didn't wait to run back home to read it. I stood in the store aisle. As O'Brien had predicted, Will's exclusive was spread across the top front page of the *White Plains Daily* along with a large photo of Persico trying to hide his face. The headline: Suspect in Bloody Killings?

Will's editors apparently had thought that by making the headline into a question, they would be protecting themselves from a potential libel suit from Gallo & Conti. Under that questioning headline was a subhead: Murder Victim and Hubby Enjoyed Sex Parties.

Will's story was tabloid fodder. In the second paragraph, District Attorney Carlton Whitaker III was quoted as saying that Persico was only one of several "persons of interest" and that it would be "premature" to jump to conclusions. But, of course, the rest of the story did exactly that. Will quoted a "courthouse source who asked not to be identified by name" but was "close to the investigation" as saying that Persico had been spotted entering the Midland Apartments on the day of the murder. The next several paragraphs quoted unnamed sources talking about "swingers clubs in Scarsdale" that Isabella Ricci had participated in with her husband.

By the time I finished reading Will's story, I was furious—at Whitaker, his three stooges, and at Will. In their hurry to make headlines, they had trashed Isabella's reputation. I didn't care about the mud that they'd flung at Persico and Marco Ricci. Those scumbags deserved it. But Isabella had been the victim of a vicious murder and now she was being crucified all over again on the front page without being able to defend herself.

Will's story also painted a bright red target on Persico's back. There was no question that the mobster was our chief murder suspect and now every-one in the paper's circulation area knew it. Will had given Tiny Nunzio an-other reason to take vigilante action against his most-hated mob rival.

Whitaker and his chiefs had intentionally left us out—a signal that I wasn't part of their team. The fact that they had most likely faked having an eyewitness also stuck in my craw.

As soon as I ran home, I dialed Will's number and it immediately went to a busy signal. Coward! He must have unplugged his phone. He had to know that I was going to be upset by this. And the more I thought about it, the more pissed off I became.

Even though it was a Saturday, I'd planned to spend the day catching up in my office. But as I was driving to work, I changed course and instead headed toward Yonkers. Some forty minutes later, I parked my car outside Persico's butcher shop, took a deep breath, questioned my own sanity, and walked through the shop's front door.

The same chubby clerk who had been cutting meat when O'Brien and I had first visited the store was waiting on customers. He did a double take when he saw me.

"I need to see Mr. Persico," I declared.

He gave me a curious look, glanced up at the camera in the corner, and then disappeared through the door behind him.

Part of me was thinking: What the hell am I doing? This is not a smart move on any level. For a moment, I thought about bolting but I didn't.

Carmine Caruso, the second in command, emerged from the back. While he had been friendly during my first visit, he was definitely not smiling now.

"What the hell you want?" he asked. "You got your headline."

"Listen," I said, "you might not believe this, but I am not convinced Mr. Persico is responsible for Isabella Ricci's death. I'm not certain he had any-thing to do with the Mancini murders. But the only way I can prove that is with his cooperation."

Caruso grunted and said, "An assistant district attorney wants to prove our boss didn't do nothin' illegal? You seen today's paper? Lady, what kinda games you playin'?"

"I had nothing to do with that lineup," I said, wondering if I was disclos-ing too much information. "I'm here on my own and alone. I don't have any witnesses with me. All I want to do is ask Mr. Persico a couple of questions. There's no way I can use his answers at trial without corroboration. In fact, my boss might fire me for coming here."

Caruso thought about what I had said and disappeared into the back room to consult with his master. I flopped down on one of the cheap metal chairs near the closest of three tables. A thirtyish-looking woman standing behind the deli counter eyeballed me. I smiled, but she glared.

What was I doing? What did I really hope to gain from this? I found myself staring at an old electric clock hanging above the exit; I was fascinated by its red minute hand, which was sweeping across its face. A smiling pig, encircled by the clock's numbers, looked back at me. NOTHING BEATS THE TASTE OF PERSICO'S PORK was printed under the pig's snout. What idiot had come up with that slogan?

I fully expected Gallo and Conti to show up at any minute and braced myself for the nasty exchange that would follow, but after waiting five minutes, Caruso stepped from behind the counter, followed by the old mobster himself.

As they approached my table, Persico called to the woman making a sandwich behind the deli counter. "Angelica, we need you!" he hollered.

The woman put aside the hoagie that she was making, wiped her hands on her white apron, and came forward, still glaring at me. "Stand up and face me," she ordered.

"I need to check for a wire," she explained, and then before I could protest, she dropped down and expertly began frisking my legs.

"Is this really necessary?" I asked Persico.

Caruso answered. "If you wanna talk to the boss, it is."

Having inspected my legs, Angelica announced, "I need to check under your shirt."

I'd not expected this but again, she moved quickly, reaching under my T-shirt and racing her hands up and down my sides and then simultaneously along my back and front. It happened in seconds. She turned, nodded, and had started back to her station when Persico reached out and took her arm. "You stay," he ordered.

Angelica looked angry and I wondered if something was going on between them. She turned and faced me.

I now had Caruso, Persico, and Angelica standing directly in front of me, waiting for me to speak. "That was a first," I said, making no attempt to hide my indignation.

Caruso said, "You never been frisked by a cop? Trust me, they ain't gentle like Angelica."

"How about a lineup?" Persico said. "You ever have to go through one of them?"

"Yeah," Caruso said, immediately chiming in. "You ever been called down to a station and been ambushed by photographers?"

"No, but I've never been a murder suspect," I replied.

Persico said, "Why'd you come here?"

"Look, I already told you that everyone thinks you were having an affair with Isabella Ricci."

Angelica seemed shocked for a second and then caught herself.

"I don't believe that," I continued.

Persico's eyes locked on mine. "I'd never seen that broad before that Friday. I didn't even know who she was."

"Wait," I said. "You didn't know it was Isabella Ricci, Tiny Nunzio's daughter, in that apartment?"

"You deaf?"

"Then why did you go there?"

"That's none of your business," he said.

"It is if you want me to help you."

"I already got an entire law firm," he said. "I don't need your help."

"Was it because of some feud between you and Tiny Nunzio?"

"You deaf *and* dumb?" he replied. "I just told you, I didn't know that broad was his daughter."

I was thinking about his answer when he turned the tables. "Your boyfriend—did you come here to help him get another big story in tomorrow's paper?"

I got a sudden chill. I had no idea that the Butcher knew about Will and me. I didn't like it. Clearly, he had sources either at the courthouse, the newspaper, or the police department. Maybe all three.

"If you want my help," I said, "tell me why you went to that apartment."

Persico turned and began walking toward the meat counter.

Our tête-à-tête was over. Just to make certain that I didn't chase after Persico, Caruso stepped between us.

"For a prosecutor," Caruso said coldly, "youse got yourself a nice pair a legs. I could use a broad like youse in one of our clubs. Youse ever want a legit job, gimme a call." He gave me a truly evil smirk.

I was angrier at myself than I was at Persico. I'd thought I might be able to get the gangster to talk to me as a person. I wondered how many of his victims had tried that same tactic, pleading for their lives only to have him scoff at them. I looked at Caruso and replied, "Nice try, asshole. Maybe after I convict your boss of murder."

21

O'BRIEN WAS WAITING AT OUR OFFICE WHEN I PARKED my car and let myself in through the building's back door. He was holding an open copy of the newspaper in one hand and a cup of coffee in the other.

"I'd like to be there when Tiny Nunzio reads that his only daughter was being forced to spread 'em and bend over at wild sex parties," he said.

"Spread 'em and bend over?"

"Yeah. Remember? My New Year's Eve resolution? I'm trying to expand my vocabulary." O'Brien chuckled to himself and said, "Marco Ricci's butt has got to be super puckered right now."

"Super puckered? That's increasing your vocabulary?"

He shrugged. But he was right. Marco Ricci had to be even more terrified of Tiny Nunzio knowing that the mobster had read about Isabella's forced sexual swinging.

"He'll be Nunzio's secondary target," I predicted, "after Persico."

O'Brien nodded in agreement and put down the newspaper. "Your boyfriend's opened a real Pandora's box."

"Citing Greek mythology now," I teased. "That's more impressive than super puckered."

"I read the first few pages of that Pandora story back in high school. The teacher tricked me. I thought Pandora's box was something else."

I gave him a blank stare.

"A certain part of her lower anatomy."

"You're quite a detective, O'Brien."

Eager to change the subject, he said: "I expected you two hours ago. Where you been?"

I hesitated, not sure I wanted to tell him, but then I said, "I went to the butcher shop."

O'Brien's smile vanished along with his New Year's resolution. "Why the fuck did you do that?"

"I felt bad about the fake police lineup and I thought I might be able to break through to him if he realized I was different from Whitaker and his cronies. I wanted him to know that I was trying to solve these killings and not simply prosecute him."

"How'd that work for you?"

"Not well, although I did get a job offer," I said with a sly smile.

"Doing what? We're both going to need new jobs after Whitaker finds out you met with Persico without permission."

"Carmine Caruso said I had nice legs. He offered me a job in one of his titty clubs."

I expected O'Brien to laugh, but instead he spun the toothpick in his mouth several times and in a serious voice said, "Dani, you don't want to get personal with guys like Caruso or Persico."

"What do you mean, get personal?"

"Right now, they think you're an asshole prosecutor. That's how you want to keep it. If they begin to think you have some sort of fondness or friendship with them—that could be dangerous."

"I was just trying to talk to him as a fellow human being."

"Persico's not a human being. He's your enemy. If he thinks you like him, he'll see that as a weakness and he'll exploit it. And if you develop even the slightest hint of a friendship, you stop being just another asshole prosecutor. The moment you do something he doesn't like, he'll feel betrayed. He'll think you're toying with him and Nicholas Persico isn't someone you toy with."

"I don't want to be his friend," I said.

"That's not my point. Let me spell this out for you. Let's say two bums are sitting outside the courthouse, panhandling. Every day, we walk by them and I tell them to 'go get a job.' But you're too nice to do that. You give them a quarter. Then one day, you got no change and you say, 'Sorry, I don't have a quarter.' Who are they going to get angry at? Not me. I'm just another asshole. But they got expectations from you. Persico is like that. Don't give him expectations."

I'd learned to trust O'Brien's street smarts so I paid attention. But now that he was finished with his lecture, I said, "My encounter with him was not a total waste. I did get one piece of useful information."

"Yeah. What's that?"

"Persico said he didn't know it was Isabella Ricci when he went into that apartment."

"He's jerking your chain. If he wasn't banging that broad, why'd he go there?"

I shrugged. "Look, Mancini said Isabella was meeting someone twice a week like clockwork and had been for three months. Persico says he didn't know who Isabella was until he met her that afternoon. If he's telling the truth, then Isabella wasn't having an affair with him. She was meeting someone else."

"Agent Coyle's logbooks should show who's tellin' the truth," O'Brien said.

Someone banged on the glass front door of our offices.

"You expecting visitors?" I asked.

"Not me," O'Brien replied, rising from his chair. "I'll handle it." He walked down the long hallway to the storefront door and returned moments later with a FedEx package.

"Saturday delivery," he said. "Must be important."

The label identified the sender as Walter Coyle, Special Agent, New York Field Office.

"The FBI's logs," I said excitedly, opening the box.

There was a note inside.

Dear Dani: This is information you need. You can thank me by accepting my dinner invitation. With much affection, Walter Coyle

"That file doesn't look like FBI logs," O'Brien said, eyeing the two-inch-thick bundle.

"It's an FBI background investigation."

"On Persico or Nunzio?" he asked.

"Neither," I said. "It's about Will Harris."

22

O'BRIEN WAS HEE-HAWING.

"A gangster says he likes your legs, then an FBI agent sends you a background investigation of your boyfriend," he said. "What is it with you and men?"

"I certainly didn't ask Agent Coyle to investigate Will."

O'Brien checked his wristwatch and said, "I'd love to read about Will's skeletons, but I got to drive over to the Midland Apartments to see when our stalker rented his apartment."

Continuing, O'Brien said, "But first, this being Saturday, I'm going to grab a bite with my backup girlfriend. You hungry?"

He was referring to Ellen, a divorced waitress at a greasy spoon diner on the outskirts of White Plains. He'd taken me there once and I still wasn't sure if it was the flirtatious Ellen or the fact that cops didn't pay for their meals that drew him to the joint. I was certain it wasn't the artery-clogging food.

"No thanks," I said. "All that grease and gravy is murder on the hips."

O'Brien reached down and jiggled his watermelon belly as he walked to the door. "A little gut on a man my age makes him even more attractive."

"To whom?" I said. "Your number-one girlfriend, Miss Potts? Or your backup, Ellen?"

"So says the attorney with a reporter, a mobster, and an FBI agent chasing her tail."

Now alone, I began poring over the FBI file.

In large letters across the top of the first page was an acronym:

COINTELPRO, for Counter-Intelligence Program. Beginning in the late 1950s, the FBI used surveillance, wiretaps, anonymous letters, and other tactics to identify and disrupt groups that it considered anti-American. At first it targeted the Communist Party of the USA but by the 1960s, the program had spread to watching civil rights and antiwar groups. The page directly in front of me had a passport-size, black-and-white mug shot of Will, taken from his University of Chicago student ID. Back then he'd had shoulder-length, stringy hair and a mountain man beard.

According to the file, Will had first caught the bureau's eye when he participated in a three-day sit-in inside the university's administration building in May 1965. He had belonged to Students for a Democratic Society, an organization that had declared war on the U.S. government and had planted bombs in federal buildings. Most of the field reports in the file described Will's participation at various SDS protests against the Vietnam War. In one photograph, Will was burning an American flag. In another, he was giving the finger to a soldier in uniform returning from the war. About three pages into the report, there was a section marked PERSONAL RELATIONSHIPS.

> The subject lives with Melissa Jamesforth in an apartment two blocks from the University of Chicago campus. Jamesforth, who goes by the name Moonbeams, and Harris are believed to be heavy marijuana smokers. But neither has been arrested for the use of illegal substances. They might have experimented with LSD. In 1969, Jamesforth gave birth to a baby girl out of wedlock. The baby is named Stardust and Harris is believed to be her biological father.

I nearly dropped the file along with my jaw. Will had never told me that he had fathered a child. I knew that he'd been married briefly in college, but that was to a woman named Carol who had moved with him to White Plains and worked at the *White Plains Daily.* Will had never mentioned Jamesforth, aka Moonbeams.

My phone rang. I thought it might be O'Brien so I answered.

"Good morning, sunshine," Agent Coyle said.

"How did you know I'm at work?" I asked.

"Where else would an A.D.A. with three murders on her plate be on a Saturday?" he replied. "Did you like my present?"

"If you're talking about the roses, they're beautiful but inappropriate," I said. "If you're asking me about Will's COINTELPRO file, it pisses me off that you sent it."

"But you're reading it, aren't you?" he replied. "Listen, don't kill the messenger. I thought you'd want to know what kind of man you're dating."

"I already know what kind of man I'm dating," I said. "Sending me this file violates Will's privacy."

"You want to see my bureau file? I've got nothing to hide," he replied. "Look, I don't think you should be wasting your time with a schmuck who burns our flag and gives the finger to our country's fighting men."

"Will's not a schmuck," I said defensively. "He was in college. It was a different time."

"You forgive him for walking in lockstep with Jane Fonda and Ho Chi Minh? I doubt your father or grandfather would approve."

I'd never mentioned both that my father and grandfather were World War II veterans and ardent patriots. Obviously, Agent Coyle had checked into my background, too.

"I'm sending Will's file back first thing Monday," I said. "You're lucky I don't file a complaint against you."

"With whom? Jack Longhorn?" he replied. "Listen, Dani, the real reason I'm calling is to set up a time for us to go over the logbooks. I'm available tonight or any time next week for dinner."

"We're not having dinner," I said. "Will wasn't happy that you sent me flowers and I'm not happy about you sending me this file."

"I don't care what Will thinks," he replied. "But I do care about your opinion, so let me clear up any misconceptions. Yes, I'm interested in dating you. I apologize if that's too blunt, but I believe honesty is the foundation of all relationships, whether they are work related or romantic. And I hope ours will be the latter."

"I'm in a committed relationship," I said. "I expect you to respect that. You can bring the logs to my office during regular working hours or Detective O'Brien and I will come into the city to read them."

"I don't think you've finished reading Will's file yet, have you?" he asked.

"I'm not sure why that matters," I replied.

"Oh, it matters. If you read his entire file, I don't think you'll be in a committed relationship much longer. Check your calendar and call me back about the logs."

He hung up.

For a moment, I thought about shoving Will's file back into the FedEx envelope it came in. But I couldn't do it. I quickly thumbed through several more pages about Will and SDS until I reached more personal information.

On February 15, 1970, at 2 a.m., Chicago police were called to the apartment where Melissa Jamesforth, aka Moonbeams, and subject William Harris were residing. Neighbors had reported that a woman was screaming hysterically in the unit. Upon entering the apartment, they found Moonbeams distraught and collapsed on the floor wailing: "I just killed my baby." The body of an infant, identified as Stardust Jamesforth, was found in a nearby crib. The child's mother said that she had smothered Stardust. She and Harris had celebrated Valentine's Day at an SDS party and had unknowingly eaten a brownie spiked with a hallucinatory substance, she said. During the night, she had been awakened by her baby's crying and had put a pillow over the infant's mouth to silence her, accidentally causing the child's death. Subject Harris slept through the episode but had been awakened by Jamesforth's screaming. Moonbeams Jamesforth was arrested and later convicted of involuntary manslaughter and sentenced to ten years in prison. William Harris was never charged.

Will had never whispered a word about any of this to me. If he had kept this from me, what other secrets was he hiding? I was starting to feel as if I didn't know Will at all.

PART THREE

MORE THAN
MEETS THE EYE

*The world is full of obvious things which nobody
by any chance ever observes.*

—ARTHUR CONAN DOYLE

23

REPORTERS AT THE *WHITE PLAINS DAILY* TOOK TURNS once a month working a graveyard shift, just in case there was some late-breaking news worth a last-minute, page-one bulletin. Whenever Will worked Saturday nights, we didn't bother getting together. It was Will's turn to fulfill this late-night duty and I was glad. I needed time to sort things out. I focused on work that I'd fallen behind on completing. I didn't answer the phone. I didn't want to think about Will or Agent Coyle.

Just after 5 p.m., my desk phone began ringing and wouldn't stop. I decided to check my beeper in case there was an emergency, but I noticed I didn't have it. I must have placed it on my bathroom counter while getting dressed that morning and left it there by accident.

I heard the front door of our office open, followed by O'Brien's booming voice. "Dani, you still here?"

"In my office."

"Why the hell aren't you answering your phone? We got another homicide!"

"Who?"

"Isabella's husband, Marco Ricci. They whacked him in his own goddamn bedroom."

I rushed out with O'Brien to his unmarked car.

O'Brien didn't know much about Ricci's murder, only that one of the security guards at Ricci's house had found his body in the bedroom. "But someone gave him an Italian necktie last night," O'Brien warned me.

"Nunzio?" I asked.

"Makes sense. What the hell did Ricci think would happen when he turned a mobster's only daughter into a whore?"

I drive too fast, but compared to O'Brien, I'm a snail. I've always suspected one reason why O'Brien became a cop was to avoid paying speeding fines. As he endlessly switched lanes, speeding up only to brake and change lanes again, O'Brien told me about his midmorning visit to the Midland Apartments.

"The freak lied to us," O"Brien said. "He moved into that building one week after her. He was stalking her."

"If you move your entire family into a building because you're fixated on a woman, that's more than stalking. It's obsession and obsession over a woman who continues to reject you is—"

O'Brien finished my sentence. "A damn good motive for murder."

I said, "Gilmore told us that he was home that day."

"I already checked with the post office," O'Brien said, "and he was off all day from work."

"So he really could have seen Persico leave the apartment," I said, "and slipped inside to confront her."

O'Brien said, "There's something else you need to hear about him. Wanna take a wild guess?"

I wasn't in the mood. "Just tell me."

"Gilmore's got a rap sheet. Five years ago, he got busted for rape, but the victim failed to show so the charge got kicked. The victim was a nineteen-year-old student, and get this, he'd threatened her with a knife."

When a man is arrested for raping a woman, there are a lot more unreported rapes in his past.

O'Brien said, "He cut off her clothes—the rape victim."

O'Brien and I like to bounce theories off each other. It helps us see the flaws in our thinking. "Let's assume for the moment that Donnie Gilmore—and not Persico—murdered Isabella. That solves her killing. Now who killed Roman and Maggie Mancini?"

"Maybe Nunzio—like your FBI boyfriend says," O'Brien said, teasingly. "Or Persico. To get rid of a witness. Take your pick."

"That leaves us with Marco Ricci?"

"Oh, I don't even need to see the scene to make that call. My money is on

Tiny Nunzio," O'Brien said. He hesitated and then added, "Whitaker is going to have a boner for months. If we're right about any of this, his office will try Gilmore for Isabella's murder, Persico for whacking the Mancinis, and Nunzio for taking revenge on Marco Ricci. He'll be on TV so much people will think he's a new anchorman."

I thought about what he'd just suggested. "Something isn't right."

"Yeah, what's that?"

"The timing," I said. "You said someone gave Marco Ricci an Italian necktie last night."

"Yeah, that's right. But they just found his body a couple of hours ago."

"Will's story didn't come out until this morning," I said. Once again, a murder had taken place before Will's story hit the streets. This time the article was about Isabella's swinging and Persico's lineup.

"I don't think Tiny needed the newspaper to tell him that Marco was a sleaze," O'Brien noted. "Or Nunzio could have someone at the paper on his payroll, feeding him tips."

An officer waved us through the gated entrance at Ricci's estate. I followed O'Brien inside the French mansion to the cavernous living room, where detectives were interrogating Pete and his fellow security guards.

As soon as Pete spotted us, he hollered at O'Brien. "Tommy Boy, thank God you're here. They think we're involved."

"Where's the body?" I asked.

Pete glanced toward a second-floor railing that overlooked the atrium great room. "Master's on the left," Pete said.

"I'll handle this," O'Brien said, with a nod to Pete and the detectives. "You go ahead."

A double staircase led to the second floor, where a narrow walkway connected bedrooms that ringed the great room. I walked toward a police officer standing watch. He recognized me from a battered woman case and opened one of the bedroom's double doors.

I thought I'd stepped into a whorehouse or, at least, what I imagined one would look like. The bedroom's walls were covered with a bright red velvet wallpaper, the ceiling was painted sunshine yellow, and the shag carpet was ink black with white animal skins tossed around the foot of a giant four-poster, king-size water bed. It had black satin sheets and a black fake fur

bedspread. The ceiling above it was mirrored. The headboard was uphol-
stered with alternating black and red leather stripes with gold buttons. On
each side of the headboard were long, black leather straps and furry handcuffs.

On the wall directly above the massive headboard was a painting of a
nude couple—Marco and Isabella—posing as Adam and Eve, complete with
a snake hanging from a branch. Isabella was reaching toward an apple that
the serpent held in its fangs.

On the bed, Marco Ricci was lying lifeless, tied with rope to the four bed-
posts. He was nude, spread eagle. His head had been pushed back, revealing
the ugly slit where his throat had been cut and his tongue pulled through.
But the Italian necktie was not the worst of it.

His penis had been cut off.

I heard O'Brien's voice as he entered the bedroom.

"Christ almighty!" he said. "Someone cut off his dick."

"We got a more specific time of death yet?" I asked.

"Coroner estimates between midnight and six a.m., just like the Mancini
murders."

"How'd the killer get past the guards?"

"Pete don't have a clue. He was out front. One guard was inside the
house, the other out on the grounds."

"I don't believe in ghosts," I said. I checked the master bedroom's four windows. They were locked, plus the house had a sophisticated burglar alarm
system.

"The inside guard didn't hear screams?" I asked. Marco's mouth had not
been gagged.

"Television was playing too loud. He found Marco about an hour ago. He
wondered why he hadn't come out of his bedroom."

"Who turned off the TV?" Its screen was dark.

"The guard. Turned it off so he could call it in."

I walked over and turned it on. The volume was turned up as high as possible.

"The guard touched the television and the phone," I said, turning off the
set. "Anything else?"

"He says no."

"What'd Pete tell you?"

"Just another Friday night. Some punks racing through the neighborhood too fast in their cars. Dogs barking. No visitors. Ricci ate dinner with the guard inside around eight o'clock and then went upstairs. A couple of hours later, the guard hears the TV blasting. Stayed that way all night."

"Remind me to never hire Pete or his friends to protect me," I said.

Marco's red bikini briefs and a black silk robe were lying on the shag carpet next to the water bed.

O'Brien said, "Cutting his dick off sends a pretty clear message."

"What's that?"

"You don't cheat on my daughter."

"I agree, but how'd Nunzio know? I think it's time for us to go across the river and ask him," I said.

"You're getting a two-fer today. You started with Persico and now you want to question Nunzio. We bothering with a search warrant?"

"What for?"

O'Brien nodded toward Ricci's body.

"I don't see his dick lying around. Somebody's got to have it. Maybe Nunzio."

24

VERONA, NEW JERSEY, IS AN HOUR'S DRIVE FROM WHITE Plains and is located across the Hudson River in a valley tucked between the First and Second Watchung Mountains. The town was once part of Caldwell Township, named after a preacher and local Revolutionary War hero, James Caldwell, who used burning pages from his church's Bibles to ignite the ammo in soldiers' cannons that helped drive the British troops from the valley. Verona's image-conscious citizens later voted to secede from the township because they wanted to disassociate themselves from a well-known local insane asylum and reform school. Apparently, today's residents weren't as worried as they had been about their image, since they had welcomed Giuseppe "Tiny" Nunzio into their fold.

I'd learned from Will Harris that Nunzio had gotten his nickname Tiny because of his slight build as a teenager, which he'd put to good use slipping through air-conditioning ducts to commit burglaries. But the Nunzio who peered out from behind security bars protecting the front door of his Personette Avenue house was anything but slim. He must have tipped the scales at more than 300 pounds. He had silver hair, large black glasses, was in his fifties, and was wearing baggy black trousers, house slippers, and an open-necked tan shirt.

I introduced myself and O'Brien and said, "We just wanted to ask you a few questions about your daughter's murder—"

Nunzio slammed the door in our faces. Next to the doorbell was a five-by-seven-inch framed photograph of Isabella Ricci with a black cloth draped around it—an old Italian custom that meant the house's occupants were in mourning. I pushed the bell and kept pushing until the door flew open again.

This time, there was a heavyset woman staring at us.

"What the hell is wrong with you?" she demanded. "Isabella was put to rest yesterday and you people can't give us a frickin' weekend for mourning?"

"We're trying to catch whoever killed Isabella," I said calmly, trying to make our impromptu visit sound much more noble than it was. "That's why we'd like to speak to your husband."

"Tiny ain't my husband," she said in an angry voice. "He's my father-in-law and he don't want to talk to you. Now get the hell off our front porch and leave us alone."

She slammed the door shut.

"Smooth move, counselor," O'Brien said. "Calling her Tiny's wife."

"She looks older," I replied.

The screeching brakes of an approaching car made us both turn around. A slender man wearing white tennis shorts and an athletic shirt emblazoned with his country club's emblem hurried from behind the wheel of a blue Cadillac.

"Reuben Myers, the Nunzio family's attorney," he announced as he walked up the sidewalk. "Why are you folks here?"

"I'm Dani Fox, an assistant district attorney in Westchester County, New York, and this is Detective Thomas O'Brien."

"I recognize you from television," he said. "But you're in New Jersey now, not Westchester County. It would have been prudent to have called me during regular working hours if you wished to speak to my client. Coming here on a Saturday, the day after his daughter was buried, is, quite frankly, both rude and highly unprofessional."

It's one thing to get an ethics lecture from a professor at some highly regarded university or even from an esteemed judge, but from a paid mouthpiece from the mob? I didn't give a damn that we'd interrupted his indoor tennis match at his club or upset his Mafia capo's grieving.

"Your client has another funeral to attend," I said matter-of-factly.

"Whose?"

"His son-in-law, Marco Ricci."

Suddenly, Myers looked concerned. "Have you told Mr. Nunzio?"

"We figured he already knew," O'Brien chimed in.

"What are you implying?" Myers asked.

"You're a smart guy, you figure it out," O'Brien said.

Obviously, O'Brien hadn't liked the dressing down that Myers had given us, either.

Myers slipped between us and rang the Nunzios' doorbell. He called out, "Maria, it's Reuben Myers. Please let me in. I need to speak to Mr. Nunzio."

The curtains in a side window of the Victorian house moved and someone peeked out onto the porch. Seconds later, the front door opened and Nunzio's daughter-in-law unlocked the reinforced security gate, letting Myers through. She shot me a hateful look and said to Myers, "Why are they still here?"

Once again, she slammed the door shut. If she kept that up, Nunzio was going to need new hinges.

O'Brien toyed with his toothpick while I shifted my weight from one foot to another and tried to keep my mind from wandering back to Will. Myers and Nunzio left us standing outside alone for about five minutes before the attorney came out. Since the door slammed behind him, I assumed that Maria was still on sentry duty.

"Have you come to ask my client if he was involved in the murder of Marco Ricci?" Myers asked me.

"Actually," I said, "I didn't say Marco Ricci had been murdered. I just said he was dead."

"Let's not play word games, shall we?" Myers replied. "You wouldn't have driven from Westchester on a Saturday if someone hadn't killed Ricci."

"Let's not play any games at all," I replied, although I doubted that was going to happen. "Marco Ricci was murdered and yes, it has crossed our minds that your client might have been involved. You know, given the story in today's paper."

"What story?"

"I thought we weren't going to play games."

Either Myers was good at playing dumb, really was dumb, or really hadn't read about Marco Ricci forcing Isabella to take part in Scarsdale sex parties.

I said, "You asked why we are here. Let's start with the fact that your client is an alleged member of a known criminal enterprise and that Marco

Ricci hired security guards to protect him from your client the morning after Isabella was found murdered."

With a straight face, Myers replied, "My client is a hardworking businessman. There was no reason for Mr. Ricci to be afraid of him."

"Now we're not only playing games, we're pretending," I said.

O'Brien decided to join in. "Listen, if she'd been my daughter and her
husband was bending her over like that, I'd have wanted him dead, too."

I wondered for a moment if O'Brien was trying to use the Reid Technique to sound sympathetic, but then I decided he was simply telling the
truth.

Myers continued to stare at us blankly. He seemed at a complete loss for
words, unlike the lawyers at Gallo & Conti, who were undoubtedly charging the Butcher a much higher hourly fee.

Hoping to snap Myers out of his fog, I asked, "Is your client willing to
answer a few questions about his daughter, her death, and his relationship
with Marco Ricci?"

"My client has an ironclad alibi," he said.

"That's interesting, because we haven't told you when Ricci was murdered," I replied.

"It doesn't really matter. Since Isabella's murder," Myers explained, "Mr.
Nunzio has been housebound in mourning. The only time he has left this
house has been to attend her funeral mass and burial. We have plenty of witnesses who can vouch for that."

"I'm sure you do," I said with a hint of sarcasm.

A city police cruiser appeared and parked next to Myers's Cadillac. The
Verona Police Department officer who stepped from it called out to us. "The
Nunzios are complaining about trespassers."

"I'm Assistant District Attorney Dani Fox. This is Detective O'Brien."

"You got a warrant?"

"No. We came to learn if Mr. Nunzio wanted to give us a statement vol-
untarily about a homicide."

"He doesn't," Myers declared.

The officer said, "Then you two need to vacate these premises. This is
private property and the owners have said you aren't welcome here."

For some stupid reason, he started to reach for O'Brien's arm.

"Touch me, buddy-boy," O'Brien said, "and you'll be wearing a cast for a month."

Apparently thinking better of it, the officer pulled back his right hand, which he then rested on the grip of his still-holstered pistol. In an authoritative voice, he said, "If you don't vacate these premises, I'm going to arrest you."

I didn't want this standoff escalating, particularly since it was clear that the Verona police were more interested in keeping Nunzio happy than helping us.

"We'll leave," I said. "We were just trying to save Mr. Nunzio from possibly having to appear before a grand jury." I practically yelled that last comment because I suspected Nunzio was probably hiding behind the door, listening as best he could to our conversation.

The house's front door opened and Nunzio appeared in the doorway. He waved Myers over to speak to him. They exchanged whispers and then the attorney spoke to us.

"Can you tell me how Mr. Ricci was murdered?" he asked.

"An Italian necktie," I said, loud enough for Nunzio to hear. "The killer also mutilated his body. But if you want the gory details, your client needs to talk to us."

Nunzio looked directly at me, as if he were memorizing my face, then shut the door. I took the fact that he hadn't slammed it as a sign that he was satisfied. Or maybe he was worried about those hinges.

25

I T WAS AFTER NINE O'CLOCK IN THE EVENING WHEN O'BRIEN dropped me at the DVU to get my Triumph, so I drove straight home. Wilbur was waiting anxiously for his dinner and the red light on my answering machine was blinking.

"Hi, sweetheart."

It was Mom.

"Are you coming for lunch tomorrow? I'll make one of your favorites. We could go to Mass and then eat. It's been a while and Father McHenry asks me every week when he might be seeing you. I'll be up late tonight, as always, so call me." The image of sitting down with Mom for a meal of okra and tomatoes, stewed with meat, poured over white rice was appealing. The image of sitting next to her listening to a Mass was not.

The next message was Will. "You probably heard Marco Ricci was murdered. The editors have called everyone in. We're redoing tomorrow's entire front page. Can you believe this? When was the last time Westchester County had four murders in a row? We've got photos of Isabella, Roman and Maggie Mancini, and now Marco Ricci lined up. I hope you realize that I haven't called you for any inside information. I'm respecting our new professional boundaries."

Will hesitated and then said, "Dani, I'm sorry I was jealous last night about that FBI prick. Remember, I do love you. See you tomorrow. Oh, did you see my story about Persico? Another exclusive for my résumé."

Apparently, Will had no clue how angry I was about his morning exclusive. I put my anger aside. All I wanted was a hot bath and good night's rest.

The third message was Chief Steinberg. "The boss is giving the press a short statement today about Marco Ricci. He wants to see you and O'Brien in his office tomorrow—yes, on Sunday—at two o'clock. We need to discuss what you two are doing to get this matter under control. Are you ready to indict Persico? One more thing. Has that FBI agent called you? I want answers tomorrow and don't be late."

The final message was from Agent Coyle. "We need to meet ASAP now that Marco Ricci is dead. I've got our logs to show you. We're hearing rumors the Battaglias and the Gacciones are about to go to war. Call me on my home line tonight no matter how late it is. I can drive out to White Plains. It's time to end this jurisdictional bullshit and combine our efforts."

Although I was exhausted, I wanted to see those FBI logs. I called the home number that Coyle had left. He picked up on the first ring.

"I can be in White Plains in an hour," he said. "Want me to come to your house?"

"No, there's an IHOP that's open twenty-four hours in Yonkers, on Central Park Avenue," I said. "You will be bringing the logs this time, right? I'm not wasting my time if you forget them again."

"They're in my car. Hey, I heard you tried to speak to Nunzio today. You got guts. I'd like to hear how that went."

"Show me the logs first," I said.

I wasn't sure how he'd heard about our visit. My best guess was that the FBI had a wiretap on Nunzio's home phone and had heard him call his attorney. Either that or Coyle had a snitch in Nunzio's crew.

Before hanging up, I added, "I'll be bringing the package you sent me about Will Harris. And I want to make this perfectly clear: This meeting at IHOP is going to be purely professional. It will not be a date, got that?"

"See you in an hour," he said.

It would take me less time to get to the Yonkers IHOP than it would Agent Coyle so I decided to give my mom a quick call.

"I only have a few minutes," I began, hoping to keep our conversation short. "I'm heading out for a meeting with the FBI."

"At this hour? Is it with that fellow who wants to date you?"

"Yes, but this is purely professional. It's an emergency. I don't have time to explain. I'm calling because I won't have time for lunch tomorrow because O'Brien and I have to be at the D.A.'s office at two o'clock."

"Honey, you still need to eat," she said, sounding very much like a mother.

"Mom, I can't. But let's do breakfast in the morning."

"If you swing by at nine," she offered, "we can eat here and then go to the eleven o'clock Mass."

I decided to give in. Maybe a good breakfast and some divine inspiration would help me deal with the murders and what I'd learned about Will.

"Okay, see you at nine," I said. I told her that I loved her, grabbed my purse and keys, and hurried outside.

I got to the IHOP before Agent Coyle and surveyed the place out of habit. About a dozen customers were seated in booths. A waitress with a badge that read: HI! I'M PATTI! agreed to let me sit in a booth away from the other diners. I ordered a Dr Pepper and was relieved when I saw Coyle arrive carrying a bulky accordion file.

Taking a seat across from me, he said, "Thanks for seeing me so late."

"Those the logs?" I asked.

"Yes," he replied, but he didn't pass the file folder to me or open it. Instead, he picked up a menu and said, "You ordering something? I'm hungry."

Our waitress appeared and Coyle ordered a burger, extra fries, and a slice of apple pie à la mode.

"How about you?" he said.

I realized that I hadn't eaten all day, so I decided to have breakfast as dinner and ordered pancakes with hot maple syrup. I was still eyeing the closed file, but Coyle clearly wanted to make polite chitchat.

"I'll pay for that pie and ice cream tomorrow when I work out," he said.

"I don't think the pie and ice cream is the only problem," I said. "It's the greasy burger with extra fries."

Coyle had always been wearing business suits when we'd met previously, but tonight he was in blue jeans and a navy high-collared sweater, which he proceeded to take off, because it was warm in the diner. The T-shirt underneath it showed ripped biceps. I couldn't help noticing again that he was incredibly handsome. Coyle said, "I'll throw in a few extra miles tomorrow. I like to run five miles each morning and then lift weights for an hour. I'm a bit compulsive about it."

He was clearly trying to impress me and it was working.

"I run each morning, too," I said. "Dark chocolate is my vice, Junior Mints in particular."

"I'll send candy instead of roses next time."

"Unless you have a habit of sending roses and chocolates to every prosecutor you meet, including the men, I'd prefer you knock it off with the gifts."

"If I send roses to Detective O'Brien, I can send chocolates to you?" he asked with a grin.

"If you send roses to O'Brien, he'd probably punch your lights out."

"It might be worth it," he said.

"Agent Coyle," I replied, "I think it's important that we keep our relationship professional. Now, can I see the logs, please?"

"I've been told that sometimes I can be too aggressive," he said, ignoring my request. "I guess the enthusiasm and intensity that make me a good agent can be a bit intimidating to women. But you're opinionated and independent and aggressive, too. Otherwise you wouldn't be where you are in a man's field. It probably intimidates most men. Am I right?"

"Can I see the daily logs?"

"I'm trying to compliment you," he said. "As I said earlier, I'd like to be friends."

"No. You've made it clear that you want to be more than friends and I've made it clear that I'm not comfortable with that right now."

He smiled. "Right now. I'll take that to mean that I might have a chance later." Without waiting for me to respond, he slid the accordion file across the Formica-topped table.

I immediately opened it. Coyle glanced around to see if anyone was watching us or was in earshot. Satisfied, he said, "What I brought you are summaries, not the full logs."

"Why only summaries?" I asked. Was this another trick by Jack Longhorn?

"The summaries highlight how Persico spent his day. The full logs have more details. A summary would report that one of our best agents met with

Assistant District Attorney Dani Fox at an IHOP restaurant at ten-thirty on a Saturday night. The daily log would describe the conversation that the agent had with Ms. Fox and note such information as whether or not Ms. Fox had gazed into the agent's eyes longingly during dinner."

"Cute," I said.

"Illustrations are sometimes more effective than long explanations," he replied proudly.

"So if I told the agent to stop flirting, then that would be in the daily log report but not in the daily summary."

Coyle groaned and feigned a pained look. "That's right. The summary would simply mention that the agent and Fox met. The log would describe how—despite his witty personality and their easy rapport—he got shot down."

Thankfully, waitress Patti arrived with our food. Coyle waited until she was gone to continue.

"I can't let you see the daily logs because they contain sensitive information, such as the names of undercover FBI agents and the numeric IDs of our confidential sources. But there's no harm in letting you see the summaries."

"You promised to show me the full logs earlier," I said. "What happened?"

"Jack Longhorn," Coyle answered candidly. "He told me to only show you the summary reports."

I scanned the first entry in Persico's file.

Suspect picked up at 8:30 a.m. at home. Driven in limo, New York license 65183-LV, to butcher shop. At 1:45 p.m. driven home to lunch and then returned to work at 3:30 p.m. Driven home at 7:30 p.m. Didn't go out anymore that night.

"These summaries don't contain much information," I complained.

Coyle said, "It's the best I can do." He took a big bite of his burger.

"Do you know if Persico uses any other limos besides this one when he rides to work?" I asked.

"Persico stopped driving years ago after someone tried to assassinate him in his family car. The limo is the only vehicle that he rides in: it has armor plating and bullet-resistant windows."

I flipped through the daily summaries, stopping when I reached the stack that covered the month of October 1979. I was specifically looking for notations that would show if Persico had visited the Midland Apartments every Tuesday and Friday afternoon during that month.

I scanned them quickly. There was no record of him ever being followed to the apartment complex in October. None for November, either. But when I got to the December summaries, there was a mention of the Midland Apartments.

Persico's car had been observed leaving the butcher shop at 2 p.m. on a Tuesday. The FBI agent shadowing him had followed the vehicle to the Midland Apartments. But the passenger who got out of the limo's backseat wasn't Persico. The agent had mistakenly assumed the mobster had been riding in the vehicle. Realizing his error, the agent had rushed back to the butcher's shop, where he'd observed Persico sitting inside the deli speaking to a customer. Unfortunately, the summary didn't identify who the passenger was who had ridden in Persico's armored car to the Midland Apartments.

I turned the daily log summary around on the table so that Coyle could read it.

"According to this notation, someone besides Persico used his limo in December to drive to the Midland Apartments on a Tuesday afternoon," I said. "Do you think the more detailed daily log for that Tuesday might help us identify who that person was?"

"Only if the agent recognized him. But I'll check that specific log when I go into the office tomorrow."

I continued flipping through the December entries, stopping on December 31, 1979, the afternoon when Isabella was murdered. The summary confirmed what I'd already been told. Agent Coyle had visually observed Persico entering the Midland Avenue building at 2:30 p.m. Persico's driver had remained outside in the limo. The mobster had exited the building at exactly 5:30 p.m.

Glancing up from the papers, I asked, "Did you write additional information in the daily log about Persico's visit?"

"Of course," he said. "I wrote that Persico had appeared to be in a hurry when he left the apartment building. I also noted that he'd changed his clothes later that afternoon before he went home. I found that to be suspicious."

I closed the file. "Persico was not meeting Isabella twice a week," I said, "because there's no mention of him going to the apartments on a regular basis. However, the logs show that he did visit the apartment on the day of the murder. These logs also tell us that someone else used Persico's limo to drive to the apartment on a Tuesday in December. Who else, besides Persico, has access to his personal car?"

"I don't have a clue and it doesn't really matter," Coyle said. "I saw Nicholas Persico at the apartment when Isabella was murdered. Case closed. It's immaterial whether he was having an affair with Isabella or someone else from the butcher's shop was using his car to meet her."

"You're wrong. Persico told me he didn't even know the name of the woman in that apartment. That means he was either going there because he'd been asked to—by the person who normally visited Isabella—or to talk to her about something that was important to him—maybe this other person's relationship with Isabella."

"You're wasting time worrying about it," he said.

Coyle reached over and gently touched my hand, which was resting next to my plate. "Listen, Dani," he said softly, "I've been dealing with these Mafia guys for a long time and you never really know what is happening with them. They operate in a closed society. The only facts we can be certain of are that Isabella was killed and Persico was there when it happened. The coroner puts her time of death at between three-thirty-five p.m. and six o'clock. He's our only viable suspect."

I pulled back my hand and said, "No, actually he's not."

"There's someone else? Who?" Coyle asked, visibly surprised.

"A man who lives in the Midland Apartments was stalking Isabella. He's got a criminal record for rape but he beat the charge. He used a knife to cut off that woman's clothes, just like Isabella's clothes were removed."

"How'd you find this guy?"

"By not assuming Persico was guilty and by doing some police work."

Coyle frowned. He didn't like my dig.

I said, "Our new suspect first met Isabella and her husband at a swingers club in Scarsdale. But she refused to sleep with him. He became obsessed with her and began stalking her—to the point that he actually moved his family into the Midland Apartments so that he could keep an eye on Isabella."

"Let's assume he was stalking her like you said," Coyle said. "When was there time for him to kill Isabella? I mean, Persico was with her."

"Your report says Persico left at five-thirty," I said. "The coroner estimates that she was killed between three-thirty-five and six o'clock. That means our suspect could have gotten into that apartment after Persico left. How long does it take for someone to torture and kill a woman?"

"I'm not an expert in torturing and killing women," he said, grinning. "But I suspect thirty minutes is long enough."

I didn't think his comment was funny and he noticed.

"There's just one little hole in your theory," he said. "I read the reports and the killer used an electrical cord cut from a clock to tie her hands. That clock stopped at three-thirty-five p.m. And that was when Persico was in that apartment. He didn't leave until five-thirty, remember?"

He was right. "I can't explain that," I said. "But I think our new suspect is worth further investigation."

"I agree," he said. "What's his name? I'll run a background check on him."

I hesitated. "Thanks, but our guys can handle that. Besides, I don't think my boss is ready to invite the FBI into our investigation just yet."

"He might not have a choice," Coyle said, "especially if Tiny Nunzio killed Marco Ricci. He would have had to cross state lines and that gives us the jurisdiction to jump in."

I checked my watch. It was nearly midnight and I needed to get some sleep. Mom was expecting me for breakfast and Mass. Whitaker was expecting O'Brien and me at 2 p.m. and he wasn't going to be happy to hear that I'd met with Coyle without first alerting Chief of Staff Steinberg—despite the late hour.

"It's late and I need to get some sleep," I said. "It has been a hell of a day."

"I'll follow you home."

"That's not necessary."

"It's too late for you to be driving around alone. Besides, the drive back into Manhattan from your house isn't that much out of my way back to Manhattan."

"How do you know that?" I asked. "You've never been to my house—have you?"

"I was talking about White Plains in general."

There was something about the way he said it that made me think he was lying. He'd warned me that he was aggressive when it came to women. Driving by my house was downright creepy. On the other hand, he was an FBI agent and used to investigating people. I wasn't sure what to make of Agent Coyle.

"I don't want you following me home," I said.

"It's what a gentleman would do," he replied.

There was a slight edge to his voice, which made me think that his comment was supposed to be a slight against Will. That reminded me of the FedEx package that I'd brought to give back to him.

"Here's the background information that you sent me," I said, sliding it across the table.

"Your boyfriend is a real piece of work," Coyle said. "I'm not sure you should trust him."

I slipped out of the booth and said, "And you, Agent Coyle. Are you someone I should trust?"

26

As I UNLOCKED MY CAR IN THE IHOP PARKING LOT, I began second-guessing myself.

Was I being too harsh on Coyle? Was I upset with him because he had shattered my image of Will? If I knew something horrible about one of my girlfriend's boyfriends, would I tell her about it or keep it quiet?

I noticed a black sedan fall in behind me as I pulled away from the parking lot. It looked like an unmarked police car and any second doubts that I had about Coyle vanished. If he was tailing me after I had specifically told him that I didn't want to be followed home, I was going to be furious.

The sedan stayed well behind me until I reached the driveway to my house. Then it sped up and kept driving down my street. It was nearly 1 a.m. by now and I had never felt so tired. What a day. Going directly into my bedroom, I kicked off my shoes, stepped out of my pants, and heard the doorbell rang.

Damn it!

I could have strangled Coyle. Didn't he know that no meant no? I slipped back into my jeans and marched across the living room, where I checked the door's peephole. No one was outside on my front porch.

Unbolting the door, I opened it a crack and peeked outside. There wasn't anyone there. The porch felt cold on my bare feet when I stepped out and called: "Hello? Who rang the bell? Coyle, are you out here?"

No answer. Back inside, I threw the dead bolt and headed to my bedroom. Just as I was about to enter it, someone grabbed me from behind. A leather-gloved hand swept across my mouth and a deep male voice said, "Don't fight!"—which is exactly what I did.

I immediately kicked backward with my right foot, but hit only air. I tried to bite the intruder's hand, but the glove was thick. Making a fist, I punched backward, but he dodged my blows and, having wrapped his left hand around my waist, swept me off the floor. I grabbed his right hand with both of mine and tried to pull his fingers away from my face so that I could scream. He jerked my head sideways, pinning it against his shoulder, and said, "I'll break your neck."

A second man appeared wearing a ski mask. He grabbed my hands and quickly handcuffed me. That didn't stop me from swinging at his head but he jerked my cuffed hands back, shoving them against my chest. He'd stepped closer when he did that and I kicked him in the groin as hard as I could with my bare feet, causing him to step back and groan.

He recovered, raced forward, and punched me in the gut, knocking the air out of me. As I was gasping for breath, I felt the jab of a needle into my left arm and within seconds, I felt woozy. I fought to stay focused but whatever it was was too powerful.

I woke up. I had no idea what time it was. I opened my eyes and saw only black. Ink black. Nothing. Terrified, I gasped for air and the blackness covered my mouth, causing me to gag and immediately cough, sending it away from my mouth. I realized that I had a black hood covering my head. It was a heavy cloth that I had sucked toward me.

Dozens of questions raced through my mind, although it was still running slowly because of the injection. Where was I? What time was it? How much time had passed? Who had abducted me? Why? Were they going to kill me?

I took inventory. My hands were now behind my back and still handcuffed. I felt ropes on my chest and realized that I was tied to a chair. My legs had been tied together at my ankles. I couldn't move. I listened and heard a humming noise that sounded like the buzz that comes from fluorescent lights. I was helpless.

A door opened and I heard a man's voice. "That cunt awake yet? You gave her too much juice."

Even though I couldn't see his face, I recognized who it was. Giuseppe Tiny Nunzio.

I remained perfectly still.

A different male voice said, "I'll take care of it."

I heard the door close but knew I was not alone. Suddenly I felt ice-cold water splash down on me, causing the heavy fabric of the hood to cling to my skin, forcing me to gag for air. I was petrified and if I was going to survive, I was going to have to be tough. I needed to take command of the situation.

"I don't know who you are," I said, after catching my breath. "But I am an assistant district attorney. Do you have any idea what kind of shit you are going to have coming down on you?"

"I know you," a male voice—not Nunzio's—replied. "You answer a few questions and you go home. No trouble. You don't, you die. Got it?"

So much for me taking command of the situation. I was glad, however, that he hadn't removed my hood. That was a good sign. My kidnappers didn't know that I had heard and recognized Nunzio's voice. As long as they thought that I didn't know who they were, I had a chance of surviving.

"What sort of questions?" I asked.

"Easy ones."

"Then you could have called me on the phone."

I heard him chuckle. "Funny," he said.

Something sharp poked against my neck. He moved it slowly across the front of my neck and I realized it was a knife blade.

"No more jokes, got it?" he said.

"Got it," I replied.

I heard his footsteps as he stepped away from the chair. That sound was followed but a loud click—as if a big button had been pushed down—and I heard a soft whirling noise.

"Talk into the microphone," he said, coming forward. I felt what apparently was a microphone being taped against my chest.

He began. "Did Nicholas Persico kill Isabella Ricci?"

With that one question, I understood what was happening. Tiny Nunzio had kidnapped me to get the evidence he needed to prove that the Butcher had murdered his daughter. I'd been told that the five families in New York would not sit idly by and allow a capo from New Jersey in the Gaccione family to take revenge against the de facto acting head of the Battaglia family without some sort of evidence, especially when the Nunzios and Persicos had been responsible for earlier family disappearances and murders. Kidnapping a prosecuting attorney seemed extreme. But what better evidence for Nunzio to show the five families. He would not only convince them, he would be showing off by kidnapping a court official. They'd get a good laugh out of it. A prosecutor being called as a witness by the mob to help Nunzio make his case.

"We're not confident that Persico killed her."

"What?" the male voice said, clearly surprised.

"There are other suspects."

"Persico was with her in that apartment. A witness saw him go there. The newspaper said so."

"Yes, we had an eyewitness, Roman Mancini," I said. "But someone murdered him, remember?"

"Mancini told you Persico was there. That's why Persico killed Mancini. It fits."

I knew I was taking a chance, but I decided to answer truthfully. "Maybe it fits for you, but not us. We think Tiny Nunzio killed Roman Mancini."

For a moment, my interrogator didn't speak. Then he said, "You said Nunzio. You mean Nicholas Persico."

"No, I said Tiny Nunzio and that's who I meant."

I heard a short click and the soft whirr of the tape recorder became quiet, causing me to believe that he had stopped recording. There was a high-pitched whirling noise, which I recognized from my office, when the secretaries rewound tapes on a reel-to-reel recorder. He was going to erase what I'd said about his boss.

Without any warning, a fist punched me in the abdomen, knocking the air out of my lungs.

"We're gonna try this again," he said softly. "Only this time, don't say Mr. Nunzio killed them. Got that?"

Panting, I said, "You want me to lie? I'm answering your questions."

I braced myself for another blow but instead I heard footsteps and the door opening and closing. He had left the room.

As I was sitting there, an odd thought popped into my head: *Charlie's Angels,* one of Will's favorite shows, probably because its three main characters often appeared wearing bikinis. But for whatever reason, the image of actress Jaclyn Smith appeared to me. She would find a way to easily escape from her captors by slipping her hands free from handcuffs. Unfortunately, I knew that neither Smith nor her scantily clad cohorts would be racing in to save me. Still, it was a nice fantasy. If they could escape each week, didn't I have a chance at being rescued? I shook it off. It must have been a combination of the drug and desperation.

I thought about my mom. I was supposed to meet her for breakfast and Sunday Mass. I didn't know how long I'd been knocked out, but if I'd missed breakfast, she would know something was wrong. Will had also said he would call me in the morning. Plus, I was due at Whitaker's meeting at two o'clock. Someone—besides Wilbur—had to realize that I was missing. Surely they would be searching for me.

I heard the door open and footsteps.

The same male voice that had been questioning me earlier said, "Forget about the Mancinis being killed. But just so you know, Tiny Nunzio ain't killed no one—yet."

He meant that as a threat, but I saw it as an opening.

"Tell that to his dead son-in-law," I said, again bracing for a blow.

"You ain't too smart if you think Mr. Nunzio whacked Marco Ricci."

Turning the tables, I asked, "Who else would want him dead? Of course Mr. Nunzio killed him."

He was quiet for a moment, clearly pondering the question, and then he said, "Yeah, he ain't shedding tears. But like I just told you, Mr. Nunzio ain't killed nobody yet."

He knew I was a prosecutor and there was a chance he was lying, especially if he was serious about freeing me after our interrogation. But there was something about his answer that rang true. You get a knack as a prosecutor for knowing when someone is lying. I didn't think he was, which made me wonder: Who in the hell had killed Marco Ricci if Tiny Nunzio hadn't done it?

I heard my interrogator punch a button and the reel-to-reel recorder began to slowly turn.

"Who's these other suspects you got?" he asked, referring to the Isabella Ricci murder.

I needed to be careful because I knew Nunzio and his goons would not hesitate to go after Donnie Gilmore if I told them that he had been stalking Isabella.

"Marco Ricci was another suspect," I said. "He had good reason to hire someone to kill his wife, including a life insurance policy."

"Yeah, who else you got? Like you said, Marco's dead."

"If Marco hired someone, then we'll find him," I said, stalling.

"Don't bullshit me," he snarled. "You got someone else in mind. Protecting some asshole isn't worth the pain I can cause you. Got it? You'll talk. I've had men stronger than you sitting in that chair, crying like a baby."

He was right, Donnie Gilmore was an asshole. Just the same, I wasn't going to name names. I didn't want Gilmore's blood on my hands. "Okay," I said. "Here's what I know. We got a tip someone was stalking Isabella. But I haven't had a chance to run it down. Someone she met at a sex party in Scarsdale."

I'd dealt with a lot of witnesses who lied during trials and I'd learned from them that the best way to lie is to hide behind bits and pieces of the truth. I was hoping that I had told him enough truth that he would stop peeling back the layers. To make my story even more convincing, I said, "You kidnapped me too soon. I asked an FBI agent last night in Yonkers for help identifying Isabella's stalker. If you'd waited a week or so, we'd have had him."

I had intentionally mentioned meeting with Coyle because I now suspected that it had been Nunzio and his goons following me home from IHOP. I was trying to corroborate my own story.

Apparently, my dodge worked because instead of asking me more about the stalker, he said, "Your boss called Persico in for a lineup. That means he did it. He killed Isabella."

"Not necessarily," I said. I knew I was being recorded and didn't want to explain how that lineup had been a publicity stunt, so I asked, "You ever been called in for a lineup when you were innocent? People get called in all the time. Don't you think we'd have arrested Persico by now if we knew he'd done it? You know how much heat is on us about this? If we were convinced, he'd be in jail."

My last comment must have triggered something because I heard him step away from me, turn off the recorder, and walk to the door, which I heard open and close. I assumed he was going out of the room to report to

Nunzio and to get further instructions since I was obviously not telling him the answers that they wanted to hear. Knowing what I did about the mob, I figured the next round of questioning was not going to be as easy or as painless.

I sat there listening to the only sound in the room—the annoying buzz of the fluorescent lights. And then I heard a different sound. A frightening sound. It was the sound of gunfire.

27

"DANI! YOU OKAY?"

It wasn't one of Charlie's Angels who'd come to rescue me.

It was Coyle.

I felt fingers untying the hood. He pulled it off and I squinted until my eyes could adjust while he dropped to his feet to untie my ankles and then moved to the back of the chair to undo the ropes and handcuffs.

"Lucky for you, most handcuffs use the same keys," he said. "Can you stand?"

"Yes, I think so."

He took my arm and helped pull me to my feet. For the first time, I was able to see where I had been held. We were inside an abandoned, walk-in storage freezer, which explained the odd noise the door made when it was opened and closed. As I had suspected, there was a reel-to-reel tape recorder on a table a few feet from the chair where I'd been bound. I removed the microphone that was still duct-taped to my chest.

"Nunzio and his men?" I asked.

"They won't be hurting you. I've dealt with them."

"Dead?"

He nodded.

"Where's everyone else?"

"I'm alone," he said. "I didn't have time to wait."

"They knocked me out. How long have I been here?"

"Not long."

"It felt like hours," I said. "How'd you find me?"

Coyle looked sheepish and said, "You told me not to follow you and I didn't. At first. Then I changed my mind. I turned around and drove to your house. Don't be angry at me."

"Angry? Thank you for not listening to me!"

I put my arms around him and gave him a hug. He leaned down and kissed me hard on my lips. I hadn't expected that, but I didn't resist. I wasn't sure if the reason was gratitude or if there was something that I had secretly wanted.

"We need to go," he said. "Staying here isn't safe."

Coyle led me out of the freezer door, pausing only long enough to retrieve a twelve-gauge pump shotgun that he'd apparently used during my rescue and leaned against the wall when he'd come inside the freezer. We hurried down a narrow hallway and entered what looked like an old employee lunchroom.

"Nunzio owns this old warehouse," Coyle said, "but it's been boarded up for years."

"He didn't stop using that abandoned freezer for beating people," I said.

"You could have screamed your heart out and no one would have heard."

Again, I felt grateful that Coyle had found me.

There were steel tables bolted to the floor in the lunchroom and as we started to make our way through them, I saw a body on floor. It was a man with a gaping hole in his chest.

"He was supposed to be a lookout," Coyle said.

A half-empty bottle of Jack Daniel's and a half-eaten sandwich were on the table closest to the corpse.

"Where's Nunzio?" I asked.

"A room next to the freezer along with his second in command."

"The man interrogating me," I said.

"That's right," Coyle said. "Let me guess, Nunzio was trying to get proof that the Butcher had killed Isabella."

"Just like you predicted. Only one odd thing."

"What?"

"Nunzio's underboss claimed they hadn't killed the Mancinis or Marco Ricci. That doesn't make sense."

"They were lying. Don't worry about it."

We reached an exit and stepped outside into the early morning air. A black limo was parked close by. It had to be Nunzio's.

"I'm parked around the front of the building," Coyle explained. "Follow me."

We'd hurried across the back of the warehouse and turned the corner into the building's side parking lot. I could see Coyle's unmarked car on the street. I went to the passenger's side while he opened the trunk and deposited his shotgun before getting behind the wheel.

"I need to call this in," he said, reaching for the car's two-way radio.

"Why didn't you call for backup on your way here?" I asked. It was the prosecutor in me kicking in.

I thought I saw a flash of anger in Coyle's eyes. He didn't like me questioning him.

"I told you," he said. "When I got to your house, I saw them driving away. I had no way of knowing that they'd kidnapped you. You could've been sound asleep inside your house. I followed them here. It wasn't until I saw them carrying you into the warehouse that I knew what they had done. At that point, I had to act fast. Once they got you into the warehouse I knew I was dealing with a hostage situation or worse. I got my shotgun and came in after you."

I reached over, touched his hand, and said apologetically, "I don't know what would have happened if you hadn't rescued me."

"I do," he said. "You'd have ended up buried in the Meadowlands."

"I'm not so sure. I was told they were going to let me go."

"Don't be naïve," he said.

The first wave of emergency vehicles began arriving at the warehouse within minutes. I was hustled into an ambulance that parked near the back entrance even though I assured everyone I hadn't been injured. The next familiar face I saw was O'Brien's. He knocked on the ambulance door and stepped inside, where a paramedic was taking my blood pressure.

"What the hell happened?" he asked.

"It was Nunzio and his goons. They kidnapped me outside my house. They were trying to get me to tell them that Persico killed Isabella Ricci."

"You hurt?"

"Not to worry. My childbearing days are over."

"Nunzio hit you?"

"No, one of his goons."

The paramedic gave me a thumbs-up.

There was another knock on the ambulance door.

"Let's go outside," I said.

FBI Agent Longhorn and D.A. Whitaker were waiting next to Coyle in the parking lot.

"How you doing?" Whitaker asked.

"A bit shaken, but fine."

"Nunzio has some balls kidnapping a prosecuting attorney," Whitaker said.

"Had some balls," Longhorn said, correcting him. "My boy here is quite a hero." Someone hollered my name so I turned and saw Will, who was standing on the opposite side of the bright yellow crime-scene tape that had been stretched around the warehouse's perimeter.

"Just a moment," I said, walking toward him.

Judging from Will's face, I must have looked horrible. My hair was a tangled mess. Whatever makeup I'd been wearing had been smeared by the wet hood that had been covering my face. I also was beginning to feel the impact of having bruised ribs and was walking slowly.

"Tell me you're okay," Will said. He reached out his arms to embrace me.

"I'm sore as hell, but no broken bones," I said, stopping on the opposite side of the tape, well outside his reach.

Will gave me a puzzled look. "I was afraid I'd lost you."

My intent was not to be cruel but my words came out in a burst of pent-up frustration and emotion. "Lost me? Like you lost your baby?"

Will looked hurt.

"I know about your baby, Will!" I exclaimed. "I know about the SDS protests, about Moonbeams being sent to prison, and Stardust being suffocated. I know all of it—the drugs—everything that you kept hidden from me. And that hurts—even more than what happened to me tonight."

Coyle tugged on my sleeve. "We need to go. You can deal with him later."

"Leave her alone," Will said. "This doesn't concern you."

"We're just trying to do our jobs here," Coyle said.

"He's right, Will," I said. "This isn't the time or the place."

I turned with Coyle and started to walk back toward the others.

"Are you Agent Coyle?" Will called after us.

Coyle glanced over his shoulder and shot him a cocky grin.

"Yeah, that's me. I'm the one who thinks you're an asshole."

28

"AGENT LONGHORN AND I ARE GOING TO HOLD A JOINT press conference later today," Whitaker announced the moment we got back to the ambulance.

"I'm not sure I'm up for that," I replied. I was both physically and emotionally exhausted. The last thing I needed was to have reporters shouting questions at me—assuming Whitaker and Longhorn planned to let me actually talk at their press briefing.

"Not a problem, little lady," Longhorn declared. "We'll let Agent Coyle cover for you, like he did tonight!"

I ignored his dig. Let the boys bask in the spotlight.

Agent Coyle volunteered to drive me home, but I asked O'Brien to do it. I noticed other reporters gathering outside the yellow-taped perimeter. Several television news trucks with antennas jutting from their rooftops had arrived. Word about the kidnapping and Nunzio's death was spreading.

"Let's get out of here," I said to O'Brien. "I don't need anyone taking my photo. Mom will kill me if I'm in the paper looking like this."

O'Brien escorted me to his car, but not before several photographers started snapping pictures. "Find a back way out of here, please," I told him.

Rather than drive out the front of the parking lot, past the crowd assembled there, O'Brien headed behind the warehouse into an alley that dumped us out several streets away. The sun was starting to rise.

I glanced through the passenger window at the closed buildings that lined the empty streets. I didn't see any people, but there was plenty of graffiti and trash, especially broken bottles. "O'Brien, where the hell are we?"

"A wharf area along the Hudson, on the Jersey side," he said. "Most of these warehouses closed years ago."

We rode in silence. As we approached the Holland Tunnel, I looked at the Manhattan skyline and thought about the hundreds of thousands of New Yorkers who were waking up to begin their day. They would soon be scurrying inside the city, some destined for church, others to brunch, still others to visit family or shop or go to museums. For most, this would be a routine Sunday. But I realized I was lucky to see this sunrise—thanks to Agent Coyle.

I'm not usually quiet when O'Brien and I are riding together. O'Brien noticed: "Out with it."

"I don't want to talk about it," I replied.

"It's Will?"

"I don't want to think about him."

"We'll talk about the weather."

"I just can't understand," I said, "how he could hide his past from me."

"So the FBI has some dirt on good old Will, huh?" O'Brien said with a smirk. "Big deal."

I realized that O'Brien didn't have a clue about what was in the FBI file, because only I had read it.

He said, "So what'd your reporter boyfriend do? Spray-paint graffiti on a federal building? Forget to put enough stamps on a letter? Or drive across state lines with his high school girlfriend? He don't exactly strike me as the dangerous type."

"He fathered a baby who was murdered by its mother. That's not an insignificant detail from your past that you forget to mention."

"Dani," O'Brien said in a now-serious voice, "no one hides good things from their past."

"But how could he lie to me like this? What else don't I know?"

"In Will's defense, lots of men do stupid things in college."

"Stupid things? Stupid is getting drunk and running naked across campus," I replied. "It's not failing to realize that your baby is being smothered because you're too stoned to hear."

"Coyle shouldn't have sent you Will's files," O'Brien said. "That was a dirty trick."

"He wanted to warn me."

"Bullshit! Coyle's been sniffing around you like a dog in heat."

"Thanks for that warm-and-fuzzy image."

"His John Wayne heroics at the warehouse this morning are going to be tough for Will to match."

I thought about how relieved I'd felt when I'd heard Coyle's voice in that warehouse freezer.

"Does Nunzio have sons?" I asked, abruptly changing the subject.

"Yeah, a couple, all shitheads like their old man. Why? I don't think they'll be coming after you."

"It wasn't me I was thinking about. Do you think one of them would take up their father's vigilante crusade against Persico?"

"Who cares? Let those guinea bastards all kill one another."

"You're such a tough guy," I said mockingly.

"Let me tell you a story," O'Brien said as we entered the tunnel.

I prepared myself for one of his "from the O'Brien files" reminiscences and smiled.

"When I was working the street, there was a little old man who owned a clock shop. He could fix about anything, just a self-taught Irishman tinker. People brought him stuff and he made it work. One day, this guinea bastard sees the old man's granddaughter walking into the store. She was just a kid, maybe fifteen. But she's a beauty so he waits for the shop to close and when they come out, he beats the old man to death on the sidewalk and rapes the girl."

"That's awful," I said.

O'Brien honked at the car in front of us. "That old man never lifted a finger against anyone and his poor granddaughter was never the same."

"What happened to the dirtbag?"

"Not a damn thing. He was Johnny Battaglia and his old man paid off the cops, the judges; he had everybody in his pocket."

"The same Johnny Battaglia who's in prison now? The head of the Battaglia family?"

"The same. He took over after his father died. He's the bastard pulling Persico's strings from prison. A real wop son of a bitch. I say let 'em all kill each other."

I knew O'Brien had investigated hundreds of homicides but this one seemed different.

"You knew the clock shop owner?" I asked, taking a guess.

"Knew him? I was married to his daughter but the girl wasn't mine. Her first husband died."

I knew that O'Brien had been married a couple of times, but no details.

As we emerged from the tunnel into Manhattan, he said, "I was a cop and I couldn't protect them. Sometimes, Dani, the people you love let you down."

29

MOM WAS WAITING AT MY HOUSE WHEN WE GOT there. O'Brien had tipped her off and had arranged for a squad car to be parked out front to keep pesky reporters from disturbing me. The phone was ringing when I went inside with O'Brien and Mom.

"Do me a favor, O'Brien," I said. "Unplug my phone while I feed Wilbur."

By the time I returned to the kitchen, Mom had made coffee, brought out the tabouli, and was warming up the chicken with rice that she'd brought over.

"I gotta get goin'," O'Brien said.

"You need to have some food," Mom insisted.

"Just a bite."

After two huge helpings, O'Brien pushed back from the table and I walked him to the front door.

"Thanks," I said, giving him a quick hug.

"For what? Taxi service?"

"Yeah," I said. "Taxi service."

Back in the kitchen, Mom spent two hours telling me how worried she'd been and how I need to be careful. On her way out she drew a hot bath for me. Once she was gone, I carried my portable twelve-inch television into the bathroom. I'd just begun to soak when Coyle's face appeared on the tube, flanked by a grinning Whitaker and Longhorn. "Breaking headline news!" a voice announced. "We are now going live to a press conference being held outside the Westchester County Courthouse."

Perched behind a podium, Whitaker solemnly announced, "One of my assistant district attorneys, Ms. Dani Fox, was kidnapped late last night by a known New Jersey mobster, Giuseppe Nunzio, aka Tiny Nunzio. He and two of his associates took Ms. Fox to an abandoned warehouse. Fortunately for our community and my office, Ms. Fox was freed by FBI Special Agent Walter Coyle and was not seriously injured."

An old photo of me flashed on the screen, followed by footage of me ducking into O'Brien's car earlier that morning.

Whitaker stepped to his left so that Longhorn could take center stage. After introducing himself, he picked up the story. "In a heroic act, FBI Special Agent Coyle entered the warehouse and confronted three armed men, including Tiny Nunzio. Gunfire was exchanged and the three kidnappers were fatally wounded. Agent Coyle located Ms. Fox and brought her to safety. He is with us this morning."

Looking every bit the hero in his tailored dark suit, red-white-and-blue tie, and crisp white shirt, Coyle said, "I don't think of myself as a hero. I did what any other professional law enforcement officer would have done. In our line of work, putting your life on the line to protect the public from a gangster like Giuseppe Nunzio is nothing out of the ordinary. It's what we do every day."

I was surprised at how emotional I was becoming.

Having made his one-paragraph declaration, Coyle stepped back to allow Whitaker and Longhorn to butt together at the podium and begin fielding questions.

Someone asked where I was. Whitaker said, "Recuperating after this horrific ordeal." One of the tabloid reporters asked if I had been sexually assaulted during the kidnapping. Whitaker looked more disappointed than relieved when he said that I hadn't. It would have made the story even juicier. When a reporter asked why I'd been kidnapped, Whitaker said it was because I'd been helping investigate the "unprecedented rash of mob violence" that had hit Westchester County. He spent several minutes reminding the crowd that reports of violent crime had actually dropped under his tenure.

When Longhorn was finally able to wrestle the microphone from Whitaker, he announced that Whitaker, the FBI, and the District Attorney's Office had concluded that Tiny Nunzio had been responsible for the murder of

Marco Ricci. Longhorn explained that Nunzio had murdered his former son-in-law after learning that Ricci had forced his wife to engage in "Scarsdale sex parties." The FBI chief also declared that he and Whitaker had closed the Roman and Maggie Mancini homicides at the Midland Apartments. Tiny Nunzio had been responsible for their deaths, too, Longhorn said, explaining that the unfortunate couple had gotten caught in the middle of a dispute between a New Jersey crime family and a New York one.

At that point, Whitaker reclaimed the microphone and explained that the closing of the Marco Ricci and the Mancini homicides left only the Isabella Ricci homicide still unsolved.

"My office," Whitaker announced proudly, "will present this case to a grand jury within days."

That bombshell caused reporters to begin shouting more questions, but Whitaker and Longhorn balked at answering them and instead pushed Coyle to the front.

"Unfortunately, Agent Coyle cannot answer questions about his heroic rescue efforts this morning," Longhorn said, "because the shootings in the warehouse are still being reviewed. It's standard procedure. But I can tell you that I am recommending Agent Coyle for a citation and award from the FBI for his bravery in the line of duty."

The screen went from the press conference back to the television station's newsroom, where the local anchorman said, "Agent Coyle certainly deserves our thanks and praise, and we're all wishing Assistant District Attorney Dani Fox a speedy recovery."

The station then went back to *The $50,000 Pyramid*.

Hurrying out of the tub, I plugged in my phone and paged O'Brien. When he called me back, I said, "Did you see the news conference?"

"Yeah, no surprises."

"No surprises? They're going to indict Persico for Isabella's murder. We've got to tell them about Donnie Gilmore and his record. We've got to tell them Gilmore was stalking Isabella."

"Relax, we will. Your boss and Longhorn will keep busy kissing reporters' asses all day. We'll clear this up tomorrow. You need to get some rest."

He was right. I needed to be at my best when we broke the news about Gilmore to Whitaker and his three chiefs. I unplugged the phone and slipped under the covers. I was asleep as soon as my head hit the pillow. But it didn't last. Four hours later, my entire body began to shake as if I had stuck my finger into an electrical socket. My eyes popped open and I gasped for air.

A nightmare. A bad one. I'd been sitting in the warehouse freezer. Only in my dream, Nunzio had come into the freezer and taken off my hood. He had stared into my eyes, brandishing a knife, and said: "You need a necktie!"

I was drenched in sweat.

I was afraid of having another nightmare. Awake, I could control my emotions, but how do you control your subconscious?

Plugging in my bedroom phone, I dialed a familiar number.

I caught him at his apartment. "I need a taxi. I need to talk."

"I'll pick you up in fifteen," O'Brien said, "but we're going to a place I choose."

"Great," I said. "I almost get killed by the mob and now you're going to kill me by making me eat at one of your greasy spoons."

"Stop bitching and get dressed."

30

O'BRIEN DROVE US TO THE DINER WHERE ELLEN—HIS backup girlfriend—was on duty. She acted as if a pair of Hollywood stars had arrived when she spotted us.

"Lordly Lou!" she screamed, looking away from the handful of truckers perched on stools at the diner's counter. "I saw you on the news just a bit ago."

I had slipped on a pair of jeans, a T-shirt, jacket, and baseball cap, but it obviously hadn't kept her from recognizing me. She rushed over to our booth, grabbing a glass coffeepot and ceramic mug en route for O'Brien.

"Miss Fox," she declared, "I'm so glad those gangsters didn't rape and kill you."

Conscious of all the eyes on us, I whispered, "Thank you," and ducked behind the menu.

"That FBI agent who rescued you sure is yummy."

"How about me?" O'Brien said.

"Oh sweetie pie, no one can rock my boat like you. But that don't mean a gal don't have eyes, does it, Miss Fox? No harm in looking, right?"

"I'm grateful for what Agent Coyle did," I said.

"Grateful!" Ellen repeated loudly. "Honey, grateful is when your old man picks his underwear and socks up off the floor and puts them in the laundry basket. What that hunk did for you demands a bit more than just feeling grateful."

"I think Agent Coyle knows how much I appreciate his actions," I said.

Without picking up a menu, O'Brien said, "You know what I want, darling."

"Are we talking food or something else?" she giggled.

Oh God, here we go again. "I'd like a Dr Pepper and some wheat toast with jelly," I said.

"How about a juicy steak?" she asked me. "On the house."

"Thank you, but my stomach's a bit upset," I demurred.

"Oh, baby, no problem. But it's still on the house."

O'Brien watched Ellen with appreciative eyes as she walked away. Stirring his coffee, he asked, "What's wrong?"

"Nightmares."

He took a sip. "I'm not surprised. You're not the first. I had them, too."

"When?"

"After I got shot."

"You got shot?"

"Yeah, more than once. I wear bullets well." He chuckled and continued, "The first time I was chasing this punk down an alley. Got me with a Saturday night special. Cheap piece of imported crap. I saw the flash and got knocked off my feet. The little prick swiped a Sony Walkman and I was lying in an alley looking up at the stars thinking, Goddamn it, I'm dying for a piece of junk made in Japan."

I tried to hold back a grin but couldn't.

He scowled at me. "It was only a flesh wound, but I kept reliving it every night when I got to sleep. Got so I was afraid to close my eyes."

"I didn't think anything frightened you."

He put down his mug. "Any cop who's never been scared is a liar or a fool."

I said, "Tell me about your nightmares."

"It was the same thing over and over. Chasing that punk, getting shot. The captain required me to talk to our department shrink. He said the dreams were my way of trying to figure out what I'd done wrong. My head was saying, Dummy, don't let this happen again."

O'Brien had a way of making me smile. "How'd you stop them?"

"When my thick skull finally realized I hadn't done nothin' wrong. Shit happens. It's out of my hands. It's out of your hands."

"The clockmaker," I said. "And his granddaughter. That wasn't your fault. You weren't there. Shit happens?"

A pained look crossed his face. I'd touched a nerve and O'Brien didn't like it. Thankfully, Ellen arrived carrying a massive platter of chicken fried steak and french fries smothered in white cream gravy for O'Brien and some wheat toast with burnt crusts for me.

"I told the cook to pour on extra gravy so it's just how you like it," she told O'Brien.

O'Brien twirled his ever-present toothpick in his mouth and winked at her again. "You always know how to satisfy me," he said. She giggled and sashayed away.

After she was gone, he said, "Your skull's gonna keep replaying the kidnapping until it's convinced you couldn't have done nothin' different. You wanna sleep? Do what the rest of us do. Either get drunk or deal with it." He stabbed his fork into his gravy-covered steak.

I said, "What I need is to get right back in the saddle."

Suddenly, I stopped smearing grape jelly on my toast and shook my head in disgust. "Did you just hear me?" I asked. "Back in the saddle. Jesus, I'm channeling Jack Longhorn now. My brain is fried, O'Brien."

O'Brien winked and said, "Not in a pig's eye."

"Leave pigs out of it."

"You're gonna be messed up until the cows come home," he said.

"Stop, O'Brien. I told you my gut hurts."

I couldn't think of any more Longhornisms, but O'Brien wasn't done. "See that trucker over there," he said, nodding at the counter. "He's so cheap, he'd squeeze a nickel until the buffalo craps."

"Enough, enough," I pleaded, laughing despite the pain in my ribs.

O'Brien shook his head. "Not yet. Dani, you're busier than a one-legged man at a butt-kicking contest."

"I had no idea you could outdo Longhorn," I said.

"I can outdo that prick in everything," he bragged, then got serious. "The first step to stopping those nightmares is smiling."

"And the next step," I said, "will be prosecuting Isabella Ricci's killer. We need to pay another visit to the Midland Apartments and confront Donnie Gilmore."

"And we will, Dani. But not tonight. Go home. Try to sleep. We'll meet like normal people do at eight o'clock and head over to the Midland Apartments."

"I'd like to go tonight. Now. I'm worried he'll run."

O'Brien used his last french fry to mop up what remained of the thick white gravy on his platter. "He won't. Remember little Chunky?"

"His name was Chucky."

"Yeah, but I got another smile, didn't I? You're afraid to go back to bed. But that's what you need to do. I'm driving you home now."

He was right. I was scared. O'Brien gave me a sly look and then, in a voice that mimicked Longhorn, he said, "This dinner has made me as happy as a pig in shit."

I raised my hands in surrender. "Please. No pig references."

31

B ECAUSE DONNIE GILMORE WORKED AN IRREGULAR schedule at the U.S. Postal Service, we couldn't be sure that he'd be home when O'Brien and I arrived at the Midland Apartments at 9 a.m. on Monday.

We went directly to Apartment 104 and when no one answered, O'Brien made a fist and pounded harder on the door. I heard a baby cry inside. O'Brien had awakened Chucky. The door cracked and Rachel peeked out. Her eyes were red, swollen, and filled with tears.

"We'd like to speak to you and your husband again," I said.

"Have you found him?" she asked, opening the door. Chucky was riding on her right hip, sucking hard on a pacifier.

"Who?" I replied.

"Donnie. He's missing."

We followed her into the cluttered living room and waited while she put Chucky into a corner playpen, where he continued to suck on his pacifier, oblivious to his mom's obvious distress.

"I don't know where he went," Rachel said, sniffling and taking a seat in the cluttered living room. "We've been fighting since you guys came here last time."

I found a tissue in my purse and handed it to her. Rachel said, "We had a big blowup Sunday afternoon. He stormed out and never came back."

"Do you have any idea where he might be?" I asked.

"His supervisor called really angry because Donnie didn't show up this morning when he was supposed to."

Rachel had called her husband's family and his friends, even a local bar that Gilmore patronized, but no one had seen him.

"I'm sorry I'm crying," she said. "When I opened the door, I thought you'd come to tell me he was dead."

"We came because we wanted to talk to him about the murder in your building," I said. "Detective O'Brien and I think Donnie knew more about it than he told us."

"Was he screwing her, too?" she asked.

Her candor took me by surprise. I wasn't sure how much Gilmore had told her about his sexual swinging in Scarsdale and his obsession with Isabella Ricci.

"We think he was stalking her," O'Brien said.

So much for being subtle.

In a weary voice, Rachel said, "I married him, had his kid, and then I find out he was cheating on me. I didn't really know him, did I? How's that happen?"

I thought of my own life and Will's hidden past. "Did Donnie keep a lot of secrets from you?" I asked.

Covering her face with her hands, she nodded and said, "He sure as hell did. But he didn't kill that woman. I know that."

"Did he tell you that?" O'Brien asked.

"Naw, we didn't talk about her. But he wasn't there when she was murdered."

"How do you know?" I asked. "Donnie told us that he took the day off from work to be at home with your baby while you were at your mother's house."

"Me and my mom were watching Donnie the whole time." Rachel took a deep breath to steady her emotions and said, "I was worried he was cheating. And I thought I wanted to know for sure. Now I do know and I'm not so sure I want to anymore."

"You said you were watching Donnie on the afternoon of the murder," I said, trying to get her back on track.

"Yeah. I didn't know what to do. I mean, I hadn't caught him with nobody."

"You and your mother followed him?" I said.

"Yes and no. My mom came over and we told Donnie we was going to her house but we really went across the street to a coffee shop."

"What time was this?" I asked.

"About ten in the morning. Maybe later. My mom's always late. We just sat there 'cause nothing happened. Then Donnie comes out without Chucky about noon. I followed him and mom went up to check on Chucky because we were afraid he'd left him alone."

"Was Chucky alone?" I asked.

"Naw, he had Mrs. McCurry's granddaughter babysitting. She lives next door. Donnie told her he had errands to do so she came over."

"Did Donnie see you tailing him?" O'Brien asked.

"Naw. He was in a big hurry. He went to this park a few blocks from here and met up with this woman. I seen them kiss and then go in this restaurant. The Happy Clam. He takes me there sometimes, too."

"You went inside?" I asked.

"Naw. I didn't want no big scene. I knew he'd blame me, saying I wasn't meeting his husband needs. That's what he said when we were fighting yesterday."

"Tell me about your fight," I said.

"I told him I knew he was cheating but I didn't tell him I'd followed him that afternoon. I didn't want him to know."

"What happened after you saw Donnie enter the Happy Clam with another woman?"

"I just sat in the park watching. He and her came out around two o'clock. They walked down to this hotel and went in there. I didn't know what to do, so I just hung around. He finally comes out after six o'clock. That's when he starts walking back to our place."

"You're sure it was after six o'clock?" I asked.

"Yeah. I needed to get home to feed Chucky. He eats around six. I also looked at my watch and it was like, maybe six-ten."

"You followed him home?" O'Brien asked.

"Naw, I went after that woman. I caught her just before she got to the bus stop. She was wearing a wedding ring. I said, 'Why you sleeping with my husband? We got a kid together.' She got all embarrassed because people were watching."

"Did you know her?" O'Brien asked.

She shook her head. "Naw, but I know where she works because she was wearing a uniform. She's a waitress right across the street from the post office where Donnie works."

"Would you recognize her again?" O'Brien asked.

"That bitch? You know I would. I was going to slap her, but she ran out into the street and got into a cab so I just came home."

"Did you and Donnie have a fight that night?" I asked.

"Naw, I never said nothing. I didn't know what to do. I mean, where would me and Chucky go? I needed time to think so I fixed dinner and said I'd been with my mom. And you know what really got me? That night, Donnie wants to screw because it's New Year's Eve and all. He hadn't even showered. But we didn't do it 'cause the cops showed up. Donnie was up most of the night trying to find out what was going on."

"Did he tell you anything that night about Isabella Ricci?" I asked.

"He said he didn't know her."

"Did he ever mention her husband, Marco Ricci?"

"Was Donnie screwing him, too?" She feigned a smile and said, "I'm just joking." But I could tell how hurt she'd been by her husband's infidelity.

I said, "Your husband met Isabella and Marco at a sex party in Scarsdale."

She didn't seemed shocked. "He told me about them swingers parties yesterday. Told me he'd gone a few times but he didn't mention names. Said he had to get some sexual relief for his blue balls. He blamed me." She let out a sigh and added, "I guess this marriage is over—if he has the guts to come home again. He was pretty scared that you was going to arrest him for that murder."

"Are you absolutely sure there is no way that your husband could have come back to this building that afternoon and gone into Isabella Ricci's apartment between the hours of two o'clock and six?" I asked.

"I just told you he was screwing that woman in the hotel all afternoon. You can ask her. He was cheating on me. Ask that bitch or ask the babysitter or my mom. She can tell you that I was watching him 'cause I told her all about it."

Chucky stirred, distracting her. "My kid's gonna wanna eat soon." She walked over to the playpen in the corner and rubbed his tummy, coaxing him back to sleep. When she returned to her seat, she said, "I thought that waitress bitch might tell Donnie about me going after her at the subway. But when we was fighting yesterday, he didn't say nothing about me following him. I don't think he's got a clue about me catching him."

"Why didn't you tell him?" I asked.

Rachel shrugged.

"You're his alibi," O'Brien said.

"Yeah, I know. But he doesn't know that. He was probably thinking that bitch was his only chance. He was probably thinking she wouldn't tell anyone they was together 'cause she's married and all."

"You want him to suffer?" O'Brien asked.

"Why not? Look what he's done to me and Chucky. He deserves to be in jail, don't he?"

"Not for murder," I said. "If he's innocent."

"Oh, he didn't kill that woman," she said. "But he hurt me and Chucky with his screwing around." She hesitated and then asked, "Is that dead woman the reason he moved us into this apartment building?"

O'Brien said, "We think so."

"We'll need to speak to him when he gets home," I said. "I'd like you to tell him that. And to call us."

"You going to arrest him?" she asked.

"Not if you're telling the truth," O'Brien said.

"The hotel will have records, plus the babysitter, plus the woman he was with," I said. "As long as they substantiate your story, he'll be in the clear."

"Then I wish I'd never told you about his alibi."

Hell hath no fury.

32

"I THINK SHE WAS TELLING US THE TRUTH," I SAID AS WE were riding back to White Plains. "But we'll know for sure after you investigate her story and track down the other woman and babysitter."

"If we're eliminating Donnie Gilmore as a suspect in Isabella Ricci's murder," O'Brien said, "who's left except Nicholas Persico?"

He was right. We were running out of other suspects. It seemed more and more likely that he was the killer. But my gut was still telling me that we were missing something.

"There's still a big loose end," I replied. "We still don't know who Isabella Ricci was meeting with every Tuesday and Thursday at her love nest. That person could be the key to solving this homicide."

"You said an FBI agent followed Persico's limo to the Midland Apartments by mistake once," O'Brien said.

"That's right. He was following Persico's limo but Persico wasn't in it."

"What's that tell us?"

"That Isabella's mystery lover might be someone in Persico's own family," I said.

"That's right," O'Brien replied. "He wouldn't give his car to just anyone."

"You know anything about the Butcher's family?"

"He's got a couple of sons who are definitely not peas in a pod. Names are Francis and Paul. One's legit, the other's as vicious as his old man. I'm sure the FBI has big files on 'em, or at least one of 'em. Now that you and Coyle are so buddy-buddy, you should ask him."

"We're not buddy-buddy. It's a purely professional relationship."

"I'm a detective, Dani. Don't bullshit me—or yourself."

When we reached our office, I took O'Brien's advice and telephoned Coyle. He sounded excited to hear my voice.

"Did you check your logbooks to see if there were any details about who was meeting Isabella at the Midland Apartments?" I asked.

"I sure did and we got nothing. Sorry."

"What can you tell me about Persico's family?"

"Nothing over the phone, but I'm free tonight if you'd like to have dinner," he offered. "I can brief you about the Persicos."

I thought about Will and hesitated. We were still a couple.

"Listen," Coyle said, "you can't turn down the man who saved your life. I'm a hero, remember? They said so on television."

"Then how can I refuse?" I replied.

I suggested we meet at 7 p.m. at Bistro Bistro, where we'd met the first time. The instant I hung up my phone, it rang.

It was Miss Hillary Potts and, as usual, she was curt. "The district attorney wants to see you in his office right now," she said.

"Any idea why?" I asked.

"I'm certain he will explain it when you arrive here. He wants you here immediately."

I wasn't going to get any hints from her so I thanked her, hung up the phone, and started for the door, only to have my phone ring again. I thought Miss Potts was calling me back for some reason so I grabbed it.

"Dani, don't hang up," Will said. "I know you're angry, but we can work this out. I deserve that much. How about dinner tonight? Roberto's."

"I have other plans."

"We can't resolve this if you refuse to talk to me. Change your plans. Please! We're talking about us and our relationship. This should be a priority."

"It's work. I can't. And don't lecture me about priorities."

"I'm just saying our relationship is more important than your work."

"How about your work? If I told you that we needed to talk and your newspaper deadline didn't matter, would you drop everything and show up?"

"That's different, Dani. News doesn't wait for anyone. But let's not fight, okay? Just meet me tonight at seven."

"No. I have other dinner plans."

"Are you meeting Agent Coyle?"

"I told you it's work. If it's with him or someone else shouldn't matter."

"But it does matter if it's him. Work is talking to him in an office, not across a table during a romantic dinner."

"I didn't say anything about a romantic dinner. It's a business meeting." I hesitated and then said in an icy voice, "What's wrong, Will? You afraid you can't trust me?"

"Coyle's trying to break us up."

"He's not breaking us up, you are."

"It's not just me," he replied in an irritated voice.

I replied, "You're the one who hid things from me."

"You're the one who's getting flowers from another man. This conversation is pointless," he said bitterly. "Have fun on your date." He hung up.

Now I was furious. My phone rang again and I assumed it was Will calling back to either apologize or complain some more. I grabbed the receiver and said, "Now what?"

"In my office, now!" Carlton Whitaker III said.

The fact that the district attorney had called me personally meant that this meeting was really important.

"I'm sorry, sir," I replied. "I'm coming right now."

"You should have been here ten minutes ago."

Then he hung up on me, too.

PART FOUR

FOOLS
RUSH IN

A grand jury would "indict a ham sandwich,"
if that's what you wanted.

—NEW YORK CHIEF JUDGE SOL WACHTLER

33

THE DISTRICT ATTORNEY AND HIS THREE CHIEFS WERE waiting when I walked into his office and it was clear from the first words out of Whitaker's mouth that I was not summoned to offer an opinion, but merely to listen.

"I want you to go before a grand jury this afternoon and get an indictment against Persico for the murder of Isabella Ricci," Whitaker announced.

"I'm not sure we can win it," I said.

Whitaker leaned forward from behind his desk and said in a stern voice, "I wasn't asking, I was telling. You indict him this afternoon or I'll replace you with someone who will."

Chiefs Steinberg, Myerson, and Vanderhoot all smiled. I knew that Vanderhoot, in particular, was enjoying this. Of the trio, Myerson was the only one I respected as a trial attorney and, apparently, he felt some respect toward me, too. He asked, "Why aren't you ready?"

"We still don't have a motive, for one thing," I said.

"We win cases all the time without a motive You know that," he replied.

"We still don't know who Isabella Ricci was meeting every Tuesday and Thursday in that apartment," I said.

"That shouldn't matter," Myerson said, "as long as you prove that she was murdered in the apartment and Persico was there. Whether they were lovers or just happen to be in the same place at the same time should not be an insurmountable obstacle to getting a conviction."

"We don't have any physical evidence—no murder weapon, no fingerprints, no hairs or fibers," I said.

"Miss Fox, I've heard you tell your peers that you loved circumstantial cases," Whitaker chimed in.

Having played the role of a devil's advocate, Myerson now changed tactics and began telling me why I could appear later today and get an indictment. "We already have a sitting grand jury and you should be able to get them to issue an indictment without any problems based on three pieces of evidence."

"I'm all ears," I replied without enthusiasm.

"You show them the photos of Isabella and the murder scene. That'll sicken and outrage any juror. They will want someone to pay. Next you tell them that you want to indict Nicholas Persico. His face was all over the front page of the paper the other day when we brought him in for the lineup."

I thought, Yep, you four arranged that ruse nicely. But I didn't say anything because he was still talking.

"The jurors are going to know Persico is a member of the Mafia and that his nickname is the Butcher. They will look at those horrific, graphic photographs and think that only someone as vicious as a mobster could have done that to Isabella Ricci."

"And what is my third winning component?" I asked, although I felt certain about what was coming next.

"Agent Coyle," Myerson said. "We'll get him out here this afternoon. He's clean-cut, all-American, a stellar FBI agent, and he is going to get up on that witness stand and tell the jurors that he followed Persico to the Midland Apartments on the day of the murder and that he personally saw the Butcher go into that building at two-thirty and saw him leave later that afternoon at five-thirty. By the time Coyle testifies, you'll already have established the time of death. Coyle will then testify that he saw Persico hurry back to his shop to change his clothes before going home. That should be more than enough to get him indicted."

Myerson was correct and I thought about telling him that he should take charge of the case, since he was in a rush to get Persico indicted. But I knew that insubordination would simply make everyone angry and get me removed from the case. Instead, I decided to ask why they were so intent on having me indict Persico today, given my qualms.

"Myerson, you make a convincing argument," I said, intentionally flattering him. "But why today?"

"Because I said so," Whitaker said, staring at me.

"I told you she'd fight this," Vanderhoot said. "There are plenty of other prosecutors who could do a better job. I say let one of them do it."

Steinberg shot Vanderhoot an unhappy look and said, "The district attorney and I both feel Ms. Fox is the right person for this case, given all of the work she's already done."

That was probably true, but I also assumed Steinberg had pushed Whitaker to keep me on this investigation for the same old reasons: women voters liked reading about me.

"And if I can't move forward today?" I asked.

Whitaker raised an eyebrow. "Don't get too big for your britches, Miss Fox. The fact that a mobster kidnapped you has garnered you a lot of emotional sympathy and support in our community. But it also could be used as justification for removing you from this case—and your job—given your need to recuperate after such an ordeal."

There was a reason why Whitaker had survived as district attorney for as long as he had. He knew how to play hardball. I was one step away from the unemployment line. All Whitaker had to do was announce that I was leaving because I'd been traumatized by the kidnapping. He'd look like a merciful boss.

Sitting there, I began doubting myself. Maybe they were right. Maybe Persico was the killer. Did I have any real evidence other than a nagging gut?

Looking directly at Whitaker, I said, "I serve at your pleasure, Mr. District Attorney. I will present this case to a grand jury as quickly as possible."

"No," Whitaker declared. "It will not be as quickly as possible. It will be this afternoon. Myerson will contact the FBI and make certain that Coyle is over here by two o'clock. After Persico's indicted and arrested, I want you to get an expedited trial scheduled. It will be good for the community to get all of these homicides put to bed quickly."

And good for your poll numbers, I thought.

With that little pep talk, I was shown the door, leaving the four men behind, no doubt, to discuss how best to exploit Persico's indictment. I headed across the street to get Whitaker's steamroller gassed up and ready.

34

I N NEW YORK STATE, A GRAND JURY IS COMPRISED OF
twenty-three jurors who are selected at random. It only takes twelve of
these ordinary citizens to issue an indictment, which is also called a
"true bill." Jurors say no to only about 7 percent of cases presented to a grand
jury. Such is the confidence the public puts in the police and prosecutors.

If they only knew.

Out of fairness, New York law states that anyone being accused of a
criminal charge can appear before a grand jury on his own behalf as a witness
before jurors. But I wasn't worried about that. The idea of Nicholas Persico
showing up in a grand jury room was far-fetched. He would be playing on
my home turf, and anything he said could be later used against him. And if
he perjured himself, additional changes could be filed. There was absolutely
no reason why Persico would come forward, especially since he was paying a
hefty retainer to his mouthpieces at Gallo & Conti.

Grand jury sessions are one of the few procedures that are held in secret. It
would be up to me to show that a crime had happened and identify who had
done it. I could use witnesses and present evidence. The jurors would then
decide if there was reasonable cause to believe, and legally sufficient evidence
to establish, that the individual had committed a felony. Once a grand jury
had issued an indictment, the matter would be assigned to the criminal division of the Westchester County Court.

Despite the rush, I wasn't worried about appearing before the grand jury
that afternoon. I'd presented cases before plenty of them. Myerson and Vanderhoot also had been busy getting everything set up for me. When it came

time, I entered the grand jury room and outlined my case. I called a Yonkers detective to describe the murder scene and then handed out color photographs of Isabella Ricci's body. Several jurors looked physically ill. Next came the medical examiner to establish the time of death and then Agent Coyle appeared to nail the coffin shut on Persico. It took less than an hour for the jurors to issue a true bill.

By four-thirty, the grand jury had been dismissed for the day, Myerson and Vanderhoot were congratulating each other, and Coyle was waiting for me in the hallway outside the grand jury room.

"We might as well move up our dinner date," he suggested. "I'm assuming you still want to hear about Persico and his kids. We can use the extra time to talk about what happens when the Butcher actually goes on trial. It looks like we might be seeing a lot more of each other since I'm your star witness."

I checked my watch and said, "I need to get some things squared away at my office. I could meet you at the restaurant by five-forty-five."

He smiled and quipped, "Knowing you, that means six o'clock."

"I'll try to be on time," I said as I walked away.

Back at my office, I checked the ever-growing pile of pink call-return slips on my desk. I drew a deep breath and was about to make some calls when O'Brien rapped on my door and saved me.

"You get the Butcher indicted?" he asked.

"He'll be arrested within the hour. The arrest warrant is being typed up now. You and Yonkers detectives should make the arrest. Notify his lawyers when you're at his door."

O'Brien chuckled and said, "Whitaker better hurry if he wants to make the six o'clock news."

"I'm certain he and Steinberg have that covered," I said. Changing topics, I asked, "Did Rachel Gilmore's story check out?"

He nodded. "The waitress who was shacking up with Gilmore that afternoon broke down and cried like a baby. They signed into the hotel under a fake name. John and Jane Smith. Real pros them two. The hotel manager verified it. The babysitter said Gilmore didn't get home until nearly six-thirty. I'd say he's in the clear."

"Then why's he running?" I asked.

"I put out a missing persons on him. We'll hear if he or his corpse shows up. It don't matter either way now."

"I'd like you to pull some files for me," I told him. "I want everything you can get me on Isabella's murder and I also want the files on Roman and Maggie Mancini and on Marco Ricci."

"Casting a wide net?" he said.

"I don't like how Whitaker and Longhorn tied all these murders up into a neat bow without anything but conjecture," I said. "And if I'm going to get a conviction, I've got to be prepared for Conti & Gallo. They'll point a finger at someone else."

"Maybe Marco Ricci," he said. "Defense attorneys enjoy blaming the dead. It's easier."

"I need to be prepared for whatever screwball theory they offer jurors," I said.

O'Brien said, "What did you learn from Coyle about Persico's family?"

"Oh crap!" I replied. "What time is it?"

"About ten minutes after six o'clock."

Grabbing my purse, I hurried out my office door, late as usual.

35

S PECIAL AGENT WALTER COYLE WAS JUST FINISHING A GLASS
of merlot when the maître d' seated me.

"Got held up at work," I said.

"Actually, you're early based on Dani Fox time," he joked.

"Cute."

"My comment or me personally?" he asked.

"Both."

"That's the first time you've given me a compliment," Coyle said.

"You did rescue me."

"I certainly did," he declared, raising his glass in a mocking self-salute. "And you rewarded me with an embrace and kiss."

"Actually, I hugged you and you kissed me."

"I didn't see you resist."

I could feel my face beginning to flush.

We ordered and Coyle said, "How'd I do this afternoon?"

"The grand jury loved you," I said.

"No surprises there," he replied confidently. "I make a good witness."

"At trial, it will be more difficult," I said, hoping to pop his bubble. "You didn't have Conti or Gallo going at you. They may lack certain ethics representing a mobster like Persico, but that doesn't mean they aren't skilled litigators."

"I'm sure you'll protect me in court," he said.

"Thanks for your vote of confidence, but there are lots of holes in this case. That's why I wanted to keep digging and not rush things."

"But you got outvoted."

"I didn't even get to cast one."

"Don't worry. I testified in Detroit in plenty of gang cases and I never let a defense attorney get the better of me. I'm not some run-of-the-mill cop."

Continuing, Coyle said, "I was a bit surprised this morning when you called and asked about Persico's family. Jack Longhorn had told me when I got to work that your office was going to indict the Butcher this afternoon. But my boss didn't mention anything about you going after Persico's kids."

I wondered if I'd heard him correctly. He'd just told me that Longhorn had known about our plans to seek an indictment before I had.

"How'd your boss know we were going after Persico today?" I asked in my most nonthreatening voice.

"He heard it from Vanderhoot. They talk regularly."

I thought back to my morning meeting with Whitaker and his three chiefs. Whitaker had specifically ordered Myerson, not Vanderhoot, to arrange for Coyle to appear before the grand jury.

Again, sounding nonchalant, I said, "I thought it was Myerson who arranged for you to come before the grand jury."

"He did. Myerson called me," Coyle said, "but by then, Longhorn already had spoken to Vanderhoot so I already knew I was going to be your star witness."

It was a minor detail but our conversation told me that my misgivings about Vanderhoot were well placed. He was telling the FBI about our every move inside Whitaker's office. He was a snitch for Longhorn and in return the FBI special agent in charge was helping him get a more lucrative U.S. Attorney's job.

I didn't want to call attention to what I'd just learned so I said, "You asked why I was interested in Persico's immediate family. I want to learn everything I can about someone whom I've charged with murder."

"Makes sense," Coyle said approvingly.

"I also think someone in his family was having an affair with Isabella Ricci," I added.

Coyle's easy smile vanished. "Why are you still fussing about that?" he asked in an irritated tone.

"It's a loose end that might help us understand why Persico killed her," I said.

Coyle considered this and said, "Okay, that's reasonable. What do you want to know about them?"

"I know Persico has two sons, and O'Brien told me that one of them is like his father and the other isn't."

"Detective O'Brien is right. Francis Persico is the oldest but he's the one who got away. He graduated from college, got a legitimate job, and is an investment banker on Wall Street. His wife's from a respectable Stamford, Connecticut, family. She sells real estate. They got three kids, all in private schools."

"He doesn't sound like someone who'd get involved with Isabella Ricci," I said. "What about the other brother?"

"Paul's the obvious choice. Never married and a carbon copy of the Butcher. His mob handle is 'Little Pauly.' He runs the Battaglia crime family's operations in the Bronx, where he's just as ruthless as his old man."

"Are those Persico's only kids?"

"Little Pauly is the baby in the family. Francis is the oldest. Then there's a daughter between them, Angelica. She works at the family butcher's shop."

I recognized her name. Angelica was the attractive young woman who'd frisked me when I'd paid my unofficial visit to Persico at his shop. The Butcher himself had called her over to check me for a wire and told her to listen to our conversation.

"Is Angelica in the mob?" I asked.

Coyle laughed. "C'mon. Little Pauly is the apple of his father's eye and he didn't fall far from the tree. Besides, she's a woman."

I was finding Coyle's demeaning attitude irritating. I also didn't like his use of idioms. He'd obviously been spending too much time with Special Agent Longhorn, the king of the folksy homily.

"What can you tell me about Little Pauly?" I asked.

"He was trouble from the moment he was born. He boxed in amateur bouts as a teenager and earned a reputation for his left jab, although rumors were that other fighters took dives as soon as they learned who his old man was. He's got a long rap sheet."

"What sort of crimes?"

"Everything and anything. Running cigarettes up from North Carolina.

Hijacking trucks out of Kennedy Airport. He did time in a federal country club before graduating to maximum security state prisons. He's known for having a hot temper. More Sonny Corleone than Michael."

"Is he a womanizer?"

"Thinks he is. A real Don Juan with Jersey girls. He got one pregnant a few years ago. Rumor was she was trying to force him down the aisle, since he's Catholic. Instead, they found her body in the Meadowlands. Against abortion, but not murder."

"Little Pauly Persico murdered one of his girlfriends, but you don't think he might be responsible for carving up Isabella Ricci?" I asked in a surprised voice. "Why didn't you share that information with us?"

"Little Pauly wasn't at that apartment when Isabella was murdered, re-member?" he said in a ridiculing tone. "His father was there. How many times do I have to tell you that? If we were suspicious of Little Pauly, we would have told you. But we don't just randomly share information with locals unless we think they need it."

"This is our case. You should have told us, especially since we know that someone besides Nicholas Persico was visiting Isabella at that apartment twice a week."

"You don't tell us what we should and shouldn't share with you. Don't you get it? It doesn't matter who was fucking her," Coyle said loudly. "The only thing you need to know is that Nicholas Persico was in that apartment when that woman was murdered."

Several people sitting nearby were staring. He noticed and immediately dropped his voice. "Let's talk about something else," he said.

His outburst was startling. I hadn't seen this side of Coyle before. I de-cided to go along with him.

"What would you like to talk about?" I said. "The trial? Your testimony?"

"No. Us. Our future."

"There is no us," I said.

"You're wrong," he said in a cocky voice. "You might still have feelings for that asshole reporter, but he's not right for you."

"That reporter has a name and how do you know what's right for me?"

"I know his name. Will Harris, or does he prefer some Age of Aquarius nickname like his ex-girlfriend Moonbeams?"

"That happened during the sixties," I said. "Besides, who are you to judge him?"

"Who are you to not judge him?" Will replied. "The guy lied to you about his past, for God's sake."

"He didn't lie," I said. "He just didn't tell me about it."

"Burning flags, student protests, maybe you can blow off those things now and say that he just got caught in the sixties," Coyle said, "but not telling you about his daughter and how she died, that's an entirely different matter."

I wasn't sure why I felt the need to defend Will. Maybe I still had strong feelings for him. Or maybe I just didn't like Coyle's condescending attitude. Regardless, I decided to turn the tables. "Do you think you should have sent me your confidential FBI background investigation just because you wanted to date me?"

"You're a prosecutor," he said. "The bureau sends background information to prosecutors all the time. You can't compare my decision to tell you about your former boyfriend's shortcomings to the smothering death of a baby. I was trying to protect you."

"Maybe Will thought he was trying to protect me, too, by keeping his past a secret."

"You're a lawyer. The law sees no difference between the getaway driver and his buddy who's inside holding up a bank. Will Harris was there when Moonbeams suffocated his baby. Under the law, that makes him a killer and you shouldn't be dating him."

I was beginning to get angry. Who was he to be telling me who I should and shouldn't date?

Coyle realized he was pissing me off. He smiled and said, "I think this is another topic we need to skip over. I'm sorry if you don't realize that I was trying to help you. I just didn't want you to get hurt again."

"Hurt again?"

"Yeah," he said. "Let's be honest here. I asked around at the courthouse. I heard about you and your med school boyfriend. How he cheated on you. You don't have the best history with men."

I suddenly felt the urge to stick my fork into his chest.

"How dare you investigate me?" I said, taking my napkin off my lap and tossing it on the table.

"Dani," he said softly, "don't make more of this than it is. Guys ask around when they find someone attractive. It's no big deal. I'm the good guy here. I'm willing to protect you. Hell, Will Harris isn't even putting up a fight for you."

"Are you stuck in third grade?" I replied. "What you just said was not flattering. It was insulting. I don't need a man to protect me or win me in battle."

"You didn't feel that way when you were handcuffed in the warehouse, did you?" he asked.

Now I really did want to stab him.

Coyle picked up the menu. "Let's order dessert. Something to share."

I was in no mood for dessert. I was angry at him for the belittling remarks that he'd made. I was angry because he was arrogant. I was angry because he'd attacked Will. And I was really pissed that he accused me of having a flawed character because my first boyfriend couldn't keep his pants zipped and my second had secrets hidden in his past.

"Agent Coyle, you're going to have to change your attitude about a lot of things if you are interested in dating me."

"No problem," he said flippantly. "I'll gladly let you change me."

He reached over and placed his hand on mine. I immediately started to pull my hand back and when I did, he tightened his grip and for a moment held it in place before releasing me.

I was stunned. "Don't you ever try to manhandle me again," I snapped. "I'm leaving."

"Does this mean no dessert?" he said.

In a controlled voice, I said, "Because of Persico's trial, we're going to have to work together during the coming weeks. I think we need to be clear right now that we are going to have a professional relationship and nothing more."

"Dani," he said in an accommodating voice, "I'm sorry. This evening has been a disaster. I warned you I can get too aggressive. How about if I play by your rules? We'll keep this entirely professional and then after Persico is convicted, you'll give me another chance. I mean, I did save your life, right?"

Without waiting for an answer, Coyle waved to our waiter and said, "We'd like to split a dessert."

"You'll be eating it yourself," I said, standing.

I left Coyle at the table, choosing between a cannoli and gelato.

36

EXCEPT WHEN NECESSARY, I STAYED CLEAR OF AGENT Coyle in the weeks leading up to the Persico trial. I also told Will that I needed a break to sort out our relationship. I asked him to stop calling or coming by my office or house. I wanted to focus on my work. If I felt lonely, I had my mom and Wilbur for company. I threw myself into trial preparation and got along quite nicely without either man adding to my troubles.

Ordinarily, the scheduling of a murder trial such as Persico's drags on for months, even years. But Persico didn't like being in jail and our office was eager to get the case heard quickly. Both sides agreed on an insanely expedited trial. It was set for April 1. Beginning on April Fool's Day seemed significant to me, although I wasn't certain whether it would be Persico, his lawyers, or me who would be proved a fool.

Vanderhoot called me into his office several times to ask about my strategy. But now that I knew he was a snitch for Longhorn, I was intentionally evasive. Nor did I spend much time with Myerson, but that was for a different reason. Our office's chief trial lawyer didn't want to know too much or get too involved, in case it turned out that Persico was found innocent. He wasn't going to take the blame. I sensed that Whitaker was laying the groundwork for a "blame Dani Fox" exit if this case ran amok. I began to notice that whenever Whitaker spoke to the media, he made a point of reminding everyone that I was the lead prosecutor and that Detective O'Brien and I had been deeply involved in the investigation of Isabella's murder.

The only person I could count on was O'Brien. My first request was for all the investigative files on Isabella's murder as well as the Mancini and Marco Ricci homicides. I had to put myself in the shoes of the defense to figure out what sort of cockamamie theory the law firm of Conti & Gallo might present.

When O'Brien dropped a huge stack of files on my desk, I got right to work. I removed all of the black-and-white crime scene photographs that had been taken and tacked them on my office wall. Underneath each photo, I wrote the victim's name, date and time of their death, and how they died. I stepped back and examined my display. I needed more information. I got O'Brien to get me files about Giuseppe Nunzio and Nicholas Persico. I put their photos on my wall, too. One of the girls in our office knits, so I borrowed a skein of yarn from her and began using it and thumbtacks to link commonalities between the different cases and different suspects. Before long, my display looked like a spiderweb of purple yarn.

As expected, Anthony Conti and Alonzo Gallo filed all of the prerequisite motions that one would expect before a trial of this magnitude. I have always found it frustrating that prosecutors have to show all of their cards but the defense isn't required to show anything. Even more frustrating is that defense attorneys are given wide latitude to conjure up whatever nutty theories and inventions that they want to protect their clients. This practice was especially common in domestic violence cases, where it always seemed as if the victims were the ones being put on trial. All of this pretrial maneuvering ran its normal course and before I knew it, I was standing at the prosecutor's table in the courtroom of Judge Lorenzo Cerrato, along with attorneys Anthony Conti, Alonzo Gallo, and their client.

There had been so many requests by reporters to attend the mobster's murder trial that Judge Cerrato had instructed his clerk to put numbered slips of paper into a hat and have reporters pick them out. The first thirty winners got seats. Everyone else was stuck in the hallway. Of course, none other than Will Harris was sitting in the front row directly behind me. In addition to reporters, Judge Cerrato allowed a limited number of family members from the Persico and Nunzio clans to attend. All of them were searched before they entered the courtroom, where they sat either on the left, behind the defense table, or on the right, behind me. That meant that I got the Nunzios on my side. The only spectator whom I recognized was the deceased Mafia capo's heavyset daughter-in-law, who'd confronted me when

O'Brien and I had shown up on the family's doorstep. She was flanked by two men who deputies told me were both Nunzio's sons. The dead mobster's wife and elderly mother also sat with them. On the opposite side of the courtroom, the Persico family sat on wooden benches. His supporters included his wife, his son Pauly, his daughter, Angelica, and his elderly mother. I found it amusing that both Mafia kingpins had their mother's support. There were more deputies assigned to keep order in the courtroom than usual. O'Brien told me that the Battaglia and Gaccione crime families had both sent their soldiers to keep an eye on each other during the trial but courthouse security had refused to allow anyone to enter the courthouse who couldn't show that they had a legitimate reason to be there, so the Mafia goons, as O'Brien referred to them, had taken up residence in two different restaurants near the downtown courthouse, claiming each as their turf.

My mother likes to attend cases that I prosecute, but I'd told her to stay away from this one. I didn't want either mob family knowing more than necessary about my family.

All of the media attention and anxiety about the mob had caused Judge Cerrato to implement his own set of courtroom precautions. Rather than having jurors state their names, they were assigned numbers and the attorneys were cautioned about prying too deeply into the jurors' personal lives. That made selecting a jury even trickier than usual. It took us three days to seat the jury and during that time period, Judge Cerrato made it clear that he was not going to tolerate any theatrics or posturing by either the defense or prosecution.

I liked Judge Cerrato. He was a no-nonsense judge in his late sixties with a reputation for being fair and smart when it came to applying the law. He was also known for having a quick temper and an unorthodox practice. A chain smoker of unfiltered Camels, Cerrato, already short in stature, would feel the urge for a cigarette so badly during long trials that he would scoot down in his chair on the bench so that it was almost impossible to see him. He would bend down as if he were looking for something that he'd dropped on the floor and then he'd fire up a Camel, the telltale smoke drifting upward. In addition to smoking in his courtroom, Judge Cerrato was also known to wear a pistol under his robe and there was little doubt in my mind that if trouble broke out, he wouldn't hesitate to use it. I just prayed his aim was good because he apparently had poor eyesight since he wore thick Coke-bottle glasses that seemed to triple the size of his eyeballs.

Myerson had assigned a fellow A.D.A. named Carl Cameron to assist me, but he worked for Vanderhoot in the Organized Crime Bureau so I limited his participation to the filing of routine motions and the interviewing of minor witnesses. I simply didn't trust him.

I kept my opening statement relatively brief and simply asked the jury to listen to the evidence and evaluate the credibility of the witnesses as each of them gave their testimony. I knew Conti and Gallo would be eager to jump on any mistake that I might make so I was careful not to say anything in my opening that I would be unable to substantiate in the course of the trial. I also had decided beforehand that there was no need for me to be overly dramatic or emotional, because the circumstances of the murder were sensational on their own. A verdict of guilty was only half the battle; an appeals court would decide the other half. It was my job to convince this jury that Persico was guilty while policing myself to make certain that I didn't say or do anything that opened the door later for a verdict to be overturned.

Although I felt we were rushing to judgment, I felt obligated to prosecute Persico to the best of my abilities. The public deserved no less from me and neither did Isabella. Besides, Agent Coyle hadn't wavered since the moment we'd met. He was absolutely certain that Persico was guilty.

Gallo gave the defense's opening, explaining that he would leave it up to Conti to later deliver the closing statements. Gallo was more articulate and well-mannered than I expected. He was also a man who preferred to use six words when only two were necessary. I quickly realized that the two attorneys planned to take advantage of their different courtroom styles by falling into a good cop/bad cop routine, with Gallo being the smiling, calm defender of his innocent client and Conti being the angry attack dog with bared teeth let loose when necessary.

My first several witnesses described the crime scene inside the apartment and Isabella's cause of death. I intentionally did not introduce color photos, and instead used black-and-white shots as I had done in the grand jury. Those, and the testimony of the coroner and the Yonkers detectives who investigated the murder, gave the jury a graphic view of Isabella's mutilated body. A common tactic of defense attorneys is to file an appeal based on inflammatory photographs, which the color shots of Isabella certainly could have been. I didn't need to take that risk because I knew that experienced attorneys like Gallo and Conti would be quick to exploit it.

Under my careful questioning, the lead detective established that the time of death was sometime after three-thirty-five in the afternoon and explained that he'd reached that conclusion based on the cut clock-radio cord that had been used to tie Isabella's arms.

Next up was the medical examiner, who testified that in his expert medical opinion the victim had been dead before six o'clock, creating a window of two and a half hours for the homicide to have been committed.

I was surprised that neither defense attorney challenged or cross-examined these early witnesses. Conti and Gallo were up to something and that made me nervous because I had no idea what it was. I only knew they had something up their sleeves. Persico wasn't paying them to sit idly by and watch him get convicted, and I suspected that Conti and Gallo knew better than most how dangerous it was to disappoint the Butcher.

37

Although we had lots of circumstantial evidence in this case, I'd always known that the key witness was going to be Coyle. Jurors love to hear witnesses say: "I was there. This is what I saw with my own two eyes." The fact that Coyle was the picture of a straight-shooting, all-American FBI agent would give his words even more credibility.

He was scheduled to testify during day three and the two of us spent a considerable amount of time together the week before the trial, going over his testimony and potential cross-examination. It had taken a great deal of patience on my part to deal with his arrogance and belief that he could outsmart Conti and Gallo. I kept reminding him that he needed to give yes and no answers and not challenge the defense. Many investigators consider themselves to be experts when it comes to interrogating suspects. And many of them are talented at getting someone who is guilty to confess. But interrogating a suspect at a police station and being questioned on the witness stand are two very different experiences. The rules in a courtroom are complex and so is the stage. A judge and the defense are listening to every word, looking for the most minor miscue.

I tried repeatedly to emphasize this to Coyle. But he seemed more interested in my legs than my advice. It was winter and I was wearing black tights that disappeared into my black shoes in a fluid, seamless fashion. I never thought about looking sexy—only practical. Men are just wired differently.

When he was sworn in, Coyle raised his right hand and answered loudly, "Yes, I do," when Judge Cerrato's court clerk asked him if he would swear to tell the truth and only the truth. I always like to start with softball questions because it puts a witness at ease. That's what I intended to do with Coyle, but he was so cocky that I quickly realized I could shortcut this step. I moved on by having him establish his credentials. He told jurors about his educational background, training in law enforcement, and FBI accomplishments. Next I launched into a series of carefully crafted questions that the two of us had gone over earlier. I needed to reveal to jurors that the FBI had been conducting an ongoing investigation of Persico at the time of Isabella's murder, but I had to be careful about how I did this. Judge Cerrato had warned me not to prejudice the defendant in front of the jury by labeling him as a well-known mobster. This could have been fatal on post-trial motions. As I gingerly walked Coyle through my questions, I sensed that much of what I was establishing was already known by jurors. The fact that they had been issued juror numbers rather than asked their real names had tipped them off to Persico's reputation.

After I'd established that the FBI was routinely following Persico, I had Coyle identify the FBI logbook and had it introduced as evidence. I thought Conti and Gallo might raise some sort of objection, but they stayed strangely silent.

I instructed Coyle to open the logbook and turn to December 31, 1979.

"Is there an entry in the logbook on that date?" I asked.

"Yes, it is an entry that I made," he replied.

Next I asked him to read his entry and had him explain to jurors how he saw Persico enter and leave the Midland Apartments at 2:30 p.m. and 5:30 p.m., respectively. He then recounted how he'd observed Persico wearing different clothes later that night when he left work.

Coyle looked good, dressed in a tailored three-piece wool suit. On the witness stand, he came across with confidence. He answered my questions as he'd been instructed with snappy yes and no replies. When he was required to give a more detailed response, he used short declarative sentences that were easy to understand. Several times he turned his head so that he was speaking directly to jurors and making eye contact. I felt good about his testimony when I asked him my final question.

It was now Gallo's turn to cross-examine. Rising from his chair, Gallo methodically began his cross-examination without a hint of animosity. He

seemed almost admiring of Coyle. I could see my witness being lulled in by
Gallo like a Siren beckoning unsuspecting sailors to crash on the rocks. I
knew Gallo would eventually make his move and when it happened, I suspected he would do so without drama or flair. He would simply go in for a
clean kill.

"Agent Coyle," Gallo said, "I'd like you to read from the logbook that the
prosecution has introduced as evidence."

Coyle looked pleased as he was handed the FBI file.

Continuing, Gallo said, "Now, you testified earlier that Mr. Persico had
been under surveillance for quite some time, is that correct?"

"Yes sir," Coyle said. "That's accurate."

"And this bureau logbook contains entries made by the FBI agents assigned to conduct that surveillance, is that your testimony?"

"Yes, sir."

"Please look at the entry for Tuesday, December 11, 1979. Do you see it?"

"Yes, sir," Coyle replied, and then without waiting to be asked, he began
reading it: "Tuesday, December 11, 1979. Special Agent Dixon commenced
surveillance of the Persico Butcher Shop at 1200 hours after relieving Agent
Campbell. At 1400 hours, Agent Campbell observed a limo, New York license plate 65183-LV with driver and passenger, leave from rear of Butcher
Shop. Subject followed. At 1430 hours, limo arrived at the apartment building on Midland Avenue, Yonkers, New York."

I realized that Gallo was having Coyle read the entry that I had first noticed when I'd reviewed the logs at the IHOP restaurant. It was the entry
that described how an agent had followed the car to the apartment building,
only to discover that someone besides Persico had been in the vehicle.

Coyle continued reading. "Passenger in rear seat of the vehicle exited
the vehicle. Passenger had collared overcoat and hat. Agent realized that
this was not subject Persico based on subject's overall height and size. 1435
hours, agent left Midland Avenue, Yonkers, New York, en route to Persico
Butcher Shop. 1450 hours, agent arrived at butcher shop. Subject Persico
was observed outside butcher shop speaking to unidentified man carrying
a bag. Unidentified man appears to be a customer. 1450 hours, agent remained in place for surveillance. Subject remains at butcher shop location.
1600 hours, limo, New York license plate 65183-LV, returned and drives to

rear of butcher shop. 1700 hours, Agent Dixon relieved by Agent Campbell."

Coyle shut the logbook and waited for Gallo's next question.

"Agent Coyle," Gallo said, "do you know who the person was who got dropped off at the apartment building on Midland Avenue, Yonkers, New York on Tuesday, December 11, 1979, at 1430 hours?"

"No, sir. I do not."

Gallo directed him to another entry in the logbook, this one December 31, 1979. He asked if Coyle had written that notation and the agent quickly acknowledged that he had been watching Persico that day.

"Please read us your entry," Gallo said.

"1200 hours, Agent Coyle relieves Agent Dixon at subject's place of business at butcher shop. 1410 hours, limo, New York license plate 65183-LV, leaves from rear of butcher shop with driver and passenger in rear seat. Vehicle followed by agent. 1430 hours, limo arrives at the apartment building on Midland Avenue, Yonkers, New York. Subject Persico identified by agent exiting from vehicle. Subject enters building. Driver remains in limo. 1730 hours, subject Persico identified exiting the apartment building on Midland Avenue, Yonkers, New York. Appears excited and in a hurry. Enters limo, New York license plate 65183-LV. Agent follows limo. 1755 hours, limo returns to subject's butcher shop. 1900 hours, subject Persico identified and seen getting into limo, New York license plate 65183-LV. Subject's clothing has been changed from 1730 hours identification. Driven in vehicle by driver. Subject in rear seat. Agent follows vehicle. 1930 hours, subject arrives at his home. Stays in residence for balance of night."

Gallo said, "Thank you, Agent Coyle. Now, can you please tell us if the person you were watching that afternoon was wearing a hat and overcoat?"

"Mr. Persico was only wearing an overcoat," Coyle said.

"Was it cold outside?"

"Yes sir, it was."

"Was the collar on the overcoat pulled up to protect from the cold?"

"No, sir. I could clearly see that the subject was Nicholas Persico. He had a scar on his left cheek that was clearly recognizable from prior surveillance."

I felt a sudden sense of foreboding. In his eagerness to impress jurors,

Coyle had gone off script and was giving Gallo more information than I'd wanted him to. He was supposed to be replying with yes and no answers.

Gallo said, "Agent Coyle, I want to show you a newspaper story dated January 3, 1980, that appeared in the *White Plains Daily*, written by reporter Will Harris. Have you seen this newspaper article before today?"

"Yes, sir. I read it when it came out."

"Does this article contain a description of the person seen entering the Midland building on the afternoon in question? A description given by the building's manager, Roman Mancini, to the reporter?"

"Objection," I declared. I knew where this was going and I wanted to stop it.

"State your reason," Judge Cerrato said.

"Hearsay evidence, Your Honor. It is not admissible."

"Counselor?" Cerrato asked Gallo.

"Your Honor, the description that Roman Mancini gave to reporter Harris comes into the record solely for the fact that it was said, not the truth that it may or may not contain. Therefore, the statement by Roman Mancini is admissible to impeach Agent Coyle's credibility." Gallo took two sheets of paper from a file and asked for permission to hand them to the judge's clerk.

The clerk delivered one sheet to Judge Cerrato and one to me. The sheets were copies of Section 200, from *Richardson on Evidence*, tenth edition. I knew as soon as I scanned the citation that I was sunk.

"Your objection is overruled," Judge Cerrato said.

"But your honor," I complained, "Agent Coyle cannot read that news article in front of the jury until the defense actually enters it as evidence. It can only be used to refresh his recollection at this point."

"Miss Fox, you have my ruling," Judge Cerrato said sternly. "Proceed, Mr. Gallo."

I sat down and glanced at Coyle. I had mentioned to him during our pre-trial sessions that Gallo might try to make use of Will's story, but Coyle had brushed off my warnings and had chuckled at my concerns. He'd refused to even discuss it and had assured me that he'd be able to defuse any tricks that Gallo might try.

Holding up the newspaper, Gallo said, "Now, Agent Coyle, please read what's been marked as Exhibit Number 207, where Mr. Mancini describes the person who visited the apartment on Midland Avenue on Monday, December 31, 1979."

In his clear voice, Coyle read:

When asked, Mancini said he'd only seen the face of "Vicky's" lover once because the older man generally wore a hat and turned up his collar. But on the afternoon of the murder, the woman's "boyfriend" arrived without a hat and turned-up collar, Mancini said. "He had the eyes of a stone-cold killer. Looking at his face scared me."

As soon as he finished, Gallo said, "Do you see my client sitting at the defense table?"

"Yes, sir, I do."

"And do you notice anything unusual about the left side of his face?"

Persico, who was seated with his right side facing the jury, turned so that everyone could see the long, jagged knife scar on his left check.

"It is well known that Mr. Persico has a prominent scar on his left cheek," Coyle said.

"Isn't it fair to say that Mr. Mancini would have noticed that scar if my client had entered his building?" Gallo asked.

Coyle shrugged and said, "Maybe he forgot to mention it to Will Harris or maybe the reporter forgot to put it in his article."

"Your Honor," Gallo said, "I would ask that Agent Coyle's last remark be stricken—speculation."

With a loud sigh, Judge Cerrato said, "So stricken." Addressing the jury, the judge explained that Coyle had not answered the question. Instead, he had tried to rationalize why the article did not mention a scar.

"Mr. Coyle, answer the question that is asked. Don't speculate or give us your theories," Judge Cerrato warned.

At that point, Gallo asked Coyle: "Does the statement by Mr. Mancini as reported by Will Harris in the newspaper mention a scar? Answer yes or no."

"No," Coyle said.

"Now wasn't that easy, Agent Coyle?" Judge Cerrato remarked.

I winced. It is never good to have a judge chastise a prosecution witness.

Gallo also knew this and immediately called attention to the judge's remark.

"Thank you, Your Honor, for your help. Now, Agent Coyle, in the article, Mr. Mancini is quoted as saying that he looked at the man who visited the apartment . . . and, well you tell us, what did that man see?"

"The article quotes Mr. Mancini saying the visitor had 'stone-cold eyes.' "

Gallo repeated those words. " 'Stone-cold eyes.' That means he got a pretty good look at that man's face if he saw his eyes, wouldn't you say?"

"I don't want to assume," Coyle said sarcastically.

In a stern voice, Judge Cerrato said, "Answer the question, Agent Coyle."

"Yes," Coyle said, "if Mr. Mancini was quoted accurately, then it would appear that he looked at the visitor's face."

"Now, please notice that Mr. Mancini did not say in the article that this man had a scar on his left cheek. Can you confirm?"

"That's true."

"Then how could that man going into the apartment building have been Mr. Persico?"

Coyle looked frustrated. "Mr. Persico clearly has a scar."

"That's not what I asked you," Gallo said. "If the man whom Mr. Mancini saw didn't have a scar, then he couldn't have been my client, isn't that correct?"

Coyle twisted uncomfortably in his seat. "I saw Mr. Persico enter that building," he said.

"Your Honor," Gallo protested, "he's not answering the question."

Judge Cerrato glared at Coyle and said, "I'm going to make this very simple for you, Agent Coyle. We all know Mr. Persico has a scar on his left cheek. You've just testified that Mr. Mancini did not mention that scar in the newspaper article. The defense has asked you, if the man whom Mr. Mancini said that he saw did not have a scar, could he have been Mr. Persico? Now answer that question."

"No, it couldn't have been Mr. Persico if that man didn't have a scar."

Gallo said, "Thank you, Judge and Agent Coyle."

Gallo had done a masterful job raising doubts about whether Persico had been spotted by Mancini. Now Gallo went on to further undermine Coyle's credibility.

"Would you consider yourself ambitious, Agent Coyle?" he asked.

"No more than any other agent," Coyle replied. "We all seek justice."

"Come now, Agent. There's no need for you to be modest. Isn't it true that you have moved up the ranks quicker than your peers?"

"I have been promoted much faster than others who entered the academy with me."

"Is that because you've been involved in big cases?"

"Yes, sir," Coyle proudly declared. "I helped solve a major case in Detroit that involved street gangs."

"Would getting my client convicted be considered a major notch in your belt and possibly get you another big promotion?"

I objected, pointing out that Coyle couldn't speculate on the future. The judge told Gallo to move on, but he'd accomplished what he'd wanted. He'd suggested a motive for why Coyle might lie about Persico.

"Agent Coyle," Gallo said, "in your log entry, you made a remark about Mr. Persico changing clothing after he left the apartment but before he went home for the night, did you not?"

"Yes, sir. He changed his clothes after he left the apartment."

"What did you conclude from this observation?"

"That the defendant changed clothing to get rid of the clothes he wore at the murder scene because they were covered in blood."

"I see," Gallo said thoughtfully. "There was a lot of blood on that scene, wasn't there?"

"I object," I said. "Agent Coyle was never at the scene. Calls for speculation."

"I'll withdraw my question," Gallo said. But it hardly mattered. The jurors couldn't unhear the reminder about how bloody the apartment had been.

"Did you actually see blood on Mr. Persico's shirt when you say he exited the Midland Avenue apartment?"

"No. I wasn't close enough."

"You weren't close enough," Gallo repeated. "But you were close enough to notice Mr. Persico's scar and that he had changed his clothing and you what—assumed he changed it to get rid of blood-soaked clothing, is that correct?"

"I thought it was a fair and logical assumption."

"A fair and logical assumption?" Gallo repeated. "Did you obtain a search warrant after the murder to search the butcher shop to confirm this fair and logical assumption?"

"No, sir."

"But you could have obtained a search warrant if you had wanted, isn't that correct?"

"I suppose so."

"That would have been an easy way for you to see if blood was on his clothing. In fact, it would have been damning evidence, wouldn't it?"

Strike two, I thought.

For the next several minutes, Gallo asked Coyle about several insignificant items and then he suddenly switched gears.

"Agent Coyle, are you familiar with a person named Daniel DiVenzenzo?"

I'd never heard the name before.

"Yes," Coyle answered.

I shot Coyle a curious look. Where the hell was Gallo going with this? And why hadn't Coyle warned me about this Mr. DiVenzenzo?

Gallo said, "Please explain to the court who he is."

"Objection. Relevancy?" I said, rising to my feet.

"I'm going to allow it," Judge Cerrato ruled, "but Mr. Gallo, you need to connect the dots."

"I will, Your Honor," Gallo said. "Now, Agent Coyle, isn't Daniel DiVenzenzo an alleged member of a crime family?"

"Yes, the bureau has identified him as being a member of the Battaglia crime family. He lived in Yonkers, where he was involved in numerous illegal activities that date back to his youth. Right now, he's currently in prison doing ten years for extortion."

"You seem to know a lot about Daniel DiVenzenzo, Agent Coyle. Why is that?"

Coyle beamed and said, "Because I was part of a task force that was responsible for his arrest and conviction in early January of this year after his trial in federal court."

"Now, isn't it true that the basis of his conviction was telephone conversations that the FBI secretly tape-recorded as part of its surveillance of Mr. DiVenzenzo?"

"You are correct, sir. We had permission to place taps on Mr. DiVenzenzo's telephones."

"Now, these tape recordings were introduced into evidence during the DiVenzenzo trial and were accepted as evidence by the court, is that true?"

"Yes, the bureau showed an impeccable chain of custody and clearly established the authenticity of all wiretapped and taped conversations to the satisfaction of the court."

I still had no idea where this was going so I decided to object. "Your Honor," I said, interrupting, "Mr. Gallo still has not demonstrated how any of this is relevant."

"Your Honor," Gallo replied, "a few more questions and you will see the relevancy."

"Start connecting the dots or I'm going to rule in the prosecution's favor."

Gallo said, "Agent Coyle, are you aware that my law firm represented Daniel DiVenzenzo at his criminal trial?"

With a smirk on his face, Agent Coyle looked at the jury and said, "If I'm not mistaken, you represent all the mobsters in the Battaglia family."

Judge Cerrato didn't like that response. Slamming down his gavel, he said, "Agent Coyle, stop trying to be clever. A yes-or-no answer will suffice."

Again, I winced. Each time the judge admonished Coyle, we lost points with jurors.

Gallo suddenly got a concerned look on his face. "Your Honor," he said, "may we approach the bench?"

Judge Cerrato waved us forward.

Gallo said, "I'd like to connect these dots, but I'm not sure I can do it in open court without causing a mistrial. Can we discuss this in your chambers?"

"You just now came to this conclusion?" I said sarcastically.

Judge Cerrato said, "Mr. Gallo, I'm losing my patience. I hope you can explain yourself in my chambers because I'm not happy."

Minutes later, we were standing in chambers before the judge, who was seated behind his desk, sucking an unfiltered Camel.

"This better be good," Judge Cerrato said.

Gallo replied, "Your Honor, we have copies of the tape recordings from the DiVenzenzo case with us today along with transcripts. They were turned over to my law firm before Mr. DiVenzenzo's trial by the U.S. Attorney's Office as part of pretrial discovery."

"Okay, counselor," Judge Cerrato said, "I'll bite. What's on these tape recordings?"

"The recordings and trial transcripts establish that Corrado DiVenzenzo made a telephone call to Nicholas Persico. During their conversation, Mr. DiVenzenzo can be heard complaining about the Gaccione crime family headed by Giuseppe 'Tiny' Nunzio. Mr. DiVenzenzo can be heard saying that the Gaccione family has been, in his words, 'trying to muscle in' on several lucrative contracts at refuse collection sites in Staten Island."

"Refuse collection sites? Do you mean landfills and dumps?" the judge asked.

"That's correct, Your Honor. Mr. DiVenzenzo can be heard asking Mr. Persico what he wants to do about this incursion. And Mr. Persico's response is that he does not want Mr. DiVenzenzo to do anything. He can be heard telling Mr. DiVenzenzo that under no circumstances should he or anyone else take any action against the Gaccione criminal organization, Mr. Nunzio, or anyone associated with Mr. Nunzio."

"What was the date of this telephone call?" the judge asked.

"The call was made on December 28, 1979. It was the last piece of evidence that the bureau provided to us before Mr. DiVenzenzo's trial on January 7, 1980."

"And the point of all this?" Judge Cerrato asked.

"Your Honor," Gallo said, "my law firm filed a motion before this trial for full discovery, including all 'Brady material.'"

It suddenly became clear to everyone what Gallo was doing. Brady material was a reference to the 1963 U.S. Supreme Court case *Brady v. Maryland*, which required prosecutors to give defense attorneys any and all evidence that might exonerate a defendant of a crime.

Looking at me, Gallo said, "The Westchester District Attorney's Office did not tell us about these wiretaps or about Mr. Persico's directive that no one harm anyone connected with the Gaccione family, especially Mr. Nunzio and his family."

"Your Honor," I said, "we didn't turn them over because I had absolutely no idea they existed. This is the first time I've heard of them. But in any event, I do not see how they would exonerate Persico in this murder case. They aren't relevant."

"Your Honor," Gallo replied, "these tapes establish our client's state of mind at the time of the Isabella Ricci murder. They speak directly to this case. They show he had no intent to harm any Nunzio family member and that would include Isabella Ricci, who was the daughter of Giuseppe Nunzio."

From the look on Judge Cerrato's face, I knew I had to do damage control and do it fast.

"Your Honor," I said, "the defense has just admitted to you that their client is an experienced crime boss. Surely he would have known that there was a good chance that all of his calls were being tape-recorded. This entire conversation could have been a ruse to establish any lack of criminal intent on his part. It could be a cover story. You can't believe what he says on those tapes. They are nothing more than self-serving statements."

Gallo said, "Nice try, Ms. Fox, but the facts are clear. You worked this case with Agent Coyle. He let you read his logbooks and you called him as a witness. Agent Coyle has acknowledged that he participated in the investigation of Mr. DiVenzenzo. Agent Coyle was intimately familiar with these tape recordings. His participation in both cases created a legal nexus or connection between the FBI and the District Attorney's Office. That clearly makes the tape recordings Brady material that should have been turned over by the D.A.'s office to the defense. Ms. Fox can't pick and choose what exculpatory evidence to show us."

I said, "Judge, the defense already knew about them. They already had them."

"That's not the point, counselor, and you know it," Judge Cerrato replied. "The issue is whether or not your office withheld Brady material that Agent Coyle and the FBI knew might help Mr. Persico prove his innocence. Let's go back into court."

From the irritation in his voice, this was not going well. When we returned to court, Judge Cerrato immediately asked the jury to leave. As soon as they were gone, he announced that he was going to question Agent Coyle on the record.

Coyle gave me a puzzled look.

"Agent Coyle," the judge said, "let me remind you that you are under oath and subject to a potential perjury charge."

For the first time since he'd taken the witness stand, Coyle looked nervous. Threats of perjury do that to witnesses.

Judge Cerrato got right to the point. "Agent Coyle, prior to the commencement of the Persico indictment, did the FBI make the D.A.'s office aware of tape-recorded conversations between defendant Nicholas Persico and Daniel DiVinzenzo?"

"No, sir," he said quietly. "I did not tell Ms. Fox or her associates about the tape recordings. I didn't think they were relevant to this case."

"Well, Agent Coyle, we're about to find out if they are relevant," Judge Cerrato said. Judge Cerrato ordered his bailiff to play the relevant portions of the recordings that Gallo had mentioned. By the time they stopped playing, I knew we were sunk. To make certain there were no misunderstandings, Judge Cerrato asked Coyle one more time: "Do you know if anyone in the FBI discussed these tapes with anyone in the Westchester District Attorney's Office?"

"I don't think so. I didn't tell Ms. Fox about them."

"Give me a specific yes-or-no answer. Did the FBI turn these tapes over to the Westchester County District Attorney's Office? Anyone at all—the D.A. or any of his chiefs?"

"No, sir, not to my knowledge."

"Agent Coyle," the judge asked, "did you participate directly in the investigation of Persico with the D.A.'s office?"

"Yes. I was briefed and cooperated with Chief Steven Vanderhoot, the head of the Organized Crime Bureau in the Westchester D.A.'s office, and I assisted Ms. Fox."

"Did you at any time advise either Vanderhoot or Ms. Fox about these recordings verbally?"

"No, sir."

Judge Cerrato turned his attention to me. "Ms. Fox," he said, "I will not bother to put you under oath. Did you have any knowledge of the fact, or did the FBI, or D.A.'s office advise you, that these tapes existed?"

"No, Your Honor, I had no idea before today."

"Very well. We're going to take a ten-minute recess so that Ms. Fox can consult with her boss about this case. Let me further say that I believe that what I just heard is very problematic for the prosecution. Do you understand?" he said, looking directly at me.

I did. Judge Cerrato was telling me that the prosecution was in deep trouble.

By the time I got to Whitaker's office, I was fuming. Agent Coyle and his boss should have known those tapes fell under Brady material. What I didn't know is whether my boss and his chiefs had known about the tapes and intentionally withheld them from me. From the start, I'd told them that I had reservations about indicting Persico on such little evidence and that an indictment would be driven by publicity, not evidence. I sailed by Miss Potts's desk without saying a word to her.

"He's expecting you," she called over my shoulder.

Under my breath I whispered, "No shit!"

Steinberg, Myerson, and Vanderhoot had already assumed their positions around Whitaker's desk.

It was me against them. O'Brien, my sidekick in most of these confrontations, was left cooling his heels outside the courtroom, since he wasn't an attorney. Perhaps if he'd been there, he might have calmed me down, because I was about to lose it. "I need to know if I just got fucked down there or did all of us get fucked by Coyle and Longhorn?" My ears could not believe what my mouth had just said.

Whitaker couldn't believe it, either. "Don't you dare question my integrity," he said in an angry voice. "I didn't know a damn thing about those tapes." He glanced at Vanderhoot and said, "Did those FBI bastards tell you about any of this?"

Vanderhoot said, "Absolutely not, sir. I didn't know about the tapes. I swear it."

Steinberg jumped in. "Forget about the tapes. It's too late to fix that. We need to do damage control. I say we go forward with this trial and let Judge

Cerrato or the jury take responsibility for dismissing it. It will look bad if we dismiss the charges."

"Are you kidding me?" I said. "This case needs to be dismissed immediately."

Vanderhoot chimed in. "We still have a chance. The jurors know this is a mob boss. We could get a hung jury if we keep pushing it."

Myerson joined in the chorus. "In your closing, you could emphasize how much the Persico and Nunzio families hated each other. The jurors haven't heard those tapes."

"Are you living in a dream world?" I asked, fully aware that I was being insubordinate. "We didn't give them Brady material, and if we move forward, the judge is going to let Gallo play those tapes."

The intercom buzzed and Miss Potts said, "Sir, Judge Cerrato is on line one."

Whitaker snatched the phone and put it to his ear, leaving us to wonder what Cerrato was telling him. Whitaker didn't say a word until the judge had finished his tirade. Finally, he said, "Ms. Fox doesn't have any more witnesses, but we're going forward with this trial."

I couldn't believe my ears. I was being sent to a firing squad.

A few minutes later, I was back in the courtroom with the jury seated. The judge gave Gallo permission to enter the FBI wiretaps as evidence and allowed him to play the snippet where Persico could be heard clearly instructing DiVenzenzo to not take any actions against Nunzio or any of his family members. As soon as the tape stopped, the judge asked me if I had any more witnesses.

At this point, I was simply going through the motions.

"No, Your Honor," I said. "The people rest."

"Mr. Gallo, you may begin your defense."

"Your Honor, we ask that the jury be excluded at this time. We have an application to the court."

"Fine, bailiff, remove the jury," Judge Cerrato said.

Here it comes, I thought.

Gallo immediately asked that the murder charge against his client be dismissed because the state had not established its case beyond a reasonable doubt.

Judge Cerrato looked down at me and said, "In my many years on the bench, I have not seen such a flimsy excuse for a murder charge. Ms. Fox, as a representative of the people, you are responsible for upholding the highest standards of conduct. The eyewitness identification of Persico by Agent Coyle in view of Mr. Mancini's statement in the newspaper creates substantial doubt regarding that eyewitness identification. The fact that Agent Coyle would believe that Persico had committed a murder and the FBI did not bother to obtain a search warrant for the supposed bloody clothing that Persico wore at the crime scene and changed out of at the butcher shop later that afternoon raises serious doubt in my mind regarding Agent Coyle's testimony and the value of this circumstantial evidence."

I thought about defending Coyle by stating the obvious—that an experienced killer such as the Butcher would have known to destroy bloody clothing after a murder—but it seemed pointless. Judge Cerrato was in no mood to be interrupted.

"Further," he said, "I have heard no evidence in this case that links Persico to this murder other than the circumstantial evidence that you have thrown at him, hoping it will stick. The only evidence you have is Agent Coyle's testimony, which frankly I find to be questionable in terms of its credibility and problematic in that Agent Coyle failed to turn over potentially exculpatory evidence as required by *Brady v. Maryland*. For these reasons, I am granting the defense's motion and dismissing the charge lodged against Mr. Persico."

Judge Cerrato turned his attention to the Butcher. "Sir," he said, "you are free to go and on behalf of this court, I would like to publicly apologize to you for the time that you have spent in jail awaiting this trial."

As soon as the judge left the room, Gallo and Conti hugged their client. I heard cussing from behind me and noticed the Nunzio family members hurrying from the courtroom.

Agent Coyle tugged on my arm.

"Dani," he said. "Look, I'm really sorry about how—"

"Don't talk to me!" I exclaimed. I shoved my files into my briefcase and marched out of the courtroom. A gaggle of reporters had surrounded Gallo, Conti, and their client as soon as they exited the building. I watched Gallo break away to answer questions and, undoubtedly, assail me and our office, while Conti and Persico continued toward a waiting car.

The mobster and his lawyer were about ten feet from the limousine when a man wearing a black jogging suit appeared from a car parked nearby with a raised handgun. The sound of his pistol firing caused immediate panic as reporters and onlookers scrambled for cover or fell to the ground. The attacker's first shot hit Persico in his chest, knocking him to the sidewalk. A stunned Conti stood in shock over his client, uncertain what to do. The gunman continued to shoot as he walked deliberately toward Persico, this time aiming at the Butcher's face.

Crack. Crack. Crack.

Each shot caused Persico's body to shake from the bullet's impact. I sensed movement from behind me and remained standing still as two court security guards burst from the building's entrance with their guns drawn. Both began firing at the assailant. A White Plains police officer who had been standing across the street when the first shots were fired ran toward the lone gunman. As I watched, Persico's assailant collapsed, discharging his final two shots into the sidewalk near his feet. Within seconds, it was over. Persico was dead and so was his killer. One bystander had been wounded by a stray shot. A reporter had a busted nose from being hit by a television camera when its operator swung the heavy device sideways, pointing away from Gallo to take footage of the shooter. Defense Attorney Conti was rushed to a hospital after complaining of chest pains.

The assailant who'd killed Persico would be identified later as a low-level member of the Gaccione crime family. I wondered if he had voted for Whitaker in his last campaign, because he'd certainly done our office a favor by giving the evening news a more sensational story to lead with that night than our blotched courtroom drama.

38

I FELT BEAT-UP WHEN I ARRIVED AT MY OFFICE THE FOLLOW-ing morning. I'd not slept well. I could still hear Judge Cerrato's sting-ing words in my ears. I had fallen on my sword in the courtroom for a case that I'd been reluctant to prosecute. When I reached my desk, the receptionist informed me that Agent Coyle had already called five times.

"Good to hear your voice," Coyle chirped when he came on the line.

I thought he would be apologetic and ask for forgiveness. Instead, he chattered on about how great it was that Persico had been gunned down outside the courthouse. "An assassin killed the Butcher and I took out Tiny Nunzio. All in all, yesterday didn't go so badly."

"Are you fucking kidding me?" I replied. My profanity got his attention.

"What's your problem?" he asked.

"Don't try to gloss over what happened in court," I said. "Why the hell didn't you tell me about those Brady materials?"

"I didn't think they were important."

"Judge Cerrato certainly thought they were, didn't he?" I replied sarcasti-cally. "Gallo and Conti certainly thought they were, didn't they?"

"Who cares? They're assholes. Those tape recordings were a sham. You thought so yourself when you first heard them. Persico's attorneys just got lucky exploiting a loophole but in the end justice prevailed because Persico is dead."

"Justice didn't prevail and that loophole happens to be federal law," I said. "You're an FBI agent sworn to protect those laws. I don't know whether you're a crooked cop, a moron, or both!"

"Who in the hell do you think you are to talk to me like this?" Coyle exploded.

"Who am I?" I repeated. "I'm the assistant district attorney who got her ass chewed off yesterday by a judge because of your arrogance, stupidity, and your asshole FBI ways."

"And I'm the FBI agent who saved that same ass when you were kidnapped. Don't you ever forget that!"

The gloves were off and during the next several minutes, our conversation went from ugly to uglier. At one point, I accused the FBI of intentionally withholding the Brady material to undermine our prosecution so that Jack Longhorn and the Justice Department could pursue a federal racketeering case against Persico without us. Coyle called me paranoid and accused me of having a grudge about Longhorn.

"You're being dramatic and overreacting," Coyle said. "Did it ever dawn on you that maybe you aren't as smart as you think you are?"

"And who do you think you are, Albert Einstein?" I asked. I couldn't believe that I'd actually kissed this guy.

"It's time you woke up and realized you're nothing but a two-bit local prosecutor who gets away with her uppity attitude because she has a pair of tits and nice legs. If you weren't a woman, no one would pay attention to you and your constant whining."

I'd tapped into a vicious side of Coyle that I'd not seen before. Before I could react, he let loose with attack. "You lost in court yesterday because you're a loser, just like your loser, baby-killer boyfriend. I thought maybe Longhorn was wrong about you, but what he told me was dead-on."

"Fuck you. I'm going to hang up now," I said.

"Longhorn called you a stupid cunt," he said. "And he was right!"

I slammed down my phone.

I was still fuming when O'Brien knocked on my open office door two hours later. I waved him in.

"Rough day yesterday," he said. "You got thrown to the wolves."

"I should have told Whitaker to send Vanderhoot to the wolves when they insisted I go forward with that indictment."

"That wouldn't have worked. Whitaker would have canned you for insubordination and then what? Remember that before you, no one gave a damn about battered women around here. You go, and this program goes. I go. Remember that."

He was right.

"Here's something you got to see," he said, handing me a folder. "It ain't pretty."

Inside was an eight-by-ten-inch black-and-white photograph of a nude man's body. The victim had been wrapped with chain and tied to four concrete cinder blocks.

"A dredging crew fished him out of Kensico Reservoir," O'Brien explained. "Recognize him?"

The body was too badly decomposed. I said, "Besides making me wish I hadn't eaten breakfast, what's the point of this?"

"That's Donnie Gilmore, our sexual stalker."

I took another look at the bloated face. "Oh my God! Who did this? A jealous husband?"

O'Brien said, "Check out his chest."

Someone had cut a long slit from Gilmore's pubic area up to his neck.

"That lets the gases out so he wouldn't come floating up," O'Brien said. "The killer knew what he was doing."

"Tiny Nunzio's crew?" I asked. "Maybe Nunzio found out he was stalking Isabella."

"He did more than stalk her," O'Brien said.

"We got another homicide tied to the Isabella Ricci murder," I said, rising from my desk. I walked over and taped the photo of Gilmore on my wall of murder photos.

"I thought you'd be taking them down today, not putting more up," O'Brien said as he dropped into the chair across from my desk and helped himself to some of the chocolates that I keep in a bowl for clients. "Your boss won't be pleased if he drops by and sees your display."

"Why do I have to remind you that he's your boss, too, and Whitaker hasn't ever darkened my door. He summons us to Mount Olympus."

O'Brien said, "Maybe it's time to get back to domestic abuse cases, Dani. We got other dragons to slay."

I pointed up to a photo of Isabella Ricci. It was one that was taken before her brutal murder. It was a head shot and the raven-haired beauty looked like a model. She looked happy.

"I have this here to remember what she looked like before she was cut to pieces," I said. "This is the woman I made a promise to on New Year's Eve."

"Your New Year's resolution," O'Brien said. "Sometimes, you can't keep them."

"Sometimes," I replied, "you got to." I glanced at the wall and said, "I'm missing something. It's right in front of us but I can't see it."

"Try fresh eyes."

"Fresh eyes?"

"You got a case you can't figure out. You go back to square one. Start over. Forget about everything you've already done."

Looking at my files perched in a cardboard box, he said, "The answer is somewhere in that box."

I thought about what he said and looked at the photo of Isabella Ricci.

"O'Brien," I said, "you're a genius."

"I know," he said, scooping up another handful of Junior Mints. "What took you so long to figure that out?"

"The first question that popped into my head when I walked into that apartment and saw Isabella hanging there was 'Who was her lover?' And that's the one question no one has ever answered."

"So how are you going to answer it?"

"By asking the most logical suspect. Little Pauly Persico."

39

"YOU'RE GONNA DO WHAT?" O'BRIEN ASKED, NEARLY choking on a candy.

"I'm going to ask Little Pauly if he was having an affair with Isabella Ricci."

"His father hasn't even been planted yet. Probably not the best timing for asking that hothead if he was banging Isabella."

"My gut has been telling me from day one that something isn't right about her murder. It all begins with Isabella Ricci, and if you look at these murders, the only thing they have in common is her death."

"Maybe you just got bad gas," O'Brien said. "That's why your stomach hurts."

I picked up my bag and started out the door.

"Christ almighty, wait for me," he complained, scrambling out of his chair. "I'll drive you. But you're gonna get us both killed."

Nicholas Persico's house was on a hilltop in the historic Cedar Knolls neighborhood of Bronxville, about fifteen minutes from his Yonkers butcher shop. Built in the 1920s in a Spanish style, it had a light yellow stucco exterior, a red tile roof, and was surrounded by manicured grounds. All of the windows were protected by iron grillwork but there was no wall around the property.

O'Brien parked across the street and motioned toward several black Lincolns stationed directly in front of the residence. All of them had drivers and none of those men looked especially welcoming.

"Dani, the fact that you're an A.D.A. and a woman isn't going to mean squat," he said.

I flung open the car door and started across the street. One of the chauffeurs saw me and immediately stepped from his Lincoln to block the stone walkway leading to the house. "Where you going?" he asked.

"I'm Assistant District Attorney Dani Fox from the Westchester District Attorney's Office and the man coming up behind me is Detective Thomas O'Brien," I announced.

"So what?" he replied, giving me the once-over with his eyes. "I've seen you at the courthouse. You got a lot of balls showing up here."

I started to walk around him, but he turned and blocked my path.

"You got a warrant? 'Cause this is private property," he said.

"You an attorney moonlighting as a driver?" I asked sarcastically. I noticed that four other drivers had encircled us.

"Nobody goes up to the house without an invite from the family and I know you don't got one of them."

O'Brien seemed nonplussed about the odds, but I knew he didn't want to put me in danger. He said, "Maybe we should come back later."

But I stood my ground. "Tell Little Pauly that I don't think his father killed Isabella Ricci. I'm here to help clear his name and possibly avoid more violence between the Gacciones and Battaglias."

The driver sneered. "You kidding me? Aren't you the broad who was just busting Mr. Persico's balls in court?"

"If Little Pauly hears I was here and you didn't let me talk to him, then it will be your balls that will be getting busted."

The driver pondered that for a moment and then said, "Wait here."

Everyone watched as he walked up the stone path. None of the other knuckle-draggers around us spoke. They simply tried to look threatening. It worked. Finally, the driver returned from the mountaintop.

"Little Pauly says you can come up but not the cop. And I need to check you for a wire."

"You gotta be kidding."

"Them's the rules."

"You do not put your hands on me," I said firmly. "But if there's a woman up at the house, she can frisk away."

He just stared, so I added, "And if you or anyone here lays a finger on me, I'll see to it that you're arrested for assault."

The driver looked up at the house and then back at me. Little Pauly must have been waiting. "Okay," he said. "You come but the cop stays put."

"You sure you want to go up there alone?" O'Brien asked.

"It's probably safer than being here with these guys," I said.

"You got fifteen minutes," O'Brien said. "You've already been kidnapped once."

I started to move to the steps, but the driver stopped me. "Hey, no purse. You could have a gun in there."

Actually, I did. I handed my bag to O'Brien to hold, which caused the goons watching him to break into ugly grins. I fell into step behind my tour guide and walked up the hill to the front arched door, which was painted bright red and protected by a thick iron grille. He rapped on the door and one of the biggest men I've ever seen unlocked the gate. I stepped into a narrow foyer with a large mirror and pale yellow walls.

"She ain't been checked for a wire," the driver said. "She wants a woman to frisk her."

The giant said, "Don't move—both of you." He disappeared through an archway to our left and returned moments later with a familiar face: Angelica Persico from the butcher's shop and courtroom. She had been crying and at first I thought her tears had caused her mascara to run, but on second glance, I saw that she had two black eyes. "Leave us alone," she told the two men. "I'll call you after I'm done."

"Little Pauly told me to stay put," the brute said.

"And I just told you to get the hell out of here and give us some privacy," she replied. Speaking to the driver, Angelica said, "You can go back out to the car."

Both men looked nervously at each other and did as she had ordered.

"Thank you," I said softly. "I'm not wearing a wire."

She gave me an angry look. "Take off your jacket and unbutton your blouse. Otherwise, Paul won't meet with you."

"What?"

"I need to see your chest and feel your back."

I got the impression that this was more about Little Pauly lording his power over me than checking for a wire. I happened to be wearing a pantsuit—gray pants with a gray jacket over a checkered silk top with gray and white polka dots. I removed the jacket and undid the buttons, opening my shirt a crack to expose my abdomen. I wasn't wearing a bra. "Take off the blouse or stand still while I touch you," she said.

I didn't like the idea of being topless so I said, "Feel away."

She reached her hands inside my shirt and ran her fingers along my back. Then she moved them to my front and ran them up my chest over my breasts. She was rough. Dropping to her knees, she ran her fingers along each of my legs. Satisfied, she said, "I'll tell Pauly." I'd finished buttoning my blouse and had put on my jacket when the giant lug who'd met me at the door rounded the corner, followed by a powerfully built, dark-haired man wearing an expensive black suit and Ray-Ban sunglasses.

"You tried to frame my father," he said. "Now you come here. What the hell do you want?" He removed his Ray-Bans, revealing ink-colored pupils. His nose had a ridge on it from being broken.

"I want to help clear your father's name by finding the real killer."

"Ain't you a saint," he sneered.

"I need to know the name of Isabella Ricci's lover."

"How's that going to help clear my father's name?"

"It could help me understand why your father went there."

"If he wanted you to know that, he would have told you. You're wasting my time." He turned to leave.

"Was it you?" I asked. "Were you sleeping with Isabella Ricci?"

He stopped. "You think I don't get all the pussy I want? You think I got to chase after Tiny Nunzio's daughter to get laid? You think this is some Romeo and Juliet melodrama you got going here? Is that the best you got?" He started walking back toward me and with each step he got more animated.

"You accusing me of murder? You accusing me of hanging that broad on a hook and butchering her?"

He stopped inches from my face.

"Listen, you smug bitch. I wouldn't have fucked that scag with someone else's dick. Now get out of my father's house!" he yelled. I obliged.

O'Brien was waiting at the sidewalk. The goons around him parted, like the Red Sea for Moses.

We'd driven about a block away when O'Brien asked, "Was Little Pauly banging Isabella Ricci?"

"I don't think so."

"Great, we just put our lives at risk for nothing?" he asked.

"No. I got the answer I wanted."

40

WILL WAS SITTING ON THE TOP PORCH STEP AT MY house when I arrived home after work. He stood when I approached him. "A peace offering," he said, lifting a bouquet of roses in one hand and a bottle of Dr Pepper in the other. "You said you wanted to focus on the Persico trial and needed space. Well, he's dead now."

I slipped by him without speaking and unlocked my front door. "Let's get this over with," I said unenthusiastically.

Will followed me to my kitchen, where I sat down at the table, leaving him standing awkwardly near the doorway. "May I sit down?" he asked.

"Sure."

He put the flowers and bottle on the table between us. "I've come to say, 'I'm sorry.'"

"You already did that and it wasn't enough. It still isn't."

"What else can I do?"

"I don't know. You hid information from me."

"Dani, we've been a couple long enough for you to know who I am. The past is the past. I made mistakes. I have regrets. What's the point of going over and over the same thing? The reason I'm here now is that I don't want to make another mistake. I don't want to lose you."

When I didn't immediately respond, he said, "I thought you loved me. But I'm not going to spend my life apologizing for things that happened before I even met you."

"You keep wanting this to be about what you did in college with Moon-

PART FIVE

THE PIECES COME TOGETHER

I would rather trust a woman's instinct than a man's reason.

—STANLEY BALDWIN, BRITISH PRIME MINISTER

41

I TELEPHONED ADALINA AT THE THREE B'S BEAUTY SHOP
from my house before going to work the next morning and told her
that I needed a favor.

"With your hair?" she asked.

"Always," I replied, smiling. "But no, I'd like you to do some detective
work."

"Goodie. I'd make a damn good cop."

"This has to be between the two of us."

"Honey, you'd be surprised at the secrets I keep."

"Can you find where Nicholas Persico's daughter, Angelica, gets her hair
done?"

"Them mob girls travel in packs. I'll find 'em."

When I got to work an hour later, there were six new domestic violence
cases waiting on my desk. I started to read them, but I had a difficult time
concentrating. I kept glancing at the photos on my wall—at a snapshot of
Isabella Ricci from happier days, before she'd been sliced and tortured.

"What am I missing, Isabella?" I asked aloud.

"Talking to yourself now or the dead?" O'Brien said, walking unan-
nounced into my office.

"I was thinking about you this morning in the shower," I said.

"Now that's an image."

"Not you, but what you said about fresh eyes. What if we started down
the wrong path from the very beginning on these cases?"

"How's that?"

"We've been looking at Isabella's murder and the rest of them as being mob related. Ironically, I think Gallo might have been on to something when they told us that these cases were not mob related."

"What else would they be?"

"What if they had nothing to do with the Mafia?"

"Who else would have killed them?"

"I don't know, but what if someone did? Someone not even connected to the mob?"

"Convince me."

"Okay, wash the mob out of your mind. What are the other links that tie these murders together?"

"They're all dead."

"C'mon, O'Brien, work with me."

"They knew Isabella," he said.

"That's right."

"And the killer or killers used a knife," he said. "That's it."

We both stared at the wall and for a moment were quiet. And then I saw it. Grabbing Isabella's file, I pulled her autopsy, Mancini's autopsy, and finally Marco Ricci's paperwork.

"What the hell you doing?" O'Brien asked.

"Solving these homicides," I said. I held up a finger, motioning him to be quiet, and moved from my desk to the wall, where I studied the photograph of Donnie Gilmore.

"Come here!" I said excitedly. "Look at his right hand."

O'Brien joined me. "Yeah, what am I looking at?"

"He's only got four fingers," I said.

"Maybe a fish ate one."

"Since when did sharks start swimming in the Kensico Reservoir? That finger was deliberately cut off! It's a straight cut."

Hurrying back to my desk, I held up the autopsy photos. "Every victim is missing a body part. Isabella Ricci was missing her pinkie finger, Roman Mancini was missing a toe, Maggie Mancini was missing a thumb, and Marco Ricci was—"

O'Brien interrupted me. "Missing his dick. Trust me, I remember that one."

"Now we got Gilmore missing a finger. They have that in common, too."

O'Brien twirled the toothpick in his mouth, which is what he did when he was thinking, as opposed to removing it, which is what he did when he was angry. "You ever hear about that nut the Feds caught in Montana a while back?"

"Which nut? It's a big state."

"Back in '73, a kid, girl, only about seven, turned up missing from her parents' campsite. She'd been abducted. No clues, so the locals called this new FBI unit at Quantico. They look at crime scenes. They predicted the killer was a white male, in his twenties. They said he'd kidnapped other kids. A few months later, they caught the creep and he fit the profile to a T."

I shrugged. "What's your point?"

"That killer was collecting body parts. Souvenirs. The bureau said he was a new type of killer. A one-man murder machine. This new unit specializes in nut jobs like that."

I glanced up at my wall of photos and said, "Is it really possible that one killer might have done this? And why? You've got to tell me if you think I'm crazy here."

"Call the FBI."

"Then you're the one who's crazy. Coyle and Longhorn are convinced these murders have been solved. They aren't going to help me."

"Not them. That new unit at Quantico. They got fresh eyes."

I said excitedly, "I could just kiss you, O'Brien."

"Don't, and stop thinking about me in the shower," he said. "That's creepy and I already got enough women imagining me naked."

I made a horrible look on my face while he grinned and reached for my Junior Mints, emptying the bowl on my desk. "You need more candy," he said, walking out the door.

My phone rang. It was Adalina. "You still looking for Angelica Persico? 'Cause she goes to a shop called Hair By Design, over on Broadway Avenue. One of the girls I went to beauty school with told me. She said Angelica's got a manicure appointment two hours from now."

That gave me time to call the FBI's Behavioral Science Unit before driving to Hair By Design. "Behavioral Science," a gruff voice answered. "Who do you want?"

"I want to speak to you if you're one of the FBI profilers I've read about." I quickly introduced myself and said, "I need fresh eyes on the murder of a woman."

"Was she married?" the voice asked.

"Yes," I replied.

"Then her husband did it," he said. "Or her boyfriend."

"What?" I said. I thought maybe he was joking.

"You just said you work for a domestic violence unit," he replied. "And I just told you who probably killed her. We don't waste our time on obvious cases. Goodbye."

The line went dead.

I called back and when that same voice answered, I said, "Are all profilers as rude as you are?"

In an irritated voice, he said, "Who exactly are you calling for?"

I didn't understand. "I just told you that I have a complicated murder that needs fresh eyes. I want to talk to a profiler."

"Young lady," he said, "I know you want to speak to a profiler. What I don't know is on whose behalf you are calling for."

I got it. Because I was a woman, he mistakenly assumed I was someone's secretary.

"I'm calling on behalf of myself, or to make it ever more clear for you—me, myself, and I. I'm an assistant D.A. in Westchester County, New York. I'm in charge of this murder investigation and I hope your skills as a profiler are better than your manners."

"I told you we only take tricky cases."

"I got a killer collecting body parts," I said. "I've got five bodies so far."

The line stayed silent.

I wondered if he'd hung up.

"Are you still there?" I finally asked.

"Yes. What kind of body parts?"

"Fingers, toes, a thumb, and a penis."

"A penis, now that's interesting. Send me what you got, especially photographs."

"It would help if I knew your name."

"Special Agent Todd Wheeler."

"The first victim was a woman named Isabella Ricci," I said.

"Wait while I grab a pencil."

When he came back on line, I spelled Isabella's name.

"Keep going," he said.

I gave him the other victims' names and said, "Let me give you some background about each—"

Wheeler interrupted. "I got their names. For now, that's all I need. I'm not interested in anybody else's opinion. Just send the police reports and the photos. I'll call you back if I'm interested. Don't call me again. I'm busy. Goodbye."

42

P ROMINENTLY DISPLAYED IN THE WINDOW AT HAIR BY
Design was a neon sign advertising UNISEX CUTS, but I didn't see
any men when I entered the Yonkers boutique. Good, I thought.
If Angelica Persico was here, she was here without bodyguards.

The seven chairs were occupied by twenty-something customers sporting
big, rock band, teased hairstyles. The smell of aerosol spray permeated the
noisy salon. Angelica was having her nails polished near the rear of the shop.
The manicurist at the table next to her didn't have a customer, so I walked
over and sat down.

Angelica gave me a casual glance and then did a double take. She spoke in
Italian to the woman who'd just begun working on my nails.

"I'm sorry," the manicurist told me, "but I got another customer coming in."

I surveyed the shop and said, "When she arrives, I'll gladly step aside. But
why don't you go ahead for now?"

The manicurist gave Angelica a frightened glance and said, "I'm sorry but
it's time for my break now." She walked away, leaving me at her table. During
this entire exchange, Angelica had looked straight ahead, ignoring me and
pretending she had nothing to do with what had just happened.

I wasn't going to be rebuffed so easily. Besides, I really could have used a
manicure. "Angelica," I said, "I want to ask you about your father and Isabella Ricci."

"Leave me alone," she said.

"I don't believe your father killed her," I said.

"You prosecuted him!" she said angrily. She spoke again in Italian, this time to the woman polishing her nails, who immediately put down her tools and left the table.

Confronting me, Angelica said, "My father was just murdered. Have you no respect?"

It was time for my trump card.

"I know your secret," I said.

She pushed her chair back from the table and stood to leave. I whispered: "It's you."

I saw tears forming in her eyes. "Leave me alone," she said, her lips quivering.

I reached up and gently touched her arm. "I don't want to hurt or embarrass you. I just need to know the truth—for your father's sake."

She pushed my hand away. "Why? So you can sell some story to the tabloids? So you can be on television?"

"No, so I can catch the real killer."

"I can't be seen talking to you."

By this point, everyone in the shop was watching us.

I took a business card from my purse and pressed it into her hand. "Call me."

She read the number and announced in a voice loud enough for everyone to hear, "I told you to leave me alone!" She threw my card back at me and marched through the shop and out its doorway.

I started to follow her but one of the hairstylists stepped in front of me, causing me to stop. Several customers said something in Italian and for a moment, I thought I might have to literally fight my way out of the shop. "I'm an officer of the court!" I yelled. "Get out of my way before I have you arrested!"

The woman moved aside.

By the time I reached the sidewalk, Angelica was nowhere to be seen.

Our receptionist at the Domestic Violence Unit was waiting with yet another stack of pink return-call slips when I entered our lobby.

"Some woman just called," the receptionist said.

I was only half listening. I'd lost count on how many callbacks I needed to make and didn't care that another had been added to my list.

Continuing, the receptionist said, "She refused to leave her name but said you two had just gotten your nails done and if you wanted to talk, you needed to call her in the next ten minutes or she'd been gone."

"When did she call?"

"About ten minutes ago," the receptionist said, curiously eyeing my unpolished nails.

I hurried to my office and dialed the return number. It rang once, twice, three times. Then a fourth, fifth, and sixth time. I was too late. Just as I was about to hang up, someone answered. "Angelica?" I asked.

"Are you tape-recording our conversation?" she replied.

"No," I answered truthfully.

"Are you planning on having me testify?"

"At what?" I said. "I don't know where any of this is leading."

For a moment, I thought she might hang up, but she didn't.

"I don't want to appear in court," she said. "If you call me, I will deny everything. Do you understand?"

I thought about telling her that she wouldn't really have a choice if I put her on the witness stand, but there was no point in possibly frightening her even more than she already was. "I understand you don't want to be called," I said.

"In the shop, you said, 'It's you.' What did you mean?"

"You're the reason why your father went to that apartment and confronted Isabella Ricci. You're her secret lover."

I could hear her breathing and crying.

"We were so careful," she said. "How did you find out?"

"Isabella's lover always wore a hat and coat. Why? Her lover refused to speak to Roman Mancini when they met each other in the stairwell. Why? But the giveaway was your father's limo. He would never have allowed anyone else at the butcher's shop to use his car except for a family member. That left only you and your brothers. One of them is married and Little Pauly has his own car and driver. That left you—you worked at the shop, you had access to your father's car anytime you wanted it."

"I used it for errands," she said. "Whenever we ran out of deli supplies, I had his driver take me out. When I first began going on Tuesdays and Fridays, no one noticed. Then my father got suspicious. He thought I was meeting some man. If it had been a man—even a married man—he wouldn't have said much. But a woman—he couldn't stand that."

"He beat you?"

"Of course he did. He called me names. Said I was violating God's sacred laws."

"But you kept seeing her."

"I loved her. She loved me."

"Your father went to see her to put an end to it."

"He was going to threaten her. He thought she was just some butch bull dyke."

"What happened in that apartment?"

"He couldn't scare her. He couldn't do nothing. Not when she told him she was Giuseppe Nunzio's daughter. If she'd been a nobody, he could have killed her. But not Nunzio's kid. She was alive when he left that day."

"How do you know that? You weren't there."

"He told me. When he came back to the shop. He called me a disgrace. He took off his belt and beat me. For the first time, I fought back. I ripped his shirt."

That must have been why Persico had changed his clothing that afternoon, I thought. But I didn't interrupt her.

"I thought he'd kill me, but Carmine Caruso stopped him. You got to understand, he couldn't kill Nunzio's daughter, but he could kill me. He threatened to kill me if I ever saw her again."

"Your father was in that apartment between the hours of three-thirty and five-thirty when Isabella was tortured and killed," I said.

"No, he wasn't."

"Yes, he was," I replied. "An FBI agent was tailing him."

"That agent lied. We got proof."

"Agent Coyle lied?" I said, genuinely surprised. "What proof?"

"Videotapes."

"What tapes?" I asked, dumbfounded.

"That Friday, Carmine Caruso made me stay in my father's office while he went to the apartment. I was watching the monitors that we got at the shop. They show the front lobby and back door. I was watching for my father. I was scared he'd killed Isabella. When he came back, the time was on the screen like it always was. It was three-thirty. If you don't believe me, ask my father's attorneys."

"Gallo and Conti have that videotape?"

"Yeah, we all knew that agent was lying," she said. "My father knew."

"Why didn't anyone tell me?"

"They said you'd claim the tapes were fake. They had them at the trial, but the judge dismissed the case so they kept quiet."

"The person who murdered Isabella cut the cord from the clock radio at three-thirty-five," I said. "If your father was with you at the butcher's shop, that means the killer must have seen your father leave Isabella's place and gone in immediately afterward to kill her."

"I have to get home," she said. "I'll be missed."

"Wait? Did Isabella ever mention a man named Gilmore, who lived on the second floor with his wife? He was stalking her."

"Yes. Her father sent men to scare him. He knew better than to mess with her."

"How about Marco Ricci? Could he have killed her?"

"Marco didn't have the cojones." Angelica began to sob. "They're expecting me at home."

"Just one more name, please?" I said.

"My brother, Little Pauly?" she said. "That's who you suspect. He wasn't in Yonkers. He was in Miami. He didn't do it. He blames me for our father's death. He hates me now. They all do."

"Are you in danger? Do you need my help?"

"How? You think you can hide me in a shelter somewhere?"

"I can try. I saw your black eyes at the house."

"No. We never talked. You promised me."

43

I WAS SITTING AT MY OFFICE DESK THINKING ABOUT ANGEL-
ica Persico when my receptionist buzzed me. "Some rude and really
angry FBI guy from Virginia called while you were on the phone," she
told me. "He wants to speak to you right now."

I dialed Agent Todd Wheeler's office at the FBI's Behavioral Science Unit
and he answered on the first ring. "What the hell have you gotten me into?"
he complained.

"Not even a friendly hello?" I asked.

"I told you this morning I'm busy. I don't give a damn about what the
weather is in New York or whether you're having a good day. What I do give
a damn about is finding out why I got Jack Longhorn breathing down my
neck because of your phone call this morning."

"Jack Longhorn called you?" I asked.

"Didn't I just say that?" Anticipating my next question, Wheeler explained, "It's standard protocol whenever we get a request from local law
enforcement that we notify the appropriate FBI branch. We get a lot of loony
calls and the local offices help us weed them out. Longhorn claims you're a
weed."

I bet Longhorn had plenty to say about me. But I kept quiet.

Wheeler said, "Ten minutes after I had our secretary notify the New
York office about your phone call, I got Longhorn on the horn demanding
to know why I was wasting time digging into closed cases."

So much for keeping my investigation quiet.

Without pausing for a breath, Wheeler said, "You didn't tell me these were closed cases."

I started to speak, but Wheeler started up again. "If you'd told me that they were closed cases, then I would—"

I decided to interrupt; otherwise I wasn't going to get a word in. "Agent Wheeler," I said in a stern voice, "you told me during our call that you didn't want to hear what I had to say about the cases. All you wanted was for me to send you the police files and photographs, remember?"

"Yes," he said. "You shouldn't have listened to me."

"What kind of reply is that?" I asked. "Longhorn thinks these cases are closed but I don't think they should be. He doesn't know about the missing body parts. He's blamed these murders on the mob."

Wheeler didn't immediately respond. Clearly, he was thinking about what I'd just said. When he finally did speak, he said, "Did the FBI investigate these murders or did you locals do it?"

"We 'locals' did it. I'm gathering up our files for you."

"How badly do you want my help?" he asked.

"I called you, didn't I?"

"Longhorn is going to complain to your boss," Wheeler warned. "Can you take that sort of heat?"

"I'll handle it," I said, glancing at my wall of photos. "I made a promise that I intend to keep."

"How fast can you get me your photos and your files?"

"I can drive them down to Washington this afternoon."

"It would be better if I met you someplace away from our office. Let me think about it and call you back."

"If Longhorn is on your back, why are you doing this?"

"Longhorn's not my boss and my reasons don't concern you," he said. "You just make sure you bring me those autopsy reports." He ended our call.

I quickly collected the homicide files on my desk and then moved to the wall to gather up the photos and my note cards. Out in the hallway, I heard familiar voices. O'Brien was talking to Will.

"I'm not sure she's in her office," O'Brien said.

I turned from facing the wall just as Will knocked on my opened door. He looked in at me standing in front of my murder display.

"I thought those cases were solved," he said.

"That's why I'm taking them down."

"Don't lie to me, Dani," he said. "You're horrible at it. I can always tell when you lie."

"Unlike me, who never knew when you were lying," I replied.

Will noticed the photo of Donnie Gilmore. "Who's that guy? I recognize everyone else, but what's he got to do with the mob murders?"

"That's a very good question," a voice declared.

Will and I turned our attention away from my wall. Agent Coyle was standing in the doorway. "What are you doing here?" Will asked Coyle.

"I could ask the same question," Coyle replied.

I was angry at both of them for barging in. Addressing Coyle, I said, "I can't believe you have the nerve to show your face after our last telephone call."

He held up his hands as if he were surrendering and said, "I'm here on official business. How about lunch? A peace offering."

"I came to ask you to lunch," Will said.

"I'm not having lunch with either of you," I replied. "I want both of you out of my office. From now on, call and make an appointment. I'm busy."

"Dani, we really need to talk," Will said.

"So do we," Agent Coyle added with a smirk.

I spoke first to Will. "I'm at work. This isn't the place for us to have a personal conversation."

"Then let's go to lunch," he said.

"No!"

"Are you going to lunch with him?" Will asked.

"If I do, that's my business."

Will turned in a huff and started toward the door where Coyle was standing. The FBI agent did not step aside, but instead forced Will to turn sideways to slip by him.

"You made the smart choice," Coyle declared. "Where's a good place to grab a sandwich around here?"

"I have no intention of going to lunch with you," I said. "After what you did to me, my reputation, and the reputation of the Westchester District Attorney's Office, I don't want anything to do with you. Not to mention the fact that you called me a cunt."

"Actually, that was Longhorn," Coyle said, trying to make a joke of it. "I simply told you what he said."

"What's your official business?" I asked.

Coyle looked down at the floor as if he were ashamed. "I came to apologize for what I said in anger. It was inexcusable. It was unprofessional." He sounded sincere, but I wasn't buying it. I no longer trusted him and I didn't think that he'd driven all the way to White Plains to simply apologize to me. He had to have an ulterior motive. He said, "How about I go get us something to eat and bring it back here? Although sitting in your office will not be as comfortable as eating at a table in a nice restaurant—especially with photos of murder victims staring down at us."

"I have other plans and I'm in a hurry," I said.

Without asking permission, he crossed my office and began studying the remaining photos and note cards on my wall.

I didn't like it. "Agent Coyle, I just told you that I'm in a hurry. There's someplace I need to go."

"I didn't come here just to apologize," he said, while still examining my display. "Agent Longhorn sent me to have a friendly chitchat with you."

"What's Longhorn want?" I asked, playing dumb.

"He wants to know why you're still investigating these closed cases and he really wants to know why you went behind his back and contacted Quantico about them."

"I'm guessing Longhorn isn't a happy camper," I replied.

"None of us are and he won't be any happier when I tell him about your wall of photos." He reached up and tapped the picture of Isabella Ricci that I had taped on the wall, the one that showed her smiling months before her murder. "Longhorn sent me to tell you these are closed cases."

"I don't give a damn what Longhorn says."

Coyle chuckled and said, "I believe you. You might not care, but others do. Maybe you've forgotten that he's in charge of the New York field office and that makes him an assistant director of the FBI, which puts him near the top of the Justice Department food chain."

"He's also an asshole."

"Asshole or not, he's got powerful connections, and if he wants, he can use them."

"Are you threatening me, Agent Coyle?"

"No, not at all, just trying to educate you. To begin with, Assistant Director Longhorn can and will exert considerable pressure on your office. He can slow down requests that your local cops make to the FBI for help with lab tests and records checks. He can stop supporting joint investigations. And that's just for starters. If he really wants, he can get nasty."

"How nasty?"

"He knows District Attorney Whitaker has accepted a free membership to that exclusive country club that he loves so much. Do you think your boss wants agents snooping around the Westchester County D.A.'s office—especially at election time—asking about his membership and other perks?"

"Whitaker is clean. He's not doing anything illegal."

"You know that and I know that, but how do you think the public is going to react when word leaks out that the FBI is investigating the District Attorney's Office for possible malfeasance? We have ways of finding out potentially embarrassing things."

Agent Coyle may have thought I was totally ignorant, but I knew that Vanderhoot was his inside source. Continuing, Coyle said, "Your boss may be as clean as a whistle, but by the time the ballots are counted, the damage will already be done. He'll get booted out of office with a cloud over his head. And that's just what Longhorn can do to Whitaker." He took his gaze off the wall and looked directly at me. "What kind of skeletons do you have in your closet?" he sneered. "Maybe this Domestic Violence Unit of yours needs a bit of FBI scrutiny or maybe your mother has a few ghosts in her past."

I was boiling inside, but I didn't want to show it. I didn't want Coyle telling Longhorn how angry he'd made me. I didn't want to give him that satisfaction and I didn't want to expose my Achilles heel. "Tell me something, Agent Coyle. What is it about these cases that makes them so important that he sent you out here to threaten me?"

"Do I really have to spell it out for you?"

"Yes, I want you to spell it out for me. Each and every letter."

"Mob murders get a lot of ink. I'll let you in on a little secret. Our office is about to bring a big RICO case in New Jersey that's also going to make national headlines."

"Is that what this fuss is all about? Getting publicity for Jack Longhorn?"

"You're missing the point. Longhorn wants more agents assigned to New York. That means the FBI director has to go before Congress to ask for a bigger budget. The threat of escalating mob violence and mob activity translates into more money. The FBI gets more money, Longhorn gets more agents, we catch more criminals, people are happy. Did I spell that out clearly enough for you?"

"So if these murders weren't done by the mob then Longhorn doesn't get more agents?"

"No, he'll still get more money because of our big RICO case, but it doesn't hurt if we've got two major crime families threatening to go to war and we've got several gangland killings to show Congress. Fortunately, for Longhorn, these murder cases are all mob related. Everyone knows that, except for you!"

"Persico didn't kill Isabella Ricci," I said.

Coyle locked his eyes onto mine. "Who cares? Persico is dead."

"I care," I said. "Tell me, Agent Coyle, what time did you see Persico leave Isabella's apartment on the day of the murder?"

"It's in the official log. I also testified in court."

"You said five-thirty. But Angelica Persico told me her father left that apartment shortly before three-thirty. And when he left, Isabella was alive. Persico was back at his butcher shop when the killer cut that radio cord in Isabella's apartment and tied her up."

"She's lying," Coyle said.

"I don't think she is."

"Then you're calling me a liar!" he said between gritted teeth.

"Isn't it possible you made a mistake, just like when you forgot to share the Brady material with us?"

A flash of anger washed across his face. "You need to stop wasting everyone's time, and go back to prosecuting abusive husbands," he said. "Longhorn told me to remind you that every moment our people in Quantico spend listening to your fantasies is time they could be using to catch real killers. His exact words were 'Tell her to fuck off—now!'"

"Tell your boss I got his message and then tell him to mind his own business."

Coyle shrugged and said, "You're digging your own grave."

44

I NEEDED TO GET MY FILES AND PHOTOS TO AGENT WHEELER. Although I'd put up a good front, Coyle's ominous warning was nothing I could ignore. It was just a matter of time before Longhorn took Whitaker aside for a friendly chat about me. I needed to solve these cases before Whitaker ordered me to stop my investigation . . . or decided that I was becoming such a political liability that I could be replaced by a less troublesome, new female hire.

I called Wheeler's line.

"You decided where we should meet?" I asked.

"Quoth the raven, 'Nevermore.'"

"Sorry, I'm not following you."

"It's from an Edgar Allan Poe poem," he said. "Did you know Poe invented the detective novel? He's actually the father of modern detective work."

"That's nice but the clock is ticking. Longhorn just sent an FBI agent to my office to tell me to stop bothering you."

"People think of Baltimore when they think of Poe, but he actually wrote most of his famous works in the City of Brotherly Love."

"It's nice that you're such a big fan," I said, hoping to hurry him along.

"Poe rented a house in Philly and this year, Congress is scheduled to make it into a national memorial. I'd like to see it before the park service turns it into a tourist trap. In fact, I'd like to see it so much that I'm going to take the rest of the day off so I can visit Philadelphia on my own personal time this afternoon. Now if you just happened to be at the Poe house and you just happened to bring me your files and I just happened to look at them, then—"

"I get it," I said. "Tell me the address."

It had been about ten minutes since Coyle had exited my office. He would be reporting to Longhorn as soon as he got back to the New York FBI field office on the twenty-third floor at 26 Federal Plaza. Longhorn would then telephone my boss. I needed to get going before Whitaker could have Miss Potts summon me to his lair. Scooping up my files, I rushed out the back door of our building, to where my Triumph was parked.

What should have been a two-and-a-half-hour drive turned into a nearly four-hour trek and when I finally arrived in Philadelphia and found the Poe house, I assumed Wheeler would be furious—if he had bothered to stick around. Instead, I found him sitting on a bench quietly reading poetry. He was trim and in his forties, wearing a green tie, black suit, mismatched socks, and brown shoes. He looked up and said, "Let's see what you brought me."

"Here? Outside?" I asked.

"I noticed a restaurant a few blocks down the street that advertised an early-bird dinner special." He started walking briskly toward it without waiting for me.

After we were settled at a table away from other diners, I asked, "How many FBI profilers are there?"

"There were eleven of us when we started eight years ago. Double that now. We examine evidence from crime scenes, along with victim and witness reports, and use that information to develop a behavioral profile of an UNSUB."

"UNSUB?"

"I work in Washington for God's sake," he said. "Everything is an acronym. You should know that. FBI. CIA. MSHA. OSHA. DOT. UNSUB means Unknown Subject."

"So far, it doesn't sound like you do anything different from what a good detective would do," I said.

"Don't be insulting," he said. "First off, we're smarter. We also believe a crime reveals something about the perpetrator's behavior and that a person's behavior—if correctly analyzed—can identify him. Habits are hard to break. For instance, you. I imagine you are always late, based on your tardiness."

I ignored his jab and said, "I read about the case that your unit solved in Montana—the little girl who was kidnapped and murdered."

"Ah, the souvenir hunter," he said. "That got a lot of press because he kept trophies—just like you think your killer is doing. But the FBI didn't actually invent profiling. In the 1950s the New York police asked a psychiatrist named James Brussel for help identifying a bomber. He knew paranoia tends to peak around age thirty-five and Brussel used his knowledge about mental illnesses to describe the bomber to the cops. His profile fit perfectly and they caught him. Of course, we've greatly refined our methods." Clearly warming to the subject, he said, "Two of our best agents are about to publish an article that's going to revolutionize how murders are investigated. It will explain organized and disorganized thinking."

"Sounds important," I said, eyeing my still-unopened files and my watch.

"An organized criminal plans his crime while a disorganized one acts spontaneously. This helps tell us if the killer might have a mental defect or is acting impulsively with little or no appreciation for what he has done. Disorganized criminals tend to be young. Many are under the influence of alcohol or drugs. An organized criminal plans ahead, is calculating, and conceals his identity."

"I get it. Someone organized would wipe away his fingerprints," I said.

"Exactly," Wheeler replied.

I checked my watch one more time. By this point, I knew Longhorn had contacted Whitaker and Miss Potts was on my scent.

Wheeler noticed that I was antsy. "Did Isabella Ricci's killer leave fingerprints?" he asked.

"No. There weren't any telltale footprints, either, even though the carpet in the bedroom was soaked with blood. Does that mean we're looking for an organized killer?"

"It suggests we might be looking for an organized thinker—not killer," he said. "They're different animals. You must be precise. Your suspect may have been careful to wipe up his fingerprints and check for footprints. But that doesn't mean he planned this murder in advance. Tell me, did he bring duct tape, rope, or the murder weapon with him?"

"Yes and no," I said. "The apartment didn't have any kitchen utensils, so he had to bring his knife with him. But he didn't come prepared with anything to bind Isabella. He cut the cord from a radio clock next to her bed."

"That could suggest this was an impulsive crime, that the murderer saw an opportunity and took it. Maybe he works in a profession where he carries a knife? It also could suggest he had done this sort of act before. He knew how to use the electrical cord. I'll need to study her murder and the others."

"I brought you everything."

"Good. Behavior always reveals personality. That's our mantra," Wheeler said. "If these cases are linked and one person is responsible for all of them, then his personality will emerge from our reading and understanding of the patterns that he unconsciously follows."

"So what exactly are you looking for?"

"I can't teach you how to profile a killer in five minutes," he said.

"But you could highlight the process," I said. "Then while you're reading my files, I could be thinking about what kind of details I might know that could help us."

Wheeler said, "We look at four parts of a crime. The first is the buildup. We ask ourselves: What fantasy or plan, or both, did the murderer have in his mind before he struck? Was he dreaming about raping a woman? Was he thinking about torturing her?"

"In other words, you're looking for a motivation," I said.

"Yes, but we're not necessarily looking for an obvious one. We're looking for some underlying emotional and mental motivation that surfaces before a crime. Perhaps the killer feels an urge to kill that comes when there is a full moon."

"A full moon?"

"You have to keep an open mind," he said. "Otherwise you will miss potential clues."

Wheeler continued: "After we discuss possible motives in a case, the next analytical step is an examination of the method and manner of a crime. What type of victim or victims did the killer choose and why? Was there a common trigger? For example, were all of the victims blond-haired or were they young women in their twenties who were in college? We're looking for links that tie a series of murders together and provide us with clues about his personality."

"Isabella Ricci is the obvious link in these cases," I said.

"I'll be the judge of that. Remember, you said you wanted fresh eyes."

I nodded and Wheeler continued his tutorial. "After we look at the method and manner of a murder, we examine the body and how it was treated. Did the murderer kill the person where the victim was found or did he move the body? Was there an attempt to hide the body or did the killer want the police to see his handiwork?"

I was about to say something but decided not to interrupt.

Wheeler said, "The final stage we study is the killer's behavior after a murder. We've found that many killers actually contact the police after they commit a crime. If someone's been kidnapped, they volunteer to hand out posters and canvas the neighborhood because they get a thrill from being part of the investigation. It helps them relive their crime. It gives them joy."

I said, "That's why my killer is taking body parts, too, isn't it? So he can relive the crime?"

"Yes, but it is more than that. Missing body parts suggest we are dealing with a pure psychopath who truly enjoys killing. He will keep his trophies near him and play with them because they remind him of his prowess and the excitement that he got when he collected his souvenirs. But that is the secondary reason why I said the body parts are important in your cases."

"Tell me the main reason."

"If these autopsies show each of these victims had a body part taken, then we will know for certain that these are not mob killings, regardless of what Jack Longhorn says. We'll know they are related and, most important of all, they were done by a single, male killer. Now, give me an hour to study the files. Go away."

I found a pay phone outside the restaurant and rang O'Brien.

"Whitaker is looking for you," he said, "and he ain't happy. Something about Jack Longhorn and the Isabella Ricci case."

"Longhorn wants me to stop asking questions," I explained.

"And?"

"And I'm in Philadelphia talking to an FBI agent who works in the behavioral science unit. He's reading the murder files right now."

"In other words," O'Brien said, "you haven't backed off."

"No one has officially told me, remember? I'm out of the office."

"You gonna stay away permanently? If so, it might be a good time for me to lead a coop," he said, mistakenly sounding as if he were about to lead a revolt by chickens.

"You mean coup as in coup d'état and you're not that popular, O'Brien. I'll be back, hopefully with some solid clues to persuade Whitaker this isn't a waste of time."

"Dani," he said, in a concerned voice, "we've tangled with Longhorn before. He plays dirty. You watch yourself."

It had been only fifteen minutes since I'd left Wheeler in the restaurant studying my files, so I took a short walk to clear my head and then returned to the pay phone to place another call. This time, I telephoned my house and punched in the code to retrieve messages from my answering machine. There were two. The first was from a very severe-sounding Hillary Potts informing me that District Attorney Carlton Whitaker III wanted to speak to me immediately and that I was supposed to stop whatever I was doing and come to his office. The next message was from Will.

"Dani," he said, "I'm sorry I got upset today. I'm just so goddamned tired of having that pompous FBI prick interfering in our relationship. Anyway, I came by to tell you good news—really great news, actually. It's finally happening. The *New York Times* offered me a job. An editor there has been following my stories about the Isabella Ricci mob murders. They need a reporter in their Miami bureau to write about really big crimes. They got a guy down there named Ted Bundy who's killed thirty women. The FBI has coined a new term to describe him. He's a 'serial murderer.' The *Times* wants me down there in time for his sentencing. Dani, will you come with me?"

45

AGENT WHEELER WAS SIPPING COFFEE WHEN I REJOINED him inside the restaurant.

"This has been a most interesting afternoon," he declared. "Before you arrived I toured the Poe house and now I've read your files." He placed his cup gently on the table. "Ms. Fox, you are dealing with a serial murderer. These were not mob killings. That's window dressing. What we have here is a very organized mind, an intelligent mind, and a murderer who has done this before and thinks he is smarter than the rest of us."

I felt a chill.

"Longhorn is wrong, then?"

"Dead wrong," Wheeler answered. "Let's begin with the first murder. On first glance it appears to be a sadistic, sex-related crime. Isabella Ricci was found naked, her hands bound, pieces of her flesh brutally cut off while she was tortured. While sex nearly always plays a role in these sorts of murders, there was no semen found at the scene, no indication of rape or sodomy or ejaculation. I do not believe this was a sex crime at all, although the killer might have received a sexual rush."

"Then what was it?"

"It was a murder, however simple or complicated as that is." He paused, clearly enjoying the explanation of his findings. He was in no hurry to speed up his analytical revelations. "This UNSUB kills because he derives joy from the actual act of killing—because ending a human life makes him feel powerful, omnipotent."

"Like God?"

"Precisely, but rather than creating life, he destroys it. We're dealing with a completely narcissistic driven personality—a psychopath who is highly intelligent and is completely self-absorbed. He views our world from a very narrow perspective. It exists only for his personal pleasure. We are toys in his playground, put here for his personal amusement, and the ultimate pleasure for him is controlling, dominating, and ending a human life."

"The body parts. They're his trophies, then. Just as you suspected," I said.

"Yes, they're his prizes, his keepsakes."

"Why do you think he cut off pieces of Isabella's flesh as well as amputated her finger?"

"Ah, that's an excellent question that deserves a two-part answer," Wheeler said. "Why did he torture her? The most obvious reason is because he could. This man has no empathy for another human being, because he cares only about himself. This means he is capable of extreme cruelty without the slightest feelings of pity or revulsion. My guess is that he was sexually or physically abused as a child and his mind is still trying to cope with that abuse. He felt powerless as a child. Now he has changed roles and he is the abuser who is in charge. The torture was all about the exertion of power."

"And the second part?" I asked.

"He was toying with the authorities. He removed Isabella's skin, in part, to hide the fact that he took her finger as a trophy. He gave Italian neckties to the others to mislead, but grew bolder, claiming a finger and toe in the case of the Mancinis and finally taking Marco Ricci's penis—a rather noticeable amputation. Except for the murder of Donnie Gilmore, he has made no effort to hide his handiwork. In fact, he carefully staged each crime scene. It is as if he is daring you to catch him, leaving clues behind, but not so obvious that anyone would notice." Wheeler wiped his hand across his chin as if he were stroking an imaginary beard and said, "You haven't found any other women butchered and hanging from a ceiling. He is not taking revenge on a specific type of person. For instance, if he were rejected by a blond woman early in his life, his trigger might be blond women whom he would kill in his quest for revenge. But your victims are male and female, young and old."

"But there is a pattern, isn't there?" I asked.

"Yes," Wheeler said. "In each case, the police have suspected the homicides were Mafia inspired. Your killer is like a man who has jumped onto a train, moving from one car to the next killing his prey."

"I'm not following you," I said.

"The killer knew Isabella Ricci had ties to the Mafia. I don't know how he obtained this information, but he decided to take advantage of that theme. That train. After killing her, he began targeting victims on the same Mafia track, so to speak. When viewed through the first murder, all of the killings would seem logical to the police."

I said, "So he killed the Mancinis because Roman was an eyewitness."

"Yes, he knew the police would suspect the mob did it."

"And he killed Marco Ricci because we would think the mob killed him, too."

"Exactly, but I think this killer targeted those victims for reasons other than simply fooling you."

"What reasons?"

"How does a person who is highly narcissistic, someone who wants to be God, prove that he is superior to the rest of us mere mortals? He does it by herding us like cattle, by manipulating us, by making us do whatever he wants. Isabella was the first move in his own little Kabuki play. He staged each death to spoon-feed you clues because he was, and may still be, directing you."

"It worked," I said. "Longhorn, Coyle, even my boss, Whitaker, all believe these cases have been solved and that the persons responsible—Tiny Nunzio and Nicholas Persico—are dead."

"That's important to him," Wheeler said. "He wants to create perfect crimes because if he is caught, he is not omnipotent. Now, Ms. Fox, at some point this killer will have completed what he hoped to accomplish. He will exit the Mafia train and find a new train track to travel. Actually, my guess is that he is done in Yonkers."

"Why?"

"Because he tried to hide the last murder, Donnie Gilmore," Wheeler said. "He needed Gilmore dead. I'm not sure why. But it had something to do with our killer leading you and the police where he wanted you to go. Once he got investigators there, he was ready to bring down the curtain on his melodrama."

"So he's stopped killing?"

"No, he's not. He will continue killing until he is caught or dies. But I think he will change his targets. He might move to a different city or begin killing an entirely different type of victim. He might target drug dealers, for instance. But if he does, he will do it in a way that will mislead investigators. They will be chasing suspects who seem to be logical targets, but are actually simple pawns."

"You're telling me this UNSUB, much like a choreographer, gets his thrill from killing and then wants us to dance to the steps that he's designed for us? In these cases, he wanted us to believe that someone in the mob killed Isabella Ricci, then the Mancinis, then Marco Ricci, and finally Donnie Gilmore. And now he is done and will start an entirely new game with a new set of characters."

"That's an excellent summation of my theory," he said.

"Can you give me a profile of this guy?"

"Your killer is most likely a white male. He's between the ages of twenty-five and thirty-five. He has a higher than average IQ, but he probably didn't do well in school and is probably from a violent and/or abusive home. He might have been a bed wetter and he probably abused or tortured animals as a kid. He might have been obsessed with starting fires. And most of all, he is convinced that he is smarter than all the rest of us combined, because deep down he has a low self-image, possibly even self-loathing, so he overcompensates with feelings of grandiosity. If ridiculed, he will explode."

"If he's done this before, do you think he'll have other trophies besides his recent souvenirs?"

"I think he will."

"Where does a killer keep a finger, a toe, or a severed penis?" I asked. "It's not like he can put them on his coffee table or display them on a bookshelf."

Wheeler chuckled. "No, but he will keep them close. They will not be buried in the ground or hidden in a hard-to-access location. He'll be like a teenage boy who hides a *Playboy* magazine under his mattress, only much more clever."

Wheeler pushed back his chair and said, "When I get back to my office, I will think about possible ways that we can work around Jack Longhorn and get my team involved. But I'm not sure that will be possible. Longhorn's po-litically powerful and a stubborn ass, more politician than cop."

I knew I liked Agent Wheeler.

"But for now," Wheeler continued, "if asked, I spent my afternoon at the Poe house."

"I understand," I said.

"There's one more critical piece of advice that you need to hear."

Without waiting for me to ask, Wheeler said, "You need to be very careful. I have a feeling your killer may either be a member of law enforcement or have a direct link to it. He could be a prosecutor, like yourself, a judge, or even a reporter who specializes in true crime. Based on what you've showed me, his behavior reveals that he knows a lot about the mob and even more about how we do our jobs."

46

O'BRIEN AND I MET AT THE GREASY SPOON DINER that he loves so much. I'd spent the drive from Philadelphia pondering Agent Wheeler's final warning.

"You look like hell," O'Brien said.

"Thanks for the ego boost."

"Honestly, I've never seen you look so rattled."

"You would be, too, if you'd just spent the afternoon with an FBI profiler," I said. "I'm not sure you're going to believe what he told me." I took a deep breath and said, "The FBI profiler is convinced there is only one killer and he is toying with us."

"We got someone in Yonkers collecting body parts?" O'Brien asked.

"He thinks so and so do I. He's killing for the thrill of it and using the link with the mob to fool us. And now, here's the really frightening part. The profiler thinks it could be a cop or someone who knows our business—a newspaper reporter."

"Christ almighty!" O'Brien exclaimed. "Do you think it's someone we know?"

I hesitated, not because I was trying to be dramatic, but because I wasn't sure how O'Brien would react to my next statement.

"I think it might be Agent Coyle or Will Harris," I said.

"You're shitting me!"

I nodded, affirming that I wasn't.

O'Brien shook his head in disbelief. "You think your boyfriend is a murderer?" he asked incredulously. "You think the FBI agent who saved your kidnapped ass is a homicidal psychopath? If you tell this to Whitaker, he'll send out the men in white coats and have you hauled off to the funny farm. Hell, I'm not sure I believe you and I'm your partner."

"I know it sounds far-fetched."

"How about fucking unbelievable? Do you have any facts to back up your suspicions? You got to walk me through this. Start with Will."

"Will is fascinated by the mob."

"And so are a zillion other people. Remember that little movie called *The Godfather*? Sold-out crowds. Magazine covers?"

"Will knew Isabella Ricci. He'd been following her, trying to get an exclusive interview. He'd been to her house."

"So what? He's a reporter chasing a story."

"Will fits Agent Wheeler's overall profile. He's a white male, falls into the right age group, and comes from a broken home."

"You just described half the young men in Westchester County. Where's the smoking gun? Remember, a little thing we call evidence? Fingerprints, an eyewitness, blood on his shoes?"

"It's all circumstantial."

"No, it's worse than that. It's bullshit. Conjecture. Are you telling me you've been sleeping with a guy who cuts off a man's penis for a trophy?"

"Will hid things from me about his past."

"What's the motive?"

"The profiler said we're dealing with a thrill killer who's manipulating us. In Will's case, he got front-page exclusive stories and a job offer from the *New York Times*."

"Dani, listen to yourself. You think Will butchered five people to get a job at a newspaper? This is Will Harris. Not Norman Bates."

"Will is the same good, decent guy who once burned the American flag while shacking up with Moonbeams, getting high on brownies, and sleeping soundly while his infant daughter was smothered. The profiler said serial murderers blend in with the rest of us."

"I'm not buying it," O'Brien said. "And Agent Coyle is even a nuttier choice."

"Why, because he's an FBI agent?" I asked. "We know Coyle was at the

47

ONE OF THE ADVANTAGES OF LIVING CLOSE TO MAN-
hattan is easy access to all sorts of information. After my
morning jog, I called in sick to avoid meeting with D.A. Whitaker and headed into the city, where I found copies of the *Detroit Tribune* on
microfilm at one of New York City's public libraries.

During one of our first encounters, Agent Coyle had mentioned that his
first FBI assignment had been in Detroit. If Coyle was a serial murderer,
there was a good chance that I'd find a clue there. Based on that assumption,
I intended to first search the *Detroit Tribune* for articles about mutilated
victims.

Unfortunately, the newspaper's records didn't come with an index, which
meant I was handed four softball-sized spools of microfilm and deposited in
front of a gunmetal gray reading machine. Each spool held exactly one
year's worth of newspapers—one spool for each year that Coyle had worked
in Detroit.

After a librarian showed me how to thread the microfilm through the
cumbersome reader, I settled onto a hard metal chair and began turning a
hand crank that slid images of individual pages across a dimly lit screen.

It was tedious work. Front pages appeared and disappeared, each with
alarming headlines. The summer of 1976 had proven to be especially violent.
Looting was common in the black business community. White city residents
were fleeing to the suburbs, unemployment hit 25 percent (among young
black males it was double that) and Detroit was given a new nickname by the

Midland Apartments on the afternoon of the murder. Angelica Persico claim
he lied about when her father actually left Isabella's apartment."

"I doubt he lied," O'Brien said. "But he might have doctored those logbooks after the murder to guarantee Persico got convicted. Trust me, that
wouldn't be the first time a cop tampered with evidence. Besides, what's
Coyle's motive?"

"Maybe he wants to start a Mafia war. Or maybe he saw an opportunity
to slip in after Persico and jump on a Mafia train."

"Mafia train?"

"It's what the profiler called it," I said. "I guess you had to be there."

"You're not making sense. There has never been an FBI agent indicted for
murder. Never. They put those stiffs through all kinds of tests by shrinks."

"How'd Longhorn slip through?" I said.

O'Brien laughed. "Good one."

"The missing body parts are the key. No one is going to believe a word of
this unless I find the fingers, toe, and penis."

"How you gonna find them?" he asked. "You gonna just ask Will or Coyle
if they have an extra penis lying around? 'Cause no judge is gonna give you a
search warrant based on what you just said."

"Our killer has killed before. He'll have other trophies from previous
murders. I need to dig into both men's pasts, beginning with Agent Coyle's.
The killer's past will unmask him."

media: going from "Motor City" to "murder capital" of the nation. There were more than 850 homicides that year alone.

In August 1976, some eight thousand people of all races gathered for a rock concert at the Cobo Hall convention center on a Sunday night. Midway through the performance, 150 young men began attacking other concertgoers. Dozens of people were robbed, one woman was gang-raped by twenty men, and more than a thousand fans were beaten. The rampage lasted a full hour before police managed to get the mayhem under control. The attacks were carried out, according to the newspaper, by two rival gangs, known as the Errol Flynns and the Black Killers. Incredibly, none of the gang members was prosecuted.

It was after that riot that the Detroit police and FBI formed a joint task force specifically to target the Errol Flynns, the city's toughest gang. Founded on Detroit's east side, the gang had appropriated its name from Hollywood film legend Errol Flynn. It was one of the first gangs to use semiotic hand gestures to show gang membership and to incorporate "hip-hop" dance moves into its gang identity. Agent Walter Coyle, fresh from the academy, was assigned to that task force. The newspaper published dozens of articles about gang-related murders, but most were drive-by shootings. There was no mention of mutilated bodies until the September 5, 1977, edition of the paper appeared on my screen.

YOUTH CRUCIFIED, MUTILATED

A nineteen-year-old man was found "crucified" on a makeshift cross erected in an alley in East Detroit early yesterday morning, police said. The suspect, whose name has not been made public, was "nailed just like Jesus" to two boards attached to a chain link fence.

A member of the city's joint gang task force said the victim was a known member of the Errol Flynns and his murder appeared to be gang related. The initials *BK* were carved in his chest and his body had been further mutilated. The "Black Killers" are the Errol Flynns' rivals and a task force spokesman, who asked not to be identified, said the ritualistic killing was meant to taunt the BK gangsters.

Next to that front-page account was an especially grisly photo of the crucified youth. Two white police officers using metal shears and hammers were removing the naked body from a makeshift cross. I read the article twice but could find no mention of how the body had been "further mutilated."

A follow-up story in the next day's edition identified the victim as Marcus Smith and quoted Detroit detective Richard Kowalski saying that two of Smith's brothers had been murdered in gang-related killings in the past three years. "We must end this black-on-black crime," Kowalski warned. "It's destroying our inner-city neighborhoods."

The next day, the newspaper published another gruesome photograph about a black youth whose disemboweled body had been found naked in an alley in a neighborhood that was part of the BK gang's turf. He had been fatally shot, but his body had been sliced open and the killers had plunged an arrow into his heart.

> . . . Detroit Detective Kowalski suspects the murder was carried out by the Errol Flynns gang in retaliation for the crucifixion of Marcus Smith, age 19, whose body was found two days ago. "The killers left an arrow behind—that's the Errol Flynns' calling card," Kowalski said. The victim was allegedly a member of the Black Killers gang. "We'd hoped to forge a truce, but now war between these two gangs is inevitable," the detective said.

The front pages that appeared after that on the microfilm reader as I slowly turned the crank revealed that Detroit had been caught up for weeks in a gang war, with sixteen young men killed in a violent clashes. Detroit's mayor had asked for even more federal help to calm the panicked city.

A month later, the joint FBI task force arrested twenty-two gang members during late-night police raids. A newspaper photo showed FBI agents herding a parade of handcuffed gang members with bowed heads into a police station. One of those agents was Walter Coyle.

My eyes were tired from straining to read the poorly lighted microfilm pages. My butt hurt and I needed to make a phone call so I left my microfilm research in place.

"I'll be back in just a few minutes," I told a librarian. She directed me to a wall of pay phones near the library's main entrance. An operator connected me to the Detroit Police Department's detective division and, moments later, I was speaking to the same Detective Kowalski whom I'd been reading about in the old newspapers. "Could you answer some questions for me about the gang war you had in Detroit six years ago?" I asked.

"I guess, but if you're a prosecutor in Westchester County, why are you asking about two Detroit gangs?" he replied.

"It's complicated," I said.

"It's your dime," he replied. "Glad to help if I can."

I said, "The first victim—Marcus Smith—the kid who was crucified and had the initials *BK* carved into his chest. Do you remember him?"

"Hell yeah. That homicide started the war and you don't see too many people on crosses—unless you hang out in a Catholic church."

"The newspaper said the body was 'further mutilated,'" I said. "In what way?"

Kowalski was quiet for a moment and then said, "Why do you want to know this again?"

"Humor me. It could be important to something we've got going on here."

"Clipped off a couple toes. You'd think nailing that poor bastard to a cross would've been enough but most of those gangbangers were strung out on heroin when they were killing each other."

"Were there any other body parts missing?"

"Nope, just a couple toes."

"Now the second victim—the one with an arrow stuck in his heart—how about him? Was his body mutilated?" I asked.

"Lady, he was disemboweled. Isn't that enough for you?"

"But were any toes or fingers amputated?"

"Let me think about it. Like I said, the guy was disemboweled. One of those gangbangers must've paid attention in school 'cause they kept that poor bastard alive while they pulled out his insides."

"Sounds horrific."

"Not a good way to go. Now, let's see, yes, I remember his little pinkie finger had been amputated. We thought maybe the gangs were taking toes and fingers as trophies at first, 'cause there were lots of stories going around at the time about how guys in Vietnam had collected ears. But those two homicides were the only ones in which toes and fingers were cut off. After those two gangs started going at it, everyone just shot everyone else."

"This has been really helpful," I said, and then, as if it were an afterthought, I asked, "Hey, did you know FBI Agent Walter Coyle?"

"Wally?" Kowalski replied. "Hell yeah, I knew him. He was a young buck fresh out of the academy. A real eager beaver who took every shit job we gave him. Do you know him?"

"Yes, he works in Manhattan now," I said.

"Why you bothering me, then?" Kowalski asked jokingly. "Wally worked those first two murders. He can tell you all about them missing toes and finger. Do me a favor and remind that young buck that he still owes me ten bucks on a bet we had."

As soon as I finished talking to Detective Kowalski, I called O'Brien at the Domestic Violence Unit office.

"Real smart, calling in sick today," O'Brien said. "Did you really think that was gonna fool Whitaker? He's mad as hell. A little birdie told me Longhorn has been busting his balls, calling the office like crazy."

"I'll deal with him tomorrow. Listen, Agent Coyle worked two violent murders in Detroit—murders that sparked a gang war—and both victims were missing body parts—toes and a finger—just like our victims."

O'Brien said, "Coyle will claim it's a coincidence. It's not enough."

"But it's a start."

"Dani, the guy is an FBI agent. You're gonna need a lot more before anyone will believe you."

"I know. That's why I got to find his trophy stash."

"Are you fricking nuts? How the hell are you gonna do that? It's not like asking a guy to see his stamp collection."

"If Coyle is a serial murderer, he'd keep his souvenirs close, probably in his apartment," I said.

"Yeah, so. No way you'll get a warrant based on what you've turned up."

"I haven't thought this through yet," I said.

O'Brien said, "How about you get him to meet you, someplace public, away from his apartment? I'll do the rest."

"I can't ask you to break into his apartment illegally," I said.

"Then don't. You just find a way to keep him busy for an hour or two, out of the city."

"I could invite him to dinner. I could claim we need to patch things up and work together as professionals. Tell him I'm dropping my investigation and need to make things right with Longhorn. He'd buy that."

"When?"

"I have to do it fast. How about tonight?" I said. "I just need to finish up here."

We agreed to talk later and finalize a plan.

Before hanging up, O'Brien said, "Dani, you know if this turns to shit, it's over for you. Whitaker will fire you. Think about it. You can still back out. Everyone's happy blaming Tiny Nunzio and the Butcher for these cases. No one will ever know."

"I'll know," I replied.

Just as the librarian had promised, no one had disturbed the microfilm that I'd left at the reader. I'd only gotten through 1977 and still had two more spools to go, but I was tired of studying the films and my eyes were burning from staring at the blurry screen. Besides, I felt as if I'd already discovered what I'd come to find. I toyed with the idea of packing up, but my conscience wouldn't let me. I'm anal about details. It's part of being a competent prosecutor. I returned to scanning stories, only at a quicker pace.

Several more headlines about the rival gangs swept across the screen, but the mass arrest had broken the backs of both groups. I was about halfway through 1978 when something caught my eye. It wasn't a gruesome story about a murder or mutilation. It was a news story about Detroit's city hall. I didn't bother to read it because the text didn't matter. It was the byline that caught me cold. The reporter who'd written the story was Will Harris.

Could there be two reporters named Will Harris? One Harris working in Detroit and the other in White Plains? Will had never mentioned anything to me about working in Michigan. What were the chances that Walter Coyle and Will Harris would both be working in Detroit when a serial murderer was collecting trophies and sparking a gang war?

48

WILL HARRIS WAS SITTING IN HIS CAR PARKED outside my house when I returned that afternoon from the city. "I called your office and they said you called in sick today," he explained as he exited his car and came to me.

"I'm feeling a bit better now," I said.

"Where have you been? Did you spend the night in the city?" he asked, his voice rising.

He must have suspected that I'd been with Agent Coyle.

"No, not that it's any of your business."

Will said, "Dani, please, can we go inside and talk?"

"Let's do it here."

Will let out a loud, frustrating sigh.

"What? Now you won't even invite me into your house?" he asked.

I unlocked the door and motioned him in. We sat in my living room, which is the one room that I almost never use.

"I'm moving to Miami," he said, "if you aren't willing to go with me, then we need to talk about how we can handle a long-distance relationship."

"Not well," I said. "Since we don't seem to know how to handle a short-distance one."

"It would help if you would stop avoiding me and talk to me about us," he said.

"I'd like to ask you a question, Will," I replied. "Did you ever work as a reporter in Detroit?"

He gave me a puzzled look and said, "Why are you asking me about De-troit now?"

"Just answer my question," I said.

"What the hell, Dani? First, I've got the FBI digging into my past and now you're doing it, too. For the record, I was never employed by a Detroit news-paper, if that's your question. But I did fill in there for several months when Detroit was having a big crime wave. The *Detroit Tribune* and the White Plains paper are owned by the same parent company and the Detroit newspa-per needed temporary help. Four of us were sent to Detroit for a stint."

"You were there when those two gangs were at war?" I asked.

"Yes," he replied, "but I was assigned to city hall, not crime."

"Why'd you decide to accept that assignment?"

"Why are you interrogating me?" he replied, but he didn't wait for me to answer. "I wanted to get out of White Plains. I'd just gotten my divorce. You know my ex-wife works at our paper. I needed to clear my head. Is that a crime now?"

"You never told me about Detroit."

"Why the hell would I?" he snapped. "It was before we began dating and it wasn't important. Dani, I can see why you got angry about me not telling you about my daughter, but Detroit, that's just, just, ridiculous."

"Agent Coyle was in Detroit at the same time," I said. "Did you know that?"

"No. Did he tell you that we'd met there or something? I mean, why's that matter?"

I decided to drop it. "I guess it doesn't," I said. "I just found it curious. When are you leaving for Miami?"

"In six days. I've already given notice. My editors are being good about it. They're throwing me a party. I'd like you to come. And I'd really like for the two of us to resolve our issues before I go."

I didn't reply. I wasn't sure how I wanted to respond.

"Dani," he said, "I thought you were in love with me, but these last sev-eral weeks, I just don't know anymore. It's like you've put up this huge wall between us. I've got to know, are you dating Agent Coyle?"

"No," I said. "I'm not dating him and I'm not interested in him, either."

"Good," he replied. "How about me, us?"

"I don't know yet. I need more time. O'Brien is expecting me to call him. If you're leaving town, I'll need to drop by your apartment and pick up some things."

He checked his watch and said, "It's four o'clock. I've got to go in to the newspaper but we could meet for dinner and then go to my apartment and gather up your things."

"I'm not sure tonight is good for me. O'Brien and I might have something going on. Why don't you give me a key to your place?" I suggested. "I can shoot over there now while you're at the newspaper and grab my stuff. Then I'll get back to you about possibly having dinner tonight."

"I only have one key and I need it," he said. "But don't worry about your stuff. I can always collect it for you."

He stood and walked over to hug me, but I didn't rise out of my seat.

Bending down, he kissed my forehead and said, "I'll call you in about an hour about tonight. After you've had a chance to speak with O'Brien. We can grab a bite and I can bring your stuff, too, you unless you decide to come over and spend the night."

"I'm curious, Will," I said. "We've been dating for several months, but you never offered me a key to your apartment. Why?"

My question took him by surprise. "I don't know. I guess I never thought about it."

49

O'BRIEN HAD BEEN A BUSY BOY. HE'D DISCOVERED that Agent Coyle lived in an apartment on Manhattan's Lower East Side. "You still wanna go through with this?" O'Brien asked me.

"Do we have a choice?" I replied. "If we don't a serial murderer is going to get away. I can't let that happen."

"Then call me after you speak to Coyle, but only agree to meet him someplace really public," he said.

"There's something more I need to tell you," I said. "Will Harris was in Detroit the same time as Coyle. He was working at the newspaper there when our killer was collecting trophies. I just talked to him."

"Another coincidence?" he asked.

"I don't know, but when I said I wanted to go by his apartment and pick up some stuff, he wouldn't give me a key. He didn't want me going there by myself."

"Probably because the place is a dump," O'Brien said. "Most of us bachelors aren't real neat."

"Or maybe he didn't want me snooping around."

When I hung up with O'Brien, I dialed Coyle's direct line. The moment he heard my voice, he said, "Why the hell have you been asking questions about me in Detroit?"

Obviously, Detective Kowalski had ratted me out. My God, had Kowalski told him that I was asking about body parts? He must have.

"I was curious about gang violence. A side project I'm working on," I said, nonchalantly.

"Bullshit," he said.

"Agent Coyle, I do have other cases and other interests."

"If you had questions about Detroit, you should have called me," he said. "Instead of bothering my friends."

"Next time I will."

"So why are you calling?" he asked, curtly.

"Because I've thought about what you said, about how your boss wants me to back away from these closed cases, and how much heat he can bring down." I was trying to sound convincing. "And I've decided you're right. Your office and my office need to make peace."

"It's not your office that is pissing everyone off here," he said.

"I realize that. That's why I want to extend an olive branch."

He didn't immediately respond.

I assumed he was suspicious, especially since he'd been warned that I'd been asking questions about his days in Detroit and mutilated bodies.

"How about dinner?" I said. "On my dime. To work out any problems the two of us might still have because of the Persico trial and these closed cases."

Despite his suspicions, I figured he would take the bait. After all, the FBI profiler had told me that our serial murderer would think he was smarter than the rest of us.

"Why don't you drive in to the city?" Coyle said. "We have more choices here and if you get lucky, I'll show you my apartment."

"Do you mind terribly coming to White Plains? We can do my favorite restaurant."

"Roberto's?" he said.

"Yes, that's it. I'm surprised that you knew that."

"You shouldn't be, Ms. Fox."

There was something different about his voice. I said, "See you at eight p.m. at Roberto's. I'll make a reservation."

"I can't wait," he said.

50

I ARRIVED AT ROBERTO'S AN UNCHARACTERISTIC TEN MIN-
utes early. The restaurant was crowded and I saw several friends and a
couple whom I really didn't want to see. It was Will's editor and his
wife. I waved and smiled.

Agent Coyle arrived ten minutes late and immediately apologized, blaming traffic from the city.

"I hate to do this," I said, "but I need to make a quick phone call. Will you
excuse me? I come here all the time and already know what I want to order.
Why don't you look at the menu?"

Hurrying from the table, I used a pay phone next to the restaurant's rest-
rooms to call O'Brien's beeper. It was our prearranged signal that Coyle was
with me and it was safe for him to investigate Coyle's apartment.

When I returned to the table, Coyle was sipping a glass of pinot noir. "I
ordered a bottle," he explained. "Hope you don't mind. You said you were
buying tonight." He gave me a smug grin.

"Of course I don't mind. Have you decided what you're having?"

"Maybe a good juicy steak," he said. "Now, why don't you tell me the real
reason why you called Detective Kowalski."

It was time for us, I decided, to match wits. "I thought he might help me
solve the Isabella Ricci murder."

In a disgusted voice, he said, "So you lied when you told me that you've
agreed to close that case. I'm not surprised."

"I want to run a theory by you," I said. "It's not something I wanted to
discuss on the phone because it may sound a bit odd."

Taking a sip of his wine, he said, "This should be good."

"I don't believe Isabella, the Mancinis, Marco Ricci, or Donnie Gilmore were murdered by the mob. I don't believe Tiny Nunzio or Persico were behind any of those homicides."

"You never have," he said, "and that is odd because everyone else knows the mob did it. You're either too proud or, quite frankly, too dumb to see it."

So much for niceties, I thought.

"No, there's another person who sees it the exact same way I do."

"Yeah, who's that?"

"The real killer."

"Are you suggesting that a single killer murdered all five of them?"

"That's right."

"Then you are dumb."

Without hesitating, I said, "I believe this serial murderer was involved in at least two murders in Detroit before he came to Yonkers. In fact, I think he intentionally murdered rival gang members, which sparked the war between those two gangs there."

"This theory of yours just officially went from dumb to crazy," Coyle said.

"The evidence says otherwise."

"What possible evidence do you have that can link two mob murders in Detroit to the homicides here?"

Without flinching, I said, "Our killer thinks he's so smart he can pull off perfect crimes. And he is good. He didn't leave any physical evidence behind. He staged the murder scenes. He even helped us identify logical suspects. But he made a mistake."

"Really?" Coyle replied with a slight grin. "And what would that be?"

"The reason why I know these were not mob hits and why I know that the homicides in Detroit and Yonkers are connected is because our killer collects trophies." I paused to let that sink in.

Coyle's cool expression did not change. He did not break down. He did not confess.

We sat in silence while the waiter served our food. Once our server was gone, Coyle said, "Trophies?"

"Body parts from each victim. With Isabella it was a finger, with the

Mancinis it was a toe and thumb, with Ricci it was a penis, and with Gilmore it was a finger," I said. "He did the same in Detroit. Some toes and a finger."

"That's his mistake?"

"That's his signature. His Achilles heel is his huge ego. I told you, he thinks he is smarter than the rest of us."

"Maybe he is."

"I saw through his game."

"And what's his motive?"

"Because of his narcissistic personality, he probably believes he is ridding the world of its trash—gang members, Mafia figures," I said. "But in actuality, he kills because he thoroughly enjoys killing. Beneath his shell, he's an angry monster."

Coyle cut a large bite from his steak and said, "I worked on the Detroit task force and I was the agent who saw Nicholas Persico enter the Midland Apartments on the afternoon when Isabella Ricci was murdered. Shall I assume I am the prime suspect? That I'm an angry monster? Is that why you have been digging into my past?" He was completely calm and I found that eerie.

"Why would you be a suspect? You're an FBI agent. That makes you one of us, a good guy."

A curious look appeared on his face. He'd expected me to accuse him. "That's a relief," he said. "You have a suspect? I'd like to know who this brilliant serial murderer is?"

I intentionally glanced around Roberto's to suggest that I didn't want anyone to overhear me. Dropping my voice into a whisper, I said, "Will Harris."

Coyle broke into a huge grin. "You honestly believe that newspaper reporter is smart enough to start a gang war in Detroit and then move here and murder Isabella Ricci to spark a war between two feuding mob families?"

"As you showed me," I said in a confident voice, "Will has a dark side."

Coyle was now enjoying this. "How do you plan to catch your exboyfriend? Assuming that you have decided that he's no longer your boyfriend now that he's a serial murderer."

"I'm going to locate the body parts that he's collected. That will prove he's guilty."

"And where will you find them?"

"He'll keep them close," I said. "Probably in his apartment."

My pager buzzed and I glanced at the callback number. It was a Manhattan prefix.

"Do you need to return that call?" Coyle asked.

"Actually, I do," I said, excusing myself.

I dialed the number and O'Brien answered on the first ring. "There's nothin' here," he said. "No fingers, toes, no male organs except for mine and it's still attached."

I said, "Maybe he keeps them in his car."

"That's unlikely. What if he had an accident? Excuse me, Officer, I just happen to have an extra penis in my trunk," O'Brien deadpanned. "Maybe it's not Coyle."

"Coyle could claim the body parts in his car were evidence in an ongoing investigation."

"You're reaching," O'Brien warned.

"I don't think I am," I said. "The night he rescued me from Nunzio and his men, we went back to his car and he put his shotgun into its trunk."

"Yeah, so?"

"He had an ice chest there."

I suddenly had another thought. "O'Brien," I said in an excited voice, "if Coyle is our killer and if he takes a body part from his victims, do you think he might have collected a trophy from Tiny Nunzio?"

"Nunzio got shot twice," O'Brien said. "Once in his chest and another blast to the left side of his skull. That second one just winged him, but it tore off most of his cheek, eye, and ear. I don't remember any mutilation."

"Wait a second, did you say that the first shot was to his chest and the second to his head?"

"That's right," O'Brien said. "Look, there's nothin' in Coyle's apartment, so I'm out of here. But Dani, be careful. Don't go anywhere with him. I've been thinking and if I had to choose which man is more likely a killer, I'd say it's Walter."

Agent Coyle greeted me with a cocky smile when I returned to our table.

"I didn't order dessert," he said. "You didn't care for any dessert the last time we met and I didn't want to run up too high of a bill since I've already stuck you with a nice bottle of pinot noir."

"Thanks," I said, appreciatively.

"Actually, I'm lying to you," he said. "I've already paid the check. It was well worth it, because I've not had this good of a laugh in a long time."

"Glad I could entertain you."

"Ms. Fox, you have an amazing ability to see things no one else sees—things that don't exist. Will Harris is not bright enough to be a serial murderer. And just because some screwball in Detroit cut off toes and your victims are missing body parts is pure coincidence. Tiny Nunzio and the Butcher are responsible for the homicides in White Plains and they're both dead. The sooner you forget all this nonsense about a missing penis, toes, fingers, and ears, the better off we'll all be. C'mon, I'll walk you to your car."

"You go ahead. I need to visit the women's room before I leave. Good night, Agent Coyle, and thank you."

"Why are you thanking me?" he asked.

"For dinner, of course, and for telling me what I needed to hear from you."

He rose from his seat. "It's probably better we don't leave together anyway. If Will Harris saw us together, he might try to murder me." He laughed.

51

I T WAS A MOONLESS NIGHT WHEN I EXITED ROBERTO'S AND I was happy that I'd parked under a floodlight on the side of the restaurant. But as I rounded the building's corner, I noticed that the light was off. It had been shining when I'd arrived earlier but someone had broken it. About a dozen cars were parked in the lot. I took my car keys and hurried toward my Triumph. When I reached it, I noticed that the back tire on the driver's side was flat. So was the front tire. All four of them were flat.

"Dani," a male voice called.

I turned and saw a figure coming from the shadows.

"It's me, Will. I've been waiting for you."

"How long have you been out here?"

"Nearly the entire time you were inside with Agent Coyle."

"You followed me?"

"My editor called from the restaurant. He asked me why you were having dinner with that FBI agent from the Persico trial. He thought a story might be brewing."

"Why did you come down here?" I asked.

"I got your stuff out of my apartment. I was going to drive it to your house and ask you about dinner since you never got back to me. Then my editor called and I got angry. I couldn't believe you were having dinner with that prick instead of me."

"But you didn't come inside Roberto's."

"I wasn't going to make a scene. If you want to be with him, that's your choice. I came over here to put your personal belongings in your car. When I saw someone had flattened the tires, I got worried."

His hands were empty so I asked: "Where's my stuff?"

"I put it back in my car and waited for you. I'm parked over there." He nodded to his left.

"Will, did you flatten my tires?"

"Hell no! Dani," he said, "you should know me better than that."

We looked at each other in silence for a moment. This was a man whom I had slept with, whom I had loved, or at least thought I had loved. Was it possible that he was a serial murderer?

Will said, "You're going to need a ride home. I'll take you."

The headlights of a car blinded both of us as it drove suddenly into the parking lot, stopping a few feet away. Coyle stepped out of the car. "Looks like you might need rescuing again," he said.

"Why don't you leave us the hell alone?" Will said.

Coyle walked toward us.

My eyes darted from him to Will and then back to him.

"Thanks, Agent Coyle," I said, "but I'll be having Will drive me home." I moved closer to him.

Coyle looked at us and then reached under his jacket and removed his 9 mm Glock handgun.

"You'll both be riding with me tonight," he said.

"What the hell are you doing?" Will asked.

"I see you're not surprised," Coyle said to me.

"You gave yourself away in the restaurant," I replied.

"How'd I do that?" he asked.

"I warned you that your Achilles heel was your ego."

"So you said."

"When you told me there was no connection between the homicides in Detroit and Yonkers, you said it didn't matter there were fingers, toes, a penis, and ears missing."

Coyle shrugged and said, "So what?"

I said, "None of the murder victims was missing an ear. The only person who could have been missing an ear was Tiny Nunzio, and the reason why you knew he was missing one was that you shot him in the chest, cut off his ear, and then shot him in the head to hide that fact."

Coyle said, "Touché, Ms. Fox. But you must admit, not taking a trophy from Nunzio would have been difficult."

"Where do you keep your playthings?" I asked. "The trunk?"

"Let's take a little ride together and I'll show you," he replied. He tossed his car keys to Will. "You drive."

"I'm not driving you anywhere," Will said.

"Suit yourself. I'll simply shoot Ms. Fox now, here in this lot."

"Will, do what he says," I replied. "Agent Coyle is a serial murderer. He's the one who killed Isabella Ricci."

"What?" Will exclaimed. "I thought Persico butchered her. Not an FBI agent!"

"Enough yakking, get in my car," Coyle said.

As ordered, Will slipped behind the steering wheel while I got into the backseat with Coyle, who sat directly behind Will. While keeping his handgun pointed at me, Coyle took out a pair of handcuffs and tossed them over the car's front seat to Will.

"Cuff one of your hands to the steering wheel," he ordered.

A reluctant Will did as he was told. He slipped one of the handcuffs around the steering wheel and snapped it closed. He slipped the other handcuff around his left wrist and locked it. His right hand remained free so he could hold both sides of the wheel when he drove.

"Start the car and drive us to your apartment," Coyle ordered.

"You can't kill us," Will said. "They'll know you did it."

"Thanks to Ms. Fox here, they won't."

"What's he talking about, Dani?" Will asked as he drove the car from the restaurant's parking lot.

"Yes, Dani, why don't you tell him," Coyle jeered. "Tell Mr. Harris here about how you thought he could have been responsible for at least two murders in Detroit and five more murders here. How you thought he could be a killer."

"Dani, what's he talking about?" Will asked.

"The homicides here were done by one man," I said.

"That would be me," Coyle happily chimed in.

"Earlier tonight, I told Coyle that you were a suspect," I said.

"Me? Why me? How could you possibly think it was me?"

"Will, your background actually fit an FBI profile of our killer," I explained. "But I told Coyle about you tonight as a ruse. I wanted to keep him off track. To make him think you were my number-one suspect."

"How ironic," Coyle chimed in, "that your attempt to misguide me is going to become my alibi. I will tell everyone that during our dinner at Roberto's, Ms. Fox shared her suspicions about you with me. She told me about the missing body parts. Of course, I didn't believe her but she was insistent. When we left the restaurant, Will Harris bushwhacked us. He forced us to go to his apartment. When we got there, I tried to disarm him. During the melee, Ms. Fox was fatally shot but I managed to draw my own weapon and kill him. They'll probably give me a medal for killing you, Mr. Harris."

"O'Brien will know it's bullshit," I said. "He was searching your apartment tonight while we were at dinner."

"I thought your phone call might have been to him," Coyle replied with confidence. "But it won't matter. FBI agents are above reproach, you yourself suspected Will, and everyone will accept your serial murder theory as soon as they find an ice chest full of surprises in Will's apartment."

"The missing body parts," I said. "In your trunk."

"Yes, another irony of the evening," Coyle said. "You set out to stop me from pulling off a series of perfect murders and, in doing so, you ended up giving me two more victims to enjoy. And I will very much enjoy doing to you what I did to Isabella Ricci."

"Why did you kill her?" I asked.

"I thought you already had all of this figured out," he sneered.

"Explain it to me, please," I said, catering to his ego. "If you're going to kill us, I want to die knowing why."

"To your credit and my amazement," Coyle said, "you got much of this right. I did start that gang war in Detroit, by nailing that young Marcus Smith boy to a cross and then putting an arrow through his rival gang member's heart. Call that child's play. After that, I just sat back and watched the mayhem unfold."

"You were trying the same thing here," I said, "only with the mob."

"The bureau had been following Persico for months and hadn't caught him jaywalking," Coyle said. "When I saw him enter that apartment, I thought, At last, he's up to no good. I followed him and as soon as I saw him leave her apartment, I knew what to do."

"Did you know then that Isabella was Tiny Nunzio's daughter?" I asked.

"No, I was simply going to frame him for killing her. I needed to get rid of Persico. He was the only reason a war between the two families hadn't started. Nunzio was encroaching on his turf in Staten Island but Persico was keeping a truce. We knew from the wiretaps on Corrado DiVenzenzo's phone that if Persico was out of the way, the rest of the Battaglia crime family would attack the Gacciones."

"You knocked on her door," I said, encouraging him to tell us more.

"I knocked on her door at the same moment Persico was driving away from the apartment buildings. I showed her my FBI credentials and she let me in. You can figure out what happened next."

"When did you discover Isabella was Nunzio's daughter?" I asked.

"Not until the next day," he said. "It was as if God had reached down and touched me. I knew that the families would go to war if I turned up the heat, just like the gangs in Detroit."

"Did turning up the heat mean killing the Mancinis?" I asked.

"That drunk saw me when I came into the apartments after Persico. I couldn't take a chance of him telling anyone. I made his cow of a wife watch him die. Then I killed her. It was delicious."

"And Marco Ricci? Why him?"

"The plastic surgeon and the stalker—Donnie Gilmore—those murders were bonuses and they were entirely your fault, Ms. Fox," he said.

"Mine?"

"That's right. I had already achieved what I'd wanted, but you kept finding other suspects. I needed you to focus on Nunzio and Persico. I didn't want you bringing in Gilmore for questioning. I wanted the two families at war. Those two men's blood is on your head for not following my plan for you."

Will turned the car down a side street and I realized we were only a few blocks from his apartment. If I was going to do something, I needed to do it quickly. I was certain that once Coyle got us into Will's apartment, he'd kill Will and begin torturing me.

Will decided to join our backseat conversation. "I can't believe you thought I might be a murderer, Dani!"

I couldn't believe he was still stuck on that thought. "This isn't the best time to discuss this," I said.

Coyle said, "Oh, I disagree."

I said to Coyle, "I kept doubting my suspicions about you because you're an FBI agent."

"One of the perks of carrying a badge," he said. "But don't go all high and mighty on me. They all deserved to die. Isabella was a dyke, the Mancinis were drunks, and Marco and Gilmore were sexual perverts. They were trash."

"Who gives you the right to judge them?" I asked.

My comment clearly irked him. He slid to the middle of the car's backseat to be closer to me. I was now sitting with my back pressed against the passenger door, having turned sideways to face him.

"You don't get out too often, do you?" he said. "Charles Bronson in *Death Wish*. Clint Eastwood as Harry Callahan. No one is crying over the scum anymore."

"How about Will and me?" I said. "Are we scum, too?"

Coyle grinned. "I actually found you interesting, Ms. Fox. A challenge. I'll consider you collateral damage. And I'll be sure to tell your mother at your funeral how highly I regarded you."

I remembered what the profiler had said about a serial murderer's deep insecurities, his need to feel powerful and his anger, if ridiculed.

"So Agent Coyle, tell me one more thing. Why are you so fucked up?" I asked. "Did the kids make fun of you for wetting your bed? Did they call you Wally? Did they make fun of little Wally and not choose him to play on their teams? Or is it because you were molested? Did your daddy turn you into his little butt buddy?"

He leaned forward. The two of us were now squeezed so tightly together that I could see his pupils and feel his breath on my face. "That's it, isn't it, Wally?" I said, continuing to taunt him. "Was it your daddy who busted your cherry? Or some neighbor? An uncle? Did you secretly enjoy being molested? Did you smile when they had their way with you?"

In a swift motion, Coyle tucked his handgun into its holster under his jacket and when his hand reappeared, he was holding a butterfly knife, which

he expertly flipped open with a snap of his wrist. Its five-inch blade glim-
mered in the light from passing streetlamps. He pressed its blade against my
neck. "I was going to wait until we got to your boyfriend's apartment. But
since you've got such a potty mouth, I think we can begin our fun here. Now
what were you saying about me being a butt buddy?"

With my back still pressed against the passenger door, I looked at Will
sitting in the car's driver's seat. He turned his head and I could see a panicked look on his face as he glanced over his right shoulder at Coyle. "Don't
hurt her!" he yelled.

"Oh, I am definitely going to hurt her," Coyle replied. "And the sad thing
is that you won't be around to write about it on tomorrow's front page."

Coyle was totally fixated on me. He slowly inched the blade along my
skin, dragging it gently from my neck to my left cheek, being careful to not
cut me. "Isabella Ricci squirmed when I cut her," he announced. "You should
have seen her eyes. They're the windows into the soul, the poets say. You will
squirm, too, Ms. Fox, when I cut you. What will I see when I look into your
soul?" With the tip of his blade, he nicked my cheek, drawing first blood.

I couldn't wait any longer. I grabbed his right hand with both of mine and
shoved the knife blade away from my face to his left, pinning it against the
backseat. "Will!" I screamed.

Although Will's left hand was cuffed to the steering wheel, he shifted his
weight to his right side and reached over the front seat with his free right hand,
as if he were trying to retrieve something that he'd left in the vehicle's backseat. When Will did this, his right foot instinctively pushed down harder on
the accelerator, causing the car to bolt forward. He released his left hand from
the steering wheel so that he could extend his reach as far as possible before
being stopped by the handcuffs. The car careened out of control. With his
right hand, Will reached for Coyle's neck but before he could grab it, our car
crossed the center line and smashed into a camper parked on the left side of
the avenue.

The impact caused Will to fly forward into the steering wheel and dash-
board. Coyle's body was ejected from the middle of the backseat but the
impact wasn't forceful enough to send him through the car's windshield. He
struck it with a thud and stopped, his legs dangling behind him in the rear
compartment. The crash sent me tumbling, too, but I was the farthest from

the car's point of impact and my back had been pinned against the back passenger door. Because of my position in the backseat, I wasn't thrown over the front seat as Coyle had been. Instead, I hit the back of the front seat with my chest and shoulder, knocking the air from my lungs. Although startled, I recovered after a few moments and immediately reached for the rear passenger door to escape.

Before I could open the latch, a hand grabbed my shoulder.

"You're not going anywhere!" Coyle yelled. He had dragged himself back into the rear seat and was now holding me. His nose was bleeding but he looked otherwise unharmed.

"Yes, I am!" I shouted. I began hitting and kicking at him in a frenzy but I was trapped between him and the still-closed door.

Coyle seemed impervious to my blows. As I watched, he raised his right hand and I saw the knife blade. Helpless, I started to brace myself for the inevitable when I saw a blur behind Coyle and watched as the FBI agent's head was snapped backward. It was Will. He'd reached over the front seat and grabbed Coyle's hair.

I quickly unlatched the rear passenger door.

But Agent Coyle was not done with me yet. Even though Will was holding Coyle by his hair, the agent brought the knife blade down, plunging it into my left calf. The pain was excruciating and I cried out. Satisfied, Coyle released the knife and reached up with both of his hands to free himself from Will's grasp.

Dragging my leg with the knife still stuck in it, I opened the door and shoved myself from the backseat. My backside hit the blacktop. As I looked into the car, I could see Coyle struggling to unlock Will's hair-filled fingers. Will refused to let go.

A propane tank attached to the back of the camper ruptured, spewing gas into the evening air. The gas hit a small flame burning under the car's crumpled hood and when it ignited, flames shot into the vehicle. A terrified look swept across Agent Coyle's face as he realized what was about to happen. For a second, we locked eyes and I could see the hatred in his. He made one last effort to free himself, but Will held tight. The initial propane explosion was followed by a second boom when the flames reached both vehicles' gas tanks. Flying metal and broken glass shot from the car around me as the vehicle was lifted by the blast from the pavement and then crashed back down. I could see Coyle's body inside, now a human fireball.

"Will!" I yelled.

Something hit my head. I heard voices yelling around me but couldn't make out what they were saying. I blacked out.

52

DETECTIVE O'BRIEN WAS SITTING NEXT TO MY HOSPI-
tal bed when I opened my eyes. My head hurt like hell and my
skull and leg were wrapped in bandages. "Dani," O'Brien said,
"can you hear me?" His voice sounded like he was miles away.

"Your ears got damaged," he said. "You got busted in the head by a piece of
flying metal, got some minor burns, and, of course, a knife was found stuck in
your leg."

"Will?" I said.

O'Brien shook his head.

I felt like I was going to vomit. I wanted to scream, but I couldn't manage
it. "Coyle?"

"Dead, too."

"You need to rest," I heard my mother's voice say.

I turned my head slightly and saw her standing next to O'Brien. There
was an IV in my arm. My mother reached over and lovingly touched my
forehead.

I closed my eyes.

It was late afternoon when I awoke the second time. O'Brien and my
mother were still there.

I was less groggy but my head still hurt.

I spoke briefly to my mom and then O'Brien said to her, "Could you give
Dani and me a few minutes in private?"

"I'll go get Dani some chocolates from the gift shop," my mom volunteered. "Sweets always make you feel better, dear."

O'Brien stayed silent until she was gone. "Tell me what happened," he said.

"It was Agent Coyle. He was the serial murderer. He was forcing Will to drive us to his apartment. He was going to plant the body parts and tell everyone that Will was a serial murderer and that he had overpowered him but couldn't save me in time. He was going to torture me like he did Isabella Ricci."

"Rotten son of a bitch," O'Brien said. "I'm sorry I doubted you."

"In the car, Will and I tried to overpower him. The car crashed. I managed to get out. Will held Coyle inside. Is Will really dead or did I dream that?"

"Sorry, Dani, Will's dead."

"The last thing I saw was him grabbing Coyle's hair, keeping him from getting out of the car. He saved my life, O'Brien."

O'Brien nodded. "He was an okay guy, even for a reporter."

I tried to smile but my heart was breaking.

"Dani," he said, "you aren't gonna like what I got to tell you. But you got to hear what's happened."

"What are you talking about?"

"A whitewash," he said. "Longhorn's behind it. He swooped in and took over. The car, the body parts, anything that could show that Agent Coyle was a murderer, it's gone."

"But Will was handcuffed to the steering wheel. You can't ignore that."

"You can when the explosion did a number on their bodies. I'll spare you the details. Longhorn's told everyone that the three of you were out drinking. Says Will was drunk at the wheel."

"The bureau gets to keep its reputation clean," I said. "No one will ever know the truth now?"

"Just you and me, girl," O'Brien said. "Longhorn's covered all his bases."

"Then he won."

"This round," O'Brien said. "But what's important is that you kept your resolution. You made sure Isabella Ricci's killer got what he deserved."

I knew that was supposed to make me feel better. But it didn't. "I need you to do me a favor," I said.

"Just name it."

"Get word to Longhorn. Somehow. Tell that lying bastard that I'm not done with him. This is not the last time the two of us are going to dance. I promise you that."

O'Brien gently took my hand. "I'll do that, Dani. And I'll tell him something else."

"What's that?"

"That Dani Fox always keeps a promise."

ACKNOWLEDGMENTS

Books are rarely the result of just one person's efforts. Such is the case with *Clever Fox*.

There are many to thank: David Vigliano, who came to me when I was district attorney of Westchester County and suggested I put pen to paper. David, thanks for your persistence.

Pete Earley, my collaborator, who is focused, logical, and organized. His capacity to take real experiences and turn them into page-turners is remarkable.

Ruth Pomerance from Hyperion, who came in just in time as my editor and did a yeoman's job . . . both she and Lauren Taylor Shute were always willing to take time to address my editorial questions.

Again, I am so grateful to publisher Ellen Archer and editor in chief Elisabeth Dyssegaard for their support as well as their confidence in the Dani Fox series.

And to all of you who give me the inspiration to write about my experiences—thank you!